Myths

of

Babylon

Myths
of
Babylon

General Editor: Jake Jackson

Associate Editor: Catherine Taylor

**FLAME TREE
PUBLISHING**

This is a FLAME TREE Book

FLAME TREE PUBLISHING
6 Melbray Mews
Fulham, London SW6 3NS
United Kingdom
www.flametreepublishing.com

First published 2018
Copyright © 2018 Flame Tree Publishing Ltd

22 21
5 7 9 8 6 4

ISBN: 978-1-78664-763-4

Special ISBN: 978-1-78755-709-3

Contributors, authors, editors and sources for this series include:
Loren Auerbach, Norman Bancroft-Hunt, E.M. Berens, Katharine
Berry Judson, Laura Bulbeck, Jeremiah Curtin, O.B. Duane, Dr
Ray Dunning, W.W. Gibbings, H. A. Guerber, Jake Jackson, Joseph
Jacobs, Judith John, J.W. Mackail, Donald Mackenzie, Chris McNab,
Professor James Riordan, Sara Robson, Lewis Spence, Rachel
Storm, K.E. Sullivan, François-Marie Arouet a.k.a. Voltaire, E.A.
Wallis Budge, Dr Roy Willis, Epiphanius Wilson, E.T.C. Werner.

A copy of the CIP data for this book is available from the British Library.

Printed and bound by Clays Ltd, Elcograf S.p.A

MIX
Paper from
responsible sources
FSC
www.fsc.org
FSC® C018072

Contents

Series Foreword

STRETCHING BACK to the oral traditions of thousands of years ago, tales of heroes and disaster, creation and conquest have been told by many different civilizations in many different ways. Their impact sits deep within our culture even though the detail in the tales themselves are a loose mix of historical record, transformed narrative and the distortions of hundreds of storytellers.

Today the language of mythology lives with us: our mood is jovial, our countenance is saturnine, we are narcissistic and our modern life is hermetically sealed from others. The nuances of myths and legends form part of our daily routines and help us navigate the world around us, with its half truths and biased reported facts.

The nature of a myth is that its story is already known by most of those who hear it, or read it. Every generation brings a new emphasis, but the fundamentals remain the same: a desire to understand and describe the events and relationships of the world. Many of the great stories are archetypes that help us find our own place, equipping us with tools for self-understanding, both individually and as part of a broader culture.

For Western societies it is Greek mythology that speaks to us most clearly. It greatly influenced the mythological heritage of the ancient Roman civilization and is the lens through which we still see the Celts, the Norse and many of the other great peoples and religions. The Greeks themselves learned much from their neighbours, the Egyptians, an older culture that became weak with age and incestuous leadership.

It is important to understand that what we perceive now as mythology had its own origins in perceptions of the divine and the rituals of the sacred. The earliest civilizations, in the crucible of the Middle East, in the Sumer of the third millennium BC, are the source to which many of the mythic archetypes can be traced. As humankind collected together in cities for the first time, developed writing and industrial scale agriculture, started to irrigate the rivers and attempted to control rather than be at the mercy of its environment, humanity began to write down its tentative explanations of natural events, of floods and plagues, of disease.

Early stories tell of Gods (or god-like animals in the case of tribal societies such as African, Native American or Aboriginal cultures) who are crafty and use their wits to survive, and it is reasonable to suggest that these were the first rulers of the gathering peoples of the earth, later elevated to god-like status with the distance of time. Such tales became more political as cities vied with each other for supremacy, creating new Gods, new hierarchies for their pantheons. The older Gods took on primordial roles and became the preserve of creation and destruction, leaving the new gods to deal with more current, everyday affairs. Empires rose and fell, with Babylon assuming the mantle from Sumeria in the 1800s BC, then in turn to be swept away by the Assyrians of the 1200s BC; then the Assyrians and the Egyptians were subjugated by the Greeks, the Greeks by the Romans and so on, leading to the spread and assimilation of common themes, ideas and stories throughout the world.

The survival of history is dependent on the telling of good tales, but each one must have the 'feeling' of truth, otherwise it will be ignored. Around the firesides, or embedded in a book or a computer, the myths and legends of the past are still the living materials of retold myth, not restricted to an exploration of origins. Now we have devices and global communications that give us unparalleled access to a diversity of traditions. We can find out about Native American, Indian, Chinese and tribal African mythology in a way that was denied to our ancestors, we can find connections, match the archaeology, religion and the mythologies of the world to build a comprehensive image of the human experience that is endlessly fascinating.

The stories in this book provide an introduction to the themes and concerns of the myths and legends of their respective cultures, with a short introduction to provide a linguistic, geographic and political context. This is where the myths have arrived today, but undoubtedly over the next millennia, they will transform again whilst retaining their essential truths and signs.

Jake Jackson
General Editor

Introduction to Ancient Babylonian Culture

T HE MYTHS OF BABYLONIA – and previously Sumer, and by extension Assyria, with which it is inextricably linked – contain themes from the cosmologies of different epochs and reflect the competing interests of the various cities of Mesopotamia, each with its own patron divinity, comprising the world's oldest urban civilization. This civilization reached its apogee in the great city of Babylon under Nebuchadnezzar (605–562 BC).

Through most of its history until the Babylonian ascendancy during 1795–1750 BC under Hammurabi, Mesopotamia, a land of 25,900 square kilometres (10,000 square miles) between the rivers Tigris and Euphrates, was a scene of rivalry between a cluster of city states, among them Ur, Eridu, Lagash and Kish. The Sumerians arrived in southern Mesopotamia about 3300 BC and spoke a tongue related to the Turkic group of South-Central Asia. Its literature, written in the wedge-shaped or cuneiform script invented by the temple priests, includes myths, epic tales and numerous hymns.

In about 1890 BC Semitic invaders from the north gained control of the country from their capital, Babylon. Later the country fell under the domination of Assyria (c. 1225 BC), before the new Babylonian empire was established by Nebuchadnezzar in 605 BC. In 539 BC Babylonia was conquered by the Persian emperor, Cyrus.

Cross-pollination

With the initial unification of the region under Babylon, conscious attempts were made by the priesthood to consolidate the mythical traditions associated with the various city-states into a coherent cosmology; and yet there are still differences between the gods as worshipped in early and later Babylonian times, and these gods are strikingly similar to those of the Assyrians, the war-like people who controlled Babylonia for much of its history and yet who revered and absorbed its gods, learning and culture.

In the first chapter of this book we will provide some historical background on the kings, conquests and literature of the Babylonian-Assyrian region (and often the histories meld with myth) to provide context to the beliefs, gods, myths and tales of the peoples of these lands, before going on to discuss specific gods, myths, superstitions, monsters and kings. There is no intention thus to follow minutely the events in the history of Babylonia and Assyria. The purpose is to depict and describe the circumstances, deeds, and times of its most outstanding figures, its most typical and characteristic rulers.

History, Religion & Myth

FOR A LONG TIME Babylon was no more than a mighty name – a gigantic skeleton whose ribs protruded here and there from the sands of Syria in colossal ruin of tower and temple. But through the labours of a band of scholars and explorers whose lives and work must be classed as among the most romantic passages in the history of human effort we have been enabled to view the wondrous panorama of human civilization as it evolved in the valleys of the Tigris and Euphrates.

We are dealing with a race austere and stern, a race of rigorous religious devotees and conquerors, the Romans of the East – but not an unimaginative race, for the Babylonians and Assyrians came of that stock which gave to the world its greatest religions, Judaism, Christianity, and Islam, a race not without the sense of mystery and science, for Babylon was the mother of astrology and magic, and established the beginnings of the study of the stars; and, lastly, of commerce, for the first true financial operations and the first houses of exchange were founded in the shadows of her temples and palaces.

The Akkadians

T HE BOUNDARIES OF THE LAND where the races of Babylonia
and Assyria evolved one of the most remarkable and original
civilizations in the world's history are the two mighty rivers of
Western Asia, the Tigris and Euphrates, Assyria being identical with
the more northerly and mountainous portion, and Babylonia with
the southerly part, which inclined to be flat and marshy. Both tracts
of country were inhabited by people of the same race, save that the
Assyrians had acquired the characteristics of a population dwelling
in a hilly country and had become to some extent intermingled
with Hittite and Amorite elements. But both were branches of an
ancient Semitic stock, the epoch of whose entrance into the land
it is impossible to fix. In the oldest inscriptions discovered we find
those Semitic immigrants at strife with the indigenous people of
the country, the Akkadians, with whom they were subsequently
to mingle and whose beliefs and magical and occult conceptions
especially they were afterward to incorporate with their own.

Who, then, were the Akkadians whom the Babylonian Semites came to displace
but with whom they finally mingled? Great and bitter has been the controversy
which has raged around the racial affinities of this people. Some have held that
they were themselves of Semitic stock, others that they were of a race more
nearly approaching the Mongol, the Lapp, and the Basque. In such a book as
this, the object of which is to present an account of the Babylonian mythology, it
is unnecessary to follow the protagonists of either theory into the dark recesses
where the conflict has led them. But the probability is that the Akkadians,
who are usually represented upon their monuments as a beardless people
with oblique eyes, were connected with that great Mongolian family which has
thrown out tentacles from its original home in central Asia to the frozen regions
of the Arctic, the north of Europe, the Turkish Empire, aye, and perhaps to
America itself! Akkadian in its linguistic features and especially in its grammatical
structure shows a resemblance to the Ural-Altaic group of languages which

embraces Turkish and Finnish, and this is in itself good evidence that the people who spoke it belonged to that ethnic division. But the question is a thorny one, and pages, nay, volumes might be occupied in presenting the arguments for and against such a belief.

It was from the Akkadians, however, that the Babylonian Semites received the germs of their culture; indeed it may be avowed that this aboriginal people carried them well on the way toward civilization. Not only did they instruct the Semitic new-comers in the arts of writing and reading, but they strongly biased their religious beliefs, and so inspired them with the idea of the sanctity of their own faith that the later Babylonian priesthood preserved the old Akkadian tongue among them as a sacred language, just as the Roman priesthood has retained the use of the dead Latin speech. Indeed, the proper pronunciation of Akkadian was an absolute necessity to the successful performance of religious ritual, and it is passing strange to observe that the Babylonian priests composed new religious texts in a species of dog-Akkadian, just as the monks of the Middle Ages composed their writings in dog-Latin! – with such zeal have the religious in all ages clung to the cult of the ancient, the mystic and half-forgotten thing unknown to the vulgar.

When we first encounter Babylonian civilization we find it grouped round about two nuclei, Nippur in the North and Eridu in the South. The first had grown up around a sanctuary of the god En-lil, who held sway over the ghostly animistic spirits which at his bidding might pose as the friends or enemies of men. A more 'civilized' deity held sway at Eridu, which was the home of Ea, or Oannes, the god of light and wisdom, who exercised his knowledge of the healing art for the benefit of his votaries. From the waters of the Persian Gulf, whence he rose each morning, he brought knowledge of all manner of crafts and trades, arts and industries, for the behoof of his infant city, even the mystic and difficult art of impressing written characters on clay. It is a beautiful picture which we have from the old legend of this sea-born wisdom daily enlightening the life of the little white city near the waters. The Semites possessed a deep and almost instinctive love of wisdom. In the writings attributed to Solomon and in the rich and wondrous Psalms of David – those deep mines of song and sagacity – we find the glories of wisdom again and again extolled. Even yet there are few peoples among whom the love of scholarship, erudition, and religious wisdom is more cultivated for its own sake than with the Jews.

These rather different cultures of the North and South, working toward a common centre, met and fused at a period prior to the commencement of history, and we even find the city of Ur, whence Abram came, a near neighbour of Eridu, colonized by Nippur! The culture of Eridu prevailed nevertheless, and its mightiest offshoot was the ultimate centre of Euphratean civilization – Babylon itself. The first founders of the city were undoubtedly of Sumerian stock – the expression 'Sumerian' being that in vogue among modern scholars for the older 'Akkadian', and therefore interchangeable with it.

The Semite Conquerors

IT WAS PROBABLY ABOUT THE TIME of the juncture of the civilizations of Eridu and Nippur that the Semites entered the country.

There are indications which lead to the belief that, as in the case of the Semitic immigrants in Egypt, they came originally from Arabia. The Semite readily accepted the Sumerian civilization which he found flourishing in the valley of the Euphrates, and adapted the Sumerian system of writing to his own language, in what manner will be indicated later. But the Sumerians themselves were not above borrowing from the rich Semitic tongue, and many of the earliest Sumerian texts we encounter are strongly Semitized. But although the Semites appear to have filtered into Sumerian territory by way of Eridu and Ur, the first definite notices we have of their presence within it are in the monuments of the more northern portion of that territory, in what is known as Akkad, in the neighbourhood of Bagdad, where they founded a small kingdom in much the same manner as the Jutes founded the kingdom of Kent. The earliest monuments, however, come from Lagash, the modern Tello, some thirty miles north of Ur, and recount the dealings of the high-priest of that place with other neighbouring dignitaries. The priests of Lagash became kings, and their conquests extended beyond the confines of Babylonia to Elam on the east, and southward to the Persian Gulf.

Sargon, A Babylonian Conqueror

B UT THE FIRST GREAT SEMITIC EMPIRE in Babylonia was that founded by the famous Sargon of Akkad. As is the case with many popular heroes and monarchs whose deeds are remembered in song and story – for example, Perseus, OEdipus, Cyrus, Romulus, and our own King Arthur – the early years of Sargon were passed in obscurity.

Sargon is, in fact, one of the 'fatal children'. He was, legend stated, born in concealment and sent adrift, like Moses, in an ark of bulrushes on the waters of the Euphrates, whence he was rescued and brought up by one Akki, a husbandman. But the time of his recognition at length arrived, and he received the crown of Babylonia. His foreign conquests were extensive. On four successive occasions he invaded Syria and Palestine, which he succeeded in welding into a single empire with Babylonia. Pressing his victories to the margin of the Mediterranean, he erected upon its shores statues of himself as an earnest of his conquests. He also overcame Elam and northern Mesopotamia and quelled a rebellion of some magnitude in his own dominions. His son, Naram-Sin, claimed for himself the title of 'King of the Four Zones', and enlarged the empire left him by his father, penetrating even into Arabia. A monument unearthed by J. de Morgan at Susa depicts him triumphing over the conquered Elamites. He is seen passing his spear through the prostrate body of a warrior whose hands are upraised as if pleading for quarter. His head-dress is ornamented with the horns emblematic of divinity, for the early Babylonian kings were the direct vicegerents of the gods on earth.

Even at this comparatively early time (c. 3800 BC) the resources of the country had been well exploited by its Semitic conquerors, and their absorption of the Sumerian civilization had permitted them to make very considerable progress in the enlightened arts. Some of their work in bas-relief, and even in the lesser if equally difficult craft of gem-cutting, is among the finest efforts of Babylonian art. Nor were they deficient in more utilitarian fields. They constructed roads through the most important portions of the empire, along which a service of posts carried messages at stated intervals, the letters conveyed by these being stamped or franked by clay seals, bearing the name of Sargon.

The First Library in Babylonia

Sargon is also famous as the first founder of a Babylonian library. This library appears to have contained works of a most surprising nature, having regard to the period at which it was instituted. One of these was entitled *The Observations of Bel*, and consisted of no less than seventy-two books dealing with astronomical matters of considerable complexity; it registered and described the appearances of comets, conjunctions of the sun and moon, and the phases of the planet Venus, besides recording many eclipses. This wonderful book was long afterward translated into Greek by the Babylonian historian Berossus, and it demonstrates the great antiquity of Babylonian astronomical science even at this very early epoch. Another famous work contained in the library of Sargon dealt with omens, the manner of casting them, and their interpretation – a very important side-issue of Babylonian magico-religious practice.

Among the conquests of this great monarch, whose splendour shines through the shadows of antiquity like the distant flash of arms on a misty day, was the fair island of Cyprus. Even imagination reels at the well-authenticated assertion that five thousand seven hundred years ago the keels of a Babylonian conqueror cut the waves of the Mediterranean and landed upon the shores of flowery Cyprus stern Semitic warriors, who, loading themselves with loot, erected statues of their royal leader and returned with their booty. In a Cyprian temple Luigi Palma di Cesnola (1832–1904), the soldier, diplomat and amateur archaeologist, discovered, down in the lowest vaults, a haematite cylinder which described its owner as a servant of Naram-Sin, the son of Sargon, so that a certain degree of communication must have been kept up between Babylonia and the distant island, just as early Egypt and Crete were bound to each other by ties of culture and commerce.

The High-Priest Gudea

B UT THE EMPIRE which Sargon had founded was doomed to precipitate ruin. The seat of power was diverted southward to Ur. In the reign of Dungi, one of the monarchs who ruled from this southern sphere, a great vassal of the throne, Gudea, stands out as one of the most remarkable characters in early Babylonian antiquity.

This Gudea (c. 2700 BC) was high-priest of Lagash, a city perhaps thirty miles north of Ur, and was famous as a patron of the architectural and allied arts. He ransacked western Asia for building materials. Arabia supplied him with copper for ornamentation, the Amames mountains with cedar-wood, the quarries of Lebanon with stone, while the deserts adjacent to Palestine furnished him with rich stones of all kinds for use in decorative work, and districts on the shores of the Persian Gulf with timber for ordinary building purposes. His architectural ability is vouched for by a plan of his palace, measured to scale, which is carved upon the lap of one of his statues in the Louvre.

Hammurabi the Great

L IKE THAT WHICH PRECEDED IT, the dynasty of Ur fell, and Arabian or Canaanite invaders usurped the royal power in much the same manner as the Shepherd Kings seized the sovereignty of Egypt. A subsequent foreign yoke, that of Elam, was thrown off by Hammurabi (also known as 'Khammurabi'), perhaps the most celebrated and most popularly famous name in Babylonian history.

This brilliant, wise, and politic monarch did not content himself with merely expelling the hated Elamites, but advanced to further conquest with such success that in the thirty-second year of his reign (2338 BC) he had formed

Babylonia into a single monarchy with the capital at Babylon itself. Under the fostering care of Hammurabi, Babylonian art and literature unfolded and blossomed with a luxuriance surprising to contemplate at this distance of time. It is astonishing, too, to note how completely he succeeded in welding into one homogeneous whole the various elements of the empire he carved out for himself. So surely did he unify his conquests that the Babylonian power as he left it survived undivided for nearly fifteen hundred years. The welfare of his subjects of all races was constantly his care, No one satisfied of the justice of his cause feared to approach him. The legal code which he formulated and which remains as his greatest claim to the applause of posterity is a monument of wisdom and equity. If Sargon is to be regarded as the Arthur of Babylonian history surely Hammurabi is its Alfred. The circumstances of the lives of the two monarchs present a decidedly similar picture. Both had in their early years to free their country from a foreign yoke, both instituted a legal code, were patrons of letters and assiduous in their attention to the wants of their subjects.

If a great people has frequently evolved a legal code of sterling merit there are cases on record where such an institution has served to make a people great, and it is probably no injustice to the Semites of Babylonia to say of them that the code of Hammurabi made them what they were. A copy of this world-famous code was found at Susa by J. de Morgan, and is now in the Louvre.

A Court Murder

What the Babylonian chronologists called 'the First Dynasty of Babylon' fell in its turn, and it is claimed that a Sumerian line of eleven kings took its place. Their sway lasted for 368 years – a statement which is obviously open to question. These were themselves overthrown and a Kassite dynasty from the mountains of Elam was founded by Kandis (c. 1780 BC) which lasted for nearly six centuries. These alien monarchs failed to retain their hold on much of the Asiatic and Syrian territory which had paid tribute to Babylon and the suzerainty of Palestine was likewise lost to them. It was at this epoch, too, that the high-priests of Asshur in the north took the title of king, but they appear to have been subservient to Babylon in some degree. Assyria grew gradually in power. Its people were hardier and more warlike than the art-loving and religious folk of Babylon, and little by little they encroached upon the weakness of the southern kingdom until at length an affair of tragic proportions entitled them to direct interference in Babylonian politics.

The circumstances which necessitated this intervention are not unlike those of the assassination of King Alexander of Serbia and Draga, his Queen, that happened 3000 years later. The Kassite king of Babylonia had married the daughter of Assur-yuballidh of Assyria. But the match did not meet with the approval of the Kassite faction at court, which murdered the bridegroom-king. This atrocious act met with swift vengeance at the hands of Assur-yuballidh of Assyria, the bride's father, a monarch of active and statesmanlike qualities, the author of the celebrated series of letters to Amen-hetep IV of Egypt, unearthed at Tel-el-Amarna. He led a punitive army into Babylonia, hurled from the throne the pretender placed there by the Kassite faction, and replaced him with a scion of the legitimate royal stock. This king, Burna-buryas, reigned for over twenty years, and upon his decease the Assyrians, still nominally the vassals of the Babylonian Crown, declared themselves independent of it. Not content with such a revolutionary measure, under Shalmaneser I (1300 BC) they laid claim to the suzerainty of the Tigris-Euphrates region, and extended their conquests even to the boundaries of far Cappadocia, the Hittites and numerous other confederacies submitting to their yoke. Shalmaneser's son, Tukulti-in-Aristi, took the city of Babylon, slew its king, Bitilyasu, and thus completely shattered the claim of the older state to supremacy. He had reigned in Babylon for some seven years when he was faced by a popular revolt, which seems to have been headed by his own son, Assur-nazir-pal, who slew him and placed Hadad-nadin-akhi on the throne. This king conquered and killed the Assyrian monarch of his time, Bel-kudur-uzur, the last of the old Assyrian royal line, whose death necessitated the institution of a new dynasty, the fifth monarch of which was the famous Tiglath-pileser I.

Tiglath-Pileser

T IGLATH-PILESER, or Tukulti-pal-E-sana, to confer on him his full Assyrian title, came to the throne about 1120 BC, and soon commenced the career of active conquest which was to render his name one of the most famous in the warlike annals of Assyria.

Campaigns in the Upper Euphrates against alien immigrants who had settled there were followed by the conquest of the Hittites of Subarti, in Assyrian territory. Pressing northward toward Lake Van in the Kurdish country he subsequently turned his arms westward and overran Malatia. Cappadocia and the Aramaeans of Northern Syria next felt the force of his arms, and he penetrated on this occasion even to the sources of the Tigris. He left behind him the character of a great warrior, a great hunter, and a great builder, restoring the semi-ruinous temples of Asshur and Hadad or Rimmon in the city of Asshur.

It is not until the reign of Assur-nazir-pal III (c. 883 BC) that we are once more enabled to take up the thread of Assyrian history with any degree of certainty. In this reign artistic development appears to have proceeded apace; but it cannot be said of Assur-nazir-pal that in him culture went hand in hand with humanity, the records of his cruelties being long and revolting. His successor, Shalmaneser II, possessed an insatiable thirst for military glory, and during his reign of thirty-five years overthrew a great confederacy of Syrian chiefs which included Ahab, King of Israel. He was disturbed during the latter part of his reign by the rebellion of his eldest son. But his second son, Samsi-Rammon, came to his father's assistance, and his faithful adherence secured him the succession to the throne in 824 BC.

Semiramis the Great

I T WAS PROBABLY IN THE REIGN of Tiglath-pileser that the queen known in legend as Semiramis lived. It would have been wonderful indeed had the magic of her name not been connected

with romance by the Oriental imagination. Semiramis! The name sparkles and scintillates with gems of legend and song. Myth, magic, and music encircle it and sweep round it as fairy seas surround some island paradise. It is a central rose in the chaplet of legend, it has been enshrined in music perhaps the most divine and melodious which the songful soul of Italy has ever conceived – yet not more beauteous than itself.

Let us introduce into the iron chain of Assyrian history the golden link of the legend of this Helen of the East, and having heard the fictions of her greatness let us attempt to remove the veils which hide her real personality from view and look upon her as she was – Sammuramat the Babylonian, queen and favourite of Samsi-Rammon, who crushed the assembled armies of Media and Chaldea, and whose glories are engraved upon a column which, setting forth the tale of her conquests, describes her in all simplicity as "A woman of the palace of Samsi-Rammon, King of the World."

Legend says that Ninus, King of Assyria, having conquered the Babylonians, proceeded toward Armenia with the object of reducing the people of that country. But its politic king, Barsanes, unable to meet him by armed force, made a voluntary submission, accompanied by presents of such magnificence that Ninus was placated. But, insatiable in his desire for conquest, he turned his eyes to Media, which he speedily subdued. His next ambition was to bring under his rule the territory between the Tanais and the Nile. This great task occupied him for no less than seventeen years, by which time all Asia had submitted to him, with the single exception of Bactria, which still maintained its independence. Having laid the foundations of the city of Nineveh, he resolved to proceed against the Bactrians. His army was of dimensions truly mythical, for he was said to be accompanied by 7,000,000 of infantrymen, 2,000,000 of horse-soldiers, with the addition of 200,000 chariots equipped with scythes.

It was during this campaign, says Diodorus Siculus, that Ninus first beheld Semiramis. Her precise legendary or mythical origin is obscure. Some writers aver that she was the daughter of the fish-goddess Ataryatis, or Derketo, and Oannes, the Babylonian god of wisdom, who has already been alluded to. Ataryatis was a goddess of Ascalon in Syria, and after birth her daughter Semiramis was miraculously fed by doves until she was found by one Simmas, the royal shepherd, who brought her up and married her to Onnes, or Menon, one of Ninus's generals. He fell by his own hand, and Ninus thereupon took Semiramis to wife, having profoundly admired her ever since her conduct at the capture of Bactria, where she had greatly distinguished herself. Not long afterward Ninus died, leaving a son called Ninyas.

During her son's minority Semiramis assumed the regency, and the first great work she undertook was the interment of her husband, whom she buried with great splendour, and raised over him a mound of earth no less than a mile and a quarter high and proportionally wide, after which she built Babylon. This city being finished, she made an expedition into Media; and wherever she went left memorials of her power and munificence. She erected vast structures, forming lakes and laying out gardens of great extent, particularly in Chaonia and Ecbatana. In short, she levelled hills, and raised mounds of an immense height, which retained her name for ages. After this she invaded Egypt and conquered Ethiopia, with the greater part of Libya; and having accomplished her wish, and there being no enemy to cope with her, excepting the kingdom of India, she resolved to direct her forces toward that quarter. She had an army of 3,000,000 foot, 500,000 horse, and 100,000 chariots. For the passing of rivers and engaging the enemy by water she had procured 2000 ships, to be so constructed as to be taken to pieces for the advantage of carriage: which ships were built in Bactria by men from Phoenicia, Syria, and Cyprus. With these she fought a naval engagement with Strabrobates, King of India, and at the first encounter sunk a thousand of his ships. After this she built a bridge over the river Indus, and penetrated into the heart of the country. Here Strabrobates engaged her. Being deceived by the numerous appearance of her elephants, he at first gave way, for being deficient in those animals she had procured the hides of 3000 black oxen, which, being properly sewn and stuffed with straw, presented the appearance of so many elephants. All this was done so naturally that even the real elephants of the Indian king were deceived. But the stratagem was at last discovered, and Semiramis was obliged to retreat, after having lost a great part of her army. Soon after this she resigned the government to her son Ninyas, and died. According to some writers, she was slain by his hand.

It was through the researches of Professor Lehmann-Haupt of Berlin that the true personal significance of Semiramis was recovered. Until the year

1910 the legends of Diodorus and others were held to have been completely disproved and Semiramis was regarded as a purely mythical figure. Jacob Bryant (1715–1804) in his *Ancient Mythology*, published at the beginning of the nineteenth century, proves the legendary status of Semiramis to his own satisfaction. He says: "It must be confessed that the generality of historians have represented Semiramis as a woman, and they describe her as a great princess who reigned in Babylon; but there are writers who from their situation had opportunities of better intelligence, and by those she is mentioned as a deity. The Syrians, says Athenagoras, worshipped Semiramis, and adds that she was esteemed the daughter of Dercatus and the same as the Suria Dea.... Semiramis was said to have been born at Ascalon because Atargatus was there worshipped under the name of Dagon, and the same memorials were preserved there as at Hierapolis and Babylon. These memorials related to a history of which the dove was the principal type. It was upon the same account that she was said to have been changed to a dove because they found her always depicted and worshipped under that form.... From the above I think it is plain that Semiramis was an emblem and that the name was a compound of Sama-ramas, or ramis, and it signified 'the divine token', a type of providence, and as a military ensign, (for as such it was used) it may with some latitude be interpreted 'the standard of the most High'. It consisted of the figure of a dove, which was probably encircled with the iris, as those two emblems were often represented together. All who went under that standard, or who paid any deference to that emblem, were styled Semarim or Samorim. It was a title conferred upon all who had this device for their national insigne."

There is much more of this sort of thing, typical of the mythic science of the eighteenth and early nineteenth centuries. It is easy to see how myth became busy with the name of the Assyrian Queen, whose exploits undoubtedly aroused the enthusiasm not only of the Assyrians themselves but of the peoples surrounding them. Just as any great work in ancient Britain was ascribed to the agency of Merlin or Arthur, so such monuments as could not otherwise be accounted for were attributed to Semiramis. Western Asia is monumentally eloquent of her name, and even the Behistun inscriptions of Darius have been placed to her credit. Herodotus states that one of the gates of Babylon was called after her, and that she raised the artificial banks that confined the river Euphrates. Her fame lasted until well into the Middle Ages, and the Armenians called the district round Lake Van, Shamiramagerd.

There is very little doubt that her fame became mingled with that of the goddess Ishtar: she possesses the same Venus-like attributes, the dove is her emblem, and her story became so inextricably intertwined with that of the Babylonian goddess that she ultimately became a variant of her. The story of Semiramis is a triumphant vindication of the manner in which by certain mythical processes a human being can attain the rank of a god or goddess, for Semiramis was originally very real indeed. A column discovered in 1909 describes her as "a woman of the palace of Samsi-rammon, King of the World, King of Assyria, King of the Four Quarters of the World." This dedication indicates that Semiramis, or, to give her her Assyrian title, Sammuramat, evidently possessed an immense influence over her husband, Samsi-rammon, and that perhaps as queen-mother that influence lasted for more than one reign, so that the legend that after a regency of forty-two years she delivered up the kingdom to her son, Ninyas, may have some foundation in fact. She seems to have made war against the Medes and Chaldeans. The story that on relinquishing her power she turned into a dove and disappeared may mean that her name, Sammuramat, was easily connected with the Assyrian *summat*, the word for 'dove'; and for a person of her subsequent legendary fame the mythical connection with Ishtar is easily accounted for.

The Second Assyrian Empire

WHAT IS KNOWN AS the Second Assyrian Empire commenced with the reign of Tiglath-pileser III, who organized a great scheme of provincial government. This plan appears to have been the first forecast of the feudal system, for each province paid a fixed tribute and provided a military contingent.

Great efforts were made to render the army as irresistible as possible with the object of imposing an Assyrian supremacy upon the entire known world.

Tiglath overran Armenia, defeated the Medes and Hittites, seized the seaports of Phoenicia and the trade routes connecting them with the centres of Assyrian commerce, and finally conquered Babylon, where in 729 BC he was invested with the sovereignty of 'Asia'. Two years later he died, but his successor, Shalmaneser IV, carried on the policy he had initiated. He had, however, only five years of life in which to do so, for at the end of that period the usurping general Sargon, who laid claim to be a descendant of Sargon the Great of Akkad, seized the royal power of Babylon. He was murdered in 705 BC, and his son Sennacherib, of Biblical fame, appears to have been unable to carry on affairs with the prudence or ability of his father. He outraged the religious feelings of the people by razing to the ground the city of Babylon, because of the revolt of the citizens. The campaign he made against Hezekiah, King of Judah, was marked by a complete failure. Hezekiah had allied himself with the Philistine princes of Ascalon and Ekron, but when he saw his Egyptian allies beaten at the battle of Eltekeh he endeavoured to buy off the invaders by numerous presents, though without success. The wonderful deliverance of Jerusalem from the forces of Sennacherib, recorded in Scripture, and sung by Byron in his *Hebrew Melodies*, appears to have a good foundation in fact. It seems that the Assyrian army was attacked and almost decimated by plague, which obliged Sennacherib to return to Nineveh, but it is not likely that the phenomenon occurred in the watch of a night. Sennacherib was eventually murdered by his two sons, who, the deed accomplished, fled to Armenia. Of all the Assyrian monarchs he was perhaps the most pompous and the least fitted to rule. The great palace at Nineveh and the great wall of that city, eight miles in circumference, were built at his command.

His son and successor, Esar-haddon, initiated his reign by sending back the sacred image of Merodach to its shrine at Babylon, which city he restored. He was solemnly declared king in the restored temple of Merodach, and during his reign both Babylonia and Assyria enjoyed quiet and contentment. War with Egypt broke out in 670 BC, and the Egyptians were thrice defeated with heavy loss. The Assyrians entered Memphis and instituted a protectorate over part of the country. Two years later Egypt revolted, and while marching to quell the outbreak Esar-haddon died on the road – his fate resembling that of Edward I, who died while on his way to overcome the Scottish people, then in rebellion against his usurpation.

Assur-bani-pal: Sardanapalus the Splendid?

SAR-HADDON WAS SUCCEEDED by Assur-bani-pal, known to Greek legend as Sardanapalus. How far the legendary description of him squares with the historical it is difficult to say. The former states that he was the last king of Assyria, and the thirtieth in succession from Ninyas. Effeminate and corrupt, he seems to have been a perfect example of the *roi fainéant*. The populace of the conquered provinces, disgusted with his extravagances, revolted, and an army led by Arbaces, satrap of Medea, and Belesys, a Babylonian priest, surrounded him in Nineveh and threatened his life. Sardanapalus, however, throwing off his sloth, made such a vigorous defence that for two years the issue was in doubt. The river Tigris at this juncture overflowed and undermined part of the city wall, thus permitting ingress to the hostile army. Sardanapalus, seeing that resistance was hopeless, collected his wives and treasures in his palace and then set it on fire, so that all perished.

It is a strange coincidence that the fate which legend ascribes to Sardanapalus was probably that which really overtook the brother of Assur-bani-pal, Samas-sum-yukin. It is likely that the self-immolation of Sardanapalus is merely a legendary statement of a rite well known to Semitic religion, which was practised at Tarsus down to the time of Dio Chrysostom, and the memory of which survives in other Greek legends, especially those of Heracles-Melcarth and Queen Dido. At Tarsus an annual festival was held and a pyre erected upon which the local Heracles or Baal was burned in effigy. This annual commemoration of the death of the god in fire probably had its origin in the older rite in which an actual man or sacred animal was burned as representing the deity.

The Golden Bough contains an instructive passage concerning the myth of Sardanapalus. Sir James Frazer writes: "There seems to be no doubt that the name Sardanapalus is only the Greek way of representing Ashurbanapal, the name of the greatest and nearly the last King of Assyria. But the records of the real monarch which have come to light within recent years give little support to the fables that attached to his name in classical tradition. For they prove that, far from being the effeminate weakling he seemed to the Greeks of a later age, he was a warlike and enlightened monarch, who carried the arms of Assyria to distant lands and fostered at home the growth of science and letters. Still, though the historical reality of King Ashurbanapal is as well attested as that of Alexander or Charlemagne, it would be no wonder if myths gathered, like clouds, around the great figure that loomed large in the stormy sunset of Assyrian glory. Now the two features that stand out most prominently in the legends of Sardanapalus are his extravagant debauchery and his violent death in the flames of a great pyre, on which he burned himself and his concubines to save them from falling into the hands of his victorious enemies. It is said that the womanish king, with painted face and arrayed in female attire, passed his days in the seclusion of the harem, spinning purple wool among his concubines and wallowing in sensual delights; and that in the epitaph which he caused to be carved on his tomb he recorded that all the days of his life he ate and drank and toyed, remembering that life is short and full of trouble, that fortune is uncertain, and that others would soon enjoy the good things which he must leave behind. These traits bear little resemblance to the portrait of Ashurbanapal either in life or death; for after a brilliant career of conquest the Assyrian king died in old age, at the height of human ambition, with peace at home and triumph abroad, the admiration of his subjects and the terror of his foes. But if the traditional characteristics of Sardanapalus harmonize but ill with what we know of the real monarch of that name, they fit well enough with all that we know or can conjecture of the mock kings who led a short life and a merry during the revelry of the Sacaea, the Asiatic equivalent of the Saturnalia. We can hardly doubt that for the most part such men, with death staring them in the face at the end of a few days, sought to drown care and deaden fear by plunging madly into all the fleeting joys that still offered themselves under the sun. When their brief pleasures and sharp sufferings were over, and their bones or ashes mingled with the dust, what more natural that on their tomb – those mounds in which the people saw, not untruly, the graves of the lovers of Semiramis – there should be carved some such lines as those which tradition placed in the mouth of the great Assyrian king, to remind the heedless passer-by of the shortness and vanity of life?"

According to Sir James Frazer, then, the real Sardanapalus may have been one of those mock kings who led a short but merry existence before a sacrifice ended their convivial career. We have analogous instances in the sacrifice of Sandan at Tarsus and that of the representative of the Mexican god, Tezcatlipoca. The legend of Sardanapalus is thus a distorted reminiscence of the death of a magnificent king sacrificed in name of a god.

When the real Assur-bani-pal succeeded Esar-haddon as King of Assyria, his brother Samas-sum-yukin was created Viceroy of Babylonia, but shortly after he claimed the kingship itself, revived the old Sumerian language as the official tongue of the Babylonian court, and initiated a revolt which shook the Assyrian empire from one end to the other. A great struggle ensued between the northern and southern powers, and at last Babylon was forced to surrender through starvation, and Samas-sum-yukin was put to death.

Assur-bani-pal, like Sardanapalus, his legendary counterpart, found himself surrounded by enemies. Having conquered Elam as well as Babylonia, he had to face the inroads of hordes of Scythians, who poured over his frontiers. He succeeded in defeating and slaying one of their chiefs, Dugdamme, whom in an inscription he calls a "limb of Satan", but shortly after this he died himself. His empire was already in a state of decay, and had not long to stand.

The First Great Library

BUT IF ASSUR-BANI-PAL WAS EFFEMINATE and lax in government, he was the first great patron of literature. It is to his magnificent library at Nineveh that we owe practically all that we have preserved of the literature that was produced in Babylonia. He saw that the southern part of his empire was far more intellectual and cultured than Assyria, and he despatched numerous scribes to the temple schools of the south, where they copied extensively from their archives every description of literary curiosity – hymns, legends, medical prescriptions, myths and rituals were all included in the great library at Nineveh. These have been restored to us through the labours of the archaeologists Sir Austen Henry Layard (1817–94) and Hormuzd Rassam (1826–1910).

It is a most extraordinary instance of antiquarian zeal in an epoch which we regard as not far distant from the beginnings of verifiable history.

Nearly twenty thousand fragments of brick, bearing the results of Assur-bani-pal's researches, are housed in the British Museum, and this probably represents only a portion of his entire collection. Political motives have been attributed to Assur-bani-pal in thus bringing together such a great library. It has been argued that he desired to make Assyria the centre of the religious influence of the empire. This wouldderogate greatly from the view that sees in him a king solely fired with the idea of preserving and retaining all that was best in ancient Babylonian literature in the north as well as in the south, and having beside him for his own personal use those records which many circumstances prove he was extremely desirous of obtaining. Thus we find him sending officials on special missions to obtain copies of certain works. It is also significant that Assur-bani-pal placed his collection in a library and not in a temple – a fact which discounts the theory that his collection of literature had a religious-political basis.

The Last Kings of Assyria

A FTER THE DEATH of Assur-bani-pal, the Scythians succeeded in penetrating into Assyria, through which they pushed their way as far as the borders of Egypt, and the remains of the Assyrian army took refuge in Nineveh.

The end was now near at hand. The last King of Assyria was probably Sin-sar-iskin, the Sarakos of the Greeks, who reigned for some years and who even tells us through the medium of inscriptions that he intended to restore the ruined temples of his land. War broke out with Babylonia, however, and Cyaxares, the Scythian King of Ecbatana, came to the assistance of the Babylonians. Nineveh was captured by the Scythians, sacked and destroyed, and the Assyrian empire was at an end.

Nebuchadnezzar

BUT STRANGELY ENOUGH the older seat of power, Babylon, still flourished to some extent. By superhuman exertions, Nebuchadnezzar II (or Nebuchadrezzar), who reigned for forty-three years, sent the standard of Babylonia far and wide through the known world. In 567 BC he invaded Egypt. In one of his campaigns he marched against Jerusalem and put its king, Jehoiakim, to death, but the king whom the Babylonian monarch set up in his place was deposed and the royal power vested in Zedekiah. Zedekiah revolted in 558 BC and once more Jerusalem was taken and destroyed, the principal inhabitants were carried captive to Babylon, and the city was reduced to a condition of insignificance.

This, the first exile of the Jews, lasted for seventy years. The story of this captivity and of Nebuchadnezzar's treatment of the Jewish exiles is graphically told in the Book of Daniel, whom the Babylonians called Belteshazzar. Daniel refused to eat the meat of the Babylonians, probably because it was not prepared according to Jewish rite. He and his companions ate pulse and drank water, and fared upon it better than the Babylonians on strong meats and wines. The King, hearing of this circumstance, sent for them and found them much better informed than all his magicians and astrologers. Nebuchadnezzar dreamed dreams, and informed the Babylonian astrologers that if they were unable to interpret them they would be cut to pieces and their houses destroyed, whereas did they interpret the visions they would be held in high esteem. They answered that if the King would tell them his dream they would show the interpretation thereof; but the King said that if they were wise men in truth they would know the dream without requiring to be told it, and upon some of the astrologers of the court replying that the request was unreasonable, he was greatly incensed and ordered all of them to be slain. But in a vision of the night the secret was revealed to Daniel, who begged that the wise men of Babylon be not destroyed, and going to a court official he offered to interpret the dream. He told the King that in his dream he had beheld a great image, whose brightness and form were terrible. The head of this image was of fine gold, the breast and arms of silver, and the other parts of brass, excepting the legs which were of iron, and the feet which were partly of that metal and partly of clay. But a stone was cast at it which smote the image upon its feet and it brake into pieces and the wind swept away the remnants. The stone that had smitten it became a great mountain and filled the whole earth.

Then Daniel proceeded to the interpretation. The King, he said, represented the golden head of the image; the silver an inferior kingdom which would rise after Nebuchadnezzar's death; and a third of brass which should bear rule over all the earth. The fourth dynasty from Nebuchadnezzar would be as strong as iron, but since the toes of the image's feet were partly of iron and partly of clay, so should that kingdom be partly strong and partly broken. Nebuchadnezzar was so awed with the interpretation that he fell upon his face and worshipped Daniel, telling him how greatly he honoured the God who could have revealed such secrets to him; and he set him as ruler over the whole province of Babylon, and made him chief of the governors over all the wise men of that kingdom.

But Daniel's three companions – Shadrach, Meshach, and Abednego – refused to worship a golden image which the King had set up, and he commanded that they should be cast into a fiery furnace, through which they passed unharmed.

This circumstance still more turned the heart of Nebuchadnezzar in the direction of the God of Israel. A second dream which he had, he begged Daniel to interpret. He said he had seen a tree in the midst of the earth of more than natural height, which flourished and was exceedingly strong, so that it reached to heaven. So abundant was the fruit of this tree that it provided meat for the whole earth, and so ample its foliage that the beasts of the field had shadow under it, and the fowls of the air dwelt in its midst. A spirit descended from heaven and called aloud, demanding that the tree should be cut down and its leaves and fruit scattered, but that its roots should be left in the earth surrounded by a band of iron and brass. Then, ordering that the tree should be treated as if it were a man, the voice of the spirit continued to ask that it should be wet with the dew of heaven, and that its portion should be with the beasts in the grass of the earth. "Let his heart be changed from a man's," said the voice, "and let a beast's heart be given him; and let seven times pass over him."

Then was Daniel greatly troubled. He kept silence for a space until the King begged him to take heart and speak. The tree, he announced, represented

Nebuchadnezzar himself, and what had happened to it in the vision would come to pass regarding the great King of Babylon. He would be driven from among men and his dwelling would be with the beasts of the field. He would be made to eat grass as oxen and be wet with the dew of heaven, and seven times would pass over him, till he knew and recognized that the Most High ruled in the kingdom of man and gave it to whomsoever he desired.

Twelve months after this Nebuchadnezzar was in the midst of his palace at Babylon, boasting of what he had accomplished during his reign, when a voice from heaven spoke, saying: "O King Nebuchadnezzar, to thee it is spoken, the kingdom is departed from thee," and straightway was Nebuchadnezzar driven from man and he did eat grass as an ox and his body was wet with the dew of heaven, till his hair was grown like eagle's feathers and his nails like bird's claws.

At the termination of his time of trial Nebuchadnezzar lifted his eyes to heaven, and praising the Most High admitted his domination over the whole earth. Thus was the punishment of the boaster completed.

It has been stated with some show of probability that the judgment upon Nebuchadnezzar was connected with that weird disease known as lycanthropy, from the Greek words *lukos*, a wolf, and *anthropos*, a man. It develops as a kind of hysteria and is characterized by a belief on the part of the victim that he has become an animal. There are, too, cravings for strange food, and the afflicted person runs about on all fours. Among primitive peoples such a seizure is ascribed to supernatural agency, and garlic or onion – the common scourge of vampires – is held to the nostrils.

The Last of the Babylonian Kings

NABONIDUS (555–539 BC) was the last of the Babylonian kings – a man of a very religious disposition and of antiquarian tastes. He desired to restore the temple of the moon-god at Harran and to restore such of the images of the gods as had been removed to the ancient shrines. But first he desired to find out whether this procedure would meet with the approval of the god Merodach.

To this end he consulted the augurs, who opened the liver of a sheep from which they drew favourable omens. But on another occasion he aroused the hostility of the god and incidentally of the priests of E-Sagila by preferring the sun-god to the great Bel of Babylon. He tells us in an inscription that when restoring the temple of Shamash at Sippar he had great difficulty in unearthing the old foundation-stone, and that, when at last it was unearthed, he trembled with awe as he read thereon the name of Naram-sin, who, he says, ruled 3,200 years before him. But destiny lay in wait for him, for Cyrus the Persian invaded Babylonia in 538 BC, and after defeating the native army at Opis he pressed on to Babylon, which he entered without striking a blow. Nabonidus was in hiding, but his place of concealment was discovered. Cyrus, pretending to be the avenger of Bel-Merodach for the slights the unhappy Nabonidus had put upon the god, had won over the people, who were exceedingly angry with their monarch for attempting to remove many images of the gods from the provinces to the capital. Cyrus placed himself upon the throne of Babylon and about a year before his death (529 BC) transferred the regal power to his son, Cambyses. Assyrian-Babylonian history here ceases and is merged into Persian. Babylonia recovered its independence after the death of Darius. A king styling himself Nebuchadnezzar III arose, who reigned for about a year (521–520 BC), at the end of which time the Persians once more returned as conquerors. A second revolt in 514 BC caused the partial destruction of the walls, and finally the great city of Babylon became little better than a quarry out of which the newer city of Seleucia and other towns were built.

The History of Berossus

I T WILL BE OF INTEREST to examine at least one of the ancient authorities upon Babylonian history. Berossus, a priest of Bel at Babylon, who lived about 250 BC, compiled from native documents a history of his country, which he published in Greek. His writings have perished, but extracts from them have been preserved by Josephus and Eusebius.

There is a good deal of myth in Berossus' work, especially when he deals with the question of cosmology, the story of the deluge, and so forth; also the 'facts' which he places before us as history cannot be reconciled with those inscribed on the monuments. He seems indeed to have arranged his history so that it should exactly fill the assumed period of 36,000 years, beginning with the creation of man and ending with the conquest of Babylon by Alexander the Great. Berossus tells of a certain Sisuthrus (Ut-Napishtim), whose history will be recounted in full in another chapter. He then relates a legend of the advent of the fish-man or fish-god, Oannes, from the waters of the Persian Gulf. Indeed he alludes to three beings of this type, who, one after another, appeared to instruct the Babylonians in arts and letters.

Berossus' Account of the Deluge

MORE IMPORTANT is his account of the deluge. There is more than one Babylonian version of the deluge: that which is to be found in the *Gilgamesh Epic* is given in the chapter dealing with that poem. As Berossus' account is quite as important, we shall give it in his own words:

"After the death of Ardates, his son (Sisuthrus) succeeded and reigned eighteen sari. In his time happened the great deluge; the history of which is given in this manner. The Deity, Cronus, appeared to him in a vision; and gave him notice, that upon the fifteenth day of the month Daesius there would be a flood, by which mankind would be destroyed. He therefore enjoined him to commit to writing a history of the beginning, procedure, and final conclusion of all things, down to the present term; and to bury these accounts securely in the City of the Sun at Sippara. He then ordered Sisuthrus to build a vessel, and to take with him into it his friends and relations; and trust himself to the deep. The latter implicitly obeyed: and having conveyed on board everything necessary to sustain life, he took in also all species of animals, that either fly, or rove upon the surface of the earth. Having asked the Deity where he was to go, he was answered, To the gods: upon which he offered up a prayer for the good of mankind. Thus he obeyed the divine admonition: and the vessel, which he built, was five stadia in length, and in breadth two. Into this he put everything which he had got ready; and last of all conveyed into it his wife, children, and friends.

"After the flood had been upon the earth, and was in time abated, Sisuthrus sent out some birds from the vessel; which not finding any food, nor any place to rest their feet, returned to him again. After an interval of some days; he sent them forth a second time: and they now returned with their feet tinged with mud. He made trial a third time with these birds: but they returned to him no more: from whence he formed a judgment, that the surface of the earth was now above the waters. Having therefore made an opening in the vessel, and finding upon looking out, that the vessel was driven to the side of a mountain, he immediately quitted it, being attended with his wife, children, and the pilot. Sisuthrus immediately paid his adoration to the earth: and having constructed an altar, offered sacrifices to the gods. These things being duly performed, both Sisuthrus, and those who came out of the vessel with him, disappeared. They, who remained in the vessel, finding that the others did not return, came out with many lamentations and called continually on the name of Sisuthrus. Him they saw no more; but they could distinguish his voice in the air, and could hear him admonish them to pay due regard to the gods; and likewise inform them, that it was upon account of his piety that he was translated to live with the gods; that his wife and children, with the pilot, had obtained the same honour. To this he added, that he would have them make the best of their way to Babylonia, and search for the writings at Sippara, which were to be made known to all mankind. The place where these things happened was in Armenia. The remainder having heard these words, offered sacrifices to the gods; and, taking a circuit, journeyed towards Babylonia."

Berossus adds that the remains of the vessel were to be seen in his time upon one of the Corcyrean mountains in Armenia; and that people used to scrape off the bitumen, with which it had been outwardly coated, and made use of it by way of an antidote for poison or amulet. In this manner they returned to Babylon; and having found the writings at Sippara, they set about building cities and erecting temples; and Babylon was thus inhabited again.

The Tower of Babel

MANY ATTEMPTS HAVE BEEN MADE to attach the legend of the confusion of tongues to certain ruined towers in Babylonia, especially to that of E-Sagila, the great temple of Merodach, and some remarks upon this most interesting tale may not be out of place at this point.

The myth is not found in Babylonia itself, and in its best form may be discovered in Scripture. In the Bible story we are told that every region was of one tongue and mode of speech. As men journeyed westward from their original home in the East, they encountered a plain in the land of Shinar where they settled. In this region they commenced building operations, constructed a city, and laid the foundations of a tower, the summit of which they hoped would reach to heaven itself. It would appear that this edifice was constructed with the object of serving as a great landmark to the people so that they should not be scattered over the face of the earth, and the Lord came down to view the city and the tower, and he considered that as they were all of one language this gave them undue power, and that what they imagined to themselves under such conditions they would be able to achieve. So the Lord scattered them abroad over the face of every region, and the building of the tower ceased and the name of it was called 'Babel', because at that place the single language of the people was confounded. Of course it is merely the native name of Babylon, which translated means 'gate of the god', and has no such etymology as the Scriptures pretend, – the Hebrews confusing their verb *balal* 'to confuse or confound', with the word *babel*.

Nimrod, the Mighty Hunter

A

I**T IS STRANGE** that the dispersion of tribes at Babel should be connected with the name of Nimrod, who figures in Biblical as well as Babylonian tradition as a mighty hunter. Epiphanius states that from the very foundation of this city (Babylon) there commenced an immediate scene of conspiracy, sedition, and tyranny, which was carried on by Nimrod, the son of Chus the AEthiop.

Around this dim legendary figure a great deal of learned controversy has raged. Before we examine his legendary and mythological significance, let us see what legend and Scripture say of him. In the Book of Genesis (chap. x, 8, *ff.*) he is mentioned as "a mighty hunter before Yahweh: wherefore it is said, Even as Nimrod the mighty hunter before the Lord." He was also the ruler of a great kingdom. "The beginning of his kingdom was Babel, and Erech, and Accad, and Calneh in the land of Shinar. Out of that land went forth Asshur" (that is, by compulsion of Nimrod) "and built Nineveh," and other great cities. In the Scriptures Nimrod is mentioned as a descendant of Ham, but this may arise from the reading of his father's name as *Cush*, which in the Scriptures indicates a coloured race. The name may possibly be *Cash* and should relate to the Cassites.

It appears then that the sons of Cush or Chus, the Cassites, according to legend, did not partake of the general division of the human race after the fall of Babel, but under the leadership of Nimrod himself remained where they were. After the dispersion, Nimrod built Babylon and fortified the territory around it. It is also said that he built Nineveh and trespassed upon the land of Asshur, so that at last he forced Asshur to quit that territory. The Greeks gave him the name of Nebrod or Nebros, and preserved or invented many tales concerning him and his apostasy, and concerning the tower which he is supposed to have erected. He is described as a gigantic person of mighty bearing, and a contemner of everything divine; his followers are represented as being equally presumptuous and overbearing. In fact he seems to have appeared to the Greeks very much like one of their own Titans.

Nimrod has been identified both with Merodach, the tutelar god of Babylon, and with Gilgamesh, the hero of the epic of that name, with Orion, and with others. The name, according to Petrie, has even been found in Egyptian documents of the XXII Dynasty as 'Nemart'.

Nimrod seems to be one of those giants who rage against the gods, as do the Titans of Greek myth and the Jotunn of Scandinavian story. All are in fact earth-gods, the disorderly forces of nature, who were defeated by the deities who stood for law and order. The derivation of the name Nimrod may mean 'rebel'. In all his later legends, for instance, those of them that are related by Philo in his *De Gigantibus* (a title which proves that Nimrod was connected with the giant race by tradition), he appears as treacherous and untrustworthy. The theory that he is Merodach has no real foundation either in scholarship or probability. As a matter of fact the Nimrod legend seems to be very much more archaic than any piece of tradition connected with Merodach, who indeed is a god of no very great antiquity.

Abram and Nimrod

Many Jewish legends bring Abram into relationship with Nimrod, the mythical King of Babylon. According to legend Abram was originally an idolater, and many stories are preserved respecting his conversion. Jewish legend states that the Father of the Faithful originally followed his father Terah's occupation, which was that of making and selling images of clay; and that, when very young, he advised his father "to leave his pernicious trade of idolatry by which he imposed on the world."

The Jewish Rabbins relate that on one occasion, his father Terah having undertaken a considerable journey, the sale of the images devolved on him, and it happened that a man who pretended to be a purchaser asked him how old he was. "Fifty years," answered the Patriarch. "Wretch that thou art," said the man, "for adoring at that age a thing which is only one day old!" Abram was astonished; and the exclamation of the old man had such an effect upon him, that when a woman soon after brought some flour, as an offering to one of the idols, he took an axe and broke them to pieces, preserving only the largest one, into the hand of which he put the axe. Terah returned home and inquired what this havoc meant. Abram replied that the deities had quarrelled about an offering which a woman had brought, upon which the larger one had seized an axe and destroyed the others. Terah replied that he must be in jest, as it was impossible that inanimate statues could so act; and Abram immediately retorted on his father his own words, showing him the absurdity of worshipping false deities. But Terah, who does not appear to have been convinced, delivered Abram to Nimrod, who then dwelt in the Plain of Shinar, where Babylon was built. Nimrod, having in vain exhorted Abram to worship fire, ordered him to be thrown into a burning furnace, exclaiming – "Let your God come and take you out." As soon as Haran, Abram's youngest brother, saw the fate of the Patriarch, he resolved to conform to Nimrod's religion; but when he saw his brother come out of the fire unhurt, he declared for the "God of Abram," which caused him to be thrown in turn into the furnace, and he was consumed. A certain writer, however, narrates a different version of Haran's death. He says that he endeavoured to snatch Terah's idols from the flames, into which they had been thrown by Abram, and was burnt to death in consequence.

The 'Babylonica' and the Tale of Sinonis and Rhodanes

FRAGMENTS OF BABYLONIAN HISTORY, or rather historical romance, occur in the writings of early authors other than Berossus. One of these is to be found in the *Babylonica* of Iamblichus, a work embracing no less than sixteen books, by a native of Chalchis in Coele-Syria, who was much enamoured of the mysterious ancient life of Babylonia and Assyria, and who died about AD 333. All that remains of what is palpably a romance, which may have been founded upon historical probability, is an epitome of the *Babylonica* by Photius, which, still further condensed, is as follows:

Attracted by her beauty and relying on his own great power, Garmus, King of Babylon, decided to marry Sinonis, a maiden of surpassing beauty. She, however, was already in love with another, Rhodanes, and discouraged Garmus' every advance. Her attachment became known to the King, but did not alter his determination, and to prevent the possibility of any attempt at flight on the part of the lovers, he appointed two eunuchs, Damas and Saca, to watch their movements. The penalty for negligence was loss of ears and nose, and that penalty the eunuchs suffered. In spite of their close vigilance the lovers escaped. Damas and Saca were, however, placed at the head of troops and despatched to recapture the fugitives. Their relentless search was not the lovers' only anxiety, for in seeking refuge with some shepherds in a meadow, they encountered a demon – a satyr, which in the shape of a goat haunted that part of the country. This demon, to Sinonis' horror, began to pay her all sorts of weird, fantastic attentions, and finally compelled her and Rhodanes to abandon the protection of the shepherds for the concealment offered by a cavern. Here they were discovered by Damas and his forces, and must have been captured but for the opportune arrival and attack of a swarm of poisonous bees which routed the eunuchs. When the runaways were alone again they tasted and ate some of the bees' honey, and almost immediately lost consciousness. Later Damas again attacked the cavern, but finding the lovers still unconscious he and his troops left them there for dead.

In time, however, they recovered and continued their flight into the country. A man, who afterward poisoned his brother and accused them of the crime, offered them sanctuary. Only the suicide of this man saved them from serious trouble and probably recapture, and from his house they wandered into the company of a robber. Here again the troops of Damas came upon them and burned their dwelling to the ground. In desperation the fugitives masqueraded as the ghosts of the people the robber had murdered in his house. Their ruse succeeded and once again their pursuers were thrown off the scent. They next encountered the funeral of a young girl, and witnessed her apparent return to life almost at the door of the sepulchre. In this sepulchre Sinonis and Rhodanes slept that night, and once more were believed to be dead by Damas and his soldiers. Later, however, Sinonis tried to dispose of their grave clothes and was arrested in the act. Soracchus, the magistrate of the district, decided to send her to Babylon. In despair she and Rhodanes took some poison with which they had provided themselves against such an emergency. This had been anticipated by their guards, however, with the result that a sleeping draught had been substituted for the poison, and some time later the lovers to their amazement awoke to find themselves in the vicinity of Babylon. Overcome by such a succession of misfortunes, Sinonis stabbed herself, though not fatally. Soracchus, on learning this, was moved to compassion, and consented to the escape of his prisoners.

After this the lovers embarked on a new series of adventures even more thrilling than those which had gone before. The Temple of Venus (Ishtar), situated on an island of the Euphrates, was their first destination after escaping from the captivity of Soracchus. Here Sinonis' wound was healed, and afterward they sought refuge with a cottager, whose daughter consented to dispose of some trinkets belonging to Sinonis. In doing so the girl was mistaken for Sinonis, and news that Sinonis had been seen in the neighbourhood was sent at once to Garmus. While selling the trinkets the cottage girl had become so alarmed by the suspicious questions and manner of the purchasers that she hurried home with all possible speed. On her way back her curiosity was excited by sounds of a great disturbance issuing from a house hard by, and on entering she was appalled to discover a man in the very act of taking his life after murdering his mistress. Terrified and sprinkled with blood she sped back to her father's house. On hearing the girl's story, Sinonis realised that the safety of herself and Rhodanes lay only in flight. They prepared at once to go, but before starting Rhodanes kissed the peasant girl. Sinonis, discovering what he had done by the blood on his lips, became furious with jealousy. In a transport of rage she tried to stab the girl, and on being prevented rushed to the house of Setapo, a wealthy Babylonian of evil repute. Setapo welcomed her only too cordially. At first Sinonis pretended to meet his mood, but as time went by she relented of her treatment of Rhodanes and began to cast about for some means of escape. As the evening wore on she plied Setapo with wine until he was intoxicated, then during the night she murdered him, and in the first early dawn left the house. The slaves of Setapo pursued and overtook her, however, and committed her to custody to answer for her crime.

All Babylon rejoiced with its king over the news of Sinonis' discovery. So great was Garmus' delight that he commanded that all the prisoners throughout his dominions should be released, and in this general boon Sinonis shared. Meanwhile the dog of Rhodanes had scented out the house in which the peasant girl had witnessed the suicide of the lover who had murdered his mistress, and while the animal was devouring the remains of the woman the father of Sinonis arrived at the same house. Thinking the mutilated body was that of his daughter he buried it, and on the tomb he placed the inscription: "Here lies the beautiful Sinonis." Some days later Rhodanes passed that way, and on reading the inscription added to it, "And also the beautiful Rhodanes." In his grief he would have stabbed himself had not the peasant girl who had been the cause of Sinonis' jealousy prevented him by telling him who in reality was buried there.

During these adventures Soracchus had been imprisoned for allowing the lovers to escape, and this, added to the threat of further punishment, induced him to help the Babylonian officers to trace Rhodanes. So in a short time Rhodanes was prisoner once again, and by the command of Garmus was nailed to a cross. In sight of him the King danced delirious with revengeful joy, and while he was so engaged a messenger arrived with the news that Sinonis was about to be espoused by the King of Syria, into whose dominions she had escaped. Rhodanes was taken down from the cross and put in command of the Babylonian army. This seeming change of fortune was really dictated by the treachery of Garmus, as certain inferior officers were commanded by Garmus to slay Rhodanes should he defeat the Syrians, and to bring Sinonis alive to Babylon. Rhodanes won a sweeping victory and also regained the affection and trust of Sinonis. The officers of Garmus, instead of obeying his command, proclaimed the victor king, and all ended auspiciously for the lovers.

The Sacred Literature of Babylonia

THE LITERATURE which the peculiar and individual script of cuneiform has brought down to us is chiefly religious, magical, epical, and legendary. The last three categories are dealt with elsewhere, so that it only falls here to consider the first class, the religious writings.

These are usually composed in Semitic Babylonian without any trace of Akkadian influence, and it cannot be said that they display any especial natural eloquence or literary distinction. In an address to the sun-god, which begins nobly enough with a high apostrophe to the golden luminary of day, we find ourselves descending gradually into an atmosphere of almost ludicrous dullness. The person praying desires the sun-god to free him from the commonplace cares of family and domestic annoyances, enumerating spells against all of his relatives in order that they may not place their 'ban' upon him.

In another, written in Akkadian, the penitent addresses Gubarra, Merodach, and other gods, desiring that they direct their eyes kindly upon him and that his supplication may reach them. Strangely enough the prayer fervently pleads that its utterance may *do good to the gods!* that it may let their hearts rest, their livers be quieted, and gladden them like a father and a mother who have begotten children. This is not so strange when we come to consider the nature of these hymns, many of which come perilously near the border-line of pure magic – that is, they closely resemble spells. We find, too, that those which invoke the older deities such as Gibi the fire-god, are more magical in their trend than those addressed to the later gods when a higher sense of religious feeling had probably been evolved. Indeed, it does not seem too much to say that some of these early hymns may have served the purpose of later incantations. Most of those 'magical' hymns appear to have emanated from that extremely ancient seat of religion, Eridu, and are probably relics of the time when as yet magic and religion were scarcely differentiated in the priestly or the popular mind.

Hymn to Adar

A fine hymn to Adar describes the rumbling of the storm in the abyss, the 'voice' of the god:

The terror of the splendour of Anu in the midst of heaven.

The gods, it is said, urge Adar on, he descends like the deluge, the champion of the gods swoops down upon the hostile land. Nusku, the messenger of Mul-lil, receives Adar in the temple and addresses words of praise to him:

Thy chariot is as a voice of thunder.
To the lifting of thy hands is the shadow turned.
The spirits of the earth, the great gods, return to the winds.

Many of the hymns assist us to a better understanding of the precise nature of the gods, defining as they do their duties and offices and even occasionally describing their appearance. Thus in a hymn to Nebo we note that he is alluded to as "the supreme messenger who binds all things together", "the scribe of all that has a name", "the lifter up of the stylus supreme", "director of the world", "possessor of the reed of augury", "traverser of strange lands", "opener of wells", "fructifier of the corn", and "the god without whom the irrigated land and the canal are unwatered". It is from such texts that the mythologist is enabled to piece together the true significance of many of the deities of ancient peoples.

A hymn to Nusku in his character of fire-god is also descriptive and picturesque. He is alluded to as "wise prince, the flame of heaven", "he who hurls down terror, whose clothing is splendour", "the forceful fire-god", "the exalter of the mountain peaks", and "the uplifter of the torch, the enlightener of darkness".

Babylonian Myths of Creation

FEW CREATION MYTHS are more replete with interest than those which have literary sanction. These are few in number, as, for example, the creation story in Genesis, those to be found in Egyptian papyri, and that contained in the *Popol Vuh* of the Maya of Central America.

In such an account we can trace the creation story from the first dim conception of world-shaping to the polished and final effort of a priestly caste to give a theological interpretation to the intentions of the creative deity; and this is perhaps more the case with the creation myth which had its rise among the old Akkadian population of Babylonia than with any other known to mythic science. In the account in Genesis of the framing of the world it has been discovered that two different versions have been fused to form a single story; the creation tale of the *Popol Vuh* is certainly a composite myth; and similar suspicions may rest upon the analogous myths of Scandinavia and Japan. But in the case of Babylonia we may be convinced that no other influences except those of the races who inhabited Babylonian territory could have been brought to bear upon this ancient story, and that although critical examination has proved it to consist of materials which have been drawn from more than one source, yet these sources are not foreign, and they have not undergone sophistication at the hands of any alien mythographer or interpolator.

It would seem that this Babylonian cosmogony was drawn from various sources, but it appears to be contained in its final form in what are known as the Seven Tablets of Creation, brought from the library of Assur-bani-pal at Nineveh and now in the British Museum. These have from time to time been supplemented by later finds, but we may take it that in this record we have the final official development of Babylonian belief, due to the priests of Babylon, after that city had become the metropolis of the empire.

The primary object of the Seven Tablets was to record a terrific fight between Bel and the Dragon, and the account of the creation is inserted by way of introduction. It is undoubtedly the most important find dealing with Babylonian religion that has as yet come to light.

The Birth of the Gods

A

S IN SO MANY CREATION MYTHS we find chaotic darkness brooding over a waste of waters; heaven and earth were not as yet. Naught existed save the primeval ocean, Mommu Tiawath, from whose fertile depths came every living thing. Nor were the waters distributed, as in the days of man, into sea, river, or lake, but all were confined together in one vast and bottomless abyss. Neither did god or man exist: their names were unknown and their destinies undetermined. The future was as dark as the gloom which lay over the mighty gulf of chaos. Nothing had been designed or debated concerning it.

But there came a stirring in the darkness and the great gods arose. First came Lahmu and Lahame; and many epochs later, Ansar and Kisar, component parts of whose names signify 'Host of Heaven' and 'Host of Earth'. These latter names we may perhaps accept as symbolical of the spirits of heaven and of earth respectively. Many days afterward came forth their son Anu, god of the heavens.

At this point it should be explained that the name Tiawath affords a parallel to the expression *T'hom* or 'deep' of the Old Testament. Practically the same word is used in Assyrian in the form *Tamtu*, to signify the 'deep sea'. The reader will recall that it was upon the face of the deep that the spirit of God brooded, according to the first chapter of Genesis. The word and the idea which it contains are equally Semitic, but strangely enough it has an Akkadian origin. For the conception that the watery abyss was the source of all things originated with the worshippers of the sea-god Ea at Eridu. They termed the deep *apsu*, or a 'house of knowledge' wherein their tutelar god was supposed to have his dwelling, and this word was of Akkadian descent. This *apsu*, or 'abyss', in virtue of the animistic ideas prevailing in early Akkadian times, had become personalized as a female who was regarded as the mother of Ea. She was known by another name as well as that of Apsu, for she was also entitled Zigarun, the 'heaven', or the 'mother that has begotten heaven and earth'; and indeed she seems to have had a form or variant in which she was an earth-goddess as well. But it was not the existing earth or heaven that she represented in either of her forms, but the primeval abyss, out of which both of these were fashioned.

At this point the narrative exhibits numerous defects, and for a continuation of it we must apply to Damascius, the last of the Neoplatonists, who was born in Damascus about AD 480, and who is regarded by most Assyriologists as having had access to valuable written or traditional material. Damascius stated that Anu was followed by Bel (we retain the Babylonian form of the names rather than Damascius' Greek titles), and Ea the god of Eridu. "From Ea and Dawkina," he writes, "was born a son called Belos or Bel-Merodach, whom the Babylonians regarded as the creator of the world." From Damascius we can learn nothing further, and the defective character of the tablet does not permit us to proceed with any degree of certainty until we arrive at the name of Nudimmud, which appears to be simply a variant of the name of Ea. From obscure passages it may be generally gleaned that Tiawath and Apsu, once one, or rather originally representing the Babylonian and Akkadian forms of the deep, are now regarded as mates – Tiawath being the female and Apsu, once female, in this case the male. These have a son, Moumis or Mummu, a name which at one time seems to have been given to Tiawath, so that in these changes we may be able to trace the hand of the later mythographer, who, with less skill and greater levity than is to be found in most myths, has taken upon himself the responsibility of manufacturing three deities out of one. It may be that the scribe in question was well aware that his literary effort must square with and placate popular belief or popular prejudice, and in no era and at no time has priestly ingenuity been unequal to such a task, as is well evidenced by many myths which exhibit traces of late alteration. But in dwelling for a moment on this question, it is only just to the priesthood to admit that such changes did not always emanate from them, but were the work of poets and philosophers who, for aesthetic or rational reasons, took it upon themselves to recast the myths of their race according to the dictates of a nicer taste, or in the interests of 'reason'.

A Darksome Trinity

These three, then, Tiawath, Apsu, and Mummu, appear to have formed a trinity, which bore no good-will to the 'higher gods'. They themselves, as deities of a primeval epoch, were doubtless regarded by the theological opinion of a later day as dark, dubious, and unsatisfactory. It is notorious that in many lands the early, elemental gods came into bad odour in later times; and it may be that the Akkadian descent of this trio did not conduce to their popularity with the Babylonian people. Be that as it may, alien and aboriginal gods have in all times been looked upon by an invading and conquering race with distrust as the workers of magic and the sowers of evil, and even although a Babylonian name had been accorded one of them, it may not have been employed in a complimentary sense. Whereas the high gods regarded those of the abyss with distrust, the darker deities of chaos took up an attitude towards the divinities of light which can only be compared to the sarcastic tone which Milton's Satan adopts against the Power which thrust him into outer darkness. Apsu was the most ironical of all. There was no peace for him, he declared, so long as the new-comers dwelt on high: their way was not his way, neither was it that of Tiawath, who, if Apsu represented sarcasm deified, exhibited a fierce truculence much more overpowering than the irony of her mate. The trio discussed how they might rid themselves of those beings who desired a reign of light and happiness, and in these deliberations Mummu, the son, was the prime mover. Here again the Tablets fails us somewhat, but we learn sufficient further on to assure us that Mummu's project was one of open war against the gods of heaven.

In connection with this campaign, Tiawath made the most elaborate preparations along with her companions. She laboured without ceasing. From the waters of the great abyss over which she presided she called forth the most fearful monsters, who remind us strongly of those against which Horus, the Egyptian god of light, had to strive in his wars with Set. From the deep came gigantic serpents armed with stings, dripping with the most deadly poison; dragons of vast shape reared their heads above the flood, their huge jaws armed with row upon row of formidable teeth; giant dogs of indescribable savagery; men fashioned partly like scorpions; fish-men, and countless other horrible beings, were created and formed into battalions under the command of a god named Kingu, to whom Tiawath referred as her 'only husband' and to whom she promised the rule of heaven and of fate when once the detested gods of light are removed by his mighty arm.

The introduction of this being as the husband of Tiawath seems to point either to a fusion of legends or to the interpolation of some passage popular in Babylonian lore. At this juncture Apsu disappears, as does Mummu. Can it be that at this point a scribe or mythographer took up the tale who did not agree with his predecessor in describing Tiawath, Apsu, and Mummu, originally one, as three separate deities? This would explain the divergence, but the point is an obscure one, and hasty conclusions on slight evidence are usually doomed to failure. To resume our narrative, Tiawath, whoever her coadjutors, was resolved to retain in her own hands the source of all living things, that great deep over which she presided.

Merodach Battles Tiawath

BUT THE GODS OF HEAVEN were by no means lulled into peaceful security, for they were aware of the ill-will which Tiawath bore them. They learned of her plot, and great was their wrath. Ea, the god of water, was the first to hear of it, and related it to Ansar, his father, who filled heaven with his cries of anger. Ansar betook himself to his other son, Anu, god of the sky. "Speak to the great dragon," he urged him; "speak to her, my son, and her anger will be assuaged and her wrath vanish." Duly obedient, Anu betook himself to the realm of Tiawath to reason with her, but the monster snarled at him so fiercely that in dread he turned his back upon her and departed. Next came Nudimmud to her, but with no better success.

At length the gods decided that one of their number, called Merodach, should undertake the task of combating Tiawath the terrible. Merodach asked that it might be written that he should be victorious, and this was granted him. He was then given rule over the entire universe, and to test whether or not the greatest power had passed to him a garment was placed in the midst of the gods and Merodach spoke words commanding that it should disappear. Straightway it vanished and was not. Once more spoke the god, and the garment re-appeared before the eyes of the dwellers in heaven.

The portion of the epic which describes the newly acquired glories of Merodach is exceedingly eloquent. We are told that none among the gods can now surpass him in power, that the place of their gathering has become his home, that they have given him the supreme sovereignty, and they even beg that to them who put their trust in him he will be gracious. They pray that he may pour out the soul of the keeper of evil, and finally they place in his hands a marvellous weapon with which to cut off the life of Tiawath. "Let the winds carry her blood to secret places," they exclaimed in their desire that the waters of this fountain of wickedness should be scattered far and wide. Mighty was he to look upon when he set forth for the combat. His great bow he bore upon his back; he swung his massive club triumphantly. He set the lightning before him; he filled his body with swiftness; and he framed a great net to enclose the dragon of the sea. Then with a word he created terrible winds and tempests, whirlwinds, storms, seven in all, for the confounding of Tiawath. The hurricane was his weapon, and he rode in the chariot of destiny. His helm blazed with terror and awful was his aspect. The steeds which were yoked to his chariot rushed rapidly towards the abyss, their mouths frothing with venomous foam. Followed by all the good wishes of the gods, Merodach fared forth that day.

Soon he came to Tiawath's retreat, but at sight of the monster he halted, and with reason, for there crouched the great dragon, her scaly body still gleaming with the waters of the abyss, flame darting from her eyes and nostrils, and such terrific sounds issuing from her widely open mouth as would have terrified any but the bravest of the gods. Merodach reproached Tiawath for her rebellion and ended by challenging her to combat. Like the dragons of all time, Tiawath appears to have been versed in magic and hurled the most potent incantations against her adversary. She cast many a spell. But Merodach, unawed by this, threw over her his great net, and caused an evil wind which he had sent on before him to blow on her, so that she might not close her mouth. The tempest rushed between her jaws and held them open; it entered her body and racked her frame. Merodach swung his club on high, and with a mighty blow shattered her great flank and slew her. Down he cast her corpse and stood upon it; then he cut out her evil heart. Finally he overthrew the host of monsters which had followed her, so that at length they trembled, turned, and fled in headlong rout. These also he caught in his net and "kept them in bondage". Kingu he bound and took from him the tablets of destiny which had been granted to him by the slain Tiawath, which obviously means that the god of a later generation wrenches the power of fate from an earlier hierarchy, just as one earthly dynasty may overthrow and replace another. The north wind bore Tiawath's blood away to secret places, and at the sight Ea, sitting high in the heavens, rejoiced exceedingly. Then Merodach took rest and nourishment, and as he rested a plan arose in his mind. Rising, he flayed Tiawath of her scaly skin and cut her asunder.

We have already seen that the north wind bore her blood away, which probably symbolises the distribution of rivers over the earth. Then did Merodach take the two parts of her vast body, and with one of them he framed a covering for the heavens. Merodach next divided the upper from the lower waters, made dwellings for the gods, set lights in the heaven, and ordained their regular courses.

As the tablet poetically puts it, "he lit up the sky establishing the upper firmament, and caused Anu, Bel, and Ea to inhabit it." He then founded the constellations as stations for the great gods, and instituted the year, setting three constellations for each month, and placing his own star, Nibiru, as the chief light in the firmament. Then he caused the new moon, Nannaru, to shine forth and gave him the rulership of the night, granting him a day of rest in the middle of the month. There is another mutilation at this point, and we gather that the net of Merodach, with which he had snared Tiawath, was placed in the heavens as a constellation along with his bow. The winds also appear to have been bound or tamed and placed in the several points of the compass; but the whole passage is very obscure, and doubtless information of surpassing interest has been lost through the mutilation of the tablet.

We shall probably not be far in error if we regard the myth of the combat between Merodach and Tiawath as an explanation of the primal strife between light and darkness. Among the most primitive peoples, the solar hero has at one stage of his career to encounter a grisly dragon or serpent, who threatens his very existence. In many cases this monster guards a treasure which mythologists of a generation ago almost invariably explained as that gold which is spread over the sky at the hour of sunset. The assigning of solar characteristics to all slayers of dragons and their kind was a weakness of the older school of mythology, akin to its deductions based on philological grounds; but such criticism as has been directed against the solar theory – and it has been extensive – has not always been pertinent, and in many cases has been merely futile. In fact the solar theory suffered because of the philological arguments with which it was bound up, and neither critics nor readers appeared to discriminate between these. But we should constantly bear in mind that to attempt to elucidate or explain myths by any one system, or by one hard and fast hypothesis, is futile. On the other hand nearly all systems which have yet attempted to elucidate or disentangle the terms of myth are capable of application to certain types of myth. The dragon story is all but universal: in China it is the monster which temporarily swallows the sun during eclipse; in Egypt it was the great serpent Apep, which battled with Ra and Horus, both solar heroes; in India it is the serpent Vritra, or Ahi, who is vanquished by Indra; in Australia and in some parts of North America a great frog takes the place of the dragon. In the story of Beowulf the last exploit of the hero is the slaying of a terrible fire-breathing dragon which guards a hidden treasure-hoard; and Beowulf receives a mortal wound in the encounter. In the Volsung Saga the covetous Faffnir is turned into a dragon and is slain by Sigurd. These must not be confounded with the monsters which cause drought and pestilence. It is a sun-swallowing monster with which we have here to deal.

The tablets here allude to the creation of man; the gods, it is stated, so admired the handiwork of Merodach, that they desired to see him execute still further marvels. Now the gods had none to worship them or pay them homage, and Merodach suggested to his father, Ea, the creation of man out of his divine blood. Here once more the tablets fail us, and we must turn to the narrative of the Chaldean writer Berossus, as preserved by no less than three authors of the classical age. Berossus states that a certain woman Thalatth (that is, Tiawath) had many strange creatures at her bidding. Belus (that is, Bel-Merodach) attacked and cut her in twain, forming the earth out of one half and the heavens out of the other, and destroying all the creatures over which she ruled. Then did Merodach decapitate himself, and as his blood flowed forth the other gods mingled it with the earth and formed man from it. From this circumstance mankind is rational, and has a spark of the divine in it. Then did Merodach divide the darkness, separate the heavens from the earth, and order the details of the entire universe. But those animals which he had created were not able to bear the light, and died. A passage then occurs which states that the stars, the sun and moon, and the five planets were created, and it would seem from the repetition that there were two creations, that the first was a failure, in which Merodach had, as it were, essayed a first attempt, perfecting the process in the second creation. Of course it may be conjectured that Berossus may have drawn from two conflicting accounts, or that those who quote him have inserted the second passage.

The Sumerian incantation, which is provided with a Semitic translation, adds somewhat to our knowledge of this cosmogony. It states that in the beginning nothing as yet existed, none of the great cities of Babylonia had yet been built, indeed there was no land, nothing but sea. It was not until the veins of Tiawath had been cut through that paradise and the abyss appear to have been separated and the gods created by Merodach. Also did he create *annunaki* or gods of the earth, and established a wondrous city as a place in which they might dwell. Then men were formed with the aid of the goddess Aruru, and finally vegetation, trees, and animals. Then did Merodach raise the great temples of Erech and Nippur. From this account we see that instead of Merodach being alluded to as the son of the gods, he is regarded as their creator. In the library of Nineveh was also discovered a copy of a tablet written for the great temple of Nergal at Cuthah. Nergal himself is supposed to make the statement which it contains. He tells us how the hosts of chaos and confusion came into being. At first, as in the other accounts, nothingness reigned supreme, then did the great gods create warriors with the bodies of birds, and men with the faces of ravens. They founded them a city in the ground, and Tiawath, the great dragon, did suckle them. They were fostered in the midst of the mountains, and under the care of the 'mistress of the gods' they greatly increased and became heroes of might. Seven kings had they, who ruled over six thousand people. Their father was the god Benani, and their mother the queen, Melili. These beings, who might almost be called tame gods of evil, Nergal states that he destroyed. Thus all accounts agree concerning the original chaotic condition of the universe. They also agree that the powers of chaos and darkness were destroyed by a god of light.

The creation tablets are written in Semitic and allude to the great circle of the gods as already fully developed and having its full complement. Even the later deities are mentioned in them. This means that it must be assigned to a comparatively late date, but it possesses elements which go to show that it is a late edition of a much earlier composition – indeed the fundamental elements in it appear, as has been said, to be purely Akkadian in origin, and that would throw back the date of its original form to a very primitive period indeed. It has, as will readily be seen, a very involved cosmogony. Its characteristics show it to have been originally local, and of course Babylonian, in its secondary origin, but from time to time it was added to, so that such gods as were at a later date adopted into the Babylonian pantheon might be explained and accounted for by it; but the legend of the creation arising in the city of Babylon, the local folk-tale known and understood by the people, was never entirely shelved by the more consequential and polished epic, which was perhaps only known and appreciated in literary and aesthetic circles, and bore the same relation to the humbler folk-story that Milton's *Paradise Lost* bears to the medieval legends of the casting out of Satan from heaven.

Although it is quite easy to distinguish influences of extreme antiquity in the Babylonian creation myth, it is clear that in the shape in which it has come down to us it has been altered in such a manner as to make Merodach reap the entire credit of Tiawath's defeat instead of En-lil, or the deity who was his predecessor as monarch of the gods. Jastrow holds that the entire cosmological tale has been constructed from an account of a conflict with a primeval monster and a story of a rebellion against Ea; that these two tales have become fused, and that the first is again divisible into three versions, originating one at Uruk and the other two at Nippur at different epochs. The first celebrates the conquest of Anu over Tiawath, the second exalts Ninib as the conqueror, and the third replaces him by En-lil. We thus see how it was possible for the god of a conquering or popular dynasty to have a complete myth made over to him, and how at last it was competent for the mighty Merodach of Babylon to replace an entire line of deities as the central figure of a myth which must have been popular with untold generations of Akkadian and Babylonian people.

The Writings of Oannes

This myth, related by Ea or Oannes (a mythical being who taught mankind wisdom) regarding the creation of the world, bears a very close relation to that told earlier of Merodach and Tiawath.

"Moreover," says Polyhistor (a Greek scholar from the 1st century BC), "Oannes wrote concerning the generation of mankind; of their different ways of life, and of civil polity; and the following is the purport of what he said: 'There was nothing but darkness, and an abyss of water, wherein resided most hideous beings, which were produced of a twofold principle. Men appeared with two wings, some with four, and with two faces. They had one body, but two heads; the one of a man, the other of a woman. They were likewise in their several organs both male and female. Other human figures were to be seen with the legs and horns of goats. Some had horses' feet: others had the limbs of a horse behind; but before were fashioned like men, resembling hippocentaurs. Bulls likewise bred there with the heads of men; and dogs with fourfold bodies, and the tails of fishes. Also horses with the heads of dogs: men too, and other animals, with the heads and bodies of horses, and the tails of fishes. In short, there were creatures with the limbs of every species of animals. Add to these, fishes, reptiles, serpents, with other wonderful animals; which assumed each other's shape and countenance. Of all these were preserved delineations in the temple of Belus at Babylon. The person, who was supposed to have presided over them, had the name of Omorca. This in the Chaldaic language is Thalath; which the Greeks express *thalassa*, the sea: but according to the most probable theory, it is equivalent to *selene*, the moon. All things being in this situation, Belus came, and cut the woman-creature asunder: and out of one half of her he formed the earth, and of the other half the heavens. At the same time he destroyed the animals in the abyss. All this, Berossus said, was an allegorical description of nature. For the whole universe consisting of moisture, and, animals being continually generated therein, the Deity (Belus) above-mentioned cut off his own head, upon which the other gods mixed the blood, as it gushed out, with the earth, and from this men were formed. On this account it is, that they are rational, and partake of divine knowledge. This Belus, whom men call Dis, divided the darkness, and separated the heavens from the earth; and reduced the universe to order. But the animals so lately created, not being able to bear the prevalence of light, died. Belus upon this, seeing a vast space quite uninhabited, though by nature very fruitful, ordered one of the gods to take off his head; and when it was taken off, they were to mix the blood with the soil of the earth; and from thence to form other men and animals, which should be capableof bearing the light. Belus also formed the stars, and the sun, and moon, together with the five planets.'"

Early Babylonian Gods

THE EARLIEST BABYLONIAN religious ideas – that is, subsequent to the entrance of that people into the country watered by the Tigris and Euphrates – were undoubtedly coloured by those of the non-Semitic Sumerians whom they found in the country. They adopted the alphabet of that race, and this affords strong presumptive evidence that the immigrant Semites, as an unlettered people, would naturally accept much if not all of the religion of the more cultured folk whom they found in possession of the soil.

There is no necessity in this place to outline the nature of animistic belief at any length – it is sufficient to state here succinctly that animism is a condition of thought or belief in which man considers everything in the universe along with himself to be the possessor of 'soul', 'spirit', or at least volition. Thus, the wind, water, animals, the heavenly bodies, all live, move, and have their being, and because of his fear of or admiration for them, man placates or adores them until at length he almost unconsciously exalts them into a condition of godhead. Have we any reason to think that the ancient Semites of Babylonia regarded the universe as peopled by gods or godlings of such a type? The proofs that they did so are not a few.

Spirits and Gods

S PIRITS SWARMED in ancient Babylonia, as the reader will observe when he comes to peruse the chapter dealing with the magical ideas of the race. And here it is important to note that the determinative or symbolic written sign for 'spirit' is the same as that for 'god'. Thus the god and the spirit must in Babylonia have had a common descent.

The manner in which we can distinguish between a god and a spirit, however, is simple. Lists of the 'official' gods are provided in the historical texts, whereas spirits and demons are not included therein. But this is not to say that no attempt had been made to systematize the belief in spirits in Babylonia, for just as the great gods of the universe were apportioned their several offices, so were the spirits allotted almost exactly similar powers. Thus the *Annunaki* were perhaps regarded as the spirits of earth and the *Igigi* as spirits of heaven. So, at least, are they designated in an inscription of Rammannirari I. The grouping evidently survived from animistic times, when perhaps the spirits which are embraced in these two classes were the only 'gods' of the Babylonians or Sumerians, and from whose ranks some of the great gods of future times may have been evolved. In any case they belong to a very early period in the Babylonian religion and play no unimportant part in it almost to the end. The god Anu, the most ancient of the Babylonian deities, was regarded as the father of both companies, but other gods make use of their services. They do not appear to be well disposed to humanity. The Assyrian kings were wont to invoke them when they desired to inculcate a fear of their majesty in the people, and from this it may be inferred that they were objects of peculiar fear to the lower orders of the population – for the people often cling to the elder cults and the elder pantheons despite the innovations of ecclesiastical politicians, or the religious eccentricities of kings. There can, however, be no doubt as to the truly animistic character of early Babylonian religion. Thus in the early inscriptions one reads of the spirits of various kinds of diseases, the spirit of the south wind, the spirits of the mist, and so forth. The *bit-ili* or sacred stones marking the residence of a god were probably a link between the fetish and the idol, remaining even after the fully developed idol had been evolved.

Totemism in Babylonian Religion

SIGNS OF TOTEMISM are not wanting in the Babylonian as in other religious systems. Many of the gods are pictured as riding upon the backs of certain animals, an almost certain indication that at one time they had themselves possessed the form of the animal they bestrode.

Religious conservatism would probably not tolerate the immediate abolition of the totem-shape, so this means was taken of gradually 'shelving' it. But some gods retained animal form until comparatively late times. Thus the sun-god of Kis had the form of an eagle, and we find that Ishtar took as lovers a horse, an eagle, and a lion – surely gods who were represented in equine, aquiline, and leonine forms. The fish-form of Oannes, the god of wisdom, is certainly a relic of totemism. Some of the old ideographic representations of the names of the gods are eloquent of a totemic connection. Thus the name of Ea, the god of the deep, is expressed by an ideograph which signifies 'antelope'. Ea is spoken of as 'the antelope of the deep', 'the lusty antelope', and so forth. He was also, as a water-god, connected with the serpent, a universal symbol of the flowing stream. The strange god Uz, probably an Akkadian survival, was worshipped under the form of a goat. The sun-god of Nippur, Adar, was connected with the pig, and was called 'lord of the swine'. Merodach may have been a bull-god. In early astronomical literature we find him alluded to as 'the bull of light'. The storm-god Zu, as is seen by his myth, retained his bird-like form. Another name of the storm-bird was Lugalbanda, patron god of the city of Marad, near Sippara. Like Prometheus – also once a bird-god, as is proved by many analogous myths – he stole the sacred fire from heaven for the service and mental illumination of man.

The Great Gods

🐾

IN THE PHASE in which it becomes first known to us, Babylonian religion is neither Semitic nor Akkadian, but Semitic-Akkadian: that is, the elements of both religious forms are so intermingled in it that they cannot be distinguished one from another; but very little that is trustworthy can be advanced concerning this shadowy time. Each petty state (and these were numerous in early Babylonia) possessed its own tutelar deity, and he again had command over a number of lesser gods. When all those pantheons were added together, as was the case in later days, they afforded the spectacle of perhaps the largest assembly of gods known to any religion.

The most outstanding of these tribal divinities, as they might justly be called, were Merodach, who was worshipped at Babylon; Shamash, who was adored at Sippar; Sin, the moon-god, who ruled at Ur; Anu, who held sway over Erech and Der; Ea, the Oannes of legend, whose city was Eridu; Bel, who ruled at Nippur, or Niffur; Nergal of Cuthah; and Ishtar, who was goddess of Nineveh. The peoples of the several provinces identified their prominent gods one with another, and indeed when Assyria rose to rivalry with Babylonia, its chief divinity, Asshur, was naturally identified with Merodach.

In the previous chapter we have seen how Merodach gained the lordship of heaven. The rise of this god to power was comparatively recent. Prior to the days of Hammurabi (the all-conquering sixth king of the First Babylonian Dynasty, who reigned from 1792 BC to 1750 BC) a rather different pantheon from that described in later inscriptions held sway. In those more primitive days the principal gods appear to have been Bel or En-lil, Belit or Nin-lil his queen, Nin-girsu, Ea, Nergal, Shamash, Sin, Anu, and other lesser divinities. There is indeed a sharp distinction between the pre- and post-Hammurabic types of religion. Attempts had been made to form a pantheon before Hammurabi's day, but his exaltation of Merodach, the patron of Babylon, to the head of the Babylonian pantheon was destined to destroy these. A glance at the condition of the great gods before the days of Hammurabi will assist us to understand their later developments.

Bel

BEL, OR, TO GIVE HIM HIS EARLIER NAME, EN-LIL, is spoken of in very early inscriptions, especially in those of Nippur; of which city he was the tutelar deity. He was described as the 'lord of the lower world', and much effort seems to have been made to reach a definite conception of his position and attributes. His name had also been translated 'lord of mist'.

The title 'Bel' had been given to Merodach by Tiglath-pileser I about 1200 BC, after which he was referred to as 'the older Bel'. The chief seat of his worship was at Nippur, where the name of his temple, E-Kur or 'mountain-house', came to be applied to a sanctuary all over Babylonia. He was also addressed as the 'lord of the storm' and as the 'great mountain', and his consort Nin-lil is also alluded to as 'lady of the mountain'. Jastrow rightly concludes that "there are substantial reasons for assuming that his original city was on the top of some mountain, as is so generally the case of storm-deities.... There being no mountains in the Euphrates valley, however, the conclusion is warranted that En-lil was the god of a people whose home was in a mountainous region and who brought their god with them when they came to the Euphrates valley."

En-lil is undoubtedly of the class of tempest-deities who dwell on mountain peaks. No text appears to have been found which alludes to him as of a red colour. The flashing of the lightning through the clouds which veil the mountain summits usually generates a belief in the mind of primitive man that the god who is concealed by the screen of vapour is red in hue and quick in movement. The second tablet of a text known as the 'crying storm' alludes to En-lil as a storm-god. Addressing him it says: "Spirit that overcomes no evildoing, spirit that has no mother, spirit that has no wife, spirit that has no sister, spirit that has no brother; that knows no abiding place, the evil-slaying spirit that devastates the fold, that wrecks the stall, that sweeps away son and mother like a reed. As a huge deluge it tears away dwellings, consumes the provisions of the home, smites mankind everywhere, and wickedly drowns the harvests of the land. Devoted temples it devastates, devoted men it afflicts, him that clothes himself in a robe of majesty the spirit lays low with cold, him of wide pasture lands with hunger it lays low. When En-lil, the lord of lands, cries out at sunset the dreadful word goes forth unto the spacious shrine, 'Destroy'."

Nippur, the city of En-lil, was of Sumerian origin, so we must connect the earliest cult of En-lil with the Sumerian aborigines. Many of his lesser names point to such a conclusion. But he greatly outgrew all local circumstances, and among other things he appears to have been a god who fostered vegetation. Some authorities appear to be of opinion that because En-lil was regarded as a god of vegetation the change was owing to his removal from a mountainous region to a more level neighbourhood. The truth is, it would be difficult to discover a god who wielded the powers of the wind and rain who was not a patron of agriculture, but as he sends beneficent rains, so also may he destroy and devastate, as we have seen from the foregoing text. The noise of the storm was spoken of as his 'word'. Probably, too, because he was a very old god he was regarded in some localities as a creator of the world. The great winged bull of Assyrian art may well often represent En-lil: no symbol could better typify the tempest which the Babylonians regarded as rushing and rioting unrestrained over country and city, overturning even tower and temple with its violence, and tumbling the wretched reed huts of the lower caste into the dust.

The word *lil* which occurs in the name En-lil, signifies a 'demon', and En-lil may therefore mean the 'chief-demon'. This shows the very early, animistic nature of the god. There appear to be other traditions of him as a war-god, but these are so obscure as scarcely to be worth notice. In the trinity which consisted of Bel, Ea, and Anu, he is regarded as the 'god of the earth', that is, the earth is his sphere, and he is at times addressed as 'Bel, the lord of the lands.'

We find the 'word' of the wind or storm-god alluded to in the *Popol Vuh* of the Kiches of Central America, where Hurakan (the deity from whose name we probably get our word 'hurricane') sweeps over the face of the primeval deep, voicing his commands.

Bel and the Dragon

🐒

THE PICTURESQUE LEGEND of Bel and the Dragon which appears in the Apocrypha, and which was at one time appended to the Book of Daniel, shows us the manner in which Bel was worshipped at Babylon, and how he was supposed to take human shape, devour food, and behave very much as a man might. The legend states that the Babylonians lavished every day upon the idol of Bel twelve great measures of fine flour, and forty sheep, and six vessels of wine. King Cyrus of Persia, who had overthrown the Babylonian kingdom, went daily to worship Bel, and asked Daniel why he did not do likewise. The prophet replied that his religion did not permit him to worship idols, but rather the living God who had created the heavens and the earth.

"Then said Cyrus: 'Thinkest thou not that Bel is the living God? Seest thou not how much he eats and drinks every day?'

"Then Daniel smiled and said, 'O King, be not deceived, for he is but clay within and brass without, and can never eat or drink anything.'

"Cyrus was exceedingly angry, and calling for his priests said to them, 'If ye tell me not who this is that devoureth these expenses ye shall die, but if ye can show me that Bel devours them Daniel shall die, for he hath spoken blasphemy against Bel;'" and to this Daniel cheerfully agreed.

It would have been surprising had not the provisions vanished, because we are told that the priests of Bel were threescore and ten in number and had numerous wives and children. So Cyrus and Daniel betook themselves to the temple of Bel, and the priests asked them to bless the meat and wine before Bel, and to shut the door fast and seal it with the King's own signet, stating that if they came on the morrow they would find that Bel had eaten up all of the provisions.

But they had taken good care to protect themselves, for they had made a secret entrance underneath the great table in the temple which they used constantly, so that they might consume the good things that were set before the idol.

And Cyrus did as the priests asked, setting the meat and wine before the statue of Bel, but Daniel commanded his servants to bring ashes, which they strewed throughout the temple in the presence of the King; then they went out and shut the door and sealed it with the King's signet.

And in the night time the priests with their wives and families entered the temple by the secret way and speedily consumed the provisions.

In the morning Cyrus and Daniel betook themselves to the temple, and the King broke the seals and opened the door, and when he perceived that all the provisions had vanished he called out with a loud voice, "Great art thou, O Bel, and with thee is no deceit at all."

But Daniel laughed, and barring the King's way into the temple requested him to look at the pavement and mark well whose footsteps he saw there.

And Cyrus replied, "I see the footsteps of men, women, and children."

He at once called the priests, who when they saw that their stratagem had been discovered showed him the secret way into the temple; and in his rage Cyrus slew them and delivered Bel into Daniel's power. The prophet speedily destroyed the idol and the temple which sheltered it.

Now in that temple was a great dragon worshipped by the people of Babylon, and the King said to Daniel: "Wilt thou also say that this is of brass, for behold! he lives, he eats and drinks, therefore should thou worship him!"

But Daniel shook his head and said to Cyrus: "Give me leave, O King, and I will slay this dragon without sword or staff."

Then Daniel took pitch and fat and hair and boiled them all together, and shaped them into great pieces. These he placed in the dragon's mouth, and shortly the dragon burst asunder.

Now the people of Babylon became greatly incensed at these doings and clamoured to Cyrus, asking him to deliver Daniel up to them, or else they would destroy him and all belonging to him. And, continues the legend, Cyrus being afraid for his crown delivered Daniel to the people, who cast him into a lions' den where he remained for six days. Seven lions were in the den and their food was removed from them so that they might be the fiercer, and the Apocrypha story, which differs considerably from that given in the sixth chapter of the Book of Daniel, states that the angel of the Lord took up a certain prophet called Habbacuc, who was about to carry a mess of pottage to certain reapers, and taking him by the hair of the head, conveyed him all the way from Palestine to Babylon along with the food, which he set at Daniel's feet. Daniel partook of the meal, and Habbacuc was conveyed back to Palestine in the same manner as that in which he had come.

And on the seventh day Cyrus came to the den to mourn for Daniel, and when he looked in Daniel was there. So impressed was Cyrus with the power of Daniel's God that he resolved to worship Him in future, and seizing those who had been instrumental in casting the Hebrew prophet into the den, he thrust them before the lions, and they were devoured in a moment.

Beltis

BELTIS, OR NIN-LIL, the wife of En-lil, shared his authority over Nippur, where she had a temple which went back in antiquity to the First Dynasty of Ur.

As has been said, she was also called the 'lady of the mountain', and as such she had a sanctuary at Girsu, a quarter of Lagash. In certain inscriptions she is described as 'the mother of the gods'. The name Beltis meant 'lady', and as such was accorded to her as being 'the' lady, but it was afterwards given to many other goddesses.

Nergal

NERGAL WAS THE PATRON GOD of Cuthah, eastward from Babylon. He was a god of extremely ancient origin, and indeed the first inscription which alludes to him is dated about 2700 BC. He is mentioned in the Old Testament (2 Kings xvii 30) as an idol whom the Babylonians who re-peopled Israel brought with them.

Nergal seems to have had a close connection with the nether world, indeed he is practically the head of its pantheon. He appears to have been a god of gloom and death, and his name may signify 'the lord of the great dwelling place', that is, the grave. His city, Cuthah, may possibly have been renowned as a burial-place. We find him associated with pestilence and famine, but he has also a solar significance. He is indeed the sun in its malevolent form, fierce and destroying, for in myth the sun can be evil as well as good. We thus find the solar power depicted as a fierce warrior slaying his thousands and tens of thousands. Again it is quite possible for a solar deity to have an underworld connection, seeing that the sun is supposed to travel through that gloomy region during the night. We thus see how Nergal could combine so many seemingly conflicting attributes. As god of the dead he has a host of demons at his command, and it may be these who do his behests in spreading pestilence and war. Where he goes violent death follows in his wake. At times he is called the 'god of fire', the 'raging king', 'he who burns', and the 'violent one', and he is identified with the fierceness of flame. In this respect he is not at all unlike the Scandinavian Loki who typifies the malevolence of fire.

The Tale of Dibarra the Destroyer

DIBARRA WAS PROBABLY A VARIANT of Nergal, in his guise as solar destroyer. Concerning him a strange myth is recounted as follows:

"The sons of Babylon were as birds and thou their falconer. In a net thou didst catch them, enclose them, and destroy them, O warrior Dibarra. Leaving the city, thou didst pass to the outside, taking on the form of a lion, thou didst enter the palace. The people saw thee and drew their weapons."

So spoke Ishum, the faithful attendant of Dibarra, by way of beginning an account of the havoc wrought in the valley of Euphrates by the war- and plague-god. "Spare no one," is the gist of his commands to his satellites. "Have neither fear nor pity. Kill the young as well as the old and rob Babylon of all its treasures."

Accordingly against the first city a large army was dispatched to carry out these instructions, and the battle with bow and sword was begun, a strife which ended so disastrously for the soldiers and inhabitants that their blood flowed "like torrents of water through the city's highways." This defeat the great lord Merodach was compelled to witness, powerless to help or avert it. Enraged at his helplessness and overcome with fury, he cursed his enemies until he is said to have lost consciousness because of his grief.

From this scene of devastation Dibarra turned his attention to Erech, appointing others of his host to mete out to this city the fate of Babylon. Ishtar, goddess of Erech, saw her devoted city exposed to plunder, pillage, and bloodshed, and had to endure the agony of inactivity experienced by Merodach. Nothing she could do or say would stay the violence of Dibarra's vengeance.

"O warrior Dibarra, thou dost dispatch the just, thou dost dispatch the unjust; who sins against thee thou dost dispatch, and the one who does not sin against thee thou dost dispatch."

These words were used by Ishum, Dibarra's servant, in a subsequent address to the god of war. He knew his lord's craving for battle and bloodshed was still unappeased, and he himself was planning a war more terrible than any he had yet conducted, a conflict not only world-wide but which was to embrace heaven itself. So in order to gain Dibarra's consent to the hideous destruction he anticipated, he continued to pander to his war-like tendencies.

Said he: "The brightness of Shul-panddu I will destroy, the root of the tree I will tear out that it no longer blossom. Against the dwelling of the king of gods I will proceed."

To all of which the warrior-god listened with growing pleasure, until fired by his myrmidon's words he cried out in sudden fierce resolve – "Sea-coast against sea-coast, Subartu against Subartu, Assyrian against Assyrian, Elamite against Elamite, Cassite against Cassite, Sutaean against Sutaean, Kuthean against Kuthean, Lullubite against Lullubite, country against country, house against house, man against man. Brother is to show no mercy towards brother; they shall kill one another."

"Go, Ishum," he added later, "carry out the word thou hast spoken in accordance with thy desire."

And with alacrity Ishum obeyed, "directing his countenance to the mountain of Khi-khi. This, with the help of the god Sibi, a warrior unequalled, he attacked and destroyed all the vineyards in the forest of Khashur, and finally the city of Inmarmaon. These last atrocious acts roused Ea, the god of humanity, and filled him with wrath," though what attitude he adopted towards Dibarra is not known.

"Listen all of you to my words, because of sin did I formerly plan evil, my heart was enraged and I swept peoples away."

This was Dibarra's defence when eventually he was propitiated and all the gods were gathered together in council with him. Ishum at this point changing his tactics urged on Dibarra the necessity for pacifying the gods he had incensed.

"Appease," said he, "the gods of the land who are angry. May fruits and corn flourish, may mountains and seas bring their produce."

As he had listened to Ishum before, Dibarra listened again, and the council of the gods was closed by his promising prosperity and protection to those who would fittingly honour him.

"He who glorifies my name will rule the world. Who proclaims the glory of my power will be without rival. The singer who sings of my deeds will not die through pestilence, to kings and nobles his words will be pleasing. The writer who preserves them will escape from the grasp of the enemy, in the temple where the people proclaim my name, I will open his ear. In the house where this tablet is set up, though war may rage and the god Sibi work havoc, sword and pestilence will not touch him – he will dwell in safety. Let this song resound for ever and endure for eternity. Let all lands hear it and proclaim my power. Let the inhabitants of all places learn to glorify my name."

Shamash

S HAMASH, GOD OF THE SUN, was one of the most popular
deities of the Babylonian and Assyrian pantheon. We find him
mentioned first in the reign of E-Anna-Tum, or about 4200 BC. He
is called the son of Sin, the moon-god, which perhaps has reference
to the fact that the solar calendar succeeded the lunar in Babylonia
as in practically all civilizations of any advancement.

The inscriptions give due prominence to Shamash's status as a great lord of light,
and in them he is called the 'illuminator of the regions', 'lord of living creatures',
'gracious one of the lands', and so forth. He is supposed to throw open the gates
of the morning and raise his head over the horizon, lighting up the heaven and
earth with his beams. The knowledge of justice and injustice and the virtue of
righteousness were attributed to him, and he was regarded as a judge between
good and evil, for as the light of the sun penetrates everywhere, and nothing can
be hidden from its beams, it is not strange that it should stand as the symbol for
justice. Shamash appears at the head of the inscription which bears the laws of
Hammurabi, and here he stands as the symbol for justice. The towns at which
he was principally worshipped were Sippar and Larsa, where his sanctuary was
known as E-Babbara, or the 'shining house'. Larsa was probably the older of the
two centres, but from the times of Sargon, Sippar became the more important,
and in the days of Hammurabi ranked immediately after Babylon. In fact it
appears to have threatened the supremacy of the capital to some extent, and
Nabonidus, the last King of Babylon, as we shall remember, offended Merodach
and his priests by his too eager notice of Shamash.

During the whole course of Babylonian history, however, Shamash retained
his popularity, and was perhaps the only sun-god who was not absorbed by
Merodach. One finds the same phenomenon in ancient Mexico, where various
solar deities did not succeed in displacing or absorbing Totec, the ancient god
of the sun *par excellence*. But Shamash succeeded in absorbing many small
local sun-gods, and indeed we find his name used as that of the sun throughout
Semitic lands. There were several solar deities, such as Nergal, and Ninib, whom

Shamash did not absorb, probably for the reason that they typify various phases of the sun. There is reason to believe that in ancient times even Shamash was not an entirely beneficent solar deity, but, like Nergal, could figure as a warrior on occasion. But in later times he was regarded as the god who brings light and life upon all created things, and upon whom depends everything in nature from man to vegetable.

Shamash's consort was Aa, who was worshipped at Sippar along with him. Her cult seems to have been one of great antiquity, but she does not appear to have any distinctive character of her own. She was supposed to receive the sun upon his setting, and from this circumstance it has been argued she perhaps represents the 'double sun', from the magnified disk which he presents at sunset; but this explanation is perhaps rather too much on allegorical lines. Jastrow thinks that she may have been evolved from the sun-god of a city on the other side of the Euphrates from Sippar. "Such an amalgamation of two originally male deities into a combination of male and female, strange as it may seem to us," he says, "is in keeping with the lack of sharp distinction between male and female in the oldest forms of Semitic religions. In the old cuneiform writing the same sign is used to indicate 'lord' or 'lady' when attached to deities. Ishtar appears amongst the Semites both as male and female. Sex was primarily a question of strength; the stronger god was viewed as masculine, the weaker as feminine."

Ea

EA WAS THE THIRD of the great Babylonian triad of gods, which consisted of Anu, En-lil, and himself. He was a god of the waters, and like Anu is called the 'father of the gods'. As a god of the abyss he appears to have been also a deity of wisdom and occult power, thus allegorically associated with the idea of depth or profundity.

Ea was the father of Merodach, who consulted him on the most important matters connected with his kingship of the gods. Indeed he was consulted by individuals of all classes who desired light to be thrown upon their crafts or businesses. Thus he was the god of artisans in general – blacksmiths, stone-cutters, sailors, and artificers of every kind. He was also the patron of prophets and seers. As the abyss is the place where the seeds of everything were supposed to fructify, so he appears to have fostered reproduction of every description. He was supposed to dwell beside Anu, who inhabited the pole of the ecliptic. The site of his chief temple was at Eridu, which at one time stood, before the waters receded, upon the shore of the Persian Gulf. Ea, under his Greek name of Oannes, was supposed to bring knowledge and culture to the people of Eridu. There are many confusing myths connected with him, and he seems in some measure to enter into the Babylonian myth of the deluge. Alexander Polyhistor, Apollodorus, and Eusebius, copying from Berossus, state that he rose from the sea upon his civilizing mission, and Abydenus says that in the time of Daon, the shepherd king of the city of Pantibiblon (meaning the 'city where books were gathered together'), "Annedatus appeared again from the Eruthrean sea, in the same form as those who had showed themselves before, having the shape of a fish blended with that of a man. Then reigned Aedorachus of Pantibiblon for the term of eighteen sari. In his days there appeared another personage from the sea of Eruthra, like those above, having the same complicated form between fish and man: his name was Odacon." From remarks by Apollodorus it would seem that these beings were messengers from Oannes, but the whole passages are very obscure.

The chief extract from the fragments of Berossus concerning Oannes states that: "In the first year there made its appearance from a part of the Eruthrean sea, which bordered upon Babylonia, an animal endowed with reason, who was called Oannes. According to the accounts of Apollodorus the whole body of the animal was like that of a fish; and had under a fish's head another head, and also feet below, similar to those of a man, subjoined to the fish's tail. His speech, too, was articulate and human; and there was a representation of him to be seen in the time of Berossus. This Being in the daytime used to converse with men; but took no food at that season; and he gave them an insight into letters and science, and every kind of art. He taught them to construct houses, to found temples, to compile laws, and explained to them the principles of geometrical knowledge. He made them distinguish the seeds of the earth, and showed them how to collect fruits; in short, he instructed them in everything which could tend to soften manners and humanize mankind. From that time, so universal were his instructions, nothing material has been added by way of improvement. When the sun set, it was the custom of this Being to plunge again into the sea, and abide all the night in the deep." After this there appeared other creatures like Oannes, of which Berossus promises to give an account when he comes to the history of the kings.

It is not often that one finds a fish-god acting as a culture hero, although we find in Mexican myth a certain deity alluded to as the "old fish-god of our flesh." Allegorical mythology would have seen in Ea a hero arriving from another clime in a wave-tossed vessel, who had landed on the shores of the Persian Gulf, and had instructed the rude inhabitants thereof in the culture of a higher civilization. There is very little doubt that Ea has a close connection in some manner with the Noah legend of the deluge. For example, a Sumerian text exists in which it would seem as if the ship of Ea was described, as the timbers of which its various parts were constructed are mentioned, and the refugees it saved consisted of Ea himself, Dawkina his wife, Merodach, and Inesh, the pilot of Eridu, along with Nin-igi-nagir-sir.

Of course it would seem natural to the Babylonians to regard the Persian Gulf as the great abyss whence all things emanated. As Jastrow very justly remarks: "In the word of Ea, of a character more spiritual than that of En-lil, he commands, and what he plans comes into existence – a wholly beneficent power he blesses the fields and heals mankind. His most striking trait is his love of humanity. In conflicts between the gods and mankind, he is invariably on the side of the latter. When the gods, at the instance of En-lil as the 'god of storms', decide to bring on a deluge to sweep away mankind, it is Ea who reveals the secret to his favourite, Ut-Napishtim (Noah), who saves himself, his family, and his belongings on a ship that he is instructed to build." The waters personified by him are not those of the turbulent and treacherous ocean, but those of irrigating streams and commerce-carrying canals. He is thus very different from the god En-lil, the 'lord of heaven' who possesses so many attributes of destruction. Ea in his benevolent way thwarts the purpose of the riotous god of tempest, which greatly enrages En-lil, and it has been thought that this myth suggests the rivalry which perhaps at one time existed between the two religious centres of Eridu and Nippur, cities of Ea and En-lil respectively. In an eloquent manner Ea implores En-lil not to precipitate another deluge, and begs that instead of such wholesale destruction man may be punished by sending lions and jackals, or by famines or pestilences. En-lil hearkens to his speech, his heart is touched, and he blesses Utnapishtim and his wife. If this myth is a piece of priestcraft, it argues better relations between the ecclesiastical authorities at Eridu and Nippur. Ea had many other names, the chief of which, Nin-a-gal, meaning 'god of great strength', alluded to his patronage of the smith's art. He was also called En-ki, which describes him as 'lord of the earth' through which his waters meandered. In such a country as Babylonia earth and water are closely associated, as under that soil water is always to be found at a distance of a few feet: thus the interior of the earth is the domain of Ea.

The Story of Adapa and the South Wind

HERE IS THE STORY OF ADAPA, the son of Ea, who, but for his obedience to his father's command, might have attained deification and immortality.

One day when Adapa was out in his boat fishing the South Wind blew with sudden and malicious violence, upsetting the boat and flinging the fisherman into the sea. When he succeeded in reaching the shore Adapa vowed vengeance against the South Wind, which had used him so cruelly.

"Shutu, thou demon," he cried, "I will stretch forth my hand and break thy wings. Thou shalt not go unpunished for this outrage!"

The hideous monster laughed as she soared in the air above him, flapping her huge wings about her ungainly body. Adapa in his fury leapt at her, seized her wings, and broke them, so that she was no longer able to fly over the broad earth. Then he went his way, and related to his father what he had done.

Seven days passed by, and Anu, the lord of heaven, waited for the coming of the South Wind. But Shutu came not; the rains and the floods were delayed, and Anu grew impatient. He summoned to him his minister Ilabrat.

"Wherefore doth Shutu neglect her duty?" he asked. "What hath chanced that she travels not afield?"

Ilabrat bowed low as he made answer: "Listen, O Anu, and I will tell thee why Shutu flieth not abroad. Ea, lord of the deep and creator of all things, hath a son named Adapa, who hath crushed and broken the wings of thy servant Shutu, so that she is no more able to fly."

"If this be true," said Anu, "summon the youth before me, and let him answer for his crime."

"Be it so, O Anu!"

When Adapa received the summons to appear in heaven he trembled greatly. It was no light thing to answer to the great gods for the ill-usage of their servant, the demon Shutu. Nevertheless he began to make preparations for his journey, and ere he set out his father Ea instructed him as to how he should comport himself in the assembly of the gods.

"Wrap thyself not in a vesture of gold, O my son, but clothe thee in the garments of the dead. At the gates of heaven thou wilt find Tammuz and Gishzida guarding the way. Salute the twain with due respect, I charge thee, baring thy head and showing all deference to them. If thou dost find favour in their eyes they will speak well of thee before Anu. And when thou standest within the precincts of heaven, don the garment that is given thee to wear, and anoint thy head with the oil that is brought thee. But when the gods offer thee food and drink, touch them not; for the food will be the 'Meat of Death', and the drink the 'Water of Death'; let neither pass within thy lips. Go now, my son, and remember these my instructions. Bear thyself with humility, and all will be well."

Adapa bade his father farewell and set out on his journey to heaven. He found all as his father had predicted; Tammuz and Gishzida received him at the portals of the divine dwelling, and so humble was Adapa's attitude that they were moved with compassion towards him. They led him into the presence of Anu, and he bowed low before the great god.

"I am come in answer to thy summons," said he. "Have mercy upon me, O thou Most High!"

Anu frowned upon him.

"It is said of thee," he made answer, "that thou hast broken the wings of Shutu, the South Wind. What manner of man art thou, who darest destroy Shutu in thy wrath? Knowest thou not that the people suffer for lack of nourishment; that the herb droopeth, and the cattle lie parched on the scorching ground? Tell me why hast thou done this thing?"

"I was out on the sea fishing," said Adapa, "and the South Wind blew violently, upsetting my boat and casting me into the water. Therefore I seized her wings and broke them. And lo! I am come to seek thy pardon."

Then Tammuz and Gishzida, the deities whose favour Adapa had won at the gates of heaven, stepped forth and knelt at the feet of their king.

"Be merciful, O Anu! Adapa hath been sorely tried, and now is he truly humble and repentant. Let his treatment of Shutu be forgotten."

Anu listened to the words of Tammuz and Gishzida, and his wrath was turned away.

"Rise, Adapa," he said kindly; "thy looks please me well. Thou hast seen the interior of this our kingdom, and now must thou remain in heaven for ever, and we will make thee a god like unto us. What sayest thou, son of Ea?"

Adapa bowed low before the king of the gods and thanked him for his pardon and for his promise of godhead.

Anu therefore commanded that a feast be made, and that the 'Meat of Life' and the 'Water of Life' be placed before Adapa, for only by eating and drinking of these could he attain immortality.

But when the feast was spread Adapa refused to partake of the repast, for he remembered his father's injunctions on this point. So he sat in silence at the table of the gods, whereupon Anu exclaimed:

"What now, Adapa? Why dost thou not eat or drink? Except thou taste of the food and water set before thee thou canst not hope to live for ever."

Adapa perceived that he had offended his divine host, so he hastened to explain. "Be not angry, most mighty Anu. It is because my lord Ea hath so commanded that I break not bread nor drink water at thy table. Turn not thy countenance from me, I beseech thee."

Anu frowned. "Is it that Ea feared I should seek thy life by offering thee deadly food? Truly he that knows so much, and hath schooled thee in so many different arts, is for once put to shame!"

Adapa would have spoken, but the lord of heaven silenced him.

"Peace!" he said; then to his attendants – "Bring forth a garment that he may clothe himself, and oil bring also to anoint his head."

When the King's command had been carried out Adapa robed himself in the heavenly garment and anointed his head with the oil. Then he addressed Anu thus:

"O Anu, I salute thee! The privilege of godhead must I indeed forego, but never shall I forget the honour that thou wouldst have conferred upon me. Ever in my heart shall I keep the words thou hast spoken, and the memory of thy kindness shall I ever retain. Blame me not exceedingly, I pray thee. My lord Ea awaits my return."

"Truly," said Anu, "I censure not thy decision. Be it even as thou wilt. Go, my son, and peace go with thee!"

And thus Adapa returned to the abode of Ea, lord of the dead, and there for many years he lived in peace and happiness.

Anu

ALONG WITH EN-LIL AND EA, Anu makes up the universal triad. He is called the 'father of the gods', but appears to be descended from still older deities. His name is seldom discovered in the inscriptions prior to the time of Hammurabi, but such notices as occur of him seem to have already fixed his position as a ruler of the sky. His cult was specially associated with the city of Erech. It is probable that in the earliest days he had been the original Sumerian sky-father, as his name is merely a form of the Sumerian word for 'heaven'. This idea is assisted by the manner in which his name is originally written in the inscriptions, as the symbol signifying it is usually that employed for 'heaven'.

It is plain, therefore, that Anu was once regarded as the expanse of heaven itself, just as are the 'sky-fathers' of numerous primitive peoples. Several writers who deal with Anu appear to be of the opinion that a god of the heavens is an 'abstraction'. "Popular fancy," says Jastrow, "deals with realities and with personified powers whose workings are seen and felt.

It would as little, therefore, have evolved the idea that there was a power to be identified with the heavens as a whole, of which the azure sky is a symbol, as it would personify the earth as a whole, or the bodies of waters as a whole. It is only necessary to state the implications involved to recognize that the conception of a triad of gods corresponding to three theoretical divisions of the universe is a bit of learned speculation. It smacks of the school. The conception of a god of heaven fits in moreover with the comparatively advanced period when the seats of the gods were placed in the skies and the gods identified with the stars." A merely superficial acquaintance with the nature of animism and the sky-myths of primitive and barbarian peoples would lead us to the conclusion that the opposite is the case. In Egyptian, Polynesian, and North American Indian myth the sky itself is directly personalized. Egyptian mythological illustration depicts the sky in female form, for in Egyptian myth the sky is the mother and the earth the father of everything. Lang has shown that the sky-father is frequently personalized as a "magnified non-natural man" among races which possess no theological schools. We do not say that the arrangement of Anu, Ea, and En-lil into a triad is not "a bit of learned speculation," but to state that early animism did not first personalize the sky and the earth and the sea is rash in the extreme. When Deucalion and Pyrrha in the Greek myth asked the gods how they might best replenish the earth with the human race, they were instructed to cast "the bones of their mother" behind them, and these bones they interpreted as the stones and rocks and acted accordingly. So would primitive man all the world over have interpreted this advice, for universally he believes the very soil upon which he walks to be the great mother which produced his ancestors, out of whose dust or clay they were formed, and who still nourishes and preserves him.

Jastrow proceeds to state that "Anu was originally the personification of some definite power of nature, and everything points to this power having been the sun in the heavens. Starting from this point of view we quite understand how the great illuminer of heaven should have been identified with the heavens in an artificially devised theological system, just as En-lil became in this system the designation of the earth and of the region above the earth viewed as a whole." The very fact that in the earliest times Anu was identified with the expanse of the sky itself, and that the symbol used to denote him meant 'heaven', is against this supposition. Again, the theory suffers from lack of analogy. In what other mythology is there to be found a sky-god who at one time possessed a solar significance? The converse might be the case. Some sky-gods have attained the solar connection because of their rule over the entire expanse of the heavens, just as they have attained the power of wielding lightning and the wind. But we are at a loss to recall any deity originally of distinctive solar attributes who later took the position of a sky-god.

Anu was regarded as head of the triad and the father of En-lil. We are told that the goddess Aruru first shaped man in the image of Anu, who must thus have attained an anthropomorphic condition. He appears also to have been regarded as the conqueror of primeval chaos. His consort was Anatu, probably a later feminine form of himself.

Ishtar

ISHTAR WAS UNDOUBTEDLY a goddess of Semitic origin and symbolized the fertility of the earth. She was the 'great mother' who fostered all vegetation and agriculture. It is probable that her cult originated at Erech, and in the course of centuries and under many nominal changes dispersed itself throughout the length and breadth of western Asia and even into Greece and Egypt.

It is probable that a number of lesser goddesses, such as Nanâ and Anunit, may have become merged in the conception of this divinity, and that lesser local deities of the same character as herself may have taken her name and assisted to swell her reputation. She is frequently addressed as 'mother of the gods', and indeed the name 'Ishtar' became a generic designation for 'goddess'. But these were later honours. When her cult centred at Erech, it appears to have speedily blossomed out in many directions, and, as has been said, lesser cults probably eagerly identified themselves with that of the great earth-mother, so that in time her worship became more than a Babylonian cult. Indeed, wherever people of Semitic speech were to be found, there was the worship of Ishtar. As Ashteroth, or Astarte, she was known to Canaanites, Phoenicians, and Greeks, and there is some likelihood that the cult of Aphrodite had also its beginnings in that of Ishtar. She could also arguably be the Esther of the Scriptures.

Astrologically Ishtar was identified with the planet Venus, but so numerous were the attributes surrounding her taken from other goddesses with which she had become identified that they threatened to overshadow her real character, which was that of the great and fertile mother. More especially did her identification with Nin-lil, the consort of En-lil, the storm-god, threaten to alter her real nature, as in this guise she was regarded as a goddess of war. It is seldom that a goddess of fertility or love achieves such a distinction. Gods possessing an agricultural significance are nearly always war-gods, but that is because they bring the fertilizing thunder-clouds and therefore possess the lightning arrow or spear. But Ishtar is specifically a goddess of the class of Persephone or Isis, and her identification with battle must be regarded as purely accidental. In later times in Assyria she was conceived as the consort of Asshur, head of the Assyrian pantheon, in days when a god or goddess who did not breathe war was of little use to a people like the Assyrians, who were constantly employed in hostilities, and this circumstance naturally heightened her reputation as a warlike divinity. But it is at present her original character with which we are occupied, indeed in some texts we find that, so far from being able to protect herself, Ishtar and her property are made the prey of the savage En-lil, the storm-god. "His word sent me forth," she complains; "as often as it comes to me it casts me prostrate upon my face. The unconsecrated foe entered my courts, placed his unwashed hands upon me, and caused me to tremble. Putting forth his hand he smote me with fear. He tore away my robe and clothed his wife therein: he stripped off my jewels and placed them upon his daughter. Like a quivering dove upon a beam I sat. Like a fleeing bird from my cranny swiftly I passed. From my temple like a bird they caused me to fly." Such is the plaint of Ishtar, who in this case appears to be quite helpless before the enemy.

The myth which best illustrates her character is that which speaks of her journey to Aralu, the underworld.

The Descent of Ishtar into Hades

THE POEM FEATURING ISHTAR'S DESCENT to the underworld, which in its existing form consists of 137 lines in cuneiform characters, appears to be incomplete. We are not told therein what was the purpose of the goddess in journeying to the 'House of No-return', but we gather from various legends and from the concluding portion of the poem itself that she went there in search of her bridegroom Tammuz, the sun-god of Eridu.

The importance of the myth of Ishtar and Tammuz lies partly in the fact that, travelling westwards to Greece by way of Phoenicia, it furnished a groundwork for classic myths of the Adonis-Attis type, which still provide mythologists with matter for endless speculation.

Tammuz and Ishtar

The myth of Tammuz is one of high antiquity, dating possibly from 4000 BC or even earlier. Both Tammuz and Ishtar were originally non-Semitic, the name of the former deity being derived from the Akkadian Dumu-zi, 'son of life', or 'the only son', perhaps a contraction of Dumu-zi-apsu, 'offspring of the spirit of the deep', as Professor Sayce indicates. The 'spirit of the deep' is, of course, the water-god Ea, and Tammuz apparently typifies the sun, though he is not, as will presently be seen, a simple solar deity, but a god who unites in himself the attributes of various departmental divinities. An ancient Akkadian hymn addresses Tammuz as "Shepherd and lord, husband of Ishtar the lady of heaven, lord of the underworld, lord of the shepherd's seat;" as grain which lies unwatered in the meadow, which beareth no green blade; as a sapling planted in a waterless place; as a sapling torn out by the root. Professor Sayce identifies him with that Daonus, or Daos, whom Berossus states to have been the sixth king of Babylonia during the mythical period. Tammuz is the shepherd of the sky, and his flocks and herds, like those of St Ilya in Slavonic folk-lore, are the cloud-cattle and the fleecy vapours of the heavens.

Ishtar has from an early period been associated with Tammuz as his consort, as she has, indeed, with Merodach and Assur and other deities. Yet she is by no means a mere reflection of the male divinity, but has a distinct individuality of her own, differing in this from all other Babylonian goddesses and betraying her non-Semitic origin. The widespread character of the worship of Ishtar is remarkable. None of the Babylonian or Assyrian deities were adopted into the pantheons of so many alien races. From the Persian Gulf to the pillars of Hercules she was adored as the great mother of all living. She has been identified with Dawkina, wife of Ea, and is therefore mother of Tammuz as well as his consort. This dual relationship may account for that which appears in later myths among the Greeks, where Smyrna, mother of Adonis, is also his sister. Ishtar was regarded sometimes as the daughter of the sky-god Anu, and sometimes as the child of Sin, the lunar deity. Her worship in Babylonia was universal, and in time displaced that of Tammuz himself. The love of Ishtar for Tammuz represents the wooing of the sun-god of spring-time by the goddess of fertility; the god is slain by the relentless heat of summer, and there is little doubt that Ishtar enters Aralu in search of her youthful husband.

The Descent

The poem we are about to consider briefly deals with a part only of the myth – the story of Ishtar's descent into Aralu. It opens thus: "To the land of No-return, the region of darkness, Ishtar, the daughter of Sin, turned her ear, even Ishtar, the daughter of Sin, turned her ear, to the abode of darkness, the dwelling of Irkalla, to the house whose enterer goes not forth, to the road whence the wayfarer never returns, to the house whose inhabitants see no light, to the region where dust is their bread and their food mud; they see no light, they dwell in darkness, they are clothed, like the birds, in a garment of feathers. On the door and the bolt hath the dust fallen." The moral contained in this passage is a gloomy one for mortal man; he who enters the dread precincts of Aralu goes not forth, he is doomed to remain for ever in the enveloping darkness, his sustenance mud and dust. The mention of the dust which lies "on door and bolt" strikes a peculiarly bleak and dreary note; like other primitive races the ancient Babylonians painted the other world not definitely as a place of reward or punishment, but rather as a weak reflection of the earth-world, a region of darkness and passive misery which must have offered a singularly uninviting prospect to a vigorous human being. The garment of feathers is somewhat puzzling. Why should the dead wear a garment of feathers? Unless it be that the sun-god, identified in some of his aspects with the eagle, descends into the underworld in a dress of feathers, and that therefore mortals who follow him must appear in the nether regions in similar guise. The description above quoted of the Babylonian Hades tallies with that given in dream to Eabani by the temple-maiden Ukhut (Gilgamesh epic, tablet seven).

At the Gates of Aralu

Coming to the gate of Aralu, Ishtar assumes a menacing aspect, and threatens to break down the door and shatter its bolts and bars if she be not admitted straightway. The keeper of the gate endeavours to soothe the irate deity, and goes to announce her presence to Eresh-ki-gal (Allatu), the mistress of Hades. From his words it would appear that Ishtar has journeyed thither in search of the waters of life, wherewith to restore her husband Tammuz to life. Allatu receives the news of her sister's advent with a bitter tirade, but nevertheless instructs the keeper to admit her, which he proceeds to do.

Ishtar on entering the sombre domains is obliged to pass through seven gates, at each of which she is relieved of some article of dress or adornment (evidently in accordance with the ancient custom of Aralu), till at last she stands entirely unclad. At the first gate the keeper takes from her "the mighty crown of her head"; at the second her earrings are taken; at the third her necklace; at the fourth the ornaments of her breast; at the fifth her jewelled girdle; at the sixth her bracelets; and at the seventh the cincture of her body. The goddess does not part with these save under protest, but the keeper of the gate answers all her queries with the words: "Enter, O lady, it is the command of Allatu." The divine wayfarer at length appears before the goddess of the underworld, who shows her scant courtesy, bidding the plague-demon, Namtar, smite her from head to foot with disease – in her eyes, side, feet, heart, and head.

During the time that Ishtar is confined within the bounds of Aralu all fertility on the earth is suspended, both in the animal and vegetable kingdoms. Knowledge of this disastrous state of affairs is conveyed to the gods by their messenger, Pap-sukal, who first tells the story to Shamash, the sun-god. Shamash weeps as he bears the matter before Ea and Sin, gods of the earth and the moon respectively; but Ea, to remedy the sterility of the earth, creates a being called Ashushu-namir, whom he dispatches to the underworld to demand the release of Ishtar. Allatu is greatly enraged when the demand is made "in the name of the great gods," and curses Ashushu-namir with a terrible curse, condemning him to dwell in the darkness of a dungeon, with the garbage of the city for his food. Nevertheless she cannot resist the power of the conjuration, wherefore she bids Namtar, the plague-demon, release the Annunaki, or earth-spirits, and place them on a golden throne, and pour the waters of life over Ishtar. Namtar obeys; in the words of the poem he "smote the firmly-built palace, he shattered the threshold which bore up the stones of light, he bade the spirits of earth come forth, on a throne of gold did he seat them, over Ishtar he poured the waters of life and brought her along." Ishtar is then led through the seven gates of Arula, receiving at each the article of attire whereof she had there been deprived. Finally she emerges into the earth-world, which resumes its normal course. Then follow a few lines addressed to Ishtar, perhaps by the plague-demon or by the keeper of the gates. "If she (Allatu) hath not given thee that for which the ransom is paid her, return to her for Tammuz, the bridegroom of thy youth. Pour over him pure waters and precious oil. Put on him a purple robe, and a ring of crystal on his hand. Let Samkhat (the goddess of joy) enter the liver...." These lines indicate with sufficient clearness that Ishtar descended into Hades in order to obtain the waters of life and thus revive her bridegroom Tammuz. The poem does not relate whether or not her errand was successful, but we are left to conjecture that it was. There still remain a few lines of the poem, not, however, continuing the narrative, but forming a sort of epilogue, addressed, it may be, to the hearers of the tale. Mention is made in this portion of mourners, "wailing men and wailing women," of a funeral pyre and the burning of incense, evidently in honour of the god Tammuz.

Nin-Girsu

GIRSU WAS A PART OF THE CITY of Lagash, and the name Nin-Girsu means 'Lord of Girsu'. Gods frequently had lordship over a city quarter, one of the best-known instances of this being that of Huitzilopochtli, who ruled over that part of the city of Tenochtitlan, called Mexico, which afterwards gave its name to the entire community.

Girsu had originally been a city itself and had become merged into Lagash, so its god was probably of ancient origin. Nin-Girsu is frequently alluded to as 'the warrior of Bel' – he who broke through the hostile ranks to aid the worshippers of the great god of the netherworld. Like many combatant deities, however, he presided over local agriculture, and in this connection he was known as Shul-gur, 'Lord of the corn heaps'. He is even identified with Tammuz.

Bau

IN ANCIENT INSCRIPTIONS, especially those of Gudea, Urbau, and Uru-kagina, the goddess Bau is alluded to as the great mother of mankind, who restores the sick to health. She is called 'chief daughter of Anu', and seems to play the part of a fate to some extent.

She has also an agricultural side to her character. Gudea was especially devoted to her, and has left it on record that she "filled him with eloquence." Her temple was at Uru-Azagga, a quarter of Lagash, and as the goddess of that neighbourhood she would, of course, have come into close contact with Nin-Girsu. Indeed she is spoken of as his consort, and when Uru-Azagga became part of Lagash, Bau was promoted as tutelar goddess of that city and designated 'Mother of Lagash'. She has been identified with the primeval watery depths, the primitive chaos, and this identification has been founded on the similarity between the name Bau and the Hebrew *bohu*, the word for 'chaos', but proof is wanting to support the conjecture. A closely allied form of her seems to be Ga-tum-dug, a goddess who has probably a common origin with Bau, and who certainly is in some manner connected with water – perhaps with the clouds.

Nannar

NANNAR WAS THE MOON-GOD OF UR, the city whence came Abram, and with that place he was connected much as was Shamash with Sippar – that is to say, Ur was his chief but not his only centre of adoration.

Why Nannar came to have his principal seat at Ur it would be difficult to say. The name Ur signifies 'light', so it may be that a shrine dedicated to Nannar existed upon the site of this city and constituted its nucleus. In Babylonian mythology the sun was regarded as the offspring of the moon, and it is easy to see how this conception arose in the minds of a race prone to astronomical study. In all civilizations the lunar method of computing time precedes the solar. The phases of the moon are regarded as more trustworthy and more easily followed than the more obscure changes of the brighter luminary, therefore a greater degree of importance was attached to the moon in very early times than to the sun. The moon is usually represented on Babylonian cylinders as bearing a crescent upon his head and wearing a long, flowing beard described as of the colour of lapis-lazuli – much the same shade as his beams possess in warmer latitudes. Nannar was frequently alluded to as 'the heifer of Anu', because of the horn which the moon displays at a certain phase. Many monarchs appear to have delighted in the upkeep and restoration of his temple, among them Nur-Ramman and Sin-iddina.

Nannar in Decay

B UT, AS HAPPENS TO MANY GODS, Nannar became confounded with some earthly hero – was even alluded to as a satrap (provincial governor) of Babylonia under the Median monarch Artaios – a personage unknown to history. Ctesias hands down to us a very circumstantial tale concerning him as follows:

"There was a Persian of the name of Parsondes, in the service of the king of the Medes, an eager huntsman, and an active warrior on foot and in the chariot, distinguished in council and in the field, and of influence with the king. Parsondes often urged the king to make him satrap of Babylon in the place of Nannaros, who wore women's clothes and ornaments, but the king always put the petition aside, for it could not be granted without breaking the promise which his ancestor had made to Belesys. Nannaros discovered the intentions of Parsondes, and sought to secure himself against them, and to take vengeance. He promised great rewards to the cooks who were in the train of the king, if they succeeded in seizing Parsondes and giving him up. One day, Parsondes in the heat of the chase strayed far from the king. He had already killed many boars and deer, when the pursuit of a wild ass carried him to a great distance. At last he came upon the cooks, who were occupied in preparations for the king's table. Being thirsty, Parsondes asked for wine; they gave it, took care of his horse, and invited him to take food – an invitation agreeable to Parsondes, who had been hunting the whole day. He bade them send the ass which he had captured to the king, and tell his own servants where he was. Then he ate of the various kinds of food set before him, and drank abundantly of the excellent wine, and at last asked for his horse in order to return to the king. But they brought beautiful women to him, and urged him to remain for the night. He agreed, and as soon as, overcome by hunting, wine, and love, he had fallen into a deep sleep, the cooks bound him and brought him to Nannaros. Nannaros reproached Parsondes with calling him an effeminate man, and seeking to obtain his satrapy; he had the king to thank that the satrapy granted to his ancestors had not been taken from him. Parsondes replied that he considered himself more worthy of the office, because he was more manly and more useful to the king. But Nannaros swore by Bel and Mylitta that Parsondes should be softer and whiter than a woman, called for the eunuch who was over the female players, and bade him shave the body of Parsondes and bathe and anoint him every day, put women's clothes on him, plait his hair after the manner of women, paint his face, and place him among the women who played the guitar and sang, that he might learn their arts. This was done, and soon Parsondes played and sang better at the table of Nannaros than any of the women.

"Meanwhile the king of the Medes had caused search to be made everywhere for Parsondes; and since he could nowhere be found, and nothing could be heard of him, he believed that a lion or some other wild animal had killed him when out hunting, and lamented for his loss. Parsondes had lived for seven years as a woman in Babylon, when Nannaros caused a eunuch to be scourged and grievously maltreated. This eunuch Parsondes induced by large presents to retire to Media and tell the king the misfortune which had come upon him. Then the king sent a message commanding Nannaros to give up Parsondes. Nannaros declared that he had never seen him. But the king sent a second messenger, with orders to put Nannaros to death if he did not surrender Parsondes. Nannaros entertained the messenger of the king; and when the meal was brought, 150 women entered, of whom some played the guitar, while others blew the flute. At the end of the meal, Nannaros asked the king's envoy which of all the women was the most beautiful and had played best. The envoy pointed to Parsondes. Nannaros laughed long and said, 'That is the person whom you seek', and released Parsondes, who on the next day returned home with the envoy to the king in a chariot. The king was astonished at the sight of him, and asked why he had not avoided such disgrace by death. Parsondes answered, 'In order that I might see you again and by you execute vengeance on Nannaros, which could never have been mine had I taken my life'. The king promised him that his hope should be realized, as soon as he came to Babylon. But when he came there, Nannaros defended himself on the ground that Parsondes, though in no way injured by him, had maligned him, and sought to obtain the satrapy over Babylonia. The king pointed out that he had made himself judge in his own cause, and had imposed a punishment of a degrading character; in ten days he would pronounce judgment upon him for his conduct. In terror, Nannaros hastened to Mitraphernes, the eunuch of greatest influence with the king, and promised him the most liberal rewards, 10 talents of gold and 100 talents of silver, 10 golden and 200 silver bowls, if he could induce the king to spare his life and retain him in the satrapy of Babylonia. He was prepared to give the king 100 talents of gold, 1,000 talents of silver, 100 golden and 300 silver bowls, and costly robes, with other gifts; Parsondes also should receive 100 talents of silver and costly robes. After many entreaties, Mitraphernes persuaded the king not to order the execution of Nannaros, as he had not killed Parsondes, but to exact from him the compensation which he was prepared to pay Parsondes and the king. Nannaros in gratitude threw himself at the feet of the king; but Parsondes said, 'Cursed be the man who first brought gold among men; for the sake of gold I have been made a mockery to the Babylonians.'"

It is impossible to say what the mythological meaning hidden in this tale may portend. We have the moon-god attempting to feminize an unfortunate enemy. Does this mean that Parsondes came under the influence of the moon-god – that is, that he became a lunatic?

Of the Underworld: Aralu, or Eres-ki-Gal

THE DEITIES OF THE UNDERWORLD, of the region of the dead, are usually of later origin than those of the heavens. They are frequently the gods of an older and discredited religion, and are relegated to the 'cold shades of opposition', dwelling there just as the dead are supposed to 'dwell' in the grave.

A legend exists regarding Aralu which was discovered among other texts at Tel-el-Amarna. The story goes that the gods once gave a feast to which they invited Aralu, apologizing at the same time that they were unable to go down to her and regretting that she could not ascend to them. In their dilemma they requested her to send a messenger to bring to her the viands which fell to her share. She complied with the request, and when the messenger arrived all the gods stood up to do him honour for his mistress's sake – all save Nergal. The messenger acquainted Aralu with this slight, and greatly enraged she sent him back to the dwelling of the gods to ask that the delinquent might be delivered into her hands so that she might slay him. The gods after some discussion requested the messenger to take back him who had offended the dark goddess, and in order that the envoy might the more easily discover him, all the gods were gathered together. But Nergal remained in the background. His absence was discovered, however, and he was despatched to the gloomy realm of Aralu. But he had no mind to taste death. Indeed Aralu found the tables turned, for Nergal, seizing her by the hair, dragged her from her throne and prepared to cut off her head. She begged to be allowed to speak, and upon her request being granted, she offered herself as a wife to her conqueror, along with the dominions over which she held sway. Nergal assented to her proposals and they were wed.

Nergal is the sun which passes through the gloomy underworld at night just as does the Egyptian god Osiris, and in this character he has to conquer the powers of death and the grave.

Dagon

DAGON, ALLUDED TO IN THE SCRIPTURES, was, like Oannes, a fish-god. Besides being worshipped in Erech and its neighbourhood, he was adored in Palestine and on occasion among the Hebrews themselves.

But it was in the extreme south of Palestine that his worship attained its chief importance. He had temples at Ashdod and Gaza, and perhaps his worship travelled westward along with that of Ishtar. Both were worshipped at Erech, and where the cult of the one penetrated it is likely that there would be found the rites of the other.

> *Dagon his name; sea-monster, upward man*
> *And downward fish,*

as Milton expresses it, affords one of the most dramatic instances in the Old Testament of the downfall of a usurping idol.

"And the Philistines took the ark of God, and brought it from Eben-ezer unto Ashdod.

"When the Philistines took the ark of God, they brought it into the house of Dagon, and set it by Dagon.

"And when they of Ashdod arose early on the morrow, behold, Dagon was fallen upon his face to the earth before the ark of the Lord. And they took Dagon, and set him in his place again.

"And when they arose early on the morrow morning, behold, Dagon was fallen upon his face to the ground before the ark of the Lord; and the head of Dagon and both the palms of his hands were cut off upon the threshold; only the stump of Dagon was left to him.

"Therefore neither the priests of Dagon, nor any that come into Dagon's house, tread on the threshold of Dagon in Ashdod unto this day.

"But the hand of the Lord was heavy upon them of Ashdod, and he destroyed them, and smote them with emerods, even Ashdod and the coasts thereof.

"And when the men of Ashdod saw that it was so, they said, The ark of the God of Israel shall not abide with us: for his hand is sore upon us and upon Dagon our god."

Thus in the Bible story only the 'stump' or fish's tail of Dagon was left to him. In some of the Ninevite sculptures of this deity, the head of the fish forms a kind of mitre on the head of the man, while the body of the fish appears as a cloak or cape over his shoulders and back. This is a sure sign to the mythological student that a god so adorned is in process of quitting the animal for the human form.

Nirig, or Enu-Restu

THIS DEITY IS ALLUDED TO in an inscription as "the eldest of the gods." He was especially favoured by the Kings of Assyria, and we find his name entering into the composition of several of their texts.

In a certain poem he is called the "son of Bel," and is described as being made "in the likeness of Anu." He rides, it is said, against the gods of his enemies in a chariot of lapis-lazuli, and his onset is full of the fury of the tempest. Bel, his father, commands him to set forth for the temple of Bel at Nippur. Here Nusku, the messenger of Bel, meets him, bestows a gift upon him, and humbly requests that he will not disturb the god Bel, his father, in his dwelling-place, nor terrify the earth-gods. It would appear from this passage that Nirig was on the point of taking the place of Bel, his father, but that he ever did so is improbable. As a deity of storm he is also a god of war, but he was the seed-scatterer upon the mountains, therefore he had also an agricultural significance. It is strange that in Babylonia tempest-gods possess the same functions and attributes – those of war and agriculture – as do rain or thunder, or rain-thunder, or wind and rain deities elsewhere-a circumstance which is eloquent of the power of climatic conditions in the manufacture of myth. In Mesopotamia fierce sand-storms must have given the people the idea of a savage and intractable deity, destructive rather than beneficent, as many hymns and kindred texts witness.

The Gilgamesh Epic

AS IT IS PROBABLE that the materials of the Gilgamesh epic, the great mythological poem of Babylonia, originally belong to the older epoch of Babylonian mythology, it is fitting that it should be described and considered before passing to the later developments of Chaldean religion.

The Gilgamesh epic ranks with the Babylonian myth of creation as one of the greatest literary productions of ancient Babylonia. The main element in its composition is a conglomeration of mythic matter, drawn from various sources, with perhaps a substratum of historic fact, the whole being woven into a continuous narrative around the central figure of Gilgamesh, prince of Erech. It is not possible at present to fix the date when the epic was first written. Our knowledge of it is gleaned chiefly from mutilated fragments belonging to the library of Assur-bani-pal, but from internal and other evidence we gather that some at least of the traditions embodied in the epic are of much greater antiquity than his reign. Thus a tablet dated 2100 BC contains a variant of the deluge story inserted in the eleventh tablet of the Gilgamesh epic. Probably this and other portions of the epic existed in oral tradition before they were committed to writing – that is, in the remote Sumerian period.

The epic, which centres round the ancient city of Erech, relates the adventures of a half-human, half-divine hero, Gilgamesh by name, who is king over Erech. Two other characters figure prominently in the narrative – Eabani, who evidently typifies primitive man (but also, according to certain authorities, a form of the sun-god, even as Gilgamesh himself), and Ut-Napishtim, the hero of the Babylonian deluge myth. Each of the three would seem to have been originally the hero of a separate group of traditions which in time became incorporated, more or less naturally, with the other two.

Gilgamesh may have been at one time a real personage, though nothing is known of him historically. Possibly the exploits of some ancient king of Erech furnished a basis for the narrative. His mythological character is more easily established. In this regard he is the personification of the sun. He represents, in fact, the fusion of a great national hero with a mythical being. Throughout the epic there are indications that Gilgamesh is partly divine by nature, though nothing specific is said on that head. His identity with the solar god is veiled in the popular narrative, but it is evident that he has some connection with the god Shamash, to whom he pays his devotions and who acts as his patron and protector.

The Birth of Gilgamesh

A MONG THE TRADITIONS concerning the birth of Gilgamesh is one related by Aelian (*Historia Animalium*, XII, 21) of Gilgamos (Gilgamesh), the grandson of Sokkaros – the first king to reign in Babylonia after the deluge.

Sokkaros was warned by means of divination that his daughter should bear a son who would deprive him of his throne. Thinking to frustrate the designs of fate he shut her up in a tower, where she was closely watched. But in time she bore a son, and her attendants, knowing how angry the King would be to learn of the event, flung the child from the tower. But before he reached the ground an eagle seized him up and bore him off to a certain garden, where he was duly found and cared for by a peasant. And when he grew to manhood he became King of the Babylonians, having, presumably, usurped the throne of his grandfather.

Here we have a myth obviously of solar significance, conforming in every particular to a definite type of sun-legend. It cannot have been by chance that it became attached to the person of Gilgamesh. Everything in the epic, too, is consonant with the belief that Gilgamesh is a sun-god – his connection with Shamash (who may have been his father in the tradition given by Aelian, as well as the eagle which saved him from death), the fact that no mention is made of his father in the poem, though his mother is brought in more than once, and the assumption throughout the epic that he is more than human.

Given the key to his mythical character it is not hard to perceive in his adventures the daily (or annual) course of the sun, rising to its full strength at noonday (or mid-summer), and sinking at length to the western horizon, to return in due time to the abode of men. Like all solar deities – like the sun itself – his birth and origin are wrapped in mystery. He is, indeed, one of the 'fatal children', like Sargon, Perseus, or Arthur. When he first appears in the narrative he is already a full-grown hero, the ruler and (it would seem) oppressor of Erech. His mother, Rimat-belit, is a priestess in the temple of Ishtar, and through her he is descended from Ut-Napishtim, a native of Shurippak, and the hero of the Babylonian flood-legend.

An Epic in Fragments

L ET US EXAMINE IN DETAIL the Gilgamesh epic as we have it in
the broken fragments which remain to us. The first and second
tablets are much mutilated. A number of fragments are extant
which belong to one or other of these two, but it is not easy to say
where the first ends and the second begins.

One fragment would seem to contain the very beginning of the first tablet – a sort
of general preface to the epic, comprising a list of the advantages to be derived
from reading it. After this comes a fragment whose title to inclusion in the epic
is doubtful. It describes a siege of the city of Erech, but makes no mention of
Gilgamesh. The woeful condition of Erech under the siege is thus picturesquely
detailed: "She asses (tread down) their young, cows (turn upon) their calves. Men
cry aloud like beasts, and maidens mourn like doves. The gods of strong-walled
Erech are changed to flies, and buzz about the streets. The spirits of strong-
walled Erech are changed to serpents, and glide into holes. For three years the
enemy besieged Erech, and the doors were barred, and the bolts were shot, and
Ishtar did not raise her head against the foe." If this fragment be indeed a portion
of the Gilgamesh epic, we have no means of ascertaining whether Gilgamesh
was the besieger, or the raiser of the siege, or whether he was concerned in the
affair at all.

Gilgamesh as Tyrant

N OW WE COME to the real commencement of the poem,
inscribed on a fragment which some authorities assign
to the beginning of the second tablet, but which more
probably forms a part of the first. In this portion we find
Gilgamesh filling the double role of ruler and oppressor of

Erech – the latter evidently not inconsistent with the character of a hero.

There is no mention here of a siege, nor is there any record of the coming of Gilgamesh, though, as has been indicated, he probably came as a conqueror. His intolerable tyranny towards the people of Erech lends colour to this view. He presses the young men into his service in the building of a great wall, and carries off the fairest maidens to his court. Finally his harshness constrained the people to appeal to the gods, and they prayed the goddess Aruru to create a mighty hero who would champion their cause, and through fear of whom Gilgamesh should be forced to temper his severity. The gods themselves added their prayers to those of the oppressed people, and Aruru at length agreed to create a champion against Gilgamesh. "Upon hearing these words (so runs the narrative), Aruru conceived a man (in the image) of Anu in her mind. Aruru washed her hands, she broke off a piece of clay, she cast it on the ground. Thus she created Eabani, the hero." When the creation of this champion was finished his appearance was that of a wild man of the mountains. "The whole of his body was (covered) with hair, he was clothed with long hair like a woman. His hair was luxuriant, like that of the corn-god. He knew (not) the land and the inhabitants thereof, he was clothed with garments as the god of the field. With the gazelles he ate herbs, with the beasts he slaked his thirst, with the creatures of the water his heart rejoiced." In pictorial representations on cylinder-seals and elsewhere Eabani is depicted as a sort of satyr, with the head, arms, and body of a man, and the horns, ears, and legs of a beast. As we have seen, he is a type of beast-man, a sort of Caliban, ranging with the beasts of the field, utterly ignorant of the things of civilization.

The Beguiling of Eabani

THE POEM GOES ON to introduce a new character, Tsaidu, the hunter, apparently designed by the gods to bring about the meeting of Gilgamesh and Eabani. How he first encounters

Eabani is not quite clear from the mutilated text. One reading has it that the King of Erech, learning the plan of the gods for his overthrow, sent Tsaidu into the mountains in search of Eabani, with instructions to entrap him by whatever means and bring him to Erech.

Another reading describes the encounter as purely accidental. However this may be, Tsaidu returned to Erech and related to Gilgamesh the story of his encounter, telling him of the strength and fleetness of the wild man, and his exceeding shyness at the sight of a human being. By this time it is evident that Gilgamesh knows or conjectures the purpose for which Eabani is designed, and intends to frustrate the divine plans by anticipating the meeting between himself and the wild man. Accordingly he bids Tsaidu return to the mountains, taking with him Ukhut, one of the sacred women of the temple of Ishtar. His plan is that Ukhut with her wiles shall persuade Eabani to return with her to Erech. Thus the hunter and the girl set out. "They took the straight road, and on the third day they reached the usual drinking-place of Eabani. Then Tsaidu and the woman placed themselves in hiding. For one day, for two days, they lurked by the drinking-place. With the beasts (Eabani) slaked his thirst, with the creatures of the waters his heart rejoiced. Then Eabani (approached) ..."

The scene which follows is described at some length. Ukhut had no difficulty in enthralling Eabani with the snares of her beauty. For six days and seven nights he remembered nothing because of his love for her. When at length he bethought him of his gazelles, his flocks and herds, he found that they would no longer follow him as before. So he sat at the feet of Ukhut while she told him of Erech and its king. "Thou art handsome, O Eabani, thou art like a god. Why dost thou traverse the plain with the beasts? Come, I will take thee to strong-walled Erech, to the bright palace, the dwelling of Anu and Ishtar, to the palace of Gilgamesh, the perfect in strength, who, like a mountain-bull, wieldeth power over man." Eabani found the prospect delightful. He longed for the friendship of Gilgamesh, and declared himself willing to follow the woman to the city of Erech. And so Ukhut, Eabani, and Tsaidu set out on their journey.

Gilgamesh meets Eabani

THE FEAST OF ISHTAR was in progress when they reached Erech. Eabani had conceived the idea that he must do battle with Gilgamesh before he could claim that hero as a friend, but being warned (whether in a dream, or by Ukhut, is not clear) that Gilgamesh was stronger than he, and withal a favourite of the gods, he wisely refrained from combat. Meanwhile Gilgamesh also had dreamed a dream, which, interpreted by his mother, Rimat-belit, foretold the coming of Eabani. That part of the poem which deals with the meeting of Gilgamesh and Eabani is unfortunately no longer extant, but from the fragments which take up the broken narrative we gather that they met and became friends.

The portions of the epic next in order appear to belong to the second tablet. In these we find Eabani lamenting the loss of his former freedom and showering maledictions on the temple-maiden who has lured him thither. However, Shamash, the sun-god, intervenes (perhaps in another dream or vision; these play a prominent part in the narrative), and showing him the benefits he has derived from his sojourn in the haunts of civilization, endeavours with various promises and inducements to make him stay in Erech – "Now Gilgamesh, thy friend and brother, shall give thee a great couch to sleep on, shall give thee a couch carefully prepared, shall give thee a seat at his left hand, and the kings of the earth shall kiss thy feet." With this, apparently, Eabani is satisfied. He ceases to bewail his position at Erech and accepts his destiny with calmness.

In the remaining fragments of the tablet we find him concerned about another dream or vision; and before this portion of the epic closes the heroes have planned an expedition against the monster Khumbaba, guardian of the abode of the goddess Irnina (a form of Ishtar), in the Forest of Cedars.

In the very mutilated IIIrd tablet the two heroes go to consult the priestess Rimat-belit, the mother of Gilgamesh, and through her they ask protection from Shamash in the forthcoming expedition. The old priestess advises her son and his friend how to proceed, and after they have gone we see her alone in the temple, her hands raised to the sun-god, invoking his blessing on Gilgamesh: "Why hast thou troubled the heart of my son Gilgamesh? Thou hast laid thy hand upon him, and he goeth away, on a far journey to the dwelling of Khumbaba; he entereth into a combat (whose issue) he knows not; he followeth a road unknown to him. Till he arrive and till he return, till he reach the Forest of Cedars, till he hath slain the terrible Khumbaba and rid the land of all the evil that thou hatest, till the day of his return – let Aya, thy betrothed, thy splendour, recall him to thee." With this dignified and beautiful appeal the tablet comes to an end.

The Monster Khumbaba

THE FOURTH TABLET is concerned with a description of the monster with whom the heroes are about to do battle. Khumbaba, whom Bel had appointed to guard the cedar (*i.e.*, one particular cedar which appears to be of greater height and sanctity than the others), is a creature of most terrifying aspect, the very presence of whom in the forest makes those who enter it grow weak and impotent.

As the heroes draw near, Eabani complains that his hands are feeble and his arms without strength, but Gilgamesh speaks words of encouragement to him.

The next fragments bring us into the fifth tablet. The heroes, having reached "a verdant mountain", paused to survey the Forest of Cedars. When they entered the forest the death of Khumbaba was foretold to one or other, or both of them, in a dream, and they hastened forward to the combat. Unfortunately the text of the actual encounter has not been preserved, but we learn from the context that the heroes were successful in slaying Khumbaba.

Ishtar's Love for Gilgamesh

IN THE SIXTH TABLET, which relates the story of Ishtar's love for Gilgamesh, and the slaying of the sacred bull, victory again waits on the arms of the heroes, but here nevertheless we have the key to the misfortunes which later befall them.

On his return to Erech after the destruction of Khumbaba, Gilgamesh was loudly acclaimed. Doffing the soiled and bloodstained garments he had worn during the battle, he robed himself as befitted a monarch and a conqueror. Ishtar beheld the King in his regal splendour, the flowers of victory still fresh on his brow, and her heart went out to him in love. In moving and seductive terms she besought him to be her bridegroom, promising that if he would enter her house "in the gloom of the cedar" all manner of good gifts should be his – his flocks and herds would increase, his horses and oxen would be without rival, the river Euphrates would kiss his feet, and kings and princes would bring tribute to him. But Gilgamesh, knowing something of the past history of this capricious goddess, rejected her advances with scorn, and began to revile her. He taunted her, too, with her treatment of former lovers – of Tammuz, the bridegroom of her youth, to whom she clung weepingly year after year; of Alalu the eagle; of a lion perfect in might and a horse glorious in battle; of the shepherd Tabulu and of Isullanu, the gardener of her father.

All these she had mocked and ill-treated in cruel fashion, and Gilgamesh perceived that like treatment would be meted out to him should he accept the proffered love of the goddess. The deity was greatly enraged at the repulse, and mounted up to heaven: "Moreover Ishtar went before Anu (her father), before Anu she went and she (said): 'O my father, Gilgamesh has kept watch on me; Gilgamesh has counted my garlands, my garlands and my girdles.'"

Underlying the story of Ishtar's love for Gilgamesh there is evidently a nature-myth of some sort, perhaps a spring-tide myth; Gilgamesh, the sun-god, or a hero who has taken over his attributes, is wooed by Ishtar, the goddess of fertility, the great mother-goddess who presides over spring vegetation. In the recital of her former love-affairs we find mention of the Tammuz myth, in which Ishtar slew her consort Tammuz, and other mythological fragments. It is possible also that there is an astrological significance in this part of the narrative.

The Bull of Anu

TO RESUME THE TALE: In her wrath and humiliation Ishtar appealed to her father and mother, Anu and Anatu, and begged the former to create a mighty bull and send it against Gilgamesh. Anu at first demurred, declaring that if he did so it would result in seven years' sterility on the earth; but finally he consented, and a great bull, Alu, was sent to do battle with Gilgamesh. The portion of the text which deals with the combat is much mutilated, but it appears that the conflict was hot and sustained, the celestial animal finally succumbing to a sword-thrust from Gilgamesh. Ishtar looks on in impotent anger. "Then Ishtar went up on to the wall of strong-walled Erech; she mounted to the top and she uttered a curse, (saying), 'Cursed be Gilgamesh, who has provoked me to anger, and has slain the bull from heaven.'" Then Eabani incurs the anger of the deity – "When Eabani heard these words of Ishtar, he tore out the entrails of the bull, and he cast them before her, saying, 'As for thee, I will conquer thee, and I will do to thee even as I have done to him.'" Ishtar was beside herself with rage. Gilgamesh and his companion dedicated the great horns of the bull to the sun-god, and having washed their hands in the river Euphrates, returned once more to Erech. As the triumphal procession passed through the city the people came out of their houses to do honour to the heroes. The remainder of the tablet is concerned with a great banquet given by Gilgamesh to celebrate his victory over the bull Alu, and with further visions of Eabani.

The seventh and eighth tablets are extremely fragmentary, and so much of the text as is preserved is open to various readings. It is possible that to the seventh tablet belongs a description of the underworld given to Eabani in a dream by the temple-maiden Ukhut, whom he had cursed in a previous tablet, and who had since died. The description answers to that given in another ancient text – the myth of Ishtar's descent into Hades – and evidently embodies the popular belief concerning the underworld. "Come, descend with me to the house of darkness, the abode of Irkalla, to the house whence the enterer goes not forth, to the path whose way has no return, to the house whose dwellers are deprived of light, where dust is their nourishment and earth their good. They are clothed, like the birds, in a garment of feathers; they see not the light, they dwell in darkness."

The Death of Eabani

THIS SINISTER VISION appears to have been a presage of Eabani's death. Shortly afterwards he fell ill and died at the end of twelve days.

The manner of his death is uncertain. One reading of the mutilated text represents Eabani as being wounded, perhaps in battle, and succumbing to the effects of the wound. But another makes him say to his friend Gilgamesh, "I have been cursed, my friend, I shall not die as one who has been slain in battle." The breaks in the text are responsible for the divergence. The latter reading is probably the correct one; Eabani has grievously offended Ishtar, the all-powerful, and the curse which has smitten him to the earth is probably hers. In modern folk-lore phraseology he died of ju-ju. The death of the hero brings the eighth tablet to a close.

In the ninth tablet we find Gilgamesh mourning the loss of his friend.

The Quest of Gilgamesh

On the heart of Gilgamesh, likewise, the fear of death had taken hold, and he determined to go in search of his ancestor, Ut-Napishtim, who might be able to show him a way of escape. Straightway putting his determination into effect, Gilgamesh set out

for the abode of Ut-Napishtim. On the way he had to pass through mountain gorges, made terrible by the presence of wild beasts. From the power of these he was delivered by Sin, the moon-god, who enabled him to traverse the mountain passes in safety.

At length he came to a mountain higher than the rest, the entrance to which was guarded by scorpion-men. This was Mashu, the Mountain of the Sunset, which lies on the western horizon, between the earth and the underworld. "Then he came to the mountain of Mashu, the portals of which are guarded every day by monsters; their backs mount up to the ramparts of heaven, and their foreparts reach down beneath Aralu. Scorpion-men guard the gate (of Mashu); they strike terror into men, and it is death to behold them. Their splendour is great, for it overwhelms the mountains; from sunrise to sunset they guard the sun. Gilgamesh beheld them, and his face grew dark with fear and terror, and the wildness of their aspect robbed him of his senses." On approaching the entrance to the mountain Gilgamesh found his way barred by these scorpion-men, who, perceiving the strain of divinity in him, did not blast him with their glance, but questioned him regarding his purpose in drawing near the mountain of Mashu. When Gilgamesh had replied to their queries, telling them how he wished to reach the abode of his ancestor, Ut-Napishtim, and there learn the secret of perpetual life and youthfulness, the scorpion-men advised him to turn back. Before him, they said, lay the region of thick darkness; for twelve *kasbu* (twenty-four hours) he would have to journey through the thick darkness ere he again emerged into the light of day. And so they refused to let him pass. But Gilgamesh implored, "with tears," says the narrative, and at length the monsters consented to admit him. Having passed the gate of the Mountain of the Sunset (by virtue of his character as a solar deity) Gilgamesh traversed the region of thick darkness during the space of twelve *kasbu*. Toward the end of that period the darkness became ever less pronounced; finally it was broad day, and Gilgamesh found himself in a beautiful garden or park studded with trees, among which was the tree of the gods, thus charmingly depicted in the text – "Precious stones it bore as fruit, branches hung from it which were beautiful to behold. The top of the tree was lapis-lazuli, and it was laden with fruit which dazzled the eye of him that beheld." Having paused to admire the beauty of the scene, Gilgamesh bent his steps shoreward.

The tenth tablet describes the hero's encounter with the sea-goddess Sabitu, who, on the approach of one "who had the appearance of a god, in whose body was grief, and who looked as though he had made a long journey," retired into her palace and fastened the door. But Gilgamesh, knowing that her help was necessary to bring him to the dwelling of Ut-Napishtim, told her of his quest, and in despair threatened to break down the door unless she opened to him. At last Sabitu consented to listen to him whilst he asked the way to Ut-Napishtim. Like the scorpion-men, the sea-goddess perceived that Gilgamesh was not to be turned aside from his quest, so at last she bade him go to Adad-Ea, Ut-Napishtim's ferryman, without whose aid, she said, it would be futile to persist further in his mission. Adad-Ea, likewise, being consulted by Gilgamesh, advised him to desist, but the hero, pursuing his plan of intimidation, began to smash the ferryman's boat with his axe, whereupon Adad-Ea was obliged to yield. He sent his would-be passenger into the forest for a new rudder, and after that the two sailed away.

Gilgamesh and Ut-Napishtim

U T-NAPISHTIM WAS INDEED SURPRISED when he beheld Gilgamesh approaching the strand. The hero had meanwhile contracted a grievous illness, so that he was unable to leave the boat; but he addressed his queries concerning perpetual life to the deified Ut-Napishtim, who stood on the shore. The hero of the flood was exceeding sorrowful, and explained that death is the common lot of mankind, "nor is it given to man to know the hour when the hand of death will fall upon him – the Annunaki, the great gods, decree fate, and with them Mammetum, the maker of destiny, and they determine death and life, but the days of death are not known."

The narrative is continued without interruption into the eleventh tablet. Gilgamesh listened with pardonable scepticism to the platitudes of his ancestor. "'I behold thee, Ut-Napishtim, thy appearance differs not from mine, thou art like unto me, thou art not otherwise than I am; thou art like unto me, thy heart is stout for the battle ... how hast thou entered the assembly of the gods; how hast thou found life?'"

The Deluge Myth

IN REPLY UT-NAPISHTIM INTRODUCES THE STORY of the Babylonian deluge, which, told as it is without interruption, forms a separate and complete narrative, and is in itself a myth of exceptional interest.

Presumably the warning of the deluge came to Ut-Napishtim in a vision. The voice of the god said: 'Thou man of Shurippak, son of Ubara-Tutu, pull down thy house, build a ship, forsake thy possessions, take heed for thy life! Abandon thy goods, save thy life, and bring up living seed of every kind into the ship'. The ship itself was to be carefully planned and built according to Ea's instructions. When the god had spoken Ut-Napishtim promised obedience to the divine command. But he was still perplexed as to how he should answer the people when they asked the reason for his preparations. Ea therefore instructed him how he should make reply, 'Bel hath cast me forth, for he hateth me'. The purpose of this reply seems clear, though the remaining few lines of it are rather broken. Ea intends that Ut-Napishtim shall disarm the suspicions of the people by declaring that the object of his shipbuilding and his subsequent departure is to escape the wrath of Bel, which he is to depict as falling on him alone. He must prophesy the coming of the rain, but must represent it, not as a devastating flood, but rather as a mark of the prosperity which Bel will grant to the people of Shurippak, perhaps by reason of his (Ut-Napishtim's) departure therefrom.

The Babylonian Ark

Ut-Napishtim employed many people in the construction of the ship. During four days he gathered the material and built the ship; on the fifth he laid it down;

on the sixth he loaded it; and by the seventh day it was finished. On a hull 120 cubits wide was constructed a great deck-house 120 cubits high, divided into six stories, each of which was divided in turn into nine rooms. The outside of the ship was made water-tight with bitumen, and the inside with pitch. To signalise the completion of his vessel, Ut-Napishtim gave a great feast, like that which was wont to be held on New Year's Day; oxen were slaughtered and great quantities of wine and oil provided. According to the command of Ea, Ut-Napishtim brought into the ship all his possessions, his silver and his gold, living seed of every kind, all his family and household, the cattle and beasts of the field, the handicraftsmen, all that was his.

A heavy rain at eventide was the sign for Ut-Napishtim to enter the ship and fasten the door. All night long it rained, and with the early dawn "there came up from the horizon a black cloud. Ramman in the midst thereof thundered, and Nabu and Marduk went before, they passed like messengers over mountain and plain. Uragal parted the anchor-cable. There went Ninib, and he made the storm to burst. The Annunaki carried flaming torches, and with the brightness thereof they lit up the earth. The whirlwind of Ramman mounted up into the heavens, and all light was turned into darkness." During a whole day darkness and chaos appear to have reigned on the earth. Men could no longer behold each other. The very gods in heaven were afraid and crouched "like hounds," weeping, and lamenting their share in the destruction of mankind. For six days and nights the tempest raged, but on the seventh day the rain ceased and the floods began to abate. Then, says Ut-Napishtim – "I looked upon the sea and cried aloud, for all mankind was turned back into clay. In place of the fields a swamp lay before me. I opened the window and the light fell upon my cheek, I bowed myself down, I sat down, I wept; over my cheek flowed my tears. I looked upon the world, and behold all was sea."

The Bird Messengers

At length the ship came to rest on the summit of Mount Nitsir. There are various readings of this portion of the text, thus: "After twelve (days) the land appeared;" or "At the distance of twelve (kasbu) the land appeared;" or "Twelve (cubits) above the water the land appeared." However this may be, the ship remained for six days on the mountain, and on the seventh Ut-Napishtim sent out a dove. But the dove found no resting-place, and so she returned. Then he sent out a swallow, which also returned, having found no spot whereon to rest. Finally a raven was sent forth, and as by this time the waters had begun to abate, the bird drew near to the ship "wading and croaking," but did not enter the vessel. Then Ut-Napishtim brought his household and all his possessions into the open air, and made an offering to the gods of reed, and cedar-wood, and incense. The fragrant odour of the incense came up to the gods, and they gathered, "like flies," says the narrative, around the sacrifice. Among the company was Ishtar, the Lady of the Gods, who lifted up the necklace which Anu had given her, saying: "What gods these are! By the jewels of lapis-lazuli which are upon my neck I will not forget! These days I have set in my memory, never will I forget them! Let the gods come to the offering, but Bel shall not come to the offering since he refused to ask counsel and sent the deluge, and handed over my people unto destruction."

The god Bel was very angry when he discovered that a mortal man had survived the deluge, and vowed that Ut-Napishtim should perish. But Ea defended his action in having saved his favourite from destruction, pointing out that Bel had refused to take counsel when he planned a universal disaster, and advising him in future to visit the sin on the sinner and not to punish the entire human race. Finally Bel was mollified. He approached the ship (into which it would appear that the remnants of the human race had retired during the altercation) and led Ut-Napishtim and his wife into the open, where he bestowed on them his blessing. "Then they took me," says Ut-Napishtim, "and afar off, at the mouth of the rivers, they made me to dwell."

Such is the story of the deluge which Ut-Napishtim told to Gilgamesh. No cause is assigned for the destruction of the human race other than the enmity which seems to have existed between man and the gods – particularly the warrior-god Bel. But it appears from the latter part of the narrative that in the assembly of the gods the majority contemplated only the destruction of the city of Shurippak, and not that of the entire human family. It has been suggested, indeed, that the story as it is here given is compounded of two separate myths, one relating to a universal catastrophe, perhaps a mythological type of a periodic inundation, and the other dealing with a local disaster such as might have been occasioned by a phenomenal overflow of the Euphrates.

Other Versions of the Deluge

The antiquity of the legend and its original character are clearly shown by comparison with another version of the myth, inscribed on a tablet found at Abu-Habbah (the ancient site of Sippar) and dated in the twenty-first century before our era. Notwithstanding the imperfect preservation of this text it is possible to perceive in it many points of resemblance to the Gilgamesh variant. Berossus also quotes a version of the deluge myth in his history, substituting Chronos for Ea, King Xisuthros for Ut-Napishtim, and the city of Sippar for that of Shurippak. In this version immortality is bestowed not only on the hero and his wife, but also on his daughter and his pilot. One writer ingeniously identifies these latter with Sabitu and Adad-Ea respectively.

The Quest Continues

To RETURN TO THE EPIC: The recital of Ut-Napishtim served its primary purpose in the narrative by proving to Gilgamesh that his case was not that of his deified ancestor. Meanwhile the hero had remained in the boat, too ill to come ashore; now Ut-Napishtim took pity on him and promised to restore him to health, first of all bidding him sleep during six days and seven nights.

Gilgamesh listened to his ancestor's advice, and by and by "sleep, like a tempest, breathed upon him." Ut-Napishtim's wife, beholding the sleeping hero, was likewise moved with compassion, and asked her husband to send the traveller safely home. He in turn bade his wife compound a magic preparation, containing seven ingredients, and administer it to Gilgamesh while he slept. This was done, and an enchantment thus put upon the hero. When he awoke (on the seventh day) he renewed his importunate request for the secret of perpetual life. His host sent him to a spring of water where he might bathe his sores and be healed; and having tested the efficacy of the magic waters Gilgamesh returned once more to his ancestor's dwelling, doubtless to persist in his quest for life. Notwithstanding that Ut-Napishtim had already declared it impossible for Gilgamesh to attain immortality, he now directed him (apparently at the instance of his wife) to the place where he would find the plant of life, and instructed Adad-Ea to conduct him thither.

The magic plant, which bestowed immortality and eternal youth on him who ate of it, appears to have been a weed, a creeping plant, with thorns which pricked the hands of the gatherer; and, curiously enough, Gilgamesh seems to have sought it at the bottom of the sea. At length the plant was found, and the hero declared his intention of carrying it with him to Erech. And so he set out on the return journey, accompanied by the faithful ferryman not only on the first, and watery, stage of his travels, but also overland to the city of Erech itself. When they had journeyed twenty *kasbu* they left an offering (presumably for the dead), and when they had journeyed thirty *kasbu*, they repeated a funeral chant. The narrative goes on: "Gilgamesh saw a well of fresh water, he went down to it and offered a libation. A serpent smelled the odour of the plant, advanced ... and carried off the plant. Gilgamesh sat down and wept, the tears ran down his cheeks." He lamented bitterly the loss of the precious plant, seemingly predicted to him when he made his offering at the end of twenty *kasbu*. At length they reached Erech, when Gilgamesh sent Adad-Ea to enquire concerning the building of the city walls, a proceeding which has possibly some mythological significance.

The twelfth tablet opens with the lament of Gilgamesh for his friend Eabani, whose loss he has not ceased to deplore. "Thou canst no longer stretch thy bow upon the earth; and those who were slain with the bow are round about thee. Thou canst no longer bear a sceptre in thy hand; and the spirits of the dead have taken thee captive. Thou canst no longer wear shoes upon thy feet; thou canst no longer raise thy war-cry on the earth. No more dost thou kiss thy wife whom thou didst love; no more dost thou smite thy wife whom thou didst hate. No more dost thou kiss thy daughter whom thou didst love; no more dost thou smite thy daughter whom thou didst hate. The sorrow of the underworld hath taken hold upon thee." Gilgamesh went from temple to temple, making offerings and desiring the gods to restore Eabani to him; to Ninsum he went, to Bel, and to Sin, the moon-god, but they heeded him not.

At length he cried to Ea, who took compassion on him and persuaded Nergal to bring the shade of Eabani from the underworld. A hole was opened in the earth and the spirit of the dead man issued therefrom like a breath of wind. Gilgamesh addressed Eabani thus: "Tell me, my friend, tell me, my friend; the law of the earth which thou hast seen, tell me." Eabani answered him: "I cannot tell thee, my friend, I cannot tell thee." But afterwards, having bidden Gilgamesh "sit down and weep," he proceeded to tell him of the conditions which prevailed in the underworld, contrasting the lot of the warrior duly buried with that of a person whose corpse is cast uncared for into the fields. "On a couch he lies, and drinks pure water, the man who was slain in battle – thou and I have oft seen such a one – his father and his mother (support) his head, and his wife (kneels) at his side. But the man whose corpse is cast upon the field – thou and I have oft seen such a one – his spirit rests not in the earth. The man whose spirit has none to care for it – thou and I have oft seen such a one – the dregs of the vessel, the leavings of the feast, and that which is cast out upon the streets, are his food." Upon this solemn note the epic closes.

Later Babylonian Gods

THE REIGN OF HAMMURABI is a logical point at which to observe general changes in and later introductions to the pantheon of the Babylonian gods. The political alterations in the kingdom were reflected in the divine circle. Certain gods were relegated to the cold shades of obscurity, whilst new deities were adopted and others, hitherto regarded as negligible quantities, were exalted to the heights of heavenly omnipotence.

The worship of Merodach first came into prominence in the days of Hammurabi, and his cult is so outstanding and important that we leave him until last. Meanwhile we will examine the nature of some of the gods who sprang into importance at or about the era of the great law-maker, and note changes which took place with regard to others. There is also a host of lesser deities, the majority of whom are no more than mere names. They do not seem to have achieved much popularity, or if they did it was an evanescent one. The names of some are indeed only mentioned once or twice, and so little is known concerning them as almost to leave us entirely in the dark regarding their natures or characteristics.

Nebo (Nabu)

THE POPULARITY OF NEBO (A.K.A. NABU) was brought about through his association with Merodach. His chief seat of worship was at Borsippa, opposite to Babylon, and when the latter city became the seat of the imperial power the proximity of Borsippa greatly assisted the cult of Nebo. So close did the association between the deities of the two cities become that at length Nebo was regarded as the son of Merodach – a relationship that often implies that the so-called descendant of the elder god is a serious rival, or that his cult is nearly allied to the elder worship. Nebo had acquired something of a reputation as a god of wisdom, and probably this it was which permitted him to stand separately from Merodach without becoming absorbed in the cult of the great deity of Babylon. He was credited, like Ea, with the invention of writing, the province of all 'wise' gods, and he presided over that department of knowledge which interpreted the movements of the heavenly bodies. The priests of Nebo were famous as astrologers, and with the bookish king Assur-bani-pal, Nebo and his consort Tashmit were especial favourites as the patrons of writing. By the time that the worship of Merodach had become recognised at Babylon, the cult of Nebo at Borsippa was so securely rooted that even the proximity of the greatest god in the land failed to shake it.

Even after the Persian conquest the temple-school at Borsippa continued to flourish. But although Nebo thus 'outlived' many of the greater gods it is now almost impossible to trace his original significance as a deity. Whether solar or aqueous in his nature – and the latter appears more likely – he was during the period of Merodach's ascendancy regarded as scribe of the gods, much as Thoth was the amanuensis of the Egyptian otherworld – that is to say, he wrote at the dictation of the higher deities. When the gods were assembled in the Chamber of Fates in Merodach's temple at Babylon, he chronicled their speeches and deliberations and put them on record. Indeed he himself had a shrine in this temple of E-Sagila, or 'the lofty house', which was known as E-Zila, or 'the firm house'. Once during the New Year festival Nebo was carried from Borsippa to Babylon to his father's temple, and in compliment was escorted by Merodach part of the way back to his own shrine in the lesser city. It is strange to see how closely the cults of the two gods were interwoven. The Kings of Babylonia constantly invoke them together, their names and those of their temples are found in close proximity at every turn, and the symbols of the bow and the stylus or pen, respectively typical of the father and the son, are usually discovered in one and the same inscription. Even Merodach's dragon, the symbol of his victory over the dark forces of chaos, is assigned to Nebo!

Nebo as Grain-God

But Nebo seems to have had also an agricultural side to his character. In many texts he is praised as the god "who opens up the subterranean sources in order to irrigate the fields," and the withdrawal of his favour is followed by famine and distress. This seems to favour the idea of his watery nature. His name, 'the proclaimer', does not assist us much in fixing his mythological significance, unless it was assigned to him in the role of herald of the gods.

Tashmit

NEBO'S CONSORT WAS TASHMIT. It is believed that Hammurabi, unsuccessful in suppressing the cult of Nebo, succeeded with that of his spouse. She seems to have been the same as a goddess Ealur who became amalgamated with Zarpanitum, the wife of Merodach.

The name may mean, according to some, 'the hearer', and to others a 'revelation', and in view of the character of her wise husband, was perhaps one of the original designations of Merodach himself. Tashmit had therefore but little individuality. None the less she possessed considerable popularity. On a seal-impression dating somewhere between 3500–4500 BC there are outlined two figures, male and female, supposed to represent Nebo and Tashmit. The former has a wide-open mouth and the latter ears of extraordinary size. Both are holding wild animals by the horns, and the representation is thought to be typical of the strength or power of speech and silence.

Shamash and Innana

WE FIND THAT HAMMURABI was very devoted to Shamash, the early type of sun-god. His improvements and restorations at Sippar and Larsa were extensive. The later Babylonian monarchs followed his example, and one of them, Mili-Shikhu (c. 1450 BC) even placed Shamash before Merodach in the pantheon!

The early connection between Merodach and Shamash had probably much to do with the great popularity of the latter. That this was the case, so far at least as Hammurabi was concerned, is obvious from certain of his inscriptions, in which he alludes in the same sentence to Merodach and Shamash and to their close relationship. Hammurabi appears also to have been greatly attached to the cult of a goddess Innana or Ninni ('lady' or 'great lady'), who was evidently the consort of some male deity. He improved her temple at Hallabi and speaks of her as placing the reins of power in his hands. There was another goddess of the same name at Lagash whom Gudea worshipped as 'mistress of the world', but she does not seem to have been the same as the Innana of Hallabi, near Sippar, as she was a goddess of fertility and generation, of the 'mother goddess' type, and there do not appear to be any grounds for the assertion that the goddess of Hallabi can be equated with her.

Hadad

RAMMAN OR RIMMON, identified with Hadad or Adad, is a deity of later type and introduction. Indeed Ramman may be merely a variant or subsidiary name, meaning as it does 'the thunderer', quite a common title for several types of deities. The worship of Hadad was widespread in Syria and Palestine, and he was a god of storms or rains, whose symbol was the thunderbolt or the lightning which he holds in his grasp like a fiery sword. But he bears solar emblems upon his apparel, and seems to wear a solar crown. He does not, however, appear to have had any centre of worship in Babylonia, and was probably a god of the Amorites, and becoming popular with the Babylonians, was later admitted into their pantheon. At Asshur in Assyria he was worshipped along with Anu, with whom he had a temple in common. This building, which was excavated in 1908, contains two shrines having but the one entrance, and the date of its foundation is referred so far back as BC 2400. There can be little doubt that the partnership of Hadad with Anu was a late one. Perhaps it was on Assyrian and not Babylonian soil that Hadad first entered from the alien world.

In many of his characteristics Hadad closely resembled En-lil. Like him he was designated 'the great mountain', and seems to have been conceived of as almost a counterpart of the older god. It is peculiar that while in Assyria and Babylonia Hadad has many of the characteristics of a sun-god, in his old home in Syria he possessed those of a thunder-god who dwelt among the mountains of northern Palestine and Syria and spoke in thunder and wielded the lightning. But even in Assyria the stormy characteristics of Hadad are not altogether obscured. Hadad's cult in Babylonia is probably not much older than the days of Hammurabi, in whose time the first inscriptional mention of him is made. His worship obtained a stronger hold in the times of the Kassite dynasty, for we find many of its monarchs incorporating his name with their own and altogether affording him a prominent place.

Ea in Later Times

EA DEVELOPED WITH THE CENTURIES, and about the epoch of Hammurabi appears to have achieved a high standard of godhead, probably because of the very considerable amount of theological moulding which he had received. In the later Babylonian period we find him described as the protagonist of mankind, the father of Merodach, and, along with Anu and Bel, a member of a great triad. The priests of Babylon were the sole mythographers of these days. This is in sharp contradistinction to the mythographers of Greece, who were nearly always philosophers and never priests. But they were mythographers in a secondary sense only, for they merely rearranged, re-edited, or otherwise altered already existing tales relating to the gods, usually with a view to the exaltation of a certain deity or to enable his story to fit in with those of other gods. It is only after a religion or mythological system has enjoyed a vogue more or less extended that the relationship of the gods towards one another becomes fixed.

The appointment of Merodach to the supreme position in the Babylonian pantheon naturally necessitated a rearrangement so far as the relationship of the other deities to him was concerned. This meant a re-shaping of myth and tradition generally for the purpose of ensuring consistency. The men fitted to accomplish such a task were to hand, for the age of Hammurabi was fertile in writers, scholastic and legal, who would be well equipped to carry out a change of the description indicated. Ea had not in the past enjoyed any very exalted sphere. But as the chief god of the important country in the neighbourhood of the Persian Gulf, the most ancient home of Babylonian culture, Ea would probably have exercised a great influence upon the antiquarian and historic sense of a man like Hammurabi. As the god of wisdom he would strongly appeal to a monarch whose whole career was marked by a love of justice and by sagacity and insight. From a local god of Eridu, Ea became a universal deity of wisdom and beneficence, the strong shield of man, and his benefactor by the gifts of harvest and water. Civilized and softer emotions must have begun to cluster around the cult of this kindly god who, when the angered deities resolved to destroy mankind, interceded for poor humanity and succeeded in preserving it from the divine wrath. As a god of medicine, too, Ea is humane and protective in character, and all the arts fall under his patronage. He is the culture-god of Babylon *par excellence.* He might not transcend Merodach, so he became his father. Thus did pagan theology succeed in merging the cults of deities which might otherwise have been serious rivals and mutually destructive.

Zu

Z U WAS A STORM-GOD symbolized in the form of a bird. He may typify the advancing storm-cloud, which would have seemed to those of old as if hovering like a great bird above the land which it was about to strike. The North-American Indians possess such a mythological conception in the Thunder-bird, and it is probable that the great bird called roc, so well known to readers of the *Arabian Nights*, was a similar monster – perhaps the descendant of the Zu-bird. We remember how this enormous creature descended upon the ship in which Sindbad sailed and carried him off. Certain it is that we can trace the roc or rukh to the Persian simurgh, which is again referable to a more ancient Persian form, the amru or sinamru, the bird of immortality, and we may feel sure that what is found in ancient Persian lore has some foundation in Babylonian belief. The Zu-bird was evidently under the control of the sun, and his attempt to break away from the solar authority is related in the following legend.

It is told of the god Zu that on one occasion ambition awaking in his breast caused him to cast envious eyes on the power and sovereignty of Bel, so that he determined to purloin the Tablets of Destiny, which were the tangible symbols of Bel's greatness.

At this time, it may be recalled, the Tablets of Destiny had already an interesting history behind them. We are told in the creation legend how Apsu, the primeval, and Tiawath, chaos, the first parents of the gods, afterward conceived a hatred for their offspring, and how Tiawath, with her monster-brood of snakes and vipers, dragons and scorpion-men and raging hounds, made war on the hosts of heaven. Her son Kingu she made captain of her hideous army –

> *To march before the forces, to lead the host,*
> *To give the battle-signal, to advance to the attack,*
> *To direct the battle, to control the fight.*

To him she gave the Tablets of Destiny, laying them on his breast with the words: "Thy command shall not be without avail, and the word of thy mouth shall be established." Through his possession of the divine tablets Kingu received the power of Anu, and was able to decree the fate of the gods. After several deities had refused the honour of becoming champion of heaven, Merodach was chosen. He succeeded at length in slaying Tiawath and destroying her evil host; and having vanquished Kingu, her captain, he took from him the Tablets of Destiny, which he sealed and laid on his own breast. It was this Merodach, or Marduk, who afterward became identified with Bel.

Now Zu, in his greed for power and dominion, was eager to obtain the potent symbols. He beheld the honour and majesty of Bel, and from contemplation of these he turned to look upon the Tablets of Destiny, saying within himself:

"Lo, I will possess the tablets of the gods, and all things shall be subject unto me. The spirits of heaven shall bow before me, the oracles of the gods shall be in my hands. I shall wear the crown, symbol of sovereignty, and the robe, symbol of godhead, and then shall I rule over all the hosts of heaven."

Thus inflamed, he sought the entrance to Bel's hall, where he awaited the dawn of day. The text goes on:

> *Now when Bel was pouring out the clear water, (i.e. thelight of day?)*
> *And his diadem was taken off and lay upon the throne,*
> *(Zu) seized the Tablets of Destiny,*
> *He took Bel's dominion, the power of giving commands.*
> *Then Zu fled away and hid himself in his mountain.*

Bel was greatly enraged at the theft, and all the gods with him. Anu, lord of heaven, summoned about him his divine sons, and asked for a champion to recover the tablets. But though the god Ramman was chosen, and after him several other deities, they all refused to advance against Zu.

The end of the legend is unfortunately missing, but from a passage in another tale, the legend of Etana, we gather that it was the sun-god, Shamash, who eventually stormed the mountain-stronghold of Zu, and with his net succeeded in capturing the presumptuous deity.

This legend is of the Prometheus type, but whereas Prometheus (once a bird-god) steals fire from heaven for the behoof of mankind, Zu steals the Tablets of Destiny for his own. These must, of course, be regained if the sovereignty of heaven is duly to continue, and to make the tale circumstantial the sun-god is provided with a fowler's net with which to capture the recalcitrant Zu-bird. Jastrow believes the myth to have been manufactured for the purpose of showing how the tablets of power were originally lost by the older Bel and gained by Merodach, but he has discounted the reference in the Etana legend relating to their recovery.

Bel

WE FIND A GOOD DEAL OF CONFUSION in later Babylonian religion as to whether the name 'Bel' is intended to designate the old god of that name or is merely a title for Merodach. Hammurabi certainly uses the name occasionally when speaking of Merodach, but at other times he quite as surely employs it for the older divinity, as for example when he couples the name with Anu. One of the Kassite kings, too, speaks of "Bel, the lord of lands," meaning the old Bel, to whom they often gave preference over Merodach. They also preferred the old city of Nippur and its temple to Babylon, and perhaps made an attempt at one time to make Nippur the capital of their Empire.

Some authorities appear to think it strange that Bel should have existed at all as a deity after the elevation of Merodach to the highest rank in the pantheon. It was his association with Anu and Ea as one of a triad presiding over the heavens, the earth, and the deep which kept him in power. Moreover, the very fact that he was a member of such a triad proves that he was regarded as theologically essential to the well-being of the Babylonian religion as a whole. The manufacture or slow evolution of a trinity of this description is by no means brought about through popular processes. It is, indeed, the work of a school, of a college of priests. Strangely enough Hammurabi seems to have associated Anu and Bel together, but to have entirely omitted Ea from their companionship, and it has been thought that the conception of a trinity was subsequent to his epoch. The god of earth and the god of heaven typify respectively that which is above and that which is below, and are reminiscent of the Father-sky and Mother-earth of many primitive mythologies, and there is much to say for the theory that Ea, god of the deep, although he had existed long prior to any such grouping, was a later inclusion.

The Triad of Earth, Air, and Sea

The habit of invoking the great triad became almost a commonplace in later Babylonia. They nearly always take precedence in religious inscriptions, and we even find some monarchs stating that they hold their regal authority by favour of the trinity. Whenever a powerful curse has to be launched, one may be certain that the names of the gods of the elements will figure in it.

Dawkina

D AWKINA WAS THE CONSORT OF EA, and was occasionally invoked along with him. She was a goddess of some antiquity, and, strangely enough for the mate of a water-god, she appears to have originally been connected in some manner with the earth. Therefore she was an elemental deity.

In later times Dawkina's attributes appear to have been inherited by Ishtar. According to some authorities Bel was the son of Ea and Dawkina, Bel in this case meaning Merodach. We find her name frequently alluded to in the Magical Texts, but her cult does not seem to have been very widespread.

Anu as Individual

WE HAVE ALREADY ALLUDED to Anu's position in the triad with Ea and Bel in later Babylonian times.

When he stands alone we find him taking a more human guise than as the mere elemental god of earlier days. He is frequently mentioned in the texts apart from Ea and Bel, and is occasionally alluded to along with Ramman, the god of thunder and storms, who of course would naturally stand in close relationship with the sky. We also find him connected with Dagan of Biblical celebrity. But in this case Dagan appears to be the equivalent of Bel.

The Great God Merodach And His Cult

THE ENTIRE RELIGIOUS SYSTEM of Babylonia is overshadowed by Merodach, its great patron deity. We remember how he usurped the place of Ea, and in what manner even the legends of that god were made over to him, so that at last he came to be regarded as not only the national god of Babylonia but the creator of the world and of mankind. He it was who, at the pleading of the other gods, confronted the grisly Tiawath, and having defeated and slain her, formed the earth out of her body and its inhabitants out of his own blood. It is almost certain that this cosmological myth was at one time recounted of Ea, and perhaps even at an earlier date

of Bel. The transfer of power from Ea to Merodach, however, was skilfully arranged by the priesthood, for they made Merodach the son of Ea, so that he would naturally inherit his father's attributes. In this transfer we observe the passing of the supremacy of the city of Eridu to that of Babylon. Ea, or Oannes, the fish-tailed god of Eridu, stood for the older and more southerly civilization of the Babylonian race, whilst Merodach, patron god of Babylon, a very different type of deity, represented the newer political power.

Originally Merodach appears to have been a sun-god personifying more especially the sun of the springtime. Thus he was a fitting deity to defeat the chaotic Tiawath, who personified darkness and destruction. But there is another side to him – the agricultural side. Says Jastrow (*Religion in Babylonia and Assyria*, p. 38): "At Nippur, as we shall see, there developed an elaborate lamentation ritual for the occasions when national catastrophes, defeat, failure of crops, destructive storms, and pestilence revealed the displeasure and anger of the gods." At such times earnest endeavours were made, through petitions accompanied by fasting and other symbols of contrition, to bring about a reconciliation with the angered power. This ritual, owing to the religious pre-eminence of Nippur, became the norm and standard throughout the Euphrates Valley, so that when Marduk (Merodach) and Babylonia came practically to replace En-lil and Nippur, the formulas and appeals were transferred to the solar deity of Babylon, who, representing more particularly the sun-god of spring, was well adapted to be viewed as the one to bring blessings and favours after the sorrows and tribulations of the stormy season.

Strange as it will appear, although he was patron god of Babylon he did not originate in that city, but in Eridu, the city of Ea, and probably this is the reason why he was first regarded as the son of Ea. He is also directly associated with Shamash, the chief sun-god of the later pantheon, and is often addressed as the 'god of canals' and 'opener of subterranean fountains'. In appearance he is usually drawn with tongues of fire proceeding from his person, thus indicating his solar character. At other times he is represented as standing above the watery deep, with a horned creature at his feet, which also occasionally serves to symbolize Ea. It is noteworthy, too, that his temple at Babylon bore the same name – E-Sagila, 'the lofty house', – as did Ea's sanctuary at Eridu.

We find among the cuneiform texts – a copy of an older Babylonian text – an interesting little poem which shows how Merodach attracted the attributes of the other gods to himself.

> *Ea is the Marduk (or Merodach) of canals;*
> *Ninib is the Marduk of strength;*
> *Nergal is the Marduk of war;*
> *Zamama is the Marduk of battle;*
> *Enlil is the Marduk of sovereignty and control;*
> *Nebo is the Marduk of possession;*
> *Sin is the Marduk of illumination of the night;*
> *Shamash is the Marduk of judgments;*
> *Adad is the Marduk of rain;*
> *Tishpak is the Marduk of the host;*
> *Gal is the Marduk of strength;*
> *Shukamunu is the Marduk of the harvest.*

This would seem as if Merodach had absorbed the characteristics of all the other gods of any importance so successfully that he had almost established his position as the sole deity in Babylonia, and that therefore some degree of monotheism had been arrived at.

A New-Year's Ceremony

On the first day of the Babylonian New Year an assembly of the gods was held at Babylon, when all the principal gods were grouped round Merodach in precisely the same manner in which the King was surrounded by the nobility and his officials, for many ancient faiths imagined that the polity of earth merely mirrored that of heaven, that, as Paracelsus would have said, the earth was the microcosm of the heavenly macrocosm – "as above, so below." The ceremony in question consisted in the lesser deities paying homage to Merodach as their liege lord. In this council, too, they decided the political action of Babylonia for the coming year.

It is thought that the Babylonian priests at stated intervals enacted the myth of the slaughter of Tiawath. This is highly probable, as in Greece and

Egypt the myths of Persephone and Osiris were represented dramatically before a select audience of initiates. We see that these representations are nearly always made in the case of divinities who represent corn or vegetation as a whole, or the fructifying power of springtime. The name of Merodach's consort Zarpanitum was rendered by the priesthood as 'seed producing', to mark her connection with the god who was responsible for the spring revival.

Merodach's ideograph is the sun, and there is abundant evidence that he was first and last a solar god. The name, originally Amaruduk, probably signifies 'the young steer of day', which seems to be a figure for the morning sun. He was also called Asari, which may be compared with Asar, the Egyptian name of Osiris. Other names given him are Sar-agagam, 'the glorious incantation', and Meragaga, 'the glorious charm', both of which refer to the circumstance that he obtained from Ea, his father, certain charms and incantations which restored the sick to health and exercised a beneficial influence upon mankind.

Merodach was supposed to have a court of his own above the sky, where he was attended to by a host of ministering deities. Some superintended his food and drink supply, while others saw to it that water for his hands was always ready. He had also door-keepers and even attendant hounds, and it is thought that the satellites of Jupiter, the planet which represented him, may have been dimly visible to those among the Chaldean star-gazers who were gifted with good sight. These dogs were called Ukkumu, 'Seizer', Akkulu, 'Eater', Iksuda, 'Grasper', and Iltehu, 'Holder'. It is not known whether these were supposed to assist him in shepherding his flock or in the chase, and their names seem appropriate either for sheep-dogs or hunting hounds.

Assyrian Gods

THE PANTHEON OF ASSYRIA, as befitted the religious system of a nation of soldiers, was more highly organized than that of the kindred people of Babylonia, the ranks and relationships of the gods who comprised it were more definitely fixed, it was considerably more compact than that of the southern kingdom, and its lesser luminaries were fewer.

It has been assumed that the deities of the Assyrians were practically identical in every respect with those of the Babylonians, with the single exception of Asshur, who equated with Merodach. And yet this is cannot truly be the case in reality, since ethnological differences (and these certainly existed between the peoples of the northern and southern culture-groups), climatic conditions, a different political environment – all these as well as other considerations, as important if less obvious, must have effected almost radical changes in the ideas of the gods as conceived by the Assyrians. Exactly what these changes were we shall probably never know. They are scarcely likely to be revealed by inscriptions or sacred writings which undoubtedly conserve for us little more than the purely ecclesiastical view-point, always anxious to embalm with scrupulous care the cherished theological beliefs of an older day.

We find in the Assyrian pantheon numerous foreign deities whom the Assyrian kings included among the national gods by right of conquest – Assur-bani-pal speaks of the capture of twenty gods of the Elamites. It was, of course, only upon the rise of a distinct Assyrian empire that the religion of the northern kingdom acquired traits that distinguished it from that of Babylonia.

The great gods in Assyria were even more omnipotent than in Babylonia. One cause contributing to this was the absorption of the minor local cults by deities associated with the great centres of Assyrian life. Early religion is extremely sensitive to political change, and as a race evolves from the tribal or local state and bands itself into a nation, so the local gods become national and centralized, probably in the great deity of the most politically active city in the state. Nor is it essential to this process that the deities absorbed should be of a like nature with the absorbing god. Quite often a divinity assumes the name and attributes of one with whom he had little in common.

Asshur

THE STATE RELIGION OF ASSYRIA centres in Asshur, nor was any deity ever so closely identified with an empire as he. On the fall of the Assyrian state, Asshur fell with it. Moreover all the gods of Assyria may be said to have been combined in his person. In Babylonia, Merodach was a leader of hosts. In Assyria, Asshur personified these hosts, that is, the other Assyrian gods had become attributes of Asshur, and we can only understand the remaining Assyrian gods if we regard them as lesser Asshurs, so to speak, as broken lights of the great god of battle and conquest.

Asshur originated in the city of his name situated on the west bank of the Tigris, not far from the point where the lower Zab flows into that river. It was not of course until the rise of this city to political pre-eminence that its god figured as all-powerful. There are conflicting estimates as regards his original nature, some authorities holding that he was lunar, others that he symbolized fire or water. The facts, however, point to the conclusion that he was solar in character.

Merodach had chiefly been worshipped in Babylon. As other Babylonian territories became subject to that city we do not find them placing the god of Babylon above their own local god. But it was different with Asshur. We find temples to him broadcast over Assyria. Indeed as Assyrian history advances, we see different cities alluded to as the chief centre of his worship, and he resides now at Asshur, now at Calah, now at Nineveh, now at Khorsabad. Wherever the Kings of Assyria took up their official residence there Asshur was adored, and there he was supposed to dwell. He was not symbolized by an idol or any man-like statue which would serve to give the populace an idea of his physical likeness, but was represented by a standard consisting of a pole surrounded by a disc enclosed with two wings. Above the disc was the figure of a warrior with bent bow and arrow on string. This well symbolized the military nature of the Assyrian nation and of its tutelar deity. At the same time indications are not wanting that this pole and its accompanying symbols are the remains of a totem-standard upon which has been superimposed the anthropomorphic figure of a lightning- or tempest-god. The pole is a favourite vehicle for carrying the totem symbols into battle, and it looks here as if the sun had at one time been regarded as a tribal totem. The figure of the archer at the top seems representative of a lightning- or storm-god – a mythic character frequently associated with the sun, that 'strong warrior'. By virtue of his possession of the lightning arrow the storm-god is often accepted as a god of war.

The etymology of the name of Asshur throws little light upon his character as a divinity. The city which took his name was in all probability originally called 'The city of the god Asshur'. To call it by the name of the god alone would not be unnatural. The name is derived from a root meaning 'to be gracious', and therefore means 'the gracious god', 'the good god'. But there are indications that an older form of the name had existed, and it has been asserted that the form Anshar has priority. With Kishar, a god Anshar was created as the second pair of deities to see the light, and according to one version it is Anshar who dispatches Anu, Ea, and finally Merodach to destroy the monster Tiawath. This Anshar, then, appears as possessed with authority among the gods. But we find no mention of him in the ancient texts and inscriptions of Babylonia. The version in which Anshar is alluded to may of course have been tampered with, and his inclusion in the creation myth may be regarded as a concession to Assyrian greatness. Indeed in one creation tablet we find Merodach displaced by Asshur as framer of the earth!

The Secret of Assyrian Greatness

Asshur is mentioned in the oldest Assyrian inscription known to us, that of Samsi-Ramman (c. 1850 BC), the priest-chief of Asshur, who ruled in the days when as yet the offices of king and high priest were undivided. Indeed, when the title of 'king' had come into use some 350 years later, the monarchs of Assyria still retained the right to call themselves 'priests of the god Asshur'. The entire faith in and dependence on their beloved deity on the part of these early Assyrian rulers is touching. They are his children and rely wholly upon him first for protection against their cruel enemies the Kassites and afterwards for the extension of their growing empire. No wonder that with such a faith to stimulate her Assyria became great. Faith in her tutelar god was, indeed, the secret of her greatness. The enemies of Assyria are 'the enemies of Asshur', her soldiers are 'the warriors of Asshur', and their weapons are 'the weapons of Asshur'. Before his face the enemies of Assyria tremble and are routed, he is consulted oracularly as to the making and conduct of war, and he is present on the battle-field. But the solitary nature of Asshur was remarkable. Originally he possessed 'neither kith nor kin', neither wife nor child, and the unnaturalness of his splendid isolation appears to have struck the Assyrian scribes, who in an interesting prayer attempted to connect their divinity with the greater gods of Babylonia, to find him a wife, ministers, a court and messengers:

A prayer to Asshur, the king of the gods, ruler over heaven and earth,
the father who has created the gods, the supreme
first-born of heaven and earth,
the supreme muttallu who inclines to counsel,
the giver of the sceptre and the throne.
To Nin-lil, the wife of Asshur, the begetter, the creatress of heaven and earth,
who by command of her mouth ...
To Sin, the lord of command, the uplifter of horns, the spectacle of heaven,
To the Sun-god, the great judge of the gods, who
causes the lightning to issue forth,
To Anu, the lord and prince, possessing the life
of Asshur, the father of the great gods.
To Rammon, the minister of heaven and earth, the
lord of the wind and the lightning of heaven.
To Ishtar, the queen of heaven and the stars, whose seat is exalted.
To Merodach, the prince of the gods, the interpreter
of the spirits of heaven and earth.
To Adar, the son of Mul-lil the giant, the first-born ...
To Nebo, the messenger of Asshur (Ansar) ...
To Nergal, the lord of might and strength ...
To the god who marches in front, the first-born ...
To the seven gods, the warrior deities ...
the great gods, the lords of heaven and earth.

Asshur as Conqueror

An incident which well illustrated the popularity of the Assyrian belief in the conquering power of the national god is described in an account of the expedition of Sargon against Ashdod stamped on a clay cylinder of that monarch's reign. Sargon states that in his ninth expedition to the land beside the sea, to Philistia and Ashdod, to punish King Azuri of that city for his refusal to send tribute and for his evil deeds against Assyrian subjects, Sargon placed Ahimiti, nephew of Azuri, in his place and fixed the taxes. But the people of Ashdod revolted against the puppet Sargon had placed over them, and by acclamation raised one Yaran to the throne, and fortified their dominions. They and the surrounding peoples sought the aid of Egypt, which could not help them. For the honour of Asshur, Sargon then engaged in an expedition against the Hittites, and turned his attention to the state of affairs in Philistia (c. 711 BC), hearing which Yaran, for fear of Asshur, fled to Meroc on the borders of Egypt, where he hid ignominiously. Sargon besieged and captured the city of Ashdod, with the gods, wives, children, and treasures of Yaran.

It is plain that this punitive expedition was undertaken for the personal honour of Asshur, that he was believed to accompany the troops in their campaign against the rebellious folk of Ashdod, and that victory was to be ascribed to him and to him alone. All tribute from conquered peoples became the property of Asshur, to whom it was offered by the Kings of Assyria. Even the great and proud monarchs of this warlike kingdom do not hesitate to affirm themselves the creatures of Asshur, by whom they live and breathe and by whose will they hold the royal authority, symbolized by the mighty bow conferred upon them by their divine master. That these haughty rulers were not without an element of affection as well as fear for the god they worshipped is seen from the circumstance that they frequently allude to themselves as the sons of Asshur, whose viceroys on earth they were. Asshur was, indeed, in later times the spirit of conquering Assyria personalized. We do not find him regarded as anything else than a war-god. We do not find him surrounded by any of the gentler attributes which distinguish non-militant deities, nor is it likely that his cult would have developed, had it lasted, into one distinguished for its humanizing influence or its ethical subtlety. It was the cult of a war-god pure and simple, and when Asshur was beaten at his own business of war he disappeared into the limbo of forgotten gods as rapidly as he had arisen.

Ishtar

NEXT TO ASSHUR in the affections of the Assyrian people stood Ishtar. As a goddess in Assyria she was absolutely identical with the Babylonian Ishtar, her favourite shrines in the northern kingdom being Nineveh, Arbela, and the temple of Kidmuru, also in Nineveh.

The Assyrians appear to have admitted her Babylonian origin, or at least to have confessed that theirs was originally a Babylonian Ishtar, for Tiglath-pileser I lays emphasis upon the circumstance that a shrine he raised to Ishtar in his capital is dedicated to 'the Assyrian Ishtar'. The date of this monarch is 1010 BC, or near it, so that the above is a comparatively early allusion to Ishtar in Assyrian history. The Ishtars of Arbela and Kidmuru do not appear in Assyrian texts until the time of Esar-haddon (681 BC), thus the Ishtar of Nineveh was much the most venerable of the three. Arbela was evidently a religious centre of importance, and the theory has been advanced that it became the seat of a school of prophets connected with the worship of Ishtar. Jastrow in his *Religion of Babylonia and Assyria* (1898, p. 203), writing on this point, says, "It is quite possible, if not probable, that the three Ishtars are each of independent origin. The 'queen of Kidmuru', indeed, I venture to think, is the indigenous Ishtar of Nineveh, who is obliged to yield her place to the so-called 'Assyrian Ishtar', upon the transfer of the capital of Assyria to Nineveh, and henceforth is known by one of her epithets to distinguish her from her more formidable rival. The cult of Ishtar at Arbela is probably, too, of ancient date; but special circumstances that escape us appear to have led to a revival of interest in their cults during the period when Assyria reached the zenith of her power. The important point for us to bear in mind is that no essential distinctions between these three Ishtars were made by the Assyrians. Their traits and epithets are similar, and for all practical purposes we have only one Ishtar in the northern empire."

Ishtar as a War-Goddess

Ishtar was frequently placed by the side of Asshur as a war-goddess. Ere she left the plains of Babylonia for the uplands of Assyria she had evinced certain bellicose propensities. In the Gilgamesh epic she appears as a deity of destructive and spiteful character, if not actually of warlike nature. But if the Babylonians regarded her first and foremost as the great mother-goddess, the Assyrians took but little notice of this side of her character. To them she was a veritable Valkyrie, and as the Assyrians grew more and more military so she became more the war-goddess and less the nature-mother of love and agriculture. She appeared in dreams to the war-loving Kings of Assyria, encouraging and heartening them with words of cheer to further military exploits. Fire was her raiment, and, as became a goddess of battle, her appearance was terrific. She consumed the enemies of Assur-bani-pal with flames. Still, strangely enough, in the religious texts, influenced probably by Babylonian sources, she was still to a great extent the mild and bountiful mother of nature. It is in the historical texts which ring with tales of conquest and the grandiloquent boastings of conquering monarchs that she appears as the leader of armies and the martial goddess who has slain her thousands and her tens of thousands. So has it ever been impossible for the priest and the soldier to possess the selfsame idea of godhead, and this is so in the modern no less than in the ancient world. Yet occasionally the stern Assyrian kings unbent, and it was probably in a brief interval of peace that Assur-nazir-pal alluded to Ishtar as the lady who "loves him and his priesthood." Sennacherib also spoke of the goddess in similar terms.

It is necessary to state that the name or title of Belit given to Ishtar does not signify that she is the wife or consort of Bel, but merely that she is a 'great lady', for which the title 'Belit' is a generic term. If she is at times brought into close association with Asshur she is never regarded as his wife. She is not the consort of any god, but an independent goddess in her own right, standing alone, equal with Asshur and the dependant of no other divinity. But it was later only that she ranked with Asshur, and purely because of her military reputation.

Ninib – the Assyrian Nin-Girsu

SUCH A DEITY AS NINIB (another name for Nin-girsu, the god of Lagash) was certain to find favour among the Assyrians by virtue of those characteristics which would render him a valuable ally in war. We find several kings extolling his prowess as a warrior, notably Tiglath-pileser I, and Assur-rishishi, who allude to him as "the courageous one", and "the mighty one of the gods". His old status as a sun-and-wind god, in which he was regarded as overthrowing and levelling with the ground everything which stood in his path, would supply him with the reputation necessary to a god of battles. He is associated with Asshur in this capacity, and Tiglath-pileser brackets them as those "who fulfil his desire". But Ninib's chief votary was Assur-nazir-pal (858–60 BC), who commenced his annals with a paean of praise in honour of Ninib, which so abounds in fulsome eulogy that we feel that either he must have felt much beholden to the god, or else have suffered from religious mania. The epithets he employs in praise of Ninib are those usually lavished upon the greatest of gods only. This proceeding secured immense popularity for Ninib and gave him a social and political vogue which nothing else could have given, and we find Shamsi-ramman, the grandson of Assur-nazir-pal, employing the selfsame titles in honouring him.

The great temple of Ninib was situated in Calah, the official residence of Assur-nazir-pal, and within its walls that monarch placed a tablet recording his deeds, and a great statue of the god. He further endowed his cult so that it might enjoy continuance.

We can readily understand how the especial favour shown to such a god as Ninib by an Assyrian monarch originated. Asshur would be regarded by them as much too popular and national a deity to choose as a personal patron. But more difficult to comprehend are the precise reasons which actuated the Assyrian kings, or indeed the kings of any similar ancient state, in choosing their patrons. Does a polytheistic condition of religion permit of the fine selection of patron deities, or is it not much more probable that the artful offices of ecclesiastical and political wire-pullers had much to do with moulding the preferences of the King before and after he reached the throne? The education of the monarch while yet a prince would almost certainly be entrusted to a high ecclesiastical dignitary, and although many examples to the contrary exist, we are pretty safe in assuming that whatever the complexion of the tutor's mind, that of the pupil would to some extent reflect it. On the other hand there is no resisting the conclusion that the Assyrian kings were very often vulgar parvenus, ostentatious and 'impossible', as such people usually are, and that, after the manner of their kind, they 'doted' upon everything ancient, and, possibly, everything Babylonian, just as the later Romans praised everything Greek.

Ninib as Hunter-God

But Ninib ministered to the amusement of his royal devotees as well as to their warlike desires. We find Assur-nazir-pal invoking him before commencing a long journey in search of sport, and Tiglath-pileser I, who was a doughty hunter of lions and elephants, ascribes his success to Ninib, who has placed the mighty bow in his hands.

Jensen in his *Kosmologie* points out that Ninib represents the eastern sun and the morning sun. If this is so, it is strange to find a god representing the sun of morning in the status of a war-god. It is usually when the sun-god reaches the zenith of the heavens that he slays his thousands and his tens of thousands. As a variant of Nin-girsu he would of course be identified with Tammuz. His consort was Gula, to whom Assur-nazir-pal erected a sanctuary.

Dagan

DAGAN (A.K.A. DAGON) THE FISH-GOD, who, we saw, was the same as Oannes or Ea, strangely enough rose to high rank in Assyria.

Some authorities consider him of Philistian or Aramaean origin, and do not compare him with Ea, who rose from the waters of the Persian Gulf to enlighten his people, and it is evident that the Mesopotamian-Palestinian region contained several versions of the origin of this god, ascribing it to various places. In the Assyrian pantheon he is associated with Anu, who rules the heavens, Dagan supervising the earth. It is strange to observe a deity, whose sphere must originally have been the sea, presiding over the terrestrial plane, and this transference it was which cost Dagan his popularity in Assyria, for later he became identified with Bel and disappeared almost entirely from the Assyrian pantheon.

Anu

ANU IN ASSYRIA did not differ materially from Anu in Babylon, but he suffered, as did other southern deities, from the all-pervading worship of Asshur.

Anu had a temple in Asshur's own city, which was rebuilt by Tiglath-pileser I 641 years after its original foundation. He was regarded in Assyria as lord of the Igigi and Anunnaki, or spirits of heaven and earth, probably the old animistic spirits, and to this circumstance, as well as to the fact that he belonged to the old triad along with Bel and Ea, he probably owed the prolongation of his cult. As an elemental and fundamental god opposition could not possibly displace him, and as ruler of the spirits of air and earth he would have a very strong hold upon the popular imagination. Gods who possess such powers often exist in folk-memory long after the other members of the pantheon which contained them are totally forgotten, and one would scarcely be surprised to find Anu lingering in the shadows of post-Assyrian folk-lore, if any record of such lore could be discovered. Anu was frequently associated with Ramman, but more usually with Bel and Eausas in Babylonia.

Ramman

RAMMAN ENJOYED MUCH GREATER POPULARITY in Assyria than in Babylonia, for there he exercised the functions of a second Asshur, and was regarded as destruction personified. Says an old Assyrian hymn concerning Ramman:

The mighty mountain, thou hast overwhelmed it.
At his anger, at his strength,
At his roaring, at his thundering,
The gods of heaven ascend to the sky,
The gods of the earth ascend to the earth,
Into the horizon of heaven they enter,
Into the zenith of heaven they make their way.

What a picture have we here in these few simple lines of a pantheon in dread and terror of the wrath and violence of one of its number. We can almost behold the divine fugitives crowding in flight, some into the upper regions of air to outsoar the anger of the destroyer, others seeking the recesses of the earth to hide themselves from the fierceness of his countenance, the roar of his thunderbolts, and the arrows of his lightning. Simple, almost bald, as the lines are they possess marvellous pictorial quality, bringing before us as they do the rout of a whole heaven in a few simple words.

The weapons of Ramman are lightning, deluge, hunger, and death, and woe to the nation upon whom he visits his wrath, for upon it he visits flood and famine. Thus his attributes as a storm-god are brought into play when he figures as a war deity, for just as a weather-god of the lightning wields it as a spear or dart in the fight, so Ramman as storm-god brings to bear the horrors of tempest upon the devoted head of the enemy.

So highly did the Assyrian kings value the assistance of Ramman that they sacrificed to him during the stress and bustle of a campaign in the field. They liken an attack of their troops to his onslaught, and if they wish to depict the stamping out of an adversary, his 'eating up', as Chaka's

Zulus were wont to term the process, they declare that their men swept over the enemy as Ramman might have done. Assur-nazir-pal alludes to Ramman as 'the mightiest of the gods', but as in reality that phrase was employed in connection with all the principal deities at one time or another by kings or priests who favoured them, there is no reason to suppose that anything more is intended than that Ramman occupied a place of importance in the Assyrian pantheon.

The worship of Ramman in later times came very much into prominence. It was only in the days of Hammurabi that he came into his kingdom, as it were, and even then his worship was not very firmly established in Babylonia. With the rise of the Kassite dynasty, however, we find him coming more into favour, and his name bestowed upon Babylonian kings. He seems to have formed a triad with Sin and Shamash, and in the Hymn of Hammurabi we find him appealed to along with Shamash as 'Divine Lords of Justice'. Nebuchadnezzar I appears to have held him in high esteem, although he was unfriendly to the dynasty which first brought him into prominence, and this monarch couples him with Ishtar as the divinity who has chiefly assisted him in all his great undertakings. Indeed, Nebuchadnezzar evinced much partiality for Ramman, perhaps feeling that he must placate the especial god of those he had cast from power. He speaks of him as the 'lord of the waters beneath the earth', and of the rains from heaven.

The place of Ramman's origin seems obscure. We have already dealt with his manifestations in more primitive days, but opinions appear to differ regarding the original seat of his worship, some authorities holding that it was Muru in Southern Babylonia, others that it is necessary to turn to Assyria for traces of his first worship. His cult is found in Damascus and extended as far south as the Plain of Jezreel. As Milton says:

> ... *Rimmon, whose delightful seat*
> *Was fair Damascus, on the fertile banks*
> *Of Abbana and Pharphar, lucid streams.*
> *He also 'gainst the house of God was bold*
> *A leper once he lost, and gained a king,*
> *Ahaz his sottish conqu'ror, whom he drew*

God's altar to disparage and displace
For one of Syrian mode, whereon to burn
His odious offerings, and adore the gods
Whom he had vanquish'd.

This later theory would make him of Aramaic origin, but his cult appears to have been of very considerable antiquity in Assyria, and it might have been indigenous there. Moreover, the earliest mention of his worship is in the city of Asshur. As has been indicated, he was probably a storm-god or a thunder-and-lightning god, but he was also associated with the sun-god Shamash. But whatever he may have been in Babylonia, in Assyria he was certainly the thunder-deity first and foremost.

A Babylonian text of some antiquity contains a really fine hymn to Ramman, which might be paraphrased as follows, omitting redundancies:

"O lord Ramman, thy name is the great and glorious Bull, child of heaven, lord of Karkar, lord of plenty, companion of the lord Ea. He that rides the great lion is thy name. Thy name doth charm the land, and covers it like a garment. Thy thunder shakes even the great mountain, En-lil, and when thou dost rumble the mother Nin-lil trembles. Said the lord En-lil, addressing his son Ramman: 'O son, spirit of wisdom, with all-seeing eyes and high vision, full of knowledge as the Pleiades, may thy sonorous voice give forth its utterance. Go forth, go up, who can strive with thee? The father is with thee against the cunning foe. Thou art cunning in wielding the hail-stones great and small. Oh, with thy right hand destroy the enemy and root him up!' Ramman hearkened to the words of his father and took his way from the dwelling, the youthful lion, the spirit of counsel."

In later times in Babylonia Ramman seems to have typified the rain of heaven in its beneficent as well as its fertilizing aspect. Not only did he irrigate the fields and fill the wells with water, but he was also accountable for the dreadful tempests which sweep over Mesopotamia. Sometimes he was malevolent, causing thorns to grow instead of herbs. The people, if they regarded him in some measure as a fertilizing agent, also seem to have looked upon him as a destructive and lion-like deity quite capable of desolating the country-side and 'eating up the land'. His roar is typical of him, filling all hearts with affright as it does, and signifying famine and destruction. It is not strange that Mesopotamian regions should have had so many deities of a destructive tendency when we think of the furious whirlwinds which frequently rush across the face of the land, raising sand-storms and devastating everything in their track. Ramman was well likened to the roaring lion, seeking what he may devour, and this seems to have symbolized him in the eyes of the peasant population of the land. Indeed, the Assyrians, impressed by his destructive tendencies, made a war-god of him, and considered his presence as essential to victory. No wonder that the great god of storm made a good war-god!

Shamash

THE CULT OF SHAMASH IN ASSYRIA dates from at least 1340 BC, when Pudilu built a temple to this god in the city of Asshur. He entitled Shamash 'The Protecting Deity', which name is to be understood as that of the god of justice, whose fiat is unchangeable, and in this manner Shamash differed somewhat from the Babylonian idea concerning him. In the southern kingdom he was certainly regarded as a just god, but not as *the* god of justice – a very different thing.

It is interesting as well as edifying to watch the process of evolution of a god of justice. Thus in Ancient Mexico Tezcatlipoca evolved from a tribal deity into a god who was beginning to bear all the marks and signs of a god of justice when the conquering Spaniards put an end to his career. We observe, too, that although the Greeks had a special deity whose department was justice, other divinities, such as Pallas Athene, displayed signs that they in time might possibly become wielders of the balances between man and man. In the Egyptian heavenly hierarchy Maat and Thoth both partook of the attributes of a god of justice, but perhaps Maat was the more directly symbolical of the two. Now in the case of Shamash no favours can be obtained from him by prayer or sacrifice unless those who supplicate him, monarchs though they be, can lay claim to righteousness. Even Tiglath-pileser I, mighty conqueror as he was, recognized Shamash as his judge, and, naturally, as the judge of his enemies, whom he destroys, not because they are fighting against Tiglath, but because of their wickedness. When he set captives free Tiglath took care to perform the gracious act before the face of Shamash, that the god might behold that justice dwelt in the breast of his royal servant. Tiglath, in fact, is the viceroy of Shamash upon earth, and it would seem as if he referred many cases regarding whose procedure he was in doubt to the god before he finally pronounced upon them.

Both Assur-nazir-pal and Shalmaneser II exalted the sun-cult of Shamash, and it has been suggested that the popularity of the worship of Ra in Egypt had reflected upon that of Shamash in Assyria. It must always be extremely difficult to trace such resemblances at an epoch so distant as that of the ninth century BC. But certainly it looks as if the Ra cult had in some manner influenced that of the old Babylonian sun-god. Sargon pushed the worship of Shamash far to the northern boundaries of Assyria, for he built a sanctuary to the deity beyond the limits of the Assyrian Empire – where, precisely, we do not know. Amongst a nation of warriors a god such as Shamash must have been valued highly, for without his sanction they would hardly be justified in commencing hostilities against any other race.

Sin

W E DO NOT FIND SIN, the Babylonian moon-god, extensively worshipped in Assyria. Assur-nazir-pal founded a temple to him in Calah, and Sargon raised several sanctuaries to him beyond the Assyrian frontier.

It is as a war-god chiefly that we find him depicted in the northern kingdom – why, it would be difficult to say, unless, indeed, it was that the Assyrians turned practically all the deities they borrowed from other peoples into war-gods. So far as is known, no lunar deity in any other pantheon possesses a military significance. Several are not without fear-inspiring attributes, but these are caused chiefly by the manner in which the moon is regarded among primitive peoples as a bringer of plague and blight. But we find Sin in Assyria freed from all the astrological significances which he had for the

Babylonians. At the same time he is regarded as a god of wisdom and a framer of decisions, in these respects equating very fully with the Egyptian Thoth. Assur-bani-pal alludes to Sin as 'the first-born son of Bel', just as he is alluded to in Babylonian texts, thus affording us a clue to the direct Babylonian origin of Sin.

Nusku of the Brilliant Sceptre

IT IS STRANGE that although we know that Nusku had been a Babylonian god from early times, and had figured in the pantheon of Hammurabi, it is not until Assyrian times that we gain any very definite information regarding him.

The symbols used in his name are a sceptre and a stylus, and he is called by Shalmaneser I 'The Bearer of the Brilliant Sceptre'. This circumstance associates him closely with Nabu, to designate whom the same symbols are employed. It is difficult, however, to believe that the two are one, as some writers appear to think, for Nusku is certainly a solar deity, while Nabu appears to have originally been a water-god. There are, however, not wanting cases where the same deity has evinced both solar and aqueous characteristics, and these are to be found notably among the gods of American races. Thus among the Maya of Central America the god Kukulcan is depicted with both solar and aqueous attributes, and similar instances could be drawn from lesser-known mythologies. Nusku and Nabu are, however, probably connected in some way, but exactly in what manner is obscure. In Babylonian times Nusku had become amalgamated with Gibil, the god of fire, which perhaps accounts for his virtual effacement in the southern kingdom. In Assyria we find him alluded to as the messenger of Bel-Merodach, and Assur-bani-pal addresses him as 'the highly honoured messenger of the gods'. The Assyrians do not seem to have identified him in any way with Gibil, the fire-god.

Bel-Merodach

EVEN BEL-MERODACH was absorbed into the Assyrian pantheon. To the Assyrians, Babylonia was the country of Bel, and they referred to their southern neighbours as the 'subjects of Bel'. This, of course, must be taken not to mean the older Bel, but Bel-Merodach. They even alluded to the governor whom they placed over conquered Babylonia as the governor of Bel, so closely did they identify the god with the country.

It is only in the time of Shalmaneser II – the ninth century BC – that we find the name Merodach employed for Bel, so general did the use of the latter become. Of course it was impossible that Merodach could take first place in Assyria as he had done in Babylonia, but it was a tribute to the Assyrian belief in his greatness that they ranked him immediately after Asshur in the pantheon.

Prisoner-Gods

The Assyrian rulers were sufficiently politic to award this place to Merodach, for they could not but see that Babylonia, from which they drew their arts and sciences, as well as their religious beliefs, and from which they benefited in many directions, must be worthily represented in the national religion. And just as the Romans in conquering Greece and Egypt adopted many of the deities of these more cultured and less powerful lands, thus seeking to bind the inhabitants of the conquered provinces more closely to themselves, so did the Assyrian rulers believe that, did they incorporate Merodach into their hierarchy, he would become so Assyrian in his outlook as to cease to be wholly Babylonian, and would doubtless work in favour of the stronger kingdom. In no other of the religions of antiquity as in the Assyrian was the idea so powerful that the god of the conquered or subject people should become a virtual prisoner in the land of the conquerors, or should at least be absorbed into their national worship. Some of the

Assyrian monarchs went so far as to drag almost every petty idol they encountered on their conquests back to the great temple of Asshur, and it is obvious that they did not do this with any intention of uprooting the worship of these gods in the regions they conquered, but because they desired to make political prisoners of them, and to place them in a temple-prison, where they would be unable to wreak vengeance upon them, or assist their beaten worshippers to war against them in the future.

It may be fitting at this point to emphasize how greatly the Assyrian people, as apart from their rulers, cherished the older beliefs of Babylonia. Both peoples were substantially of the same stock, and any movement which had as its object the destruction of the Babylonian religion would have met with the strongest hostility from the populace of Assyria. Just as the conquering Aztecs seem to have had immense reverence for the worship of the Toltecs, whose land they subdued, so did the less cultivated Assyrians regard everything connected, with Babylonia as peculiarly sacred. The Kings of Assyria, in fact, were not a little proud of being the rulers of Babylonia, and were extremely mild in their treatment of their southern subjects – very much more so, in fact, than they were in their behaviour toward the people of Elam or other conquered territories. We even find the kings alluding to themselves as being nominated by the gods to rule over the land of Bel.

The Assyrian monarchs strove hard not to disturb the ancient Babylonian cult, and Shalmaneser II, when he had conquered Babylonia, actually entered Merodach's temple and sacrificed to him.

The Assyrian Bel and Belit

AS FOR BEL, whose place Merodach usurped in the Babylonian pantheon, he was also recognized in Assyria, and Tiglath-pileser I built him a temple in his city of Asshur.

Tiglath prefixes the adjective 'old' to the god's name to show that he means Bel, not Bel-Merodach. Sargon, too, who had antiquarian tastes, also reverts to Bel, to whom he alludes as the 'Great Mountain', the name of the god following immediately after that of Asshur. Bel is also invoked in connection with Anu as a granter of victory. His consort Belit, although occasionally she is coupled with him, more usually figures as the wife of Asshur, and almost as commonly as a variant of Ishtar. In a temple in the city of Asshur, Tiglath-pileser I made presents to Belit consisting of the images of the gods vanquished by him in his various campaigns. Assur-bani-pal, too, regarded Belit as the wife of Asshur, and himself as their son, alluding to Belit as 'Mother of the Great Gods', a circumstance which would go to show that, like most of the Assyrian kings, his egoism rather overshadowed his sense of humour. In Assur-bani-pal's pantheon Belit is placed close by her consort Asshur. But there seems to have been a good deal of confusion between Belit and Ishtar because of the general meaning of the word Belit.

Nabu and Merodach

AS IN BABYLONIA SO IN ASSYRIA, Nabu and Merodach were paired together, often as Bel and Nabu. Especially were they invoked when the affairs of Babylonia were being dealt with.

In the seventh century BC we find the cult of Nabu in high popularity in Assyria, and indeed Ramman-Nirari III appears to have made an attempt to advance Nabu considerably. He erected a temple to the god at Calah, and granted him many resounding titles. But even so, it does not seem that Ramman-Nirari intended to exalt Nabu at the expense of Asshur. Indeed it would have been impossible for him to have done so if he had desired to. Asshur was as much the national god of the Assyrian people as Osiris was of the Egyptians. Nabu was the patron of wisdom, and protector of the arts; he guided the stylus of the scribe; and in these attributes he is very close to the Egyptian Thoth, and almost identical with another Babylonian god, Nusku. Sargon calls Nabu 'the Seer who guides the gods', and it would seem from some notices of him that he was also regarded as a leader of heavenly or spiritual forces. Those kings who were fond of erudition paid great devotion to Nabu, and many of the tablets in their literary collections close with thanksgiving to him for having opened their ears to receive wisdom.

Ea

EA WAS OF COURSE ACCEPTED into the Assyrian pantheon because of his membership in the old Assyrian triad, but he was also regarded as a god of wisdom, possibly because of his venerable reputation; and we find him also as patron of the arts, and especially of building and architecture.

Threefold was his power of direction in this respect. The great Colossi, the enormous winged bulls and mythological figures which flanked the avenues leading to the royal places, the images of the gods, and, lastly, the greater buildings, were all examples of the architectural art of which he was the patron.

Dibarra

ANOTHER BABYLONIAN DEITY who was placed in the ranks of the Assyrian pantheon was Dibarra, the plague-god, who can only be called a god through a species of courtesy, as he partook much more of a demoniac character, and was at one time almost certainly an evil spirit.

We have already alluded to the poem in which he lays low people and armies by his violence, and it was probably from one of the texts of this that Assur-bani-pal conceived the idea that those civilians who had perished in his campaigns against Babylonia had been slaughtered by Dibarra.

Lesser Gods

Some of the lesser Babylonian gods, like Damku and Sharru-Ilu, seem to have attracted a passing interest to themselves, but as little can be found concerning them in Babylonian texts, it is scarcely necessary to take much notice of them in such a chapter as this.

Most probably the Assyrians accepted the Babylonian gods on the basis not only of their native reputation, but also of the occurrence of their names in the ancient religious texts, with which their priests were thoroughly acquainted, and though, broadly speaking, they accepted practically the whole of the Babylonian religion and its gods in entirety, there is no doubt that some of these by their very natures and attributes appealed more to them than others, and therefore possessed a somewhat different value in their eyes from that assigned to them by the more peace-loving people of the southern kingdom.

Babylonian Star-Worship

ANCIENT CHALDEA WAS undoubtedly the birthplace of that mysterious science of astrology which was destined to exert such influence upon the European mind during the Middle Ages, and which indeed has not yet ceased to amuse the curious and flatter the hopes of the credulous. Whether any people more primitive than the Akkadians had studied the movements of the stars it would indeed be extremely difficult to say. This the Akkadians or Babylonians were probably the first to attempt. The plain of Mesopotamia is peculiarly suited to the study of the movements of the stars. It is level for the most part, and there are few mountains around which moisture can collect to obscure the sky. Moreover the climate greatly assists such observations.

Like most primitive people the Babylonians originally believed the stars to be pictures drawn on the heavens. At a later epoch they were described as the 'writing of heaven'; the sky was supposed to be a great vault, and the movements observed by these ancient astronomers were thought to be on the part of the stars alone. Of course it would be noticed at an early stage that some of the stars seemed fixed while others moved about. Lines were drawn between the various stars and planets, and the figures which resulted from these were regarded as omens. Again, certain groups or constellations were connected with such lines which led them to be identified with various animals, and in this we may observe the influence of animism. The Babylonian zodiac was, with the exception of the sign of Merodach, identified with the eleven monsters forming the host of Tiawath. Thus it would seem that the zodiacal system as a whole originated in Babylonia. The knowledge of the Chaldean astronomers appears to have been considerable, and it is likely that they were familiar with most of the constellations known to the later Greeks.

Legend of the Origin of Star-Worship and Idolatry

THE FOLLOWING LEGEND is told regarding the origin of astrology by Maimonides, the famous Jewish rabbi and friend of Averroes, in his commentary on the *Mischnah*:

"In the days of Enos, the son of Seth, the sons of Adam erred with great error: and the council of the wise men of that age became brutish; and Enos himself was of them that erred. And their error was this: they said, – Forasmuch as God hath *created these stars and spheres to govern the world*, and hath set them on high, and hath imparted honour unto them, and they are ministers that minister before Him, it is meet that men should laud and glorify and give them honour. For this is the will of God that we laud and magnify whomsoever He magnifieth and honoureth, even as a king would honour them that stand before him. And this is the honour of the king himself. When this thing was come up into their hearts they began to build temples unto the stars, and to offer sacrifice unto them, and to laud and magnify them with words, and to worship before them, that they might, in their evil opinion, obtain favour of their Creator. And this was the root of idolatry; for in process of time there stood up false prophets among the sons of Adam, which said, that God had commanded them and said unto them, – Worship such a star, or all the stars, and do sacrifice unto them thus and thus; and build a temple for it, and make an image of it, that all the people, women and children, may worship it. And the false prophet *showed them the image* which he had feigned out of his own heart, and said that *it was the image* of that star which was made known to him by prophecy. And they began after this manner to make images in temples, and under trees, and on the tops of mountains and hills, and assembled together and worshipped them; *and this thing was spread through all the world* to serve images, with services different one from another, and to sacrifice unto and worship them. So, in process of time, the glorious and fearful Name was forgotten out of the mouth of all living, and out of their knowledge, and they acknowledged Him not. And there was found on earth no people that knew aught, save images of wood and stone, and temples of stone which they had been trained up from their childhood to worship and serve, and to swear by their names; and the wise men that were among them, the priests and such like, thought that there was no God save the stars and spheres, for whose sake, and *in whose likeness*, they had made these images; but as for the Rock Everlasting, there was no man that did acknowledge Him or know Him save a few persons in the world, as Enoch, Methusaleh, Noah, Shem, and Heber. And in this way did the world work and converse, till that pillar of the world, Abram our father, was born."

Planets identified with Gods

THE ANCIENT CHALDEANS RECOGNIZED at an early period that eternal and unchangeable laws underlay planetary motion, and seem to have been able to forecast eclipses. Soon also did they begin to identify the several heavenly bodies with the gods. Thus the path of the sun was known as the 'way of Anu', and the course of the moon and planets they determined with reference to the sun's ecliptic or pathway. It is strange, too, that they should have employed the same ideograph for the word 'star' and the word 'god', the only difference being that in the case of a god they repeated the sign three times. If the sun and moon under animistic law are regarded as gods, it stands to reason that the stars and planets must also be looked upon as lesser deities.

Jupiter, the largest of the planets, was identified with Merodach, head of the Babylonian pantheon. We find him exercising control over the other stars in the creation story under the name Nibir. Ishtar was identified with Venus, Saturn with Ninib, Mars with Nergal, Mercury with Nabu. It is more than strange that gods with certain attributes should have become attached to certain planets in more countries than one, and this illustrates the deep and lasting influence which Semitic religious thought exercised over the Hellenic and Roman theological systems. The connection is too obvious and too exact not to be the result of close association. There are, indeed, hundreds of proofs to support such a theory. Who can suppose, for example, that Aphrodite is any other than Ishtar? The Romans identified their goddess Diana with the patroness of Ephesus. There are, indeed, traces of direct relations of the Greek goddess with the moon, and she was also, like Ishtar, connected with the lower world and the sea. The Greeks had numerous and flourishing colonies in Asia Minor in remote times, and these probably assisted in the dissemination of Asiatic and especially Babylonian lore.

The sun was regarded as the shepherd of the stars, and Nergal, the god of destruction and the underworld, as the 'chief sheep', probably because the ruddy nature of his light rendered him a most conspicuous object. Anu is the Pole Star of the ecliptic, Bel the Pole Star of the equator, while Ea, in the southern heavens, was identified with a star in the constellation Argo. Fixed stars were probably selected for them because of their permanent and elemental nature. The sun they represented as riding in a chariot drawn by horses, and we frequently notice that the figure representing the luminary on Greek vases and other remains wears the Phrygian cap, a typically Asiatic and non-Hellenic head-dress, thus assisting proof that the idea of the sun as a charioteer possibly originated in Babylonia. Lunar worship, or at least computation of time by the phases of the moon, frequently precedes the solar cult, and we find traces in Babylonian religion of the former high rank of the moon-god. The moon, for example, is not one of the flock of sheep under guidance of the sun. The very fact that the calendar was regulated by her movements was sufficient to prevent this. Like the Red Indians and other primitive folk, the Babylonians possessed agricultural titles for each month, but these periods were also under the direct patronage of some god or gods. Thus the first month, Nizan, is sacred to Anu and Bel; and the second, Iyar, to Ea. Siwan is devoted to Sin, and as we approach the summer season the solar gods are apportioned to various months. The sixth month is sacred to Ishtar, and the seventh to Shamash, great god of the sun. Merodach rules over the eighth, and Nergal over the ninth month.

The tenth, curiously enough, is sacred to a variant of Nabu, to Anu, and to Ishtar. The eleventh month, very suitably, to Ramman, the god of storms, and the last month, Adar, falling within the rainy season, is presided over by the seven evil spirits.

None of the goddesses received stellar honours. The names of the months were probably quite popular in origin. Thus we find that the first month was known as the 'month of the Sanctuary', the third as the 'period of brick-making', the fifth as the 'fiery month', the sixth as the 'month of the mission of Ishtar', referring to her descent into the realms of Allatu. The fourth month was designated 'scattering seed', the eighth that of the opening of dams, and the ninth was entitled 'copious fertility', while the eleventh was known as 'destructive rain.'

We find the gods so closely connected with ancient Chaldean astronomy as to be absolutely identified with it in every way. A number was assigned to each of the chief gods, which would seem to show that they were connected in some way with mathematical science. Thus Ishtar's number is fifteen; that of Sin, her father, is exactly double that. Anu takes sixty, and Bel and Ea represent fifty and forty. Ramman is identified with ten.

Magic, Demonology and Superstition

L IKE OTHER PRIMITIVE RACES the peoples of Chaldea scarcely discriminated at all between religion and magic. One difference between the priest and the sorcerer was that the one employed magic for religious purposes whilst the other used it for his own ends. The literature of Chaldea – especially its religious literature – teems with references to magic, and in its spells and incantations we see the prototypes of those employed by the magicians of mediaeval Europe. Indeed so closely do some of the Assyrian incantations and magical practices resemble those of the European sorcerers of the Middle Ages and of primitive peoples of the present day that it is difficult to convince oneself that they are of independent origin.

In Chaldea as in ancient Egypt the crude and vague magical practices of primeval times received form and developed into accepted ritual, just as early religious ideas evolved into dogmas under the stress of theological controversy and opinion. As there were men who would dispute upon religious questions, so were there persons who would discuss matters magical. This is not to say that the terms 'religion' and 'magic' possessed any well-defined boundaries for them. Nor is it at all clear that they do for us in this twentieth century. They overlap; and it has long been the belief of the writer that their relations are but represented by two circles which intersect one another and the areas of which partially coincide.

Our information regarding Chaldean magic is much more complete than that which we possess concerning the magic of ancient Egypt. Hundreds of spells, incantations, and omen-inscriptions have been recovered, and these not only enlighten us regarding the class of priests who practised magic, but they tell us of the several varieties of demons, ghosts, and evil spirits; they minutely describe the Babylonian witch and wizard, and they picture for us many magical ceremonies, besides informing us of the names of scores of plants and flowers possessing magical properties, of magical substances, jewels, amulets, and the like. Also they speak of sortilege or the divination of the future, of the drawing of magical circles, of the exorcism of evil spirits, and the casting out of demons.

Priestly Magicians, Wizards and Witches

THERE WERE AT LEAST TWO CLASSES OF PRIESTS who dealt in the occult – the *barû*, or seers, and the *asipû*, or wizards. The caste of the barû was a very ancient one, dating at least from the time of Hammurabi. The barû performed divination by consulting the livers of animals and also by observation of the flight of birds. We find many of the kings of Babylonia consulting this class of soothsayer. Sennacherib, for example, sought from the barû the cause of his father's violent death. The asipû, on the other hand, was the remover of taboo and bans of all sorts; he chanted the rites described in the magical texts, and performed the ceremony of atonement. It is:

> *He that stilleth all to rest, that pacifieth all.*
> *By whose incantations everything is at peace.*
> *The gods are upon his right hand and his left,*
> *they are behind and before him.*

The wizard and the witch were known as *Kassapu* or *Kassaptu*. These were the sorcerers or magicians proper, and that they were considered dangerous to the community is shown by the manner in which they are treated by the code of Hammurabi, in which it is ordained that he who charges a man with sorcery and can justify the charge shall obtain the sorcerer's house, and the sorcerer shall plunge into the river. But if the sorcerer be not drowned then he who accused him shall be put to death and the wrongly accused man shall have his house.

A series of texts known as 'Maklu' provides us, among other things, with a striking picture of the Babylonian witch. It tells how she prowls the streets, searching for victims, snatching love from handsome men, and withering beauteous women. At another time she is depicted sitting in the shade of the wall making spells and fashioning images. The suppliant prays that her magic may revert upon herself, that the image of her which he has made, and doubtless rendered into the hands of the priest, shall be burnt by the fire-god, that her words may be forced back into her mouth. "May her mouth be fat, may her tongue be salt," continues the prayer. The *haltappen-plant* along with sesame is sent against her. "O, witch, like the circlet of this seal may thy face grow green and yellow!"

An Assyrian text says of a sorceress that her bounds are the whole world, that she can pass over all mountains. The writer states that near his door he has posted a servant, on the right and left of his door has he set Lugalgirra and Allamu, that they might kill the witch.

The library of Assur-bani-pal contains many cuneiform tablets dealing with magic, but there are also extant many magical tablets of the later Babylonian Empire. These were known to the Babylonians by some name or word, indicative perhaps of the special sphere of their activities. Thus we have the Maklu ('burning'), Surpu ('consuming'), Utukki limnûti ('evil spirits'), and Labartu ('witch-hag') series, besides many other texts dealing with magical practices.

The Maklu series deals with spells against witches and wizards, images of whom are to be consumed by fire to the accompaniment of suitable spells and prayers. The Surpu series contains prayers and incantations against taboo. That against evil spirits provides the haunted with spells which will exorcise demons, ghosts, and the powers of the air generally, and place devils under a ban. In other magical tablets the diseases to which poor humanity is prone are guarded against, and instructions are given on the manner in which they may be transferred to the dead bodies of animals, usually swine or goats.

A Toothache Myth

THE ASSYRIAN PHYSICIAN had, inevitably, to be something of a demonologist, as possession by devils was held to be the cause of divers diseases, and we find incantations sprinkled among prescriptions. Occasionally, too, we come upon the fag-end of a folk-tale or dip momentarily into myth, as in a prescription for the toothache, compounded of fermented drink, the plant *sakilbir*,

and oil – probably as efficacious in the case of that malady as most modern ones are. The story attached to the cure is as follows:

When Anu had created the heavens, the earth created the rivers, the rivers the canals, and the canals the marshes, which in turn created the worm. And the worm came weeping before Ea, saying, "What wilt thou give me for my food, what wilt thou give me for my devouring?" "I will give thee ripe figs," replied the god, "ripe figs and scented wood." "Bah," replied the worm, "what are ripe figs to me, or what is scented wood? Let me drink among the teeth and batten on the gums that I may devour the blood of the teeth and the strength thereof." This tale alludes to a Babylonian superstition that worms consume the teeth.

The Word of Power

AS IN EGYPT, the word of power was held in great reverence by the magicians of Chaldea, who believed that the name, preferably the secret name, of a god possessed sufficient force in its mere syllables to defeat and scatter the hordes of evil things that surrounded and harassed mankind.

The names of Ea and Merodach were, perhaps, most frequently used to carry destruction into the ranks of the demon army. It was also necessary to know the name of the devil or person against whom his spells were directed. If to this could be added a piece of hair, or the nail-parings in the case of a human being, then special efficacy was given to the enchantment. But just as hair or nails were part of a man so was his name, and hence the great virtue ascribed to names in art-magic, ancient and modern. The name was, as it were, the vehicle by means of which the magician established a link between himself and his victim, and the Babylonians in exorcising sickness or disease of any kind were wont to recite long catalogues of the names of evil spirits and demons in the hope that by so doing they might chance to light upon that especial individual who was the cause of the malady. Even long lists of names of persons who had died premature deaths were often recited in order to ensure that they would not return to torment the living.

Babylonian Vampires

IN ALL LANDS AND EPOCHS the grisly conception of the vampire has gained a strong hold upon the imagination of the common people, and this was no less the case in Babylonia and Assyria than elsewhere.

There have not been wanting those who believed that vampirism was confined to the Slavonic race alone, and that the peoples of Russia, Bohemia, and the Balkan Peninsula were the sole possessors of the vampire legend. Recent research, however, has exposed the fallacy of this theory and has shown that, far from being the property of the Slavs or even of Aryan peoples, this horrible belief is or was the possession of practically every race, savage or civilized, that is known to anthropology. The seven evil spirits of Assyria are, among other things, vampires of no uncertain type. An ancient poem which was chanted by them commences thus (note the last lines in particular):

> *Seven are they! Seven are they!*
> *In the ocean deep, seven are they!*
> *Battening in heaven, seven are they!*
> *Bred in the depths of the ocean;*
> *Not male nor female are they,*
> *But are as the roaming wind-blast.*
> *No wife have they, no son can they beget;*
> *Knowing neither mercy nor pity,*
> *They hearken not to prayer, to prayer.*
> *They are as horses reared amid the hills,*
> *The Evil Ones of Ea;*
> *Throne-bearers to the gods are they,*

They stand in the highway to befoul the path;
Evil are they, evil are they!
Seven are they, seven are they,
Twice seven are they!

Destructive storms (and) evil winds are they,
An evil blast that heraldeth the baneful storm,
An evil blast, forerunner of the baleful storm.
They are mighty children, mighty sons,
Heralds of the Pestilence.
Throne-bearers of Ereskigal,
They are the flood which rusheth through the land.
Seven gods of the broad earth,
Seven robber(?)-gods are they,
Seven gods of might,
Seven evil demons,
Seven evil demons of oppression,
Seven in heaven and seven on earth.

Spirits that minish heaven and earth,
That minish the land,
Spirits that minish the land,
Of giant strength,
Of giant strength and giant tread,
Demons (like) raging bulls, great ghosts,
Ghosts that break through all houses,
Demons that have no shame,
Seven are they!
Knowing no care, they grind the land like corn;
Knowing no mercy, they rage against mankind,
They spill their blood like rain,
Devouring their flesh (and) sucking their veins.
Where the images of the gods are, there they quake (?)
In the Temple of Nabu, who fertilises the shoots (?) of wheat.
They are demons full of violence, ceaselessly devouring blood.

Gods Once Demons

MANY OF THE BABYLONIAN GODS retained traces of their primitive demoniacal characteristics, and this applies to the great triad, Ea, Anu, and En-lil, who probably evolved into godhead from an animistic group of nature spirits. Each of these gods was accompanied by demon groups. Thus the disease-demons were 'the beloved sons of Bel', the fates were the seven daughters of Anu, and the seven storm-demons the children of Ea. In a magical incantation describing the primitive monster form of Ea it is said that his head is like a serpent's, the ears are those of a basilisk, his horns are twisted into curls, his body is a sun-fish full of stars, his feet are armed with claws, and the sole of his foot has no heel.

Ea was 'the great magician of the gods'; his sway over the forces of nature was secured by the performance of magical rites, and his services were obtained by human beings who performed requisite ceremonies and repeated appropriate spells. Although he might be worshipped and propitiated in his temple at Eridu, he could also be conjured in mud huts. The latter, indeed, as in Mexico, appear to have been the oldest holy places.

The Legend of Ura

It is told that Ura, the dread demon of disease, once made up his mind to destroy mankind. But Ishnu, his counsellor, appeased him so that he abandoned his intention, and he gave humanity a chance of escape. Whoever should praise Ura and magnify his name would, he said, rule the four quarters of the world, and should have none to oppose him. He should not die in pestilence, and his speech should bring him into favour with the great ones of the earth. Wherever a tablet with the song of Ura was set up, in that house there should be immunity from the pestilence.

Purification

PURIFICATION BY WATER entered largely into Babylonian magic. The ceremony known as the 'Incantation of Eridu', so frequently alluded to in Babylonian magical texts, was probably some form of purification by water, relating as it does to the home of Ea, the sea-god.

Another ceremony prescribes the mingling of water from a pool 'that no hand hath touched', with tamarisk, *mastakal*, ginger, alkali, and mixed wine. Therein must be placed a shining ring, and the mixture is then to be poured upon the patient. A root of saffron is then to be taken and pounded with pure salt and alkali and fat of the *matku*-bird brought from the mountains, and with this strange mixture the body of the patient is to be anointed.

The Chamber of the Priest-Magician

LET US ATTEMPT TO DESCRIBE the treatment of a case by a priest-physician-magician of Babylonia. The following is a rather obscure one, but by the aid of imagination as well as the assistance of Babylonian representation we may construct a tolerably clear picture.

The chamber of the sage is almost certain to be situated in some nook in one of those vast and imposing fanes which more closely resembled cities than mere temples. We draw the curtain and enter a rather darksome room. The atmosphere is pungent with chemic odours, and ranged on shelves disposed upon the tiled walls are numerous jars, great and small, containing the fearsome compounds which the practitioner applies to the sufferings of Babylonian humanity. The asipu, shaven and austere, asks us what we desire of him, and in the role of Babylonian citizens we acquaint him with the fact that our lives are made miserable for us by a witch who sends upon us misfortune after misfortune, now the blight or some equally intractable and horrible disease, now an evil wind, now unspeakable enchantments which torment us unceasingly. In his capacity of physician the asipu examines our bodies, shrunken and exhausted with fever or rheumatism, and having prescribed for us, compounds the mixture with his own hands and enjoins us to its regular application. He mixes various ingredients in a stone mortar, whispering his spells the while, with many a prayer to Ea the beneficent and Merodach the all-powerful that we may be restored to health. Then he promises to visit us at our dwelling and gravely bids us adieu, after expressing the hope that we will graciously contribute to the upkeep of the house of religion to which he is attached.

Leaving the darkened haunt of the asipu for the brilliant sunshine of a Babylonian summer afternoon, we are at first inclined to forget our fears, and to laugh away the horrible superstitions, the relics of barbarian ancestors, which weigh us down. But as night approaches we grow more fearful, we crouch with the children in the darkest corner of our clay-brick dwelling, and tremble at every sound. The rushing of the wind overhead is for us the noise of the Labartu, the hag-demon, come hither to tear from us our little ones, or perhaps a rat rustling in the straw may seem to us the Alu-demon. The ghosts of the dead gibber at the threshold, and even pale Uru, lord of disease, himself may glance in at the tiny window with ghastly countenance and eager, red eyes. The pains of rheumatism assail us. Ha, the evil witch is at work, thrusting thorns into the waxen images made in our shape that we may suffer the torment brought about by sympathetic magic, to which we would rather refer our aches than to the circumstance that we dwell hard by the river-swamps.

A loud knocking resounds at the door. We tremble anew and the children scream. At last the dread powers of evil have come to summon us to the final ordeal, or perhaps the witch herself, grown bold by reason of her immunity, has come to wreak fresh vengeance. The flimsy door of boards is thrown open, and to our unspeakable relief the stern face of the asipu appears beneath the flickering light of the taper. We shout with joy, and the children cluster around the priest, clinging to his garments and clasping his knees.

The Witch-Finding

The priest smiles at our fear, and motioning us to sit in a circle produces several waxen figures of demons which he places on the floor. It is noticeable that these figures all appear to be bound with miniature ropes. Taking one of these in the shape of a Labartu or hag-demon, the priest places before it twelve small cakes made from a peculiar kind of meal. He then pours out a libation of water, places the image of a small black dog beside that of the witch, lays a piece of the heart of a young pig on the mouth of the figure and some white bread and a box of ointment beside it. He then chants something like the following: "May a guardian spirit be present at my side when I draw near unto the sick man, when I examine his muscles, when I compose his limbs, when I sprinkle the water of Ea upon him. Avoid thee whether thou art an evil spirit or an evil demon, an evil ghost or an evil devil, an evil god or an evil fiend, hag-demon, ghoul, sprite, phantom, or wraith, or any disease, fever, headache, shivering, or any sorcery, spell, or enchantment."

Having recited some such words of power the asipu then directs us to keep the figure at the head of our bed for three nights, then to bury it beneath the earthen floor. But alas! no cure results. The witch still torments us by day and night, and once more we have recourse to the priest-doctor; the ceremony is gone through again, but still the family health does not improve. The little ones suffer from fever, and bad luck consistently dogs us. After a stormy scene between husband and wife, who differ regarding the qualifications of the asipu, another practitioner is called in. He is younger and more enterprising than the last, and he has not yet learned that half the business of the physician is to 'nurse' his patients, in the financial sense of the term. Whereas the elderly asipu had gone quietly home to bed after prescribing for us, this young physician, who has his spurs to win, after being consulted goes home to his clay surgery and hunts up a likely exorcism.

Next day, armed with this wordy weapon, he arrives at our dwelling and, placing a waxen image of the witch upon the floor, vents upon it the full force of his rhetoric. As he is on the point of leaving, screams resound from a neighbouring cabin. Bestowing upon us a look of the deepest meaning our asipu darts to the hut opposite and hales forth an ancient crone, whose appearance of age and illness give her a most sinister look. At once we recognize in her a wretch who dared to menace our children when in innocent play they cast hot ashes upon her thatch and introduced hot swamp water into her cistern. In righteous wrath we lay hands on the abandoned being who for so many months has cast a blight upon our lives. She exclaims that the pains of death have seized upon her, and we laugh in triumph, for we know that the superior magic of our asipu has taken effect. On the way to the river we are joined by neighbours, who rejoice with us that we have caught the witch. Great is the satisfaction of the party when at last the devilish crone is cast headlong into the stream.

But ere many seconds pass we begin to look incredulously upon each other, for the wicked one refuses to sink. This means that she is innocent! Then, awful moment, we find every eye directed upon us, we who were so happy and light-hearted but a moment before. We tremble, for we know how severe are the laws against the indiscriminate accusation of those suspected of witchcraft. As the ancient crone continues to float, a loud murmuring arises in the crowd, and with quaking limbs and eyes full of terror we snatch up our children and make a dash for freedom.

Luckily the asipu accompanies us so that the crowd dare not pursue, and indeed, so absurdly changeable is human nature, most of them are busied in rescuing the old woman. In a few minutes we have placed all immediate danger of pursuit behind us. The asipu has departed to his temple, richer in the experience by the lesson of a false 'prescription.' After a hurried consultation we quit the town, skirt the arable land which fringes it, and plunge into the desert. She who was opposed to the employment of a young and inexperienced asipu does not make matters any better by reiterating "I told you so." And he who favoured a 'second opinion', on paying a night visit to the city, discovers that the 'witch' has succumbed to her harsh treatment; that his house has been made over to her relatives by way of compensation, and that a legal process has been taken out against him. Returning to his wife he acquaints her with the sad news, and hand in hand with their weeping offspring they turn and face the desert.

The Magic Circle

THE MAGIC CIRCLE, as in use among the Chaldean sorcerers, bears many points of resemblance to that described in mediaeval works on magic. The Babylonian magician, when describing the circle, made seven little winged figures, which he set before an image of the god Nergal. After doing so he stated that he had covered them with a dark robe and bound them with a coloured cord, setting beside them tamarisk and the heart of the palm, that he had completed the magic circle and had surrounded them with a sprinkling of lime and flour.

That the magic circle of mediaeval times must have been evolved from the Chaldean is plain from the strong resemblance between the two. Directions for the making of a mediaeval magic circle are as follows:

In the first place the magician is supposed to fix upon a spot proper for such a purpose, which must be either in a subterranean vault, hung round with black, and lighted by a magical torch, or else in the centre of some thick wood or desert, or upon some extensive unfrequented plain, where several roads meet, or amidst the ruins of ancient castles, abbeys, or monasteries, or amongst the rocks on the seashore, in some private detached churchyard, or any other melancholy place between the hours of twelve and one in the night, either when the moon shines very bright, or else when the elements are disturbed with storms of thunder, lightning, wind, and rain; for, in these places, times, and seasons, it is contended that spirits can with less difficulty manifest themselves to mortal eyes, and continue visible with the least pain.

When the proper time and place are fixed upon, a magic circle is to be formed within which the master and his associates are carefully to retire. The reason assigned by magicians and others for the institution and use of the circles is, that so much ground being blessed and consecrated by holy words and ceremonies has a secret force to expel all evil spirits from the bounds thereof, and, being sprinkled with sacred water, the ground is purified from all uncleanness; beside the holy names of God being written over every part of it, its force becomes proof against all evil spirits.

Babylonian Demons

BABYLONIAN DEMONS WERE LEGION and most of them exceedingly malevolent. The Utukku was an evil spirit that lurked generally in the desert, where it lay in wait for unsuspecting travellers, but it did not confine its haunts to the more barren places, for it was also to be found among the mountains, in graveyards, and even in the sea. An evil fate befell the man upon whom it looked.

The Rabisu is another lurking demon that secretes itself in unfrequented spots to leap upon passers-by. The Labartu, which has already been alluded to, is, strangely enough, spoken of as the daughter of Anu. She was supposed to dwell in the mountains or in marshy places, and was particularly addicted to the destruction of children. Babylonian mothers were wont to hang charms round their children's necks to guard them against this horrible hag.

The Sedu appears to have been in some senses a guardian spirit and in others a being of evil propensities. It is often appealed to at the end of invocations along with the Lamassu, a spirit of a similar type. These malign influences were probably the prototypes of the Arabian jinn, to whom they have many points of resemblance.

Many Assyrian spirits were half-human and half-supernatural, and some of them were supposed to contract unions with human beings, like the Arabian jinn. The offspring of such unions was supposed to be a spirit called Alu, which haunted ruins and deserted buildings and indeed entered the houses of men like a ghost to steal their sleep. Ghosts proper were also common enough, as has already been observed, and those who had not been buried were almost certain to return to harass mankind. It was dangerous even to look upon a corpse, lest the spirit or edimmu of the dead man should seize upon the beholder. The

Assyrians seemed to be of the opinion that a ghost like a vampire might drain away the strength of the living, and long formulae were in existence containing numerous names of haunting spirits, one of which it was hoped would apply to the tormenting ghost, and these were used for the purposes of exorcism. To lay a spirit the following articles were necessary: seven small loaves of roast corn, the hoof of a dark-coloured ox, flour of roast corn, and a little leaven. The ghosts were then asked why they tormented the haunted man, after which the flour and leaven were kneaded into a paste in the horn of an ox and a small libation poured into a hole in the earth. The leaven dough was then placed in the hoof of an ox, and another libation poured out with an incantation to the god Shamash. In another case figures of the dead man and the living person to whom the spirit has appeared are to be made and libations poured out before both of them, then the figure of the dead man is to be buried and that of the living man washed in pure water, the whole ceremony being typical of sympathetic magic, which thus supposed the burial of the body of the ghost and the purification of the living man. In the morning incense was to be offered up before the sun-god at his rising, when sweet woods were to be burned and a libation of sesame wine poured out.

If a human being was troubled by a ghost, it was necessary that he should be anointed with various substances in order that the result of the ghostly contact might be nullified.

An old text says, "When a ghost appeareth in the house of a man there will be a destruction of that house. When it speaketh and hearkeneth for an answer the man will die, and there will be lamentation."

Taboo

THE BELIEF IN TABOO was universal in ancient Chaldea. Amongst the Babylonians it was known as *mamit*. There were taboos on many things, but especially upon corpses and uncleanness of all kinds. We find the taboo generally alluded to in a text "as the barrier that none can pass".

Among all barbarous peoples the taboo is usually intended to hedge in the sacred thing from the profane person or the common people, but it may also be employed for sanitary reasons. Thus the flesh of certain animals, such as the pig, may not be eaten in hot countries. Food must not be prepared by those who are in the slightest degree suspected of uncleanness, and these laws are usually of the most rigorous character; but should a man violate the taboo placed upon certain foods, then he himself often became taboo. No one might have any intercourse with him. He was left to his own devices, and, in short, became a sort of pariah. In the Assyrian texts we find many instances of this kind of taboo, and numerous were the supplications that these might be removed. If one drank water from an unclean cup he had violated a taboo. Like the Arab he might not "lick the platter clean." If he were taboo he might not touch another man, he might not converse with him, he might not pray to the gods, he might not even be interceded for by anyone else. In fact he was excommunicate. If a man cast his eye upon water which another person had washed his hands in, or if he came into contact with a person who had not yet performed his ablutions, he became unclean. An entire purification ritual was incumbent on any Assyrian who touched or even looked upon a dead man.

It may be asked, wherefore was this elaborate cleanliness essential to avoid taboo? The answer undoubtedly is – because of the belief in the power of sympathetic magic. Did one come into contact with a person who was in any way unclean, or with a corpse or other unpleasant object, he was supposed to come within the radius of the evil which emanated from it.

Popular Superstitions

THE SUPERSTITION THAT THE EVIL-EYE of a witch or a wizard might bring blight upon an individual or community was as persistent in Chaldea as elsewhere. Incantations frequently allude to it as among the causes of sickness, and exorcisms were duly directed against it. Even to-day, on the site of the ruins of Babylon children are protected against it by fastening small blue objects to their head-gear.

Just as mould from a grave was supposed by the witches of the Middle Ages to be particularly efficacious in magic, so was the dust of the temple supposed to possess hidden virtue in Assyria. If one pared one's nails or cut one's hair it was considered necessary to bury them lest a sorcerer should discover them and use them against their late owner; for a sorcery performed upon a part was by the law of sympathetic magic thought to reflect upon the whole. A like superstition attached to the discarded clothing of people, for among barbarian or uncultured folk the apparel is regarded as part and parcel of the man. Even in our own time simple and uneducated people tear a piece from their garments and hang it as an offering on the bushes around any of the numerous healing wells in the country that they may have journeyed to. This is a survival of the custom of sacrificing the part for the whole.

If one desired to get rid of a headache one had to take the hair of a young kid and give it to a wise woman, who would "spin it on the right side and double it on the left," then it was to be bound into fourteen knots and the incantation of Ea pronounced upon it, after which it was to be bound round the head and neck of the sick man. For defects in eyesight the Assyrians wove black and white threads or hairs together, muttering incantations the while, and these were placed upon the eyes. It was thought, too, that the tongues of evil spirits or sorcerers could be 'bound', and that a net because of its many knots was efficacious in keeping evilly-disposed magicians away.

Omens and The Practice of Liver-reading

DIVINATION AS PRACTISED BY MEANS OF AUGURY was a rite of the first importance among the Babylonians and Assyrians. This was absolutely distinct from divination by astrology. The favourite method of augury among the Chaldeans of old was that by examination of the liver of a slaughtered animal.

It was thought that when an animal was offered up in sacrifice to a god that the deity identified himself for the time being with that animal, and that the beast thus afforded a means of indicating the wishes of the god. Now among people in a primitive state of culture the soul is almost invariably supposed to reside in the liver instead of in the heart or brain. More blood is secreted by the liver than by any other organ in the body, and upon the opening of a carcase it appears the most striking, the most central, and the most sanguinary of the vital parts. The liver was, in fact, supposed by early peoples to be the fountain of the blood supply and therefore of life itself. Hepatoscopy or divination from the liver was undertaken by the Chaldeans for the purpose of determining what the gods had in mind. The soul of the animal became for the nonce the soul of the god, therefore if the signs of the liver of the sacrificed animal could be read the mind of the god became clear, and his intentions regarding the future were known. The animal usually sacrificed was a sheep, the liver of which animal is most complicated in appearance. The two lower lobes are sharply divided from one another and are separated from the upper by a narrow depression, and the whole surface is covered with markings and fissures, lines and curves which give it much the appearance of a map on which roads and valleys are outlined. This applies to the freshly excised liver only, and these markings are never the same in any two livers.

Certain priests were set apart for the practice of liver-reading, and these were exceedingly expert, being able to decipher the hepatoscopic signs with great skill. They first examined the gall-bladder, which might be reduced or swollen. They inferred various circumstances from the several ducts and the shapes and sizes of the lobes and their appendices. Diseases of the liver, too, particularly common among sheep in all countries, were even more frequent among these animals in the marshy portions of the Euphrates Valley.

The literature connected with this species of augury is very extensive, and Assur-bani-pal's library contained thousands of fragments describing the omens deduced from the practice. These enumerate the chief appearances of the liver, as the shade of the colour of the gall, the length of the ducts, and so forth. The lobes were divided into sections, lower, medial, and higher, and the interpretation varied from the phenomena therein observed. The markings on the liver possessed various names, such as 'palaces', 'weapons', 'paths', and 'feet', which terms remind us somewhat of the bizarre nomenclature of astrology. Later in the progress of the art the various combinations of signs came to be known so well, and there were so many cuneiform texts in existence which afforded instruction in them, that a liver could be quickly 'read' by the *barû* or reader, a name which was afterward applied to the astrologists as well and to those who divined through various other natural phenomena.

One of the earliest instances on record of hepatoscopy is that regarding Naram-Sin, who consulted a sheep's liver before declaring war. The great Sargon did likewise, and we find Gudea applying to his 'liver inspectors' when attempting to discover a favourable time for laying the foundations of the temple of Nin-girsu. Throughout the whole history of the Babylonian monarchy in fact, from its early beginnings to its end, we find this system in vogue. Whether it was in force in Sumerian times we have no means of knowing, but there is every likelihood that such was the case.

The Ritual of Hepatoscopy

Quite an elaborate ritual grew up around the readings of the omens by the examination of the liver. The barû who officiated must first of all purify himself and don special apparel for the ceremony. Prayers were then offered up to Shamash and Hadad or Rammon, who were known as the 'lords of divination'. Specific questions were usually put. The sheep selected for sacrifice must be without blemish, and the manner of slaughtering it and the examination of its liver must be made with the most meticulous care. Sometimes the signs were doubtful, and upon such occasions a second sheep was sacrificed.

Nabonidus, the last King of Babylon, on one occasion desired to restore a temple to the moon-god at Harran. He wished to be certain that this step commended itself to Merodach, the chief deity of Babylonia, so he applied to the 'liver inspectors' of his day and found that the omen was favourable. We find him also desirous of making a certain symbol of the sun-god in accordance with an ancient pattern. He placed a model of this before Shamash and consulted the liver of a sheep to ascertain whether the god approved of the offering, but on three separate occasions the signs were unfavourable. Nabonidus then concluded that the model of the symbol could not have been correctly reproduced, and on replacing it by another he found the signs propitious. In order, however, that there should be no mistake he sought among the records of the past for the result of a liver inspection on a similar occasion, and by comparing the omens he became convinced that he was safe in making a symbol.

Peculiar signs, when they were found connected with events of importance, were specially noted in the literature of liver divination, and were handed down from generation to generation of diviners. Thus a number of omens are associated with Gilgamesh, the mythical hero of the Babylonian epic, and a certain condition of the gall-bladder is said to indicate "the omen of Urumush, the king, whom the men of his palace killed."

Bad signs and good signs are enumerated in the literature of the subject. Thus like most peoples the Babylonians considered the right side as lucky and the left as unlucky. Any sign on the right side of the gall-bladder, ducts or lobes, was supposed to refer to the king, the country, or the army, while a similar sign on the sinister side applied to the enemy. Thus a good sign on the right side applied to Babylonia or Assyria in a favourable sense, a bad sign on the right side in an unfavourable sense. A good sign on the left side was an omen favourable to the enemy, whereas a bad sign on the left side was, of course, to the native king or forces.

It would be out of place here to give a more extended description of the liver-reading of the ancient Chaldeans. Suffice it to say that the subject is a very complicated one in its deeper significance, and has little interest for the general reader in its advanced stages. Certain well-marked conditions of the liver could only indicate certain political, religious, or personal events. It will be more interesting if we attempt to visualise the act of divination by liver reading, as it was practised in ancient Babylonia, and if our imaginations break down in the process it is not the fault of the very large material they have to work upon.

The Missing Caravan

The ages roll back as a scroll, and I see myself as one of the great banker-merchants of Babylon, one of those princes of commerce whose contracts and agreements are found stamped upon clay cylinders where once the stately palaces of barter arose from the swarming streets of the city of Merodach. I have that morning been carried in my litter by sweating slaves, from my white house in a leafy suburb lying beneath the shadow of the lofty temple-city of Borsippa. As I reach my place of business I am aware of unrest, for the financial operations in which I engage are so closely watched that I may say without self-praise that I represent the pulse of Babylonian commerce. I enter the cool chamber where I usually transact my business, and where a pair of officious Persian slaves commence to fan me as soon as I take my seat. My head clerk enters and makes obeisance with an expression on his face eloquent of important news. It is as I expected – as I feared. The caravan from the Persian Gulf due to arrive at Babylon more than a week ago has not yet made its appearance, and although I had sent scouting parties as far as Ninnur, these have returned without bringing me the least intelligence regarding it.

I feel convinced that the caravan with my spices, woven fabrics, rare woods, and precious stones will never come tinkling down the great central street to deposit its wealth at the doors of my warehouses; and the thought renders me so irritable that I sharply dismiss the Persian fan-bearers, and curse again and again the black-browed sons of Elam, who have doubtless looted my goods and cut the throats of my guards and servants. I go home at an early hour full of my misfortune. I cannot eat my evening meal. My wife gently asks me what ails me, but with a growl I refuse to enlighten her upon the cause of my annoyance. Still, however, she persists, and succeeds in breaking down my surly opposition.

"Why trouble thy heart concerning this thing when thou may know what has happened to thy goods and thy servants? Get thee to-morrow to the Baru, and he will enlighten thee," she says.

I start. After all, women have sense. There can be no harm in seeing the Baru and asking him to divine what has happened to my caravan. But I bethink me that I am wealthy, and that the priests love to pluck a well-feathered pigeon. I mention my suspicions of the priestly caste in no measured terms, to the distress of my devout wife and the amusement of my soldier-son.

Restlessly I toss upon my couch, and after a sleepless night feel that I cannot resume my business with the fear of loss upon me. So without breathing a word of my intention to my wife, I direct my litter-slaves to carry me to the great temple at Borsippa.

Arrived there, I enquire for the chief Baru. He is one of the friends of my youth, but for years our paths have diverged, and it is with surprise that he now greets me. I acquaint him with the nature of my dilemma, and nodding sympathetically he assures me that he will do his utmost to assist me. Somewhat reassured, I follow him into a tiled court near the far end of which stands a large altar. At a sign from him two priests bring in a live sheep and cut its throat. They then open the carcase and extract the liver. Immediately the chief Baru bends his grey head over it. For a long time he stares at it with the keenest attention. I begin to weary, and my old doubts regarding the sacerdotal caste return. At last the grey head rises from the long inspection, and the Baru turns to me with smiling face.

"The omen is good, my son," he says, with a cheerful intonation. "The compass and the hepatic duct are short. Thy path will be protected by thy Guardian Spirit, as will the path of thy servants. Go, and fear not."

He speaks so definitely and his words are so reassuring that I seize him by the hands, and, thanking him effusively, take my leave. I go down to my warehouses in a new spirit of hopefulness and disregard the disdainful or pitying looks cast in my direction. I sit unperturbed and dictate contracts and letters of credit to my scribe.

Ha! what is that? By Merodach, it is – it is the sound of bells! Up I leap, upsetting the wretched scribe who squats at my feet, and trampling upon his still wet clay tablets, I rush to the door. Down the street slowly advances a travel-worn caravan, and at the head of it there rides my trusty brown-faced captain, Babbar. He tumbles out of the saddle and kneels before me, but I raise him in a close embrace. All my goods, he assures me, are intact, and the cause of delay was a severe sickness which broke out among his followers. But all have recovered and my credit is restored.

As I turn to re-enter my warehouse with Babbar, a detaining hand is placed on my shoulder. It is a messenger from the chief Baru.

"My brother at the temple saw thy caravan coming from afar," he says politely, "and his message to thee, my son, is that, since thou hast so happily recovered thine own, thou shouldst devote a tithe of it to the service of the gods."

Mythological Monsters and Animals

TIAWATH WAS NOT THE ONLY MONSTER known to Babylonian mythology. But she is sometimes likened to or confounded with the serpent of darkness with which she had originally no connection whatever.

This being was, however, like Tiawath, the offspring of the great deep and the enemy of the divine powers. We are told in the second verse of Genesis that "the earth was without form and void, and darkness was upon the face of the deep," and therefore resembling the abyss of Babylonian myth. We are also informed that the serpent was esteemed as "more subtle than other beast of the field," and this, it has been pointed out by Professor Sayce, was probably because it was associated by the author or authors of Genesis with Ea, the god of waters and of wisdom. To Babylonian geographers as to the Greeks, the ocean was a coiling, snake-like thing, which was often alluded to as the great serpent, and this soon came to be considered as the source of all evil and misfortune. The ancients, and especially the ancient Semites, with the exception of the Phoenicians, appear to have regarded it with dread and loathing. The serpent appears to have been called Aibu, 'the enemy'. We can see how the serpent of darkness, the offspring of chaos and confusion, became also the Hebrew symbol for mischief. He was first the source of physical and next the source of moral evil.

We will show how other animals and monsters had their place in Babylonian cult, including the gazelle, who represented Ea, and the goat, embodied in the god Uz. Adar, the sun-god of Nippur, was in the same manner connected with the pig, which may have been the totem of the city he ruled over; and many other gods had attendant animals or birds, like the sun-god of Kis, whose symbol was the eagle.

Winged Bulls

THE WINGED BULLS so closely identified with ancient Chaldean mythology were probably associated with Merodach.

These may have represented the original totemic forms of the gods in question, but we must not confound the bull forms of Merodach and Ea with those winged bulls which guarded the entrances to the temples. These, to perpetrate a double 'bull', were not bulls at all but divine beings, the gods or genii of the holy places. The human head attached to them indicated that the creature was endowed with humanity and the bull-like body symbolized strength. When the Babylonian translated the word 'bull' from the Akkadian tongue he usually rendered it 'hero' or 'strong one'. It is thought that the bull forms of Ea and Merodach must have originated at Eridu, for both of these deities were connected with the city. The Babylonians regarded the sky-country as a double of the plain in which they dwelt, and they believed that the gods as planets ploughed their way across the azure fields of air. Thus the sun was the 'Bull of Light', and Jupiter, the nearest of the planets to the ecliptic, was known as the 'Planet of the Bull of Light.'

The Dog in Babylonia

STRANGELY ENOUGH THE DOG was classed by the Babylonians as a monster animal and one to be despised and avoided. In a prayer against the powers of evil we read, "From the dog, the snake, the scorpion, the reptile, and whatever is baleful ... may Merodach preserve us." We find that although the Babylonians possessed an excellent breed of dog they were not fond of depicting them either in painting or bas-relief.

Dogs are seen illustrated in a bas-relief of Assur-bani-pal, and five clay figures of dogs now in the British Museum represent hounds which belonged to that monarch. The names of these animals are very amusing, and appear to indicate that those who bestowed them must have suffered from a complete lack of the humorous sense, or else have been blessed with an overflow of it. Translated, the names are: 'He-ran-and-barked', 'The-Producer-of-Mischief', 'The-Biter-of-his-foes', 'The-Judge-of-his-companions', and 'The-Seizer-of-enemies'. How well these names would fit certain dogs we all know or have known! Here is good evidence from the buried centuries that dog nature like human nature has not changed a whit.

But why should the dog, fellow-hunter with early man and the companion of civilized humanity, have been regarded as evil? Professor Sayce considers that the four dogs of Merodach "were not always sent on errands of mercy, and that originally they had been devastating winds."

A Dog Legend

The fragment of a legend exists which does not exhibit the dog in any very favourable light.

Once there was a shepherd who was tormented by the constant assaults of dogs upon his flocks. He prayed to Ea for protection, and the great god of wisdom sent his son Merodach to reassure the shepherd.

"Ea has heard thee," said Merodach. "When the great dogs assault thee, then, O shepherd, seize them from behind and lay them down, hold them and overcome them. Strike their heads, pierce their breasts. They are gone; never may they return. With the wind may they go, with the storm above it! Take their road and cut off their going. Seize their mouths, seize their mouths, seize their weapons! Seize their teeth, and make them ascend, by the command of Ea, the lord of wisdom; by the command of Merodach, the lord of revelation."

Gazelle and Goat Gods

THE GAZELLE OR ANTELOPE was a mythological animal in Babylonia so far as it represented Ea, who is entitled 'the princely gazelle' and 'the gazelle who gives the earth'.

But the gazelle/antelope was also appropriated to Mul-lil, the god of Nippur, who was specially called the 'gazelle god'. It is likely, therefore, that this animal had been worshipped totemically at Nippur. Scores of early cylinders represent it being offered in sacrifice to a god, and bas-reliefs and other carvings show it reposing in the arms of various deities.

The goat, too, seems to have been peculiarly sacred, and formed one of the signs of the zodiac. A god called Uz has for his name the Akkadian word for goat. Mr Hormuzd Rassam found a sculptured stone tablet in a temple of the sun-god at Sippara on which was an inscription to Sin, Shamash, and Ishtar, as being "set as companions at the approach to the deep in sight of the god Uz." This god Uz is depicted as sitting on a throne watching the revolution of the solar disc, which is placed upon a table and made to revolve by means of a rope or string. He is clad in a robe of goat-skin.

The Goat Cult

This cult of the goat appears to be of very ancient origin, and the strange thing is that it seems to have found its way into mediaeval and even into modern magic and pseudo-religion. There is very little doubt that it is the Baphomet of the knights-templar and the Sabbatic goat of the witchcraft of the Middle Ages. It seems almost certain that when the Crusaders sojourned in Asia-Minor they came into contact with the remains of the old Babylonian cult. When Philip the Fair of France arraigned them on a charge of heresy a great deal of curious evidence was extorted from them regarding the worship of an idol that they kept in their lodges. The real character of this they seemed unable to explain. It was said which the image was made in the likeness of 'Baphomet', which name was said to be a corruption of Mahomet, the general

Christian name at that period for a pagan idol, although others give a Greek derivation for the word. This figure was often described as possessing a goat's head and horns. That, too, the Sabbatic goat of the Middle Ages was of Eastern and probably Babylonian origin is scarcely to be doubted. At the witch orgies in France and elsewhere those who were afterwards brought to book for their sorceries declared that Satan appeared to them in the shape of a goat and that they worshipped him in this form. The Sabbatic meetings during the fifteenth century in the wood of Mofflaines, near Arras, had as their centre a goat-demon with a human countenance, and a like fiend was adored in Germany and in Scotland. From all this it is clear that the Sabbatic goat must have had some connection with the East. Eliphas Levi drew a picture of the Baphomet or Sabbatic goat to accompany one of his occult works, and strangely enough the symbols that he adorns it with are peculiarly Oriental – moreover the sun-disc figures in the drawing. Now Levi knew nothing of Babylonian mythology, although he was moderately versed in the mythology of modern occultism, and it would seem that if he drew his information from modern or mediaeval sources that these must have been in direct line from Babylonian lore.

The Invasion of the Monsters

THOSE MONSTERS who had composed the host of Tiawath were supposed, after the defeat and destruction of their commandress, to have been hurled like Satan and his angels into the abyss beneath. We read of their confusion in four tablets of the creation epic. This legend seems to be the original source of the belief that those who rebelled against high heaven were thrust into outer darkness. In the Book of Enoch we read of a 'great abyss' regarding which an angel said to the prophet, "This is a place of the consummation of heaven and earth," and again, in a later chapter, "These are of the stars who have transgressed the command of God, the Highest, and are bound

here till 10,000 worlds, the number of the days of their sins, shall have consummated ... this is the prison of the angels, and here they are held to eternity." Eleven great monsters are spoken of by Babylonian myth as comprising the host of Tiawath, besides many lesser forms having the heads of men and the bodies of birds. Strangely enough we find these monsters figuring in a legend concerning an early Babylonian king.

The tablets upon which this legend was impressed were at first known as 'the Cuthaean legend of creation' – a misnomer, for this legend does not give an account of the creation of the world at all, but deals with the invasion of Babylonia by a race of monsters who were descended from the gods, and who waged war against the legendary king of the period for three years. The King tells the story himself. Unfortunately the first portions of both tablets containing the story are missing, and we plunge right away into a description of the dread beings who came upon the people of Babylonia in their multitudes. We are told that they preferred muddy water to clear water. These creatures, says the King, were without moral sense, glorying in their power, and slaughtering those whom they took captives. They had the bodies of birds and some of them had the faces of ravens. They had evidently been fostered by the gods in some inaccessible region, and, multiplying greatly, they came like a storm-cloud on the land, 360,000 in number. Their king was called Benini, their mother Melili, and their leader Memangab, who had six subordinates. The King, perplexed, knew not what to do. He was afraid that if he gave them battle he might in some way offend the gods, but at last through his priests he addressed the divine beings and made offerings of lambs in sacrifice to them. He received a favourable answer and decided to give battle to the invaders, against whom he sent an army of 120,000 men, but not one of these returned alive. Again he sent 90,000 warriors to meet them, but the same fate overtook these, and in the third year he despatched an army of nearly 70,000 troops, all of whom perished to a man. Then the unfortunate monarch broke down, and, groaning aloud, cried out that he had brought misfortune and destruction upon his realm. Nevertheless, rising from his lethargy of despair, he stated his intention to go forth against the enemy in his own person, saying, "The pride of this people of the night I will curse with death and destruction, with fear, terror, and famine, and with misery of every kind."

Before setting out to meet the foe he made offerings to the gods. The manner in which he overcame the invaders is by no means clear from the text, but it would seem that he annihilated them by means of a deluge. In the last portion of the legend the King exhorts his successors not to lose heart when in great peril but to take courage from his example.

He inscribed a tablet with his advice, which he placed in the shrine of Nergal in the city of Cuthah. "Strengthen thy wall," he said, "fill thy cisterns with water, bring in thy treasure-chests and thy corn and thy silver and all thy possessions." He also advises those of his descendants who are faced by similar conditions not to expose themselves needlessly to the enemy.

It was thought at one time that this legend applied to the circumstances of the creation, and that the speaker was the god Nergal, who was waging war against the brood of Tiawath. It was believed that, according to local conditions at Cuthah, Nergal would have taken the place of Merodach, but it has now been made clear that although the tablet was intended to be placed in the shrine of Nergal, the speaker was in reality an early Babylonian king.

The Eagle

A S WE HAVE SEEN, the eagle was perhaps regarded as a symbol of the sun-god. A Babylonian fable tells how he quarrelled with the serpent and incurred the reptile's hatred. Feeling hungry he resolved to eat the serpent's young, and communicated his intention to his own family. One of his children advised him not to devour the serpent's brood, because if he did so he would incur the enmity of the god Shamash. But the eagle did not hearken to his offspring, and swooping down from heaven sought out the serpent's nest and devoured his young. On his arrival at home the serpent discovered

his loss, and at once repaired in great indignation to Shamash, to whom he appealed for justice. His nest, he told the god, was set in a tree, and the eagle had swooped upon it, destroying it with his mighty wings and devouring the little serpents as they fell from it.

"Help, O Shamash!" cried the serpent. "Thy net is like unto the broad earth, thy snare is like unto the distant heaven in wideness. Who can escape thee?"

Shamash hearkening to his appeal, described to him how he might succeed in obtaining vengeance upon the eagle.

"Take the road," said he, "and go into the mountain and hide thyself in the dead body of a wild ox. Tear open its body, and all the birds of heaven shall swoop down upon it. The eagle shall come with the rest, and when he seeks for the best parts of the carcase, do thou seize him by his wing, tear off his wings, his pinions, and his claws, pull him in pieces and cast him into a pit. There may he die a death from hunger and thirst."

The serpent did as Shamash had bidden him. He soon came upon the body of a wild ox, into which he glided after opening up the carcase. Shortly afterwards he heard the beating of the wings of numberless birds, all of which swooped down and ate of the flesh. But the eagle suspected the purpose of the serpent and did not come with the rest, until greed and hunger prompted him to share in the feast.

"Come," said he to his children, "let us swoop down and let us also eat of the flesh of this wild ox."

Now the young eagle who had before dissuaded his father from devouring the serpent's young, again begged him to desist from his purpose.

"Have a care, O my father," he said, "for I am certain that the serpent lurks in yonder carcase for the purpose of destroying you."

But the eagle did not hearken to the warning of his child, but swooped on to the carcase of the wild ox. He so far obeyed the injunctions of his offspring, however, as closely to examine the dead ox for the purpose of discovering whether any trap lurked near it. Satisfied that all was well he commenced to feed upon it, when suddenly the serpent seized upon him and held him fast. The eagle at once began to plead for mercy, but the enraged reptile told him that an appeal to Shamash was irrevocable, and that if he did not punish the king of birds he himself would be punished by the god, and despite the eagle's further protests he tore off his wings and pinions, pulled him to pieces, and finally cast him into a pit, where he perished miserably as the god had decreed.

Etana and the Eagle

In one fragmentary legend which was preserved in the tablet-library of Assur-bani-pal, the Assyrian monarch, Etana (a legendary ancient Sumerian king of the city of Kish) obtained the assistance of the Eagle to go in quest of the Plant of Birth. His wife was about to become a mother, and was accordingly in need of magical aid. A similar belief caused birth girdles of straw or serpent skins, and eagle stones found in eagles' nests, to be used in ancient Britain and elsewhere throughout Europe apparently from the earliest times.

On this or another occasion Etana desired to ascend to highest heaven. He asked the Eagle to assist him, and the bird assented, saying: "Be glad, my friend. Let me bear thee to the highest heaven. Lay thy breast on mine and thine arms on my wings, and let my body be as thy body." Etana did as the great bird requested him, and together they ascended towards the firmament. After a flight which extended over two hours, the Eagle asked Etana to gaze downwards. He did so, and beheld the ocean surrounding the earth, and the earth seemed like a mountainous island. The Eagle resumed its flight, and when another two hours had elapsed, it again asked Etana to look downwards. Then the hero saw that the sea resembled a girdle which clasped the land. Two hours later Etana found that he had been raised to a height from which the sea appeared to be no larger than a pond. By this time he had reached the heaven of Anu, Bel, and Ea, and found there rest and shelter.

Here the text becomes fragmentary. Further on it is gathered from the narrative that Etana is being carried still higher by the Eagle towards the heaven of Ishtar, "Queen of Heaven", the supreme mother goddess. Three times, at intervals of two hours, the Eagle asks Etana to look downwards towards the shrinking earth. Then some disaster happens, for further onwards the broken tablet narrates that the Eagle is falling. Down and down eagle and man fall together until they strike the earth, and the Eagle's body is shattered.

Tales of Kings

THE TALES OF THE BABYLONIAN AND ASSYRIAN KINGS which we present in this chapter are of value because they are taken at first hand from their own historical accounts of the great events which occurred during their several reigns. On a first examination these tablets appear dry and uninteresting, but when studied more closely and patiently they will be found to contain matter as absorbing as that in the most exciting annals of any country. Let us take first for example the wonderful inscriptions of Tiglath-pileser II (950 BC) which refer to his various conquests, and which were discovered by George Smith at Nimrud in the temple of Nabu.

Tiglath-pileser II

T IGLATH COMMENCES WITH THE USUAL ORIENTAL FLOURISH
of trumpets. He styles himself the powerful warrior who, in
the service of Asshur, has trampled upon his haters, swept over
them like a flood, and reduced them to shadows.

He has marched, he says, from the sea to the land of the rising sun, and
from the sea of the setting sun to Egypt. He enumerates the countless
lands that he has conquered. The cities Sarrapanu and Malilatu among
others he took by storm and captured the inhabitants to the number
of 150,000 men, women, and children, all of whom he sent to Assyria.
Much tribute he received from the people of the conquered lands – gold,
silver, precious stones, rare woods, and cattle. His custom seems to have
been to make his successful generals rulers of the cities he conquered,
and it is noticeable that upon a victory he invariably sacrificed to
the gods. His methods appear to have been drastic in the extreme.
Irritated at the defiance of the people of Sarrapanu he reduced it to
a heap of earth, and crucified King Nabu-Usabi in front of the gate of
his city. Not content with this vengeance, Tiglath carried off his wealth,
his furniture, his wife, his son, his daughters, and lastly his gods, so
that no trace of the wretched monarch's kingdom should remain. It is
noticeable that throughout these campaigns Tiglath invariably sent the
prisoners to Assyria, which shows at least that he considered human
life as relatively sacred. Probably these captive people were reduced to
slavery. The races of the neighbouring desert, too, came and prostrated
themselves before the Assyrian hero, kissing his feet and bringing him
tribute carried by sailors.

Tiglath then begins to boast about his gorgeous new residence with all
the vulgarity of a *nouveau riche*. He says that his house was decorated
like a Syrian palace for his glory. He built gates of ivory with planks of
cedar, and seems to have had his prisoners, the conquered kings of
Syria, on exhibition in the palace precincts. At the gates were gigantic

lions and bulls of clever workmanship which he describes as "cunning, beautiful, valuable," and this place he called 'The Palaces of Rejoicing'.

In a fragment which relates the circumstances of his Eastern expeditions he tells how he built a city called Humur, and how he excavated the neighbouring river Patti, which had been filled up in the past, and along its bed led refreshing waters into certain of the cities he had conquered. He complains in one text that Sarduri, the King of Ararat, revolted against him along with others, but Tiglath captured his camp and Sarduri had perforce to escape upon a mare. Into the rugged mountains he rode by night and sought safety on their peaks. Later he took refuge with his warriors in the city of Turuspa. After a siege Tiglath succeeded in reducing the place. Afterwards he destroyed the land of Ararat, and made it a desert over an area of about 450 miles. Tiglath dedicated Sarduri's couch to Ishtar, and carried off his royal riding carriage, his seal, his necklace, his royal chariot, his mace, and lastly a 'great ship', though we are not told how he accomplished this last feat.

Poet or Braggart?

It is strange to notice the inflated manner in which Tiglath speaks in these descriptions. He talks about people, races, and rulers 'sinning' against him as if he were a god, but it must be remembered that he, like other Assyrian monarchs, regarded himself as the representative of the gods upon earth. But though his language is at times boastful and absurd, yet on other occasions it is extremely beautiful and even poetic. In speaking of the tribute he received from various monarchs he says that he obtained from them "clothing of wool and linen, violet wool, royal treasures, the skins of sheep with fleece dyed in shining purple, birds of the sky with feathers of shining violet, horses, camels, and she-camels with their young ones."

He appears, too, to have been in conflict with a Queen of Sheba or Saba, one Samsi, whom he sent as a prisoner to Syria with her gods and all her possessions.

The Autobiography of Assur-bani-pal

🐾

IN A FORMER CHAPTER we outlined the mythical history of Assur-bani-pal or Sardanapalus, and in this place may briefly review the story of his life as told in his inscriptions.

He commences by stating that he is the child of Asshur and Beltis, but he evidently intends to convey that he is their son in a spiritual sense only, for he hastens to tell us that he is the "son of the great King of Riduti" (Esar-haddon). He proceeds to tell of his triumphal progress throughout Egypt, whose kings he made tributary to him. "Then," he remarks in a hurt manner, "the good I did to them they despised and their hearts devised evil. Seditious words they spoke and took evil counsel among themselves." In short, the kings of Egypt had entered into an alliance to free themselves from the yoke of Assur-bani-pal, but his generals heard of the plot and captured several of the ringleaders in the midst of their work. They seized the royal conspirators and bound them in fetters of iron. The Assyrian generals then fell upon the populations of the revolting cities and cut off their inhabitants to a man, but they brought the rulers of Egypt to Nineveh into the presence of Assur-bani-pal. To do him justice that monarch treated Necho, who is described as 'King of Memphis and Sars', with the utmost consideration, granting him a new covenant and placing upon him costly garments and ornaments of gold, bracelets of gold, a steel sword with a sheath of gold; with chariots, mules, and horses.

Dream of Gyges

Continuing, Assur-bani-pal recounts how Gyges, King of Lydia, a remote place of which his fathers had not heard the name, was granted a dream concerning the kingdom of Assyria by the god Asshur. Gyges was greatly impressed by the dream and sent to Assur-bani-pal to request his friendship, but having once sent an envoy to the Assyrian court Assur-bani-pal seemed to think that he should continue to do so regularly, and when he failed in this attention the Assyrian king prayed to Asshur to compass his discomfiture. Shortly afterwards the unhappy Gyges was overthrown by the Cimmerians, against whom Assur-bani-pal had often assisted him.

Assur-bani-pal then plaintively recounts how Saulmugina, his younger brother, conspired against him. This brother he had made King of Babylon, and after occupying the throne of that country for some time he set on foot a conspiracy to throw off the Assyrian yoke. A seer told Assur-bani-pal that he had had a dream in which the god Sin spoke to him, saying that he would overthrow and destroy Saulmugina and his fellow-conspirators. Assur-bani-pal marched against his brother, whom he overthrew. The people of Babylon, overtaken by famine, were forced to devour their own children, and in their agony they attacked Saulmugina and burned him to death with his goods, his treasures, and his wives. As we have before pointed out, this tale strangely enough closely resembles the legend concerning Assur-bani-pal himself. Swift was the vengeance of the Assyrian king upon those who remained. He cut out the tongues of some, while others were thrown into pits to be eaten by dogs, bears, and eagles. Then after fixing a tribute and setting governors over them he returned to Assyria. It is noticeable that Assur-bani-pal distinctly states that he 'fixed upon' the Babylonians the gods of Assyria, and this seems to show that Assyrian deities existed in contradistinction to those of Babylonia.

In one expedition into the land of Elam, Assur-bani-pal had a dream sent by Ishtar to assure him that the crossing of the river Itite, which was in high flood, could be accomplished by his army in perfect safety. The warriors easily negotiated the crossing and inflicted great losses upon the enemy. Among other things they dragged the idol of Susinay from its sacred grove, and he remarks that it had never been beheld by any man in Elam. This with other idols he carried off to Assyria. He broke the winged lions which flanked the gates of the temple, dried up the drinking wells, and for a month and a day swept Elam to its utmost extent, so that neither man nor oxen nor trees could be found in it – nothing but the wild ass, the serpent, and the beast of the desert. The King goes on to say that the goddess Nanâ, who had dwelt in Elam for over 1600 years, had been desecrated by so doing. "That country," he declares, "was a place not suited to her. The return of her divinity she had trusted to me. 'Assur-bani-pal', she said, 'bring me out from the midst of wicked Elam and cause me to enter the temple of Anna.'" The goddess then took the road to the temple of Anna at Erech, where the King raised to her an enduring sanctuary. Those chiefs who had trusted the Elamites now felt afflicted at heart and began to despair, and one of them, like Saul, begged his own armour-bearer to slay him, master and man killing each other. Assur-bani-pal refused to give his corpse burial, and cutting off its head hung it round the neck of Nabu-Quati-Zabat, one of the followers of Saulmugina, his rebellious brother. In another text Assur-bani-pal recounts in grandiloquent language how he built the temples of Asshur and Merodach.

"The great gods in their assembly my glorious renown have heard, and over the kings who dwell in palaces, the glory of my name they have raised and have exalted my kingdom.

Assur-bani-pal as Architect

"The temples of Assyria and Babylonia which Esar-haddon, King of Assyria, had begun, their foundations he had built, but had not finished their tops; anew I built them: I finished their tops.

"Sadi-rabu-matati (the great mountain of the earth), the temple of the god Assur my lord, completely I finished. Its chamber walls I adorned with gold and silver, great columns in it I fixed, and in its gate the productions of land and sea I placed. The god Assur into Sadi-rabu-matati I brought, and I raised him an everlasting sanctuary.

"Saggal, the temple of Merodach, lord of the gods, I built, I completed its decorations; Bel and Beltis, the divinities of Babylon and Ea, the divine judge from the temple of ... I brought out, and placed them in the city of Babylon. Its noble sanctuary a great ... with fifty talents of ... its brickwork I finished, and raised over it. I caused to make a ceiling of sycamore, durable wood, beautiful as the stars of heaven, adorned with beaten gold. Over Merodach the great lord I rejoiced in heart, I did his will. A noble chariot, the carriage of Merodach, ruler of the gods, lord of lords, in gold, silver, and precious stones, I finished its workmanship. To Merodach, king of the whole of heaven and earth, destroyer of my enemies, as a gift I gave it.

"A couch of sycamore wood, for the sanctuary, covered with precious stones as ornaments, as the resting couch of Bel and Beltis, givers of favour, makers of friendship, skilfully I constructed. In the gate ... the seat of Zirat-banit, which adorned the wall, I placed.

"Four bulls of silver, powerful, guarding my royal threshold, in the gate of the rising sun, in the greatest gate, in the gate of the temple Sidda, which is in the midst of Borsippa, I set up."

Esar-haddon, A 'Likeable' Monarch

E SAR-HADDON, THE FATHER OF ASSUR-BANI-PAL, has been called "the most likeable" of the Assyrian kings. He did not press his military conquests for the mere sake of glory, but in general for the maintenance of his own territory. He is notable as the restorer of Babu and the reviver of its culture. He showed much clemency to political offenders, and his court was the centre of literary activity.

Assur-bani-pal, his son, speaks warmly of the sound education he received at his father's court, and to that education and its enlightening influences we now owe the priceless series of cylinders and inscriptions found in his library. He does not seem to have been able to control his rather turbulent neighbours, and he was actually weak enough (from the Assyrian point of view) to return the gods of the kingdom of Aribi after he had led them captive to Assyria. He seems to have been good-natured, enlightened, and easy-going, and if he did not boast so loudly as his son he had probably greater reason to do so.

One of the descendants of Assur-bani-pal, Bel-zakir-iskun, speaks of his restoration of certain temples, especially that of Nebo, and plaintively adds: "In after days, in the time of the kings my sons ... When this house decays and becomes old who repairs its ruin and restores its decay? May he who does so see my name written on this inscription. May he enclose it in a receptacle, pour out a libation, and write my name with his own; but whoever defaces the writing of my name may the gods not establish him. May they curse and destroy his seed from the land." This is the last royal inscription of any length written in Assyria, and its almost prophetic terms seem to suggest that he who framed them must have foreseen the downfall of the civilization he represented. Does not the inscription almost foreshadow Shelley's wondrous sonnet on 'Ozymandias'?

I met a traveller from an antique land
Who said: Two vast and trunkless legs of stone
Stand in the desert. Near them, on the sand,
Half sunk, a shattered visage lies, whose frown,
And wrinkled lip, and sneer of cold command,
Tell that its sculptor well those passions read
Which yet survive, stamped on these lifeless things,
The hand that mocked them and the heart that fed;
And on the pedestal these words appear:
"My name is Ozymandias, king of kings:
Look on my works, ye mighty, and despair!"
Nothing beside remains. Round the decay
Of that colossal wreck, boundless and bare,
The lone and level sands stretch far away.

Assur-Dan III and the Fatal Eclipse

THE REIGN OF ASSUR-DAN III (773–764 BC) supplies us with a picturesque incident. This Assyrian monarch had marched several times into Syria, and had fought the Chaldeans in Babylonia. Numerous were his tributary states and widespread his power.

But disaster crept slowly upon him, and although he made repeated efforts to stave it off, these were quite in vain. Insurrection followed insurrection, and it would seem that the priests of Babylon, considering themselves slighted, joined the malcontent party and assisted to foment discord. At the critical juncture of the fortunes of Assur-Dan there happened an eclipse of the sun, and as the black shadow crept over Nineveh and the King lay upon his couch and watched the gradual blotting out of the sunlight, he felt that his doom was upon him. After this direful portent he appears to have resisted no longer, but to have resigned himself to his fate. Within the year he was slain, and his rebel son, Adad-Narari IV, sat upon his murdered father's throne. But Nemesis followed upon the parricide's footsteps, for he in turn found a rebel in his son, and the land was smitten with a terrible pestilence.

Shalmaneser I

SHALMANESER I (c. 1270) was cast in a martial and heroic mould, and an epic might arise from the legends of his conquests and military exploits.

In his time Assyria possessed a superabundant population which required an outlet, and this the monarch deemed it his duty to supply. After conquering the provinces of Mitani to the west of the Euphrates, he attacked Babylonia, and so fiercely did he deal with his southern neighbours that we find him actually gathering the dust of their conquered cities and casting it to the four winds of heaven. Surely a more extreme manner of dealing summarily with a conquered enemy has never been recorded!

A Babylon-Inspired Fairy Tale:
The Princess of Babylon

AS WITH THOSE OF ANCIENT EGYPT AND GREECE, the cultures and mythologies of ancient Mesopotamia have always held a fascination for writers and artists of the modern world, not least because they remain shrouded in a degree of mystery, which has fostered immense flights of imagination. The tale featured here was written by François-Marie Arouet, a.k.a. Voltaire (1694–1778) in 1768.

Though in fact a philosophical satire of European mores, its use of characters inspired by Babylonian names and gods and its initial setting in the exotic, opulent, romanticized world of ancient Babylon is evidence of the enduring appeal of this venerable land and its society.

Chapter 1: Royal Contest for the Hand of Formosanta

THE AGED BELUS, KING OF BABYLON, thought himself the first man upon earth; for all his courtiers told him so, and his historians proved it. We know that his palace and his park, situated at a few parafangs from Babylon, extended between the Euphrates and the Tigris, which washed those enchanted banks. His vast house, three thousand feet in front, almost reached the clouds. The platform was surrounded with a balustrade of white marble, fifty feet high, which supported colossal statues of all the kings and great men of the empire. This platform, composed of two rows of bricks, covered with a thick surface of lead from one extremity to the other, bore twelve feet of earth; and upon the earth were raised groves of olive, orange, citron, palm, cocoa, and cinnamon trees, and stock gillyflowers, which formed alleys that the rays of the sun could not penetrate.

The waters of the Euphrates running, by the assistance of pumps, in a hundred canals, formed cascades of six thousand feet in length in the park, and a hundred thousand *jets d'eau*, whose height was scarce perceptible. They afterward flowed into the Euphrates, from whence they came. The gardens of Semiramis, which astonished Asia several ages after, were only a feeble imitation of these ancient prodigies, for in the time of Semiramis, everything began to degenerate amongst men and women.

But what was more admirable in Babylon, and eclipsed everything else, was the only daughter of the king, named Formosanta. It was from her pictures and statues, that in succeeding times Praxiteles sculptured his Aphrodita, and the Venus of Medicis. Heavens! what a difference between the original and the copies! so that king Belus was prouder of his daughter than of his kingdom. She was eighteen years old. It was necessary she should have a husband worthy of her; but where was he to be found? An ancient oracle had ordained, that Formosanta could not belong to any but him who could bend the bow of Nimrod.

This Nimrod, "a mighty hunter before the Lord," (*Gen. x:9*), had left a bow seventeen Babylonian feet in length, made of ebony, harder than the iron of mount Caucasus, which is wrought in the forges of Derbent; and no mortal since Nimrod could bend this astonishing bow.

It was again said, "that the arm which should bend this bow would kill the most terrible and ferocious lion that should be let loose in the Circus of Babylon." This was not all. The bender of the bow, and the conquerer of the lion, should overthow all his rivals; but he was above all things to be very sagacious, the most magnificent and most virtuous of men, and possess the greatest curiosity in the whole universe.

Three kings appeared, who were bold enough to claim Formosanta. Pharaoh of Egypt, the Shah of India, and the great Khan of the Scythians. Belus appointed the day and place of combat, which was to be at the extremity of his park, in the vast expanse surrounded by the joint waters of the Euphrates and the Tigris. Round the lists a marble amphitheatre was erected, which might contain five hundred thousand spectators. Opposite the amphitheatre was placed the king's throne. He was to appear with Formosanta, accompanied by the whole court; and on the right and left between the throne and the amphitheatre, there were other thrones and seats for the three kings, and for all the other sovereigns who were desirous to be present at this august ceremony.

The king of Egypt arrived the first, mounted upon the bull Apis, and holding in his hand the cithern of Isis. He was followed by two thousand priests, clad in linen vestments whiter than snow, two thousand eunuchs, two thousand magicians, and two thousand warriors.

The king of India came soon after in a car drawn by twelve elephants. He had a train still more numerous and more brilliant than Pharaoh of Egypt.

The last who appeared was the king of the Scythians. He had none with him but chosen warriors, armed with bows and arrows. He was mounted upon a superb tiger, which he had tamed, and which was as tall as any of the finest Persian horses. The majestic and important mien of this king effaced the appearance of his rivals; his naked arms, as nervous as they were white, seemed already to bend the bow of Nimrod.

These three lovers immediately prostrated themselves before Belus and Formosanta. The king of Egypt presented the princess with two of the finest crocodiles of the Nile, two sea horses, two zebras, two Egyptian rats, and two mummies, with the books of the great Hermes, which he judged to be the scarcest things upon earth.

The king of India offered her a hundred elephants, each bearing a wooden gilt tower, and laid at her feet the *vedam*, written by the hand of Xaca himself.

The king of the Scythians, who could neither write nor read, presented a hundred warlike horses with black fox skin housings.

The princess appeared with a downcast look before her lovers, and reclined herself with such a grace as was at once modest and noble.

Belus ordered the kings to be conducted to the thrones that were prepared for them. "Would I had three daughters," said he to them, "I should make six people this day happy!" He then made the competitors cast lots which should try Nimrod's bow first. Their names inscribed were put into a golden casque. That of the Egyptian king came out first, then the name of the King of India appeared. The king of Scythia, viewing the bow and his rivals, did not complain at being the third.

Whilst these brilliant trials were preparing, twenty thousand pages and twenty thousand youthful maidens distributed, without any disorder, refreshments to the spectators between the rows of seats. Everyone acknowledged that the gods had instituted kings for no other cause than every day to give festivals, upon condition they should be diversified – that life is too short for any other purpose – that lawsuits, intrigues, wars, the altercations of theologists, which consume human life, are horrible and absurd – that man is born only for happiness that he would not passionately and incessantly pursue pleasure, were he not designed for it – that the essence of human nature is to enjoy ourselves, and all the rest is folly. This excellent moral was never controverted but by facts.

Whilst preparations were making for determining the fate of Formosanta, a young stranger, mounted upon an unicorn, accompanied by his valet, mounted on a like animal, and bearing upon his hand a large bird, appeared at the barrier. The guards were surprised to observe in this equipage, a figure that had an air of divinity. He had, as hath been since related, the face of Adonis upon the body of Hercules; it was majesty accompanied by the graces. His black eye-brows and flowing fair tresses, wore a mixture of beauty unknown at Babylon, and charmed all observers. The whole amphitheatre rose up, the better to view the stranger.

All the ladies of the court viewed him with looks of astonishment. Formosanta herself, who had hitherto kept her eyes fixed upon the ground, raised them and blushed. The three kings turned pale. The spectators, in comparing Formosanta with the stranger, cried out, "There is no other in the world, but this young man, who can be so handsome as the princess."

The ushers, struck with astonishment, asked him if he was a king? The stranger replied, that he had not that honour, but that he had come from a distant country, excited by curiosity, to see if there were any king worthy of Formosanta. He was introduced into the first row of the amphitheatre, with his valet, his two unicorns, and his bird. He saluted, with great respect, Belus, his daughter, the three kings, and all the assembly. He then took his seat, not without blushing. His two unicorns lay down at his feet; his bird perched upon his shoulder; and his valet, who carried a little bag, placed himself by his side.

The trials began. The bow of Nimrod was taken out of its golden case. The first master of the ceremonies, followed by fifty pages, and preceded by twenty trumpets, presented it to the king of Egypt, who made his priests bless it; and supporting it upon the head of the bull Apis, he did not question his gaining this first victory. He dismounted, and came into the middle of the circus. He tries, exerts all his strength, and makes such ridiculous contortions, that the whole amphitheatre re-echoes with laughter, and Formosanta herself could not help smiling.

His high almoner approached him:

"Let your majesty give up this idle honour, which depends entirely upon the nerves and muscles. You will triumph in everything else. You will conquer the lion, as you are possessed of the favour of Osiris. The Princess of Babylon is to belong to the prince who is most sagacious, and you have solved enigmas. She is to wed the most virtuous: you are such, as you have been educated by the priests of Egypt. The most generous is to marry her, and you have presented her with two of the handsomest crocodiles, and two of the finest rats in all the Delta. You are possessed of the bull Apis, and the books of Hermes, which are the scarcest things in the universe. No one can hope to dispute Formosanta with you."

"You are in the right," said the King of Egypt, and resumed his throne.

The bow was then put in the hands of the king of India. It blistered his hands for a fortnight; but he consoled himself in presuming that the Scythian King would not be more fortunate than himself.

The Scythian handled the bow in his turn. He united skill with strength. The bow seemed to have some elasticity in his hands. He bent it a little, but he could not bring it near a curve. The spectators, who had been prejudiced in his favour by his agreeable aspect, lamented his ill success, and concluded that the beautiful princess would never be married.

The unknown youth leaped into the arena and addressing himself to the king of Scythia said:

"Your majesty need not be surprised at not having entirely succeeded. These ebony bows are made in my country. There is a peculiar method in using them. Your merit is greater in having bent it, than if I were to curve it."

He then took an arrow and placing it upon the string, bent the bow of Nimrod, and shot the arrow beyond the gates. A million hands at once applauded the prodigy. Babylon re-echoed with acclamations; and all the ladies agreed it was fortunate for so handsome a youth to be so strong.

He then took out of his pocket a small ivory tablet, wrote upon it with a golden pencil, fixed the tablet to the bow, and then presented it to the princess with such a grace as charmed every spectator. He then modestly returned to his place between his bird and his valet. All Babylon was in astonishment; the three kings were confounded, whilst the stranger did not seem to pay the least attention to what had happened.

Formosanta was still more surprised to read upon the ivory tablet, tied to the bow, these lines, written in the best Chaldean:

> *The bow of Nimrod is that of war;*
> *The bow of love is that of happiness*
> *Which you possess. Through you this conquering God*
> *Has become master of the earth.*
> *Three powerful kings, – three rivals now,*
> *Dare aspire to the honour of pleasing you.*
> *I know not whom your heart may prefer,*
> *But the universe will be jealous of him.*

This little madrigal did not displease the princess; but it was criticised by some of the lords of the ancient court, who said that, in former times, Belus would have been compared to the sun, and Formosanta to the moon; his neck to a tower, and her breast to a bushel of wheat. They said the stranger had no sort of imagination, and that he had lost sight of the rules of true poetry, but all the ladies thought the verses very gallant. They were astonished that a man who handled a bow so well should have so much wit. The lady of honour to the princess said to her:

"Madam, what great talents are here entirely lost? What benefit will this young man derive from his wit, and his skill with Nimrod's bow?"

"Being admired!" said Formosanta.

"Ah!" said the lady, "one more madrigal, and he might well be beloved."

The king of Babylon, having consulted his sages, declared that though none of these kings could bend the bow of Nimrod, yet, nevertheless, his daughter was to be married, and that she should belong to him who could conquer the great lion, which was purposely kept in training in his great menagerie.

The king of Egypt, upon whose education all the wisdom of Egypt had been exhausted, judged it very ridiculous to expose a king to the ferocity of wild beasts in order to be married. He acknowledged that he considered the possession of Formosanta of inestimable value; but he believed that if the lion should strangle him, he could never wed this fair Babylonian. The king of India held similar views to the king of Egypt. They both concluded that the king of Babylon was laughing at them, and that they should send for armies to punish him – that they had many subjects who would think themselves highly honoured to die in the service of their masters, without it costing them a single hair of their sacred heads, – that they could easily dethrone the king of Babylon, and then they would draw lots for the fair Formosanta.

This agreement being made, the two kings sent each an express into his respective country, with orders to assemble three hundred thousand men to carry off Formosanta.

However, the king of Scythia descended alone into the arena, scimitar in hand. He was not distractedly enamored with Formosanta's charms. Glory till then had been his only passion, and it had led him to Babylon. He was willing to show that if the kings of India and Egypt were so prudent as not to tilt with lions, he was courageous enough not to decline the combat, and he would repair the honour of diadems. His uncommon valor would not even allow him to avail himself of the assistance of his tiger. He advanced singly, slightly armed with a shell casque ornamented with gold, and shaded with three horses' tails as white as snow.

One of the most enormous and ferocious lions that fed upon the Antilibanian mountains was let loose upon him. His tremendous paws appeared capable of tearing the three kings to pieces at once, and his gullet to devour them. The two proud champions fled with the utmost precipitancy and in the most rapid manner to each other. The courageous Scythian plunged his sword into the lion's mouth; but the point meeting with one of those thick teeth that nothing can penetrate, was broken; and the monster of the woods, more furious from his wound, had already impressed his fearful claws into the monarch's sides.

The unknown youth, touched with the peril of so brave a prince, leaped into the arena swift as lightning, and cut off the lion's head with as much dexterity as we have lately seen, in our carousals, youthful knights knock off the heads of black images.

Then drawing out a small box, he presented it to the Scythian king, saying to him.

"Your majesty will here find the genuine dittany, which grows in my country. Your glorious wounds will be healed in a moment. Accident alone prevented your triumph over the lion. Your valor is not the less to be admired."

The Scythian king, animated more with gratitude than jealousy, thanked his benefactor; and, after having tenderly embraced him, returned to his seat to apply the dittany to his wounds.

The stranger gave the lion's head to his valet, who, having washed it at the great fountain which was beneath the amphitheatre, and drained all the blood, took an iron instrument out of his little bag, with which having drawn the lion's forty teeth, he supplied their place with forty diamonds of equal size.

His master, with his usual modesty, returned to his place; he gave the lion's head to his bird: "Beauteous bird," said he, "carry this small homage, and lay it at the feet of Formosanta."

The bird winged its way with the dreadful triumph in one of its talons, and presented it to the princess; bending with humility his neck, and crouching before her. The sparkling diamonds dazzled the eyes of every beholder. Such magnificence was unknown even in superb Babylon. The emerald, the topaz, the sapphire, and the pyrope, were as yet considered as the most precious ornaments. Belus and the whole court were struck with admiration. The bird which presented this present surprised them still more. It was of the size of an eagle, but its eyes were as soft and tender as those of the eagle are fierce and threatening. Its bill was rose colour, and seemed somewhat to resemble Formosanta's handsome mouth. Its neck represented all the colours of Iris, but still more striking and brilliant. Gold, in a thousand shades, glittered upon its plumage. Its feet resembled a mixture of silver and purple. And the tails of those beautiful birds, which have since drawn Juno's car, did not equal the splendor of this incomparable bird.

The attention, curiosity, astonishment, and ecstasy of the whole court were divided between the jewels and the bird. It had perched upon the balustrade between Belus and his daughter Formosanta. She petted it, caressed it, and kissed it. It seemed to receive her attentions with a mixture of pleasure and respect. When the princess gave the bird a kiss, it returned the embrace, and then looked upon her with languishing eyes. She gave it biscuits and pistachios, which it received in its purple-silvered claw, and carried to its bill with inexpressible grace.

Belus, who had attentively considered the diamonds, concluded that scarce any one of his provinces could repay so valuable a present. He ordered that more magnificent gifts should be prepared for the stranger than those destined for the three monarchs, "This young man," said he, "is doubtless son to the emperor of China; or of that part of the world called Europe, which I have heard spoken of; or of Africa, which is said to be in the vicinity of the kingdom of Egypt."

He immediately sent his first equerry to compliment the stranger, and ask him whether he was himself the sovereign, or son to the sovereign of one of those empires; and why, being possessed of such surprising treasures, he had come with nothing but his valet and a little bag?

Whilst the equerry advanced toward the amphitheatre to execute his commission, another valet arrived upon an unicorn. This valet, addressing himself to the young man, said. "Ormar, your father is approaching the end of his life: I am come to acquaint you with it."

The stranger raised his eyes to heaven, whilst tears streamed from them, and answered only by saying, *"Let us depart."*

The equerry, after having paid Belus's compliments to the conqueror of the lion, to the giver of the forty diamonds, and to the master of the beautiful bird, asked the valet, "Of what kingdom was the father of this young hero sovereign?"

The valet replied:

"His father is an old shepherd, who is much beloved in his district."

During this conversation, the stranger had already mounted his unicorn. He said to the equerry:

"My lord, vouchsafe to prostrate me at the feet of King Belus and his daughter. I must entreat her to take particular care of the bird I leave with her, as it is a nonpareil like herself."

In uttering these last words he set off, and flew like lightning. The two valets followed him, and in an instant he was out of sight.

Formosanta could not refrain from shrieking. The bird, turning toward the amphitheatre where his master had been seated, seemed greatly afflicted to find him gone; then viewing steadfastly the princess, and gently rubbing her beautiful hand with his bill, he seemed to devote himself to her service.

Belus, more astonished than ever, hearing that this very extraordinary young man was the son of a shepherd, could not believe it. He dispatched messengers after him; but they soon returned with the information, that the three unicorns, upon which these men were mounted, could not be overtaken; and that, according to the rate they went, they must go a hundred leagues a day.

Everyone reasoned upon this strange adventure, and wearied themselves with conjectures. How can the son of a shepherd make a present of forty large diamonds? How comes it that he is mounted upon an unicorn? This bewildered them, and Formosanta, whilst she caressed her bird, was sunk into a profound reverie.

Chapter 2: The King of Babylon Convenes His Council, and Consults the Oracle

PRINCESS ALDEA, Formosanta's cousin-german, who was very well shaped, and almost as handsome as the King's daughter, said to her:

"Cousin, I know not whether this demi-god be the son of a shepherd, but methinks he has fulfilled all the conditions stipulated for your marriage. He has bent Nimrod's bow; he has conquered the lion; he has a good share of sense, having written for you extempore a very pretty madrigal. After having presented you with forty large diamonds, you cannot deny that he is the most generous of men. In his bird he possessed the most curious thing upon earth. His virtue cannot be equaled, since he departed without hesitation as soon as he learned his father was ill, though he might have remained and enjoyed the pleasure of your society. The oracle is fulfilled in every particular, except that wherein he is to overcome his rivals. But he has done more; he has saved the life of the only competitor he had to fear; and when the object is to surpass the other two, I believe you cannot doubt but that he will easily succeed."

"All that you say is very true," replied Formosanta: "but is it possible that the greatest of men, and perhaps the most amiable too, should be the son of a shepherd?"

The lady of honour, joining in the conversation, said that the title of shepherd was frequently given to kings – that they were called shepherds because they attended very closely to their flocks – that this was doubtless a piece of ill-timed pleasantry in his valet – that this young hero had not come so badly equipped, but to show how much his personal merit alone was above the fastidious parade of kings. The princess made no answer, but in giving her bird a thousand tender kisses.

A great festival was nevertheless prepared for the three kings, and for all the princes who had come to the feast. The king's daughter and niece were to do the honours. The king distributed presents worthy the magnificence of Babylon. Belus, during the time the repast was being served, assembled his council to discuss the marriage of the beautiful Formosanta, and this is the way he delivered himself as a great politician:

"I am old: I know not what is best to do with my daughter, or upon whom to bestow her. He who deserves her is nothing but a mean shepherd. The kings of India and Egypt are cowards. The king of the Scythians would be very agreeable to me, but he has not performed any one of the conditions imposed. I will again consult the oracle. In the meantime, deliberate among you, and we will conclude agreeably to what the oracle says; for a king should follow nothing but the dictates of the immortal gods."

He then repaired to the temple: the oracle answered in few words according to custom: *Thy daughter shall not be married until she hath traversed the globe*. In astonishment, Belus returned to the council, and related this answer.

All the ministers had a profound respect for oracles. They therefore all agreed, or at least appeared to agree, that they were the foundation of religion – that reason should be mute before them – that it was by their means that kings reigned over their people – that without oracles there would be neither virtue nor repose upon earth.

At length, after having testified the most profound veneration for them, they almost all concluded that this oracle was impertinent, and should not be obeyed – that nothing could be more indecent for a young woman, and particularly the daughter of the great king of Babylon, than to run about, without any particular destination – that this was the most certain method to prevent her being married, or else engage her in a clandestine, shameful, and ridiculous union that, – in a word, this oracle had not common sense.

The youngest of the ministers, named Onadase, who had more sense than the rest, said that the oracle doubtless meant some pilgrimage of devotion, and offered to be the princess's guide. The council approved of his opinion, but everyone was for being her equerry. The king determined that the princess might go three hundred parasangs upon the road to Arabia, to the temple whose saint had the reputation of procuring young women happy marriages, and that the dean of the council should accompany her. After this determination they went to supper.

Chapter 3: Royal Festival Given in Honour of The Kingly Visitors

I N THE CENTRE OF THE GARDENS, between two cascades, an oval saloon, three hundred feet in diameter was erected, whose azure roof, intersected with golden stars, represented all the constellations and planets, each in its proper station; and this ceiling turned about, as well as the canopy, by machines as invisible as those which direct the celestial spheres. A hundred thousand flambeaux,

inclosed in rich crystal cylinders, illuminated the gardens and the dining-hall. A buffet, with steps, contained twenty thousand vases and golden dishes; and opposite the buffet, upon other steps, were seated a great number of musicians. Two other amphitheatres were decked out; the one with the fruits of each season, the other with crystal decanters, that sparkled with the choicest wines.

The guests took their seats round a table divided into compartments that resembled flowers and fruits, all in precious stones. The beautiful Formosanta was placed between the kings of India and Egypt – the amiable Aldea next the king of Scythia. There were about thirty princes, and each was seated next one of the handsomest ladies of the court. The king of Babylon, who was in the middle, opposite his daughter, seemed divided between the chagrin of being yet unable to effect her marriage, and the pleasure of still beholding her. Formosanta asked leave to place her bird upon the table next her; the king approved of it.

The music, which continued during the repast, furnished every prince with an opportunity of conversing with his female neighbour. The festival was as agreeable as it was magnificent. A ragout was served before Formosanta, which her father was very fond of. The princess said it should be carried to his majesty. The bird immediately took hold of it, and carried it in a miraculous manner to the king. Never was any thing more astonishing witnessed. Belus caressed it as much as his daughter had done. The bird afterward took its flight to return to her. It displayed, in flying, so fine a tail, and its extended wings set forth such a variety of brilliant colours – the gold of its plumage made such a dazzling eclat, that all eyes were fixed upon it. All the musicians were struck motionless, and their instruments afforded harmony no longer. None ate, no one spoke, nothing but a buzzing of admiration was to be heard. The Princess of Babylon kissed it during the whole supper, without considering whether there were any kings in the world. Those of India and Egypt felt their spite and indignation rekindle with double force, and they resolved speedily to set their three hundred thousand men in motion to obtain revenge.

As for the king of Scythia, he was engaged in entertaining the beautiful Aldea. His haughty soul despising, without malice, Formosanta's inattention, had conceived for her more indifference than resentment. "She is handsome," said he, "I acknowledge: but she appears to me one of those women who are entirely taken up with their own beauty, and who fancy that mankind are greatly obliged to them when they deign to appear in public. I should prefer an ugly complaisant woman, that exhibited some amiability, to that beautiful statue. You have, madam, as many charms as she possesses, and you, at least, condescend to converse with strangers. I acknowledge to you with the sincerity of a Scythian, that I prefer you to your cousin."

He was, however, mistaken in regard to the character of Formosanta. She was not so disdainful as she appeared. But his compliments were very well received by the princess Aldea. Their conversation became very interesting. They were well contented, and already certain of one another before they left the table. After supper the guests walked in the groves. The king of Scythia and Aldea did not fail to seek for a place of retreat. Aldea, who was sincerity itself, thus declared herself to the prince:

"I do not hate my cousin, though she be handsomer than myself, and is destined for the throne of Babylon. The honour of pleasing you may very well stand in the stead of charms. I prefer Scythia with you, to the crown of Babylon without you. But this crown belongs to me by right, if there be any right in the world; for I am of the elder branch of the Nimrod family, and Formosanta is only of the younger. Her grandfather dethroned mine, and put him to death."

"Such, then, are the rights of inheritance in the royal house of Babylon!" said the Scythian. "What was your grandfather's name?"

"He was called Aldea, like me. My father bore the same name. He was banished to the extremity of the empire with my mother; and Belus, after their death, having nothing to fear from me, was willing to bring me up with his daughter. But he has resolved that I shall never marry."

"I will avenge the cause of your grandfather – of your father and also your own cause," said the king of Scythia. "I am responsible for your being married. I will carry you off the day after to-morrow by day-break – for we must dine to-morrow with the king of Babylon – and I will return and support your rights with three hundred thousand men."

"I agree to it," said the beauteous Aldea: and, after having mutually pledged their words of honour, they separated.

The incomparable Formosanta, before retiring to rest, had ordered a small orange tree, in a silver case, to be placed by the side of her bed, that her bird might perch upon it. Her curtains had long been drawn, but she was not in the least disposed to sleep. Her heart was agitated, and her imagination excited. The charming stranger was ever in her thoughts. She fancied she saw him shooting an arrow with Nimrod's bow. She contemplated him in the act of cutting off the lion's head. She repeated his madrigal. At length, she saw him retiring from the crowd upon his unicorn. Tears, sighs, and lamentations overwhelmed her at this reflection. At intervals, she cried out: "Shall I then never see him more? Will he never return?"

"He will surely return," replied the bird from the top of the orange tree. "Can one have seen you once, and not desire to see you again?"

"Heavens! eternal powers! my bird speaks the purest Chaldean." In uttering these words she drew back the curtain, put out her hand to him, and knelt upon her bed, saying:

"Art thou a god descended upon earth? Art thou the great Oromasdes concealed under this beautiful plumage? If thou art, restore me this charming young man."

"I am nothing but a winged animal," replied the bird; "but I was born at the time when all animals still spoke; when birds, serpents, asses, horses, and griffins, conversed familiarly with man. I would not speak before company, lest your ladies of honour should have taken me for a sorcerer. I would not discover myself to any but you."

Formosanta was speechless, bewildered, and intoxicated with so many wonders. Desirous of putting a hundred questions to him at once, she at length asked him how old he was.

"Only twenty-seven thousand nine hundred years and six months. I date my age from the little revolution of the equinoxes, and which is accomplished in about twenty-eight thousand of your years. There are revolutions of a much greater extent, so are there beings much older than me. It is twenty-two thousand years since I learnt Chaldean in one of my travels. I have always had a very great taste for the Chaldean language, but my brethren, the other animals, have renounced speaking in your climate."

"And why so, my divine bird?"

"Alas! because men have accustomed themselves to eat us, instead of conversing and instructing themselves with us. Barbarians! should they not have been convinced, that having the same organs with them, the same sentiments, the same wants, the same desires, we have also what is called a soul, the same as themselves; – that we are their brothers, and that none should be dressed and eaten but the wicked? We are so far your brothers, that the Supreme Being, the Omnipotent and Eternal Being, having made a compact with men, expressly comprehended us in the treaty. He forbade you to nourish yourselves with our blood, and we to suck yours.

"The fables of your ancient Locman, translated into so many languages, will be a testimony eternally subsisting of the happy commerce you formerly carried on with us. They all begin with these words: 'In the time when beasts spoke'. It is true, there are many families among you who keep up an incessant conversation with their dogs; but the dogs have resolved not to answer, since they have been compelled by whipping to go a hunting, and become accomplices in the murder of our ancient and common friends, stags, deers, hares, and partridges.

"You have still some ancient poems in which horses speak, and your coachmen daily address them in words; but in so barbarous a manner, and in uttering such infamous expressions, that horses, though formerly entertaining so great a kindness for you, now detest you.

"The country which is the residence of your charming stranger, the most perfect of men, is the only one in which your species has continued to love ours, and to converse with us; and this is the only country in the world where men are just."

"And where is the country of my dear incognito? What is the name of his empire? For I will no more believe he is a shepherd than that you are a bat."

"His country, is that of the Gangarids, a wise, virtuous, and invincible people, who inhabit the eastern shore of the Ganges. The name of my friend is Amazan. He is no king; and I know not whether he would so humble himself as to be one. He has too great a love for his fellow countrymen. He is a shepherd like them. But do not imagine that those shepherds resemble yours; who, covered with rags and tatters, watch their sheep, who are better clad than themselves; who groan under the burden of poverty, and who pay to an extortioner half the miserable stipend of wages which they receive from their masters. The Gangaridian shepherds are all born equal, and own the innumerable herds which cover their vast fields and subsist on the abundant verdure. These flocks are never killed. It is a horrid crime, in that favoured country, to kill and eat a fellow creature. Their wool is finer and more brilliant than the finest silk, and constitutes the greatest traffic of the East. Besides, the land of the Gangarids produces all that can flatter the desires of man. Those large diamonds that Amazan had the honour of presenting you with, are from a mine that belongs to him. An unicorn, on which you saw him mounted, is the usual animal the Gangarids ride upon. It is the finest, the proudest, most terrible, and at the same time most gentle animal that ornaments the earth. A hundred Gangarids, with as many unicorns, would be sufficient to disperse innumerable armies. Two centuries ago, a king of India was mad enough to attempt to conquer this nation. He appeared, followed by ten thousand elephants and a million of warriors. The unicorns pierced the elephants, just as I have seen upon your table beads pierced in golden brochets. The warriors fell under the sabres of the Gangarids like crops of rice mowed by the people of the East. The king was taken prisoner, with upwards of six thousand men. He was bathed in the salutary water of the Ganges, and followed the regimen of the country, which consists only of vegetables, of which nature hath there been amazingly liberal to nourish every breathing creature. Men who are fed with carnivorous aliments, and drenched with spirituous liquors, have a sharp adust blood, which turns their brains a hundred different ways. Their chief rage is a fury to spill their brother's blood, and, laying waste fertile plains, to reign over church-yards. Six full months were taken up in curing the king of India of his disorder. When the physicians judged that his pulse had become natural, they certified this to the council of the Gangarids. The council then followed the advice of the unicorns and humanely sent back the king of India, his silly court, and impotent warriors, to their own country. This lesson made them wise, and from that time the Indians respected the Gangarids, as ignorant men, willing to be instructed, revere the philosophers they cannot equal.

"Apropos, my dear bird," said the princess to him, "do the Gangarids profess any religion? have they one?"

"Yes, we meet to return thanks to God on the days of the full moon; the men in a great temple made of cedar, and the women in another, to prevent their devotion being diverted. All the birds assemble in a grove, and the quadrupeds on a fine down. We thank God for all the benefits he has bestowed upon us. We have in particular some parrots *that preach wonderfully well*.

"Such is the country of my dear Amazan; there I reside. My friendship for him is as great as the love with which he has inspired you. If you will credit me, we will set out together, and you shall pay him a visit."

"Really, my dear bird, this is a very pretty invitation of yours," replied the princess smiling, and who flamed with desire to undertake the journey, but did not dare say so.

"I serve my friend," said the bird; "and, after the happiness of loving you, the greatest pleasure is to assist you."

Formosanta was quite fascinated. She fancied herself transported from earth. All she had seen that day, all she then saw, all she heard, and particularly what she felt in her heart, so ravished her as far to surpass what those fortunate muslims now feel, who, disencumbered from their terrestrial ties, find themselves in the ninth heaven in the arms of their Houris, surrounded and penetrated with glory and celestial felicity.

Chapter 4: The Beautiful Bird is Killed by The King of Egypt

FORMOSANTA PASSED THE WHOLE NIGHT in speaking of Amazan. She no longer called him any thing but her shepherd; and from this time it was that the names of shepherd and lover were indiscriminately used throughout every nation.

Sometimes she asked the bird whether Amazan had had any other mistresses. It answered, "No," and she was at the summit of felicity. Sometimes she asked how he passed his life; and she, with transport, learned, that it was employed in doing good; in cultivating arts, in penetrating into the secrets of nature, and improving himself. She at times wanted to know if the soul of her lover was of the same nature as that of her bird; how it happened that it had lived twenty thousand years, when her lover was not above eighteen or nineteen. She put a hundred such questions, to which the bird replied with such discretion as excited her curiosity. At length sleep closed their eyes, and yielded up Formosanta to the sweet delusion of dreams sent by the gods, which sometimes surpass reality itself, and which all the philosophy of the Chaldeans can scarce explain.

Formosanta did not awaken till very late. The day was far advanced when the king, her father, entered her chamber. The bird received his majesty with respectful politeness, went before him, fluttered his wings, stretched his neck, and then replaced himself upon his orange tree. The king seated himself upon his daughter's bed, whose dreams had made her still more beautiful. His large beard approached her lovely face, and after having embraced her, he spoke to her in these words:

"My dear daughter, you could not yesterday find a husband agreeable to my wishes; you nevertheless must marry; the prosperity of my empire requires it. I have consulted the oracle, which you know never errs, and which directs all my conduct. His commands are, that you should traverse the globe. You must therefore begin your journey."

"Ah! doubtless to the Gangarids," said the princess; and in uttering these words, which escaped her, she was sensible of her indiscretion. The king, who was utterly ignorant of geography, asked her what she meant by the Gangarids? She easily diverted the question. The king told her she must go on a pilgrimage, that he had appointed the persons who were to attend her – the dean of the counsellors of state, the high almoner, a lady of honour, a physician, an apothecary, her bird, and all necessary domestics.

Formosanta, who had never been out of her father's palace, and who, till the arrival of the three kings and Amazan, had led a very insipid life, according to the *etiquette* of rank and the parade of pleasure, was charmed at setting out upon a pilgrimage. "Who knows," said she, whispering to her heart, "if the gods may not inspire Amazan with the like desire of going to the same chapel, and I may have the happiness of again seeing the pilgrim?" She affectionately thanked her father, saying she had always entertained a secret devotion for the saint she was going to visit.

Belus gave an excellent dinner to his guests, who were all men. They formed a very ill assorted company – kings, ministers, princes, pontiffs – all jealous of each other; all weighing their words, and equally embarassed with their neighbours and themselves. The repast was very gloomy, though they drank pretty freely. The princesses remained in their apartments, each meditating upon her respective journey. They dined at their little cover. Formosanta afterward walked in the gardens with her dear bird, which, to amuse her, flew from tree to tree, displaying his superb tail and divine plumage.

The king of Egypt, who was heated with wine, not to say drunk, asked one of his pages for a bow and arrow. This prince was, in truth, the most unskilful archer in his whole kingdom. When he shot at a mark, the place of the greatest safety was generally the spot he aimed at. But the beautiful bird, flying as swiftly as the arrow, seemed to court it, and fell bleeding in the arms of Formosanta. The Egyptian, bursting into a foolish laugh, retired to his place. The princess rent the skies with her moans, melted into tears, tore her hair, and beat her breast. The dying bird said to her, in a low voice:

"Burn me, and fail not to carry my ashes to the east of the ancient city of Aden or Eden, and expose them to the sun upon a little pile of cloves and cinnamon." After having uttered these words it expired. Formosanta was for a long time in a swoon, and revived again only to burst into sighs and groans. Her father, partaking of her grief, and imprecating the king of Egypt, did not doubt but this accident foretold some fatal event. He immediately went to consult the oracle, which replied: *A mixture of everything – life and death, infidelity and constancy, loss and gain, calamities and good fortune*. Neither he nor his council could comprehend any meaning in this reply; but, at length, he was satisfied with having fulfilled the duties of devotion.

His daughter was bathed in tears, whilst he consulted the oracle. She paid the funeral obsequies to the bird, which it had directed, and resolved to carry its remains into Arabia at the risk of her life. It was burned in incombustible flax, with the orange-tree on which it used to perch. She gathered up the ashes in a little golden vase, set with rubies, and the diamonds taken from the lion's mouth. Oh! that she could, instead of fulfilling this melancholy duty, have burned alive the detestable king of Egypt! This was her sole wish. She, in spite, put to death the two crocodiles, his two sea horses, his two zebras, his two rats, and had his two mummies thrown into the Euphrates. Had she possessed his bull Apis, she would not have spared him.

The king of Egypt, enraged at this affront, set out immediately to forward his three hundred thousand men. The king of India, seeing his ally depart, set off also on the same day, with a firm intention of joining his three hundred thousand Indians to the Egyptian army, the king of Scythia decamped in the night with the princess Aldea, fully resolved to fight for her at the head of three hundred thousand Scythians, and to restore to her the inheritance of Babylon, which was her right, as she had descended from the elder branch of the Nimrod family.

As for the beautiful Formosanta, she set out at three in the morning with her caravan of pilgrims, flattering herself that she might go into Arabia, and execute the last will of her bird; and that the justice of the gods would restore her the dear Amazan, without whom life had become insupportable.

When the king of Babylon awoke, he found all the company gone.

"How mighty festivals terminate," said he; "and what a surprising vacuum they leave when the hurry is over."

But he was transported with a rage truly royal, when he found that the princess Aldea had been carried off. He ordered all his ministers to be called up, and the council to be convened. Whilst they were dressing, he failed not to consult the oracle; but the only answer he could obtain was in these words, so celebrated since throughout the universe: *When girls are not provided for in marriage by their relatives, they marry themselves.*

Orders were immediately issued to march three hundred thousand men against the king of Scythia. Thus was the torch of a most dreadful war lighted up, which was caused by the amusements of the finest festival ever given upon earth. Asia was upon the point of being over-run by four armies of three hundred thousand men each. It is plain that the war of Troy, which astonished the world some ages after, was mere child's play in comparison to this; but it should also be considered, that in the Trojans quarrel, the object was nothing more than a very immoral old woman, who had contrived to be twice run away with; whereas, in this case, the cause was tripartite – two girls and a bird.

The king of India went to meet his army upon the large fine road which then led straight to Babylon, at Cachemir. The king of Scythia flew with Aldea by the fine road which led to Mount Imaus. Owing to bad government, all these fine roads have disappeared in the lapse of time. The king of Egypt had marched to the west, along the coast of the little Mediterranean sea, which the ignorant Hebrews have since called the Great Sea.

As to the charming Formosanta, she pursued the road to Bassora, planted with lofty palm trees, which furnished a perpetual shade, and fruit at all seasons. The temple in which she was to perform her devotions, was in Bassora itself. The saint to whom this temple had been dedicated, was somewhat in the style of him who was afterward adored at Lampsacus, and was generally successful in procuring husbands for young ladies. Indeed, he was the holiest saint in all Asia.

Formosanta had no sort of inclination for the saint of Bassora. She only invoked her dear Gangaridian shepherd, her charming Amazan. She proposed embarking at Bassora, and landing in Arabia Felix, to perform what her deceased bird had commanded.

At the third stage, scarce had she entered into a fine inn, where her harbingers had made all the necessary preparations for her, when she learned that the king of Egypt had arrived there also. Informed by his emissaries of the princess's route, he immediately altered his course, followed by a numerous escort. Having alighted, he placed sentinels at all the doors; then repaired to the beautiful Formosanta's apartment, when he addressed her by saying:

"Miss, you are the lady I was in quest of. You paid me very little attention when I was at Babylon. It is just to punish scornful capricious women. You will, if you please, be kind enough to sup with me to-night; and I shall behave to you according as I am satisfied with you."

Formosanta saw very well that she was not the strongest. She judged that good sense consisted in knowing how to conform to one's situation. She resolved to get rid of the king of Egypt by an innocent stratagem. She looked at him through the corners of her eyes, (which in after ages has been called ogling,) and then she spoke to him, with a modesty, grace, and sweetness, a confusion, and a thousand other charms, which would have made the wisest man a fool, and deceived the most discerning:

"I acknowledge, sir, I always appeared with a downcast look, when you did the king, my father, the honour of visiting him. I had some apprehensions for my heart. I dreaded my too great simplicity. I trembled lest my father and your rivals should observe the preference I gave you, and which you so highly deserved. I can now declare my sentiments. I swear by the bull Apis, which after you is the thing I respect the most in the world, that your proposals have enchanted me. I have already supped with you at my father's, and I will sup with you again, without his being of the party. All that I request of you is, that your high almoner should drink with us. He appeared to me at Babylon to be an excellent guest. I have some Chiras wine remarkably good. I will make you both taste it. I consider you as the greatest of kings, and the most amiable of men."

This discourse turned the king of Egypt's head. He agreed to have the almoner's company.

"I have another favour to ask of you," said the princess, "which is to allow me to speak to my apothecary. Women have always some little ails that require attention, such as vapours in the head, palpitations of the heart, colics, and the like, which often require some assistance. In a word, I at present stand in need of my apothecary, and I hope you will not refuse me this slight testimony of confidence."

"Miss," replied the king of Egypt, "I know life too well to refuse you so just a demand. I will order the apothecary to attend you whilst supper is preparing. I imagine you must be somewhat fatigued by the journey; you will also have occasion for a chambermaid; you may order her you like best to attend you. I will afterward wait your commands and convenience."

He then retired, and the apothecary and the chambermaid, named Irla, entered. The princess had an entire confidence in her. She ordered her to bring six bottles of Chiras wine for supper, and to make all the sentinels, who had her officers under arrest, drink the same. Then she recommended her apothecary to infuse in all the bottles certain pharmaceutic drugs, which make those who take them sleep twenty-four hours, and with which he was always provided. She was implicitly obeyed. The king returned with his high almoner in about half an hour's time. The conversation at supper was very gay. The king and the priest emptied the six bottles, and acknowledged there was not such good wine in Egypt. The chambermaid was attentive to make the servants in waiting drink. As for the princess, she took great care not to drink any herself, saying that she was ordered by her physician a particular regimen. They were all presently asleep.

The king of Egypt's almoner had one of the finest beards that a man of his rank could wear. Formosanta lopped it off very skillfully; then sewing it to a ribbon, she put it on her own chin. She then dressed herself in the priest's robes, and decked herself in all the marks of his dignity, and her waiting maid clad herself like the sacristan of the goddess Isis. At length, having furnished herself with his urn and jewels, she set out from the inn amidst the sentinels, who were asleep like their master. Her attendant had taken care to have two horses ready at the door. The princess could not take with her any of the officers of her train. They would have been stopped by the great guard.

Formosanta and Irla passed through several ranks of soldiers, who, taking the princess for the high priest, called her, "My most Reverend Father in God," and asked his blessing. The two fugitives arrived in twenty-four hours at Bassora, before the king awoke. They then threw off their disguise, which might have created some suspicion. They fitted out with all possible expedition a ship, which carried them, by the Straits of Ormus, to the beautiful banks of Eden in Arabia Felix. This was that Eden, whose gardens were so famous, that they have since been the residence of the best of mankind. They were the model of the Elysian fields, the gardens of the Hesperides, and also those of the Fortunate Islands. In those warm climates men imagined there could be no greater felicity than shades and murmuring brooks. To live eternally in heaven with the Supreme Being, or to walk in the garden of paradise, was the same thing to those who incessantly spoke without understanding one another, and who could scarce have any distinct ideas or just expressions.

As soon as the princess found herself in this land, her first care was to pay her dear bird the funeral obsequies he had required of her. Her beautiful hands prepared a small quantity of cloves and cinnamon. What was her surprise, when, having spread the ashes of the bird upon this funeral pyre, she saw it blaze of itself! All was presently consumed. In the place of the ashes there appeared nothing but a large egg, from whence she saw her bird issue more brilliant than ever. This was one of the most happy moments the princess had ever experienced in her whole life. There was but another that could ever be dearer to her; it was the object of her wishes, but almost beyond her hopes.

"I plainly see," said she, to the bird, "you are the phoenix which I have heard so much spoken of. I am almost ready to expire with joy and astonishment. I did not believe in your resurrection; but it is my good fortune to be convinced of it."

"Resurrection, in fact," said the phoenix to her, "is one of the most simple things in the world. There is nothing more in being born twice than once. Everything in this world is the effect of resurrection. Caterpillars are regenerated into butterflies; a kernel put into the earth is regenerated into a tree. All animals buried in the earth regenerate into vegetation, herbs, and plants, and nourish other animals, of which they speedily compose part of the substance. All particles which compose bodies are transformed into different beings. It is true, that I am the only one to whom Oromasdes has granted the favour of regenerating in my own form."

Formosanta, who from the moment she first saw Amazan and the phoenix, had passed all her time in a round of astonishment, said to him:

"I can easily conceive that the Supreme Being may form out of your ashes a phoenix nearly resembling yourself; but that you should be precisely the same person, that you should have the same soul, is a thing, I acknowledge, I cannot very clearly comprehend. What became of your soul when I carried you in my pocket after your death?"

"Reflect one moment! Is it not as easy for the great Oromasdes to continue action upon a single atom of my being, as to begin afresh this action? He had before granted me sensation, memory, and thought. He grants them to me again. Whether he united this favour to an atom of elementary fire, latent within me, or to the assemblage of my organs, is, in reality, of no consequence. Men, as well as phoenixes, are entirely ignorant how things come to pass, but the greatest favour the Supreme Being has bestowed upon me, is to regenerate me for you. Oh! that I may pass the twenty-eight thousand years which I have still to live before my next resurrection, with you and my dear Amazan."

"My dear phoenix, remember what you first told me at Babylon, which I shall never forget, and which flattered me with the hope of again seeing my dear shepherd, whom I idolize; 'we must absolutely pay the Gangarids a visit together', and I must carry Amazan back with me to Babylon."

"This is precisely my design," said the phoenix. "There is not a moment to lose. We must go in search of Amazan by the shortest road, that is, through the air. There are in Arabia Felix two griffins, who are my particular friends, and who live only a hundred and fifty thousand leagues from here. I am going to write to them by the pigeon post, and they will be here before night. We shall have time to make you a convenient palankeen, with drawers, in which you may place your provisions. You will be quite at your ease in this vehicle, with your maid. These two griffins are the most vigorous of their kind. Each of them will support one of the poles of the canopy between their claws. But, once for all, time is very precious."

He instantly went with Formosanta to order the carriage at an upholsterer's of his acquaintance. It was made complete in four hours. In the drawers were placed small fine loaves, biscuits superior to those of Babylon, large lemons, pine-apples, cocoa, and pistachio nuts, Eden wine, which is as superior to that of Chiras, as Chiras is to that of Surinam.

The two griffins arrived at Eden at the appointed time. The vehicle was as light as it was commodious and solid, and Formosanta and Irla placed themselves in it. The two griffins carried it off like a feather. The phoenix sometimes flew after it, and sometimes perched upon its roof. The two griffins winged their way toward the Ganges with the velocity of an arrow which rends the air. They never stopped but a moment at night for the travelers to take some refreshment, and the carriers to take a draught of water.

They at length reached the country of the Gangarids. The princess's heart palpitated with hope, love, and joy. The phoenix stopped the vehicle before Amazan's house; but Amazan had been absent from home three hours, without any one knowing where he had gone.

There are no words, even in the Gangaridian language, that could express Formosanta's extreme despair.

"Alas! this is what I dreaded," said the phoenix: "the three hours which you passed at the inn, upon the road to Bassora, with that wretched king of Egypt, have perhaps been at the price of the happiness of your whole life. I very much fear we have lost Amazan, without the possibility of recovering him."

He then asked the servants if he could salute the mother of Amazan? They answered, that her husband had died only two days before, and she could speak to no one. The phoenix, who was not without influence in the house, introduced the princess of Babylon into a saloon, the walls of which were covered with orange-tree wood inlaid with ivory. The inferior shepherds and shepherdesses, who were dressed in long white garments, with gold coloured trimmings, served up, in a hundred plain porcelain baskets, a hundred various delicacies, amongst which no disguised carcasses were to be seen. They consisted of rice, sago, vermicelli, macaroni, omelets, milk, eggs, cream, cheese, pastry of every kind, vegetables, fruits, peculiarly fragrant and grateful to the taste, of which no idea can be formed in other climates; and they were accompanied with a profusion of refreshing liquors superior to the finest wine.

Whilst the princess regaled herself, seated upon a bed of roses, four peacocks, who were luckily mute, fanned her with their brilliant wings; two hundred birds, one hundred shepherds and shepherdesses, warbled a concert in two different choirs; the nightingales, thistlefinches, linnets, chaffinches, sung the higher notes with the shepherdesses, and the shepherds sung the tenor and bass. The princess acknowledged, that if there was more magnificence at Babylon, nature was infinitely more agreeable among the Gangarids; but whilst this consolatory and voluptuous music was playing, tears flowed from her eyes, whilst she said to the damsel Irla:

"These shepherds and shepherdesses, these nightingales, these linnets, are making love; and for my part, I am deprived of the company of the Gangaridian hero, the worthy object of my most tender thoughts."

Whilst she was taking this collation, her tears and admiration kept pace with each other, and the phoenix addressed himself to Amazan's mother, saying:

"Madam, you cannot avoid seeing the princess of Babylon; you know –"

"I know everything," said she, "even her adventure at the inn, upon the road to Bassora. A blackbird related the whole to me this morning; and this cruel blackbird is the cause of my son's going mad, and leaving his paternal abode."

"You have not been informed, then, that the princess regenerated me?"

"No, my dear child, the blackbird told me you were dead, and this made me inconsolable. I was so afflicted at this loss, the death of my husband, and the precipitate flight of my son, that I ordered my door to be shut to everyone. But since the princess of Babylon has done me the honour of paying me a visit, I beg she may be immediately introduced. I have matters of great importance to acquaint her with, and I choose you should be present."

She then went to meet the princess in another saloon. She could not walk very well. This lady was about three hundred years old; but she had still some agreeable vestiges of beauty. It might be conjectured, that about her two hundred and fortieth, or two hundred and fiftieth year, she must have been a most charming woman. She received Formosanta with a respectful nobleness, blended with an air of interest and sorrow, which made a very lively impression upon the princess.

Formosanta immediately paid her the compliments of condolence upon her husband's death.

"Alas!" said the widow, "you have more reason to lament his death than you imagine."

"I am, doubtless, greatly afflicted," said Formosanta; "he was father to –." Here a flood of tears prevented her from going on. "For his sake only I undertook this journey, in which I have so narrowly escaped many dangers. For him I left my father, and the most splendid court in the universe. I was detained by a King of Egypt, whom I detest. Having escaped from this tyrant, I have traversed the air in search of the only man I love. When I arrive, he flies from me!" Here sighs and tears stopped her impassioned harangue.

His mother then said to her:

"When the king of Egypt made you his prisoner, – when you supped with him at an inn upon the road to Bassora, – when your beautiful hands filled him bumpers of Chiras wine, did you observe a blackbird that flew about the room?"

"Yes, really," said the princess, "I now recollect there was such a bird, though at that time I did not pay it the least attention. But in collecting my ideas, I now remember well, that at the instant when the king of Egypt rose from the table to give me a kiss, the blackbird flew out at the window giving a loud cry, and never appeared after."

"Alas! madam," resumed Amazan's mother, "this is precisely the cause of all our misfortunes; my son had dispatched this blackbird to gain intelligence of your health, and all that passed at Babylon. He proposed speedily to return, throw himself at your feet, and consecrate to you the remainder of his life. You know not to what a pitch he adores you. All the Gangarids are both loving and faithful; but my son is the most passionate and constant of them all. The blackbird found you at an inn, drinking very cheerfully with the king of Egypt and a vile priest; he afterward saw you give this monarch who had killed the phoenix, – the man my son holds in utter detestation, – a fond embrace. The blackbird, at the sight of this, was seized with a just indignation. He flew away imprecating your fatal error. He returned this day, and has related everything. But, just heaven, at what a juncture! At the very time that my son was deploring with me the loss of his father and that of the wise phoenix, the very instant I had informed him that he was your cousin german –"

"Oh heavens! my cousin, madam, is it possible? How can this be? And am I so happy as to be thus allied to him, and yet so miserable as to have offended him?"

"My son is, I tell you," said the Gangaridian lady, "your cousin, and I shall presently convince you of it; but in becoming my relation, you rob me of my son. He cannot survive the grief that the embrace you gave to the king of Egypt has occasioned him."

"Ah! my dear aunt," cried the beautiful Formosanta, "I swear by him and the all-powerful Oromasdes, that this embrace, so far from being criminal, was the strongest proof of love your son could receive from me. I disobeyed my father for his sake. For him I went from the Euphrates to the Ganges. Having fallen into the hands of the worthless Pharaoh of Egypt, I could not escape his clutches but by artifice. I call the ashes and soul of the phoenix, which were then in my pocket, to witness. He can do me justice. But how can your son, born upon the banks of the Ganges, be my cousin? I, whose family have reigned upon the banks of the Euphrates for so many centuries?"

"You know," said the venerable Gangaridian lady to her, "that your grand uncle, Aldea, was king of Babylon, and that he was dethroned by Belus's father?"

"Yes, madam."

"You know that this Aldea had in marriage a daughter named Aldea, brought up in your court? It was this prince, who, being persecuted by your father, took refuge under another name in our happy country. He married me, and is the father of the young prince Aldea Amazan, the most beautiful, the most courageous, the strongest, and most virtuous of mortals; and at this hour the most unhappy. He went to the Babylonian festival upon the credit of your beauty; since that time he idolizes you, and now grieves because he believes that you have proved unfaithful to him. Perhaps I shall never again set eyes upon my dear son."

She then displayed to the princess all the titles of the house of Aldea. Formosanta scarce deigned to look at them.

"Ah! madam, do we examine what is the object of our desire? My heart sufficiently believes you. But where is Aldea Amazan? Where is my kinsman, my lover, my king? Where is my life? What road has he taken? I will seek for him in every sphere the Eternal Being hath framed, and of which he is the greatest ornament. I will go into the star Canope, into Sheath, into Aldebaran; I will go and tell him of my love and convince him of my innocence."

The phoenix justified the princess with regard to the crime that was imputed to her by the blackbird, of fondly embracing the king of Egypt; but it was necessary to undeceive Amazan and recall him. Birds were dispatched on every side. Unicorns sent forward in every direction. News at length arrived that Amazan had taken the road toward China.

"Well, then," said the princess, "let us set out for China. I will seek him in defiance of both difficulty and danger. The journey is not long, and I hope I shall bring you back your son in a fortnight at farthest."

At these words tears of affection streamed from his mother's eyes and also from those of the princess. They most tenderly embraced, in the great sensibility of their hearts.

The phoenix immediately ordered a coach with six unicorns. Amazan's mother furnished two thousand horsemen, and made the princess, her niece, a present of some thousands of the finest diamonds of her country. The phoenix, afflicted at the evil occasioned by the blackbird's indiscretion, ordered all the blackbirds to quit the country; and from that time none have been met with upon the banks of the Ganges.

Chapter 5: Formosanta Visits China and Scythia in Search of Amazan

THE UNICORNS, IN LESS THAN EIGHT DAYS, carried Formosanta, Irla, and the phoenix, to Cambalu, the capital of China. This city was larger than that of Babylon, and in appearance quite different. These fresh objects, these strange manners, would have amused Formosanta could any thing but Amazan have engaged her attention.

As soon as the emperor of China learned that the princess of Babylon was at the city gates, he dispatched four thousand Mandarins in ceremonial robes to receive her. They all prostrated themselves before her, and presented her with an address written in golden letters upon a sheet of purple silk. Formosanta told them, that if she were possessed of four thousand tongues, she would not omit replying immediately to every Mandarin; but that having only one, she hoped they would be satisfied with her general thanks. They conducted her, in a respectful manner, to the emperor.

He was the wisest, most just and benevolent monarch upon earth. It was he who first tilled a small field with his own imperial hands, to make agriculture respectable to his people. Laws in all other countries were shamefully confined to the punishment of crimes: he first allotted premiums to virtue. This emperor had just banished from his dominions a gang of foreign Bonzes, who had come from the extremities of the West, with the frantic hope of compelling all China *to think like themselves*; and who, under pretence of teaching truths, had already acquired honours and riches. In expelling them, he delivered himself in these words, which are recorded in the annals of the empire:

"You may here do us much harm as you have elsewhere. You have come to preach dogmas of intolerance, to the most tolerant nation upon earth. I send you back, that I may never be compelled to punish you. You will be honourably conducted to my frontiers. You will be furnished with everything necessary to return to the confines of the hemisphere from whence you came. Depart in peace, if you can be at peace, and never return."

The princess of Babylon heard with pleasure of this speech and determination. She was the more certain of being well received at court, as she was very far from entertaining any dogmas of intolerance. The emperor of China, in dining with her *tête-à-tête*, had the politeness to banish all disagreeable *etiquette*. She presented the phoenix to him, who was gently caressed by the emperor, and who perched upon his chair. Formosanta, toward the end of the repast, ingenuously acquainted him with the cause of her journey, and entreated him to search for the beautiful Amazan in the city of Cambalu; and in the meanwhile she acquainted the emperor with her adventures, without concealing the fatal passion with which her heart burned for this youthful hero.

"He did me the honour of coming to my court," said the emperor of China. "I was enchanted with this amiable Amazan. It is true that he is deeply afflicted; but his graces are thereby the more affecting. Not one of my favourites has more wit. There is not a gown Mandarin who has more knowledge, – not a military one who has a more martial or heroic air. His extreme youth adds an additional value to all his talents. If I were so unfortunate, so abandoned by the Tien and Changti, as to desire to be a conqueror, I would wish Amazan to put himself at the head of my armies, and I should be sure of conquering the whole universe. It is a great pity that his melancholy sometimes disconcerts him."

"Ah! sir," said Formosanta, with much agitation and grief, blended with an air of reproach, "why did you not request me to dine with him? This is a cruel stroke you have given me. Send for him immediately, I entreat you."

"He set out this very morning," replied the emperor, "without acquainting me with his destination."

Formosanta, turning toward the phoenix, said to him:

"Did you ever know so unfortunate a damsel as myself?" Then resuming the conversation, she said:

"Sir, how came he to quit in so abrupt a manner, so polite a court, in which, methinks, one might pass one's life?"

"The case was as follows," said he. "One of the most amiable of the princesses of the blood, falling desperately in love with him, desired to meet him at noon. He set out at day-break, leaving this billet for my kinswoman, whom it hath cost a deluge of tears:

"Beautiful princess of the mongolian race. You are deserving of a heart that was never offered up at any other altar. I have sworn to the immortal gods never to love any other than Formosanta, princess of Babylon, and to teach her how to conquer one's desires in traveling. She has had the misfortune to yield to a worthless king of Egypt. I am the most unfortunate of men; having lost my father, the phoenix, and the hope of being loved by Formosanta. I left my mother in affliction, forsook my home and country, being unable to live a moment in the place where I learned that Formosanta loved another than me. I swore to traverse the earth, and be faithful. You would despise me, and the gods punish me, if I violated my oath. Choose another lover, madam, and be as faithful as I am."

"Ah! give me that miraculous letter," said the beautiful Formosanta; "it will afford me some consolation. I am happy in the midst of my misfortunes. Amazan loves me! Amazan, for me, renounces the society of the princesses of China. There is no one upon earth but himself endowed with so much fortitude. He sets me a most brilliant example. The phoenix knows I did not stand in need of it. How cruel it is to be deprived of one's lover for the most innocent embrace given through pure fidelity. But, tell me, where has he gone? What road has he taken? Deign to inform me, and I will immediately set out."

The emperor of China told her, that, according to the reports he had received, her lover had taken the road toward Scythia. The unicorns were immediately harnessed, and the princess, after the most tender compliments, took leave of the emperor, and resumed her journey with the phoenix, her chambermaid Irla, and all her train.

As soon as she arrived in Scythia, she was more convinced than ever how much men and governments differed, and would continue to differ, until noble and enlightened minds should by degrees remove that cloud of darkness which has covered the earth for so many ages; and until there should be found in barbarous climes, heroic souls, who would have strength and perseverance enough to transform brutes into men. There are no cities in Scythia, consequently no agreeable arts. Nothing was to be seen but extensive fields, and whole tribes whose sole habitations were tents and chars. Such an appearance struck her with terror. Formosanta enquired in what tent or char the king was lodged? She was informed that he had set out eight days before with three hundred thousand cavalry to attack the king of Babylon, whose niece, the beautiful princess Aldea, he had carried off.

"What! did he run away with my cousin?" cried Formosanta. "I could not have imagined such an incident. What! has my cousin, who was too happy in paying her court to me, become a queen, and I am not yet married?" She was immediately conducted, by her desire, to the queen's tent.

Their unexpected meeting in such distant climes – the uncommon occurrences they mutually had to impart to each other, gave such charms to this interview, as made them forget they never loved one another. They saw each other with transport; and a soft illusion supplied the place of real tenderness. They embraced with tears, and there was a cordiality and frankness on each side that could not have taken place in a palace.

Aldea remembered the phoenix and the waiting maid Irla. She presented her cousin with zibelin skins, who in return gave her diamonds. The war between the two kings was spoken of. They deplored the fate of soldiers who were forced into battle, the victims of the caprice of princes, when two honest men might, perhaps, settle the dispute in less than an hour, without a single throat being cut. But the principal topic was the handsome stranger, who had conquered lions, given the largest diamonds in the universe, written madrigals, and had now become the most miserable of men from believing the statements of a blackbird.

"He is my dear brother," said Aldea. "He is my lover," cried Formosanta. "You have, doubtless, seen him. Is he still here? for, cousin, as he knows he is your brother, he cannot have left you so abruptly as he did the king of China.

"Have I seen him? good heavens! yes. He passed four whole days with me. Ah! cousin, how much my brother is to blame. A false report has absolutely turned his brain. He roams about the world, without knowing to where he is destined. Imagine to yourself his distraction of mind, which is so great, that he has refused to meet the handsomest lady in all Scythia. He set out yesterday, after writing her a letter which has thrown her into despair. As for him, he has gone to visit the Cimmerians."

"God be thanked!" cried Formosanta, "another refusal in my favour. My good fortune is beyond my hopes, as my misfortunes surpass my greatest apprehensions. Procure me this charming letter, that I may set out and follow him, loaded with his sacrifices. Farewell, cousin. Amazan is among the Cimmerians, and I fly to meet him."

Aldea judged that the princess, her cousin, was still more frantic than her brother Amazan. Hut as she had herself been sensible of the effects of this epidemic contagion, having given up the delights and magnificence of Babylon for a king of Scythia; and as the women always excuse those follies that are the effects of love, she felt for Formosanta's affliction, wished her a happy journey, and promised to be her advocate with her brother, if ever she was so fortunate as to see him again.

Chapter 6: The Princess Continues Her Journey

FROM SCYTHIA THE PRINCESS OF BABYLON, with her phoenix, soon arrived at the empire of the Cimmerians, now called Russia; a country indeed much less populous than Scythia, but of far greater extent.

After a few days' journey, she entered a very large city, which has of late been greatly improved by the reigning sovereign. The empress, however, was not there at that time, but was making a journey through her dominions, on the frontiers of Europe and Asia, in order to judge of their state and condition with her own eyes, – to enquire into their grievances, and to provide the proper remedies for them.

The principal magistrate of that ancient capital, as soon as he was informed of the arrival of the Babylonian lady and the phoenix, lost no time in paying her all the honours of his country; being certain that his mistress, the most polite and generous empress in the world, would be extremely well pleased to find that he had received so illustrious a lady with all that respect which she herself, if on the spot, would have shown her.

The princess was lodged in the palace, and entertained with great splendor and elegance. The Cimmerian lord, who was an excellent natural philosopher, diverted himself in conversing with the phoenix, at such times as the princess chose to retire to her own apartment. The phoenix told him, that he had formerly traveled among the Cimmerians, but that he should not have known the country again.

"How comes it," said he, "that such prodigious changes have been brought about in so short a time? Formerly, when I was here, about three hundred years ago, I saw nothing but savage nature in all her horrors. At present, I perceive industry, arts, splendor, and politeness."

"This mighty revolution," replied the Cimmerian, "was begun by one man, and is now carried to perfection by one woman; – a woman who is a greater legislator than the Isis of the Egyptians, or the Ceres of the Greeks. Most law-givers have been, unhappily, of a narrow genius and an arbitrary disposition, which conned their views to the countries they governed. Each of them looked upon his own race as the only people existing upon the earth, or as if they ought to be at enmity with all the rest. They formed institutions, introduced customs, and established religions exclusively for themselves. Thus the Egyptians, so famous for those heaps of stones called pyramids, have dishonoured themselves with their barbarous superstitions. They despise all other nations as profane; refuse all manner of intercourse with them; and, excepting those conversant in the court, who now and then rise above the prejudices of the vulgar, there is not an Egyptian who will eat off a plate that has ever been used by a stranger. Their priests are equally cruel and absurd. It were better to have no laws at all, and to follow those notions of right and wrong engraven on our hearts by nature, than to subject society to institutions so inhospitable.

"Our empress has adopted quite a different system. She considers her vast dominions, under which all the meridians on the globe are united, as under an obligation of correspondence with all the nations dwelling under those meridians. The first and most fundamental of her laws, is an universal toleration of all religions, and an unbounded compassion for every error. Her penetrating genius perceives, that though the modes of religious worship differ, yet morality is every where the same. By this principle, she has united her people to all the nations on earth, and the Cimmerians will soon consider the Scandinavians and the Chinese as their brethren. Not satisfied with this, she has resolved to establish this invaluable toleration, the strongest link of society, among her neighbours. By these means, she obtained the title of the parent of her country; and, if she persevere, will acquire that of the benefactress of mankind.

"Before her time, the men, who were unhappily possessed of power, sent out legions of murderers to ravage unknown countries, and to water with the blood of the children the inheritance of their fathers. Those assassins were called heroes, and their robberies accounted glorious achievements. But our sovereign courts another sort of glory. She has sent forth her armies to be the messengers of peace; not only to prevent men from being the destroyers, but to oblige them to be the benefactors of one another. Her standards are the ensigns of public tranquillity."

The phoenix was quite charmed with what he heard from this nobleman. He told him, that though he had lived twenty-seven thousand nine hundred years and seven months in this world, he had never seen any thing like it. He then enquired after his friend Amazan. The Cimmerian gave the same account of him that the princess had already heard from the Chinese and the Scythians. It was Amazan's constant practice to run away from all the courts he visited, the instant any lady noticed him in particular and seemed anxious to make his acquaintance. The phoenix soon acquainted Formosanta with this fresh instance of Amazan's fidelity – a fidelity so much the more surprising, since he could not imagine his princess would ever hear of it.

Amazan had set out for Scandinavia, where he was entertained with sights still more surprising. In this place, he beheld monarchy and liberty subsisting together in a manner thought incompatible in other states; the laborers of the ground shared in the legislature with the grandees of the realm. In another place he saw what was still more extraordinary; a prince equally remarkable for his extreme youth and uprightness, who possessed a sovereign authority over his country, acquired by a solemn contract with his people.

Amazan beheld a philosopher on the throne of Sarmatia, who might be called a king of anarchy; for he was the chief of a hundred thousand petty kings, one of whom with his single voice could render ineffectual the resolution of all the rest. Eolus had not more difficulty to keep the warring winds within their proper bounds, than this monarch to reconcile the tumultuous discordant spirits of his subjects. He was the master of a ship surrounded with eternal storms. But the vessel did not founder, for he was an excellent pilot.

In traversing those various countries, so different from his own, Amazan persevered in rejecting all the advances made to him by the ladies, though incessantly distracted with the embrace given by Formosanta to the king of Egypt, being resolved to set Formosanta an amazing example of an unshaken and unparalleled fidelity.

The princess of Babylon was constantly close at his heels, and scarcely ever missed of him but by a day or two; without the one being tired of roaming, or the other losing a moment in pursuing him.

Thus he traversed the immense continent of Germany, where he beheld with wonder the progress which reason and philosophy had made in the north. Even their princes were enlightened, and had become the patrons of freedom of thought. Their education had not been trusted to men who had an interest in deceiving them, or who were themselves deceived. They were brought up in the knowledge of universal morality, and in the contempt of superstition.

They had banished from all their estates a senseless custom which had enervated and depopulated the southern countries. This was to bury alive in immense dungeons, infinite numbers of both sexes who were eternally separated from one another, and sworn to have no communication together. This madness had contributed more than the most cruel wars to lay waste and depopulate the earth.

In opposing these barbarous institutions, so inimical to the laws of nature and the best interests of society, the princes of the north had become the benefactors of their race. They had likewise exploded other errors equally absurd and pernicious. In short, men had at last ventured to make use of their reason in those immense regions; whereas it was still believed almost every where else, that they could not be governed but in proportion to their ignorance.

Chapter 7: Amazan Visits Albion

FROM GERMANY, AMAZAN ARRIVED AT BATAVIA; where his perpetual chagrin was in a good measure alleviated, by perceiving among the inhabitants a faint resemblance to his

happy countrymen, the Gangarids. There he saw liberty, security, and equality, – with toleration in religion; but the ladies were so indifferent, that none made him any advances; an experience he had not met with before. It is true, however, that had he been inclined to address them, they would not have been offended; though, at the same time, not one would have been the least in love; but he was far from any thoughts of making conquests.

Formosanta had nearly caught him in this insipid nation. He had set out but a moment before her arrival.

Amazan had heard so much among the Batavians in praise of a certain island called Albion, that he was led by curiosity to embark with his unicorns on board a ship, which, with a favourable easterly wind, carried him in a few hours to that celebrated country, more famous than Tyre, or Atlantis.

The beautiful Formosanta, who had followed him, as it were on the scent, to the banks of the Volga, the Vistula, the Elbe, and the Weser, and had never been above a day or two behind him, arrived soon after at the mouth of the Rhine, where it disembogues its waters into the German Ocean.

Here she learned that her beloved Amazan had just set sail for Albion. She thought she saw the vessel on board of which he was, and could not help crying out for joy; at which the Batavian ladies were greatly surprised, not imagining that a young man could possibly occasion so violent a transport. They took, indeed, but little notice of the phoenix, as they reckoned his feathers would not fetch near so good a price as those of their own ducks, and other water fowl. The princess of Babylon hired two vessels to carry herself and her retinue to that happy island, which was soon to possess the only object of her desires, the soul of her life, and the god of her idolatry.

An unpropitious wind from the west suddenly arose, just as the faithful and unhappy Amazan landed on Albion's sea-girt shore, and detained the ships of the Babylonian princess just as they were on the point of sailing. Seized with a deep melancholy, she went to her room, determined to remain there till the wind should change; but it blew for the space of eight days, with an unremitting violence. The princess, during this tedious period, employed her maid of honour, Irla, in reading romances; which were not indeed written by the Batavians; but as they are the factors of the universe, they traffic in the wit as well as commodities of other nations. The princess purchased of Mark Michael Rey, the bookseller, all the novels which had been written by the Ausonians and the Welch, the sale of which had been wisely prohibited among those nations to enrich their neighbours, the Batavians. She expected to find in those histories some adventure similar to her own, which might alleviate her grief. The maid of honour read, the phoenix made comments, and the princess, finding nothing in the *Fortunate Country Maid*, in *Tansai*, or in the *Sopha*, that had the least resemblance to her own affairs, interrupted the reader every moment, by asking how the wind stood.

Chapter 8: Amazan Leaves Albion to Visit the Land of Saturn

IN THE MEAN TIME, Amazan was on the road to the capital of Albion, in his coach and six unicorns, all his thoughts employed on his dear princess. At a small distance he perceived a carriage overturned in a ditch. The servants had gone in different directions in quest of assistance, but the owner kept his seat, smoking his pipe with great tranquillity, without manifesting the smallest impatience. His name was my lord What-then, in the language from which I translate these memoirs.

Amazan made all the haste possible to help him, and without assistance set the carriage to rights, so much was his strength superior to that of other men. My lord What-then took no other notice of him, than saying, "a stout fellow, by Jove!" In the meantime the neighbouring people, having arrived, flew into a great passion at being called out to no purpose, and fell upon the stranger. They abused him, called him an outlandish dog, and challenged him to strip and box.

Amazan seized a brace of them in each hand, and threw them twenty paces from him; the rest seeing this, pulled off their hats, and bowing with great respect, asked his honour for something to drink. His honour gave them more money than they had ever seen in their lives before. My lord What-then now expressed great esteem for him, and asked him to dinner at his country house, about three miles off. His invitation being accepted, he went into Amazan's coach, his own being out of order from the accident.

After a quarter of an hour's silence, my lord What-then, looking upon Amazan for a moment, said. "How d'ye do?" which, by the way, is a phrase without any meaning, adding, "You have got six fine unicorns there." After which he continued smoking as usual.

The traveler told him his unicorns were at his service, and that he had brought them from the country of the Gangarids. From thence he took occasion to inform him of his affair with the princess of Babylon, and the unlucky kiss she had given the king of Egypt; to which the other made no reply, being very indifferent whether there were any such people in the world, as a king of Egypt, or a princess of Babylon.

He remained dumb for another quarter of an hour; after which he asked his companion a second time how he did, and whether they had any good roast beef among the Gangarids.

Amazan answered with his wonted politeness, "that they did not eat their brethren on the banks of the Ganges." He then explained to him that system which many ages afterward was surnamed the Pythagorean philosophy. But my lord fell asleep in the meantime, and made but one nap of it till he came to his own house.

He was married to a young and charming woman, on whom nature had bestowed a soul as lively and sensible as that of her husband was dull and stupid. A few gentlemen of Albion had that day come to dine with her; among whom there were characters of all sorts; for that country having been almost always under the government of foreigners, the families that had come over with these princes had imported their different manners. There were in this company some persons of an amiable disposition, others of superior genius, and a few of profound learning.

The mistress of the house had none of that awkward stiffness, that false modesty, with which the young ladies of Albion were then reproached. She did not conceal by a scornful look and an affected taciturnity, her deficiency of ideas: and the embarrassing humility of having nothing to say. Never was a woman more engaging. She received Amazan with a grace and politeness that were quite natural to her. The extreme beauty of this young stranger, and the involuntary comparison she could not help making between him and her prosaic husband, did not increase her happiness or content.

Dinner being served, she placed Amazan at her side, and helped him to a variety of puddings, he having informed her that the Gangarids never dined upon any thing which had received from the gods the celestial gift of life. The events of his early life, the manners of the Gangarids, the progress of arts, religion, and government, were the subjects of a conversation equally agreeable and instructive all the time of the entertainment, which lasted till night: during which my lord What-then did nothing but push the bottle about, and call for the toast.

After dinner, while my lady was pouring out the tea, still feeding her eyes on the young stranger, he entered into a long conversation with a member of parliament; for everyone knows that there was, even then, a parliament called Wittenagemot, or the assembly of wise men. Amazan enquired into the constitution, laws, manners, customs, forces, and arts, which made this country so respectable; and the member answered him in the following manner.

"For a long time we went stark naked, though our climate is none of the hottest. We were likewise for a long time enslaved by a people who came from the ancient country of Saturn, watered by the Tiber. But the mischief we have done one another has greatly exceeded all that we ever suffered from our first conquerors. One of our princes carried his superstition to such a pitch, as to declare himself the subject of a priest, who dwells also on the banks of the Tiber, and is called the Old Man of the Seven Mountains. It has been the fate of the seven mountains to domineer over the greatest part of Europe, then inhabited by brutes in human shape.

"To those times of infamy and debasement, succeeded the ages of barbarity and confusion. Our country, more tempestuous than the surrounding ocean, has been ravaged and drenched in blood by our civil discords. Many of our crowned heads have perished by a violent death. Above a hundred princes of the royal blood have ended their days on the scaffold, whilst the hearts of their adherents have been torn from their breasts, and thrown in their faces. In short, it is the province of the hangman to write the history of our island, seeing that this personage has finally determined all our affairs of moment.

"But to crown these horrors, it is not very long since some fellows wearing black mantles, and others who cast white shirts over their jackets, having become aggressive and intolerant, succeeded in communicating their madness to the whole nation. Our country was then divided into two parties, the murderers and the murdered, the executioners and the sufferers, plunderers and slaves; and all in the name of God, and whilst they were seeking the Lord.

"Who would have imagined, that from this horrible abyss, this chaos of dissension, cruelty, ignorance, and fanaticism, a government should at last spring up, the most perfect, it may be said, now in the world; yet such has been the event. A prince, honoured and wealthy, all-powerful to do good, but without power to do evil, is at the head of a free, warlike, commercial, and enlightened nation. The nobles on one hand, and the representatives of the people on the other, share the legislature with the monarch.

"We have seen, by a singular fatality of events, disorder, civil wars, anarchy and wretchedness, lay waste the country, when our kings aimed at arbitrary power: whereas tranquillity, riches, and universal happiness, have only reigned among us, when the prince has remained satisfied with a limited authority. All order had been subverted whilst we were disputing about mysteries, but was re-established the moment we grew wise enough to despise them. Our victorious fleets carry our flag on every ocean; our laws place our lives and fortunes in security; no judge can explain them in an arbitrary manner, and no decision is ever given without the reasons assigned for it. We should punish a judge as an assassin, who should condemn a citizen to death without declaring the evidence which accused him, and the law upon which he was convicted.

"It is true, there are always two parties among us, who are continually writing and intriguing against each other, but they constantly re-unite, whenever it is needful to arm in defence of liberty and our country. These two parties watch over one another, and mutually prevent the violation of the sacred *deposit* of the laws. They hate one another, but they love the state. They are like those jealous lovers, who pay court to the same mistress, with a spirit of emulation.

"From the same fund of genius by which we discovered and supported the natural rights of mankind, we have carried the sciences to the highest pitch to which they can attain among men. Your Egyptians, who pass for such great mechanics — your Indians, who are believed to be such great philosophers — your Babylonians, who boast of having observed the stars for the course of four hundred and thirty thousand years – the Greeks, who have written so much, and said so little, know in reality nothing in comparison to our inferior scholars, who have studied the discoveries of Our great masters. We have ravished more secrets from nature in the space of an hundred years, that the human species had been able to discover in as many ages.

"This is a true account of our present state. I have concealed from you neither the good nor the bad; neither our shame nor our glory; and I have exaggerated nothing."

At this discourse Amazan felt a strong desire to be instructed in those sublime sciences his friend had spoken of; and if his passion for the princess of Babylon, his filial duty to his mother whom he had quitted, and his love for his native country, had not made strong remonstrances to his distempered heart, he would willingly have spent the remainder of his life in Albion. But that unfortunate kiss his princess had given the king of Egypt, did not leave his mind at sufficient ease to study the abstruse sciences.

"I confess," said he, "having made a solemn vow to roam about the world, and to escape from myself. I have a curiosity to see that ancient land of Saturn – that people of the Tiber and of the Seven Mountains, who have been heretofore your masters. They must undoubtedly be the first people on earth."

"I advise you by all means," answered the member, "to take that journey, if you have the smallest taste for music or painting. Even we ourselves frequently carry our spleen and melancholy to the Seven Mountains. But you will be greatly surprised when you see the descendants of our conquerors."

This was a long conversation, and Amazan had spoken in so agreeable a manner; his voice was so charming; his whole behavior so noble and engaging, that the mistress of the house could not resist the pleasure of having a little private chat with him in her turn. She accordingly sent him a little billet-doux intimating her wishes in the most agreeable language. Amazan had once more the courage to resist the fascination of female society, and, according to custom, wrote the lady an answer full of respect, – representing to her the sacredness of his oath, and the strict obligation he was under to teach the princess of Babylon to conquer her passions by his example; after which he harnessed his unicorns and departed for Batavia, leaving all the company in deep admiration of him, and the lady in profound astonishment. In her confusion she dropped Amazan's letter. My lord What-then read it next morning:

"D—n it," said he, shrugging up his shoulders, "what stuff and nonsense have we got here?" and then rode out a fox hunting with some of his drunken neighbours.

Amazan was already sailing upon the sea, possessed of a geographical chart, with which he had been presented by the learned Albion he had conversed with at lord What-then's. He was extremely astonished to find the greatest part of the earth upon a single sheet of paper.

His eyes and imagination wandered over this little space; he observed the Rhine, the Danube, the Alps of Tyrol, there specified under their different names, and all the countries through which he was to pass before he arrived at the city of the Seven Mountains. But he more particularly fixed his eyes upon the country of the Gangarids, upon Babylon, where he had seen his dear princess, and upon the country of Bassora, where she had given a fatal kiss to the king of Egypt. He sighed, and tears streamed from his eyes at the unhappy remembrance. He agreed with the Albion who had presented him with the universe in epitome, when he averred that the inhabitants of the banks of the Thames were a thousand times better instructed than those upon the banks of the Nile, the Euphrates, and the Ganges.

As he returned into Batavia, Formosanta proceeded toward Albion with her two ships at full sail. Amazan's ship and the princess's crossed one another and almost touched; the two lovers were close to each other, without being conscious of the fact. Ah! had they but known it! But this great consolation tyrannic destiny would not allow.

Chapter 9: Amazan Visits Rome

N O SOONER HAD AMAZAN LANDED on the flat muddy shore of Batavia, than he immediately set out toward the city of the Seven Mountains. He was obliged to traverse the southern part of Germany. At every four miles he met with a prince and princess, maids of honour, and beggars. He was greatly astonished every where at the coquetries of these ladies and maids of honour, in which they indulged with German good faith. After having cleared the Alps he embarked upon the sea of Dalmatia, and landed in a city that had no resemblance to any thing he had heretofore seen. The sea formed the streets, and the houses were erected in the water. The few public places, with which this city was ornamented, were filled with men and women with double faces – that which nature had bestowed on them, and a pasteboard one, ill painted, with which they covered their natural visage; so that this people seemed composed of spectres. Upon the arrival of strangers in this country, they immediately purchase these visages, in the same manner as people elsewhere furnish themselves with hats and shoes. Amazan despised a fashion so contrary to nature. He appeared just as he was.

Many ladies were introduced, and interested themselves in the handsome Amazan. But he fled with the utmost precipitancy, uttering the name of the incomparable princess of Babylon, and swearing by the immortal gods, that she was far handsomer than the Venetian girls.

"Sublime traitoress," he cried, in his transports, "I will teach you to be faithful!"

Now the yellow surges of the Tiber, pestiferous fens, a few pale emaciated inhabitants clothed in tatters which displayed their dry tanned hides, appeared to his sight, and bespoke his arrival at the gate of the city of the Seven Mountains, – that city of heroes and legislators who conquered and polished a great part of the globe.

He expected to have seen at the triumphal gate, five hundred battalions commanded by heroes, and in the senate an assembly of demi-gods giving laws to the earth. But the only army he found consisted of about thirty tatterdemalions, mounting guard with umbrellas for fear of the sun. Having arrived at a temple which appeared to him very fine, but not so magnificent as that of Babylon, he was greatly astonished to hear a concert performed by men with female voices.

"This," said he, "is a mighty pleasant country, which was formerly the land of Saturn. I have been in a city where no one showed his own face; here is another where men have neither their own voices nor beards."

He was told that these eunuchs had been trained from childhood, that they might sing the more agreeably the praises of a great number of persons of merit. Amazan could not comprehend the meaning of this.

They then explained to him very pleasantly, and with many gesticulations, according to the custom of their country, the point in question. Amazan was quite confounded.

"I have traveled a great way," said he, "but I never before heard such a whim."

After they had sung a good while, the Old Man of the Seven Mountains went with great ceremony to the gate of the temple. He cut the air in four parts with his thumb raised, two fingers extended and two bent, in uttering these words in a language no longer spoken: *"To the city and to the universe."* Amazan could not see how two fingers could extend so far.

He presently saw the whole court of the master of the world file off. This court consisted of grave personages, some in scarlet, and others in violet robes. They almost all eyed the handsome Amazan with a tender look; and bowed to him, while commenting upon his personal appearance.

The zealots whose vocation was to show the curiosities of the city to strangers, very eagerly offered to conduct him to several ruins, in which a muleteer would not choose to pass a night, but which were formerly worthy monuments of the grandeur of a royal people. He moreover saw pictures of two hundred years standing, and statues that had remained twenty ages, which appeared to him masterpieces of their kind.

"Can you still produce such work?" said Amazan.

"No, your excellency," replied one of the zealots; "but we despise the rest of the earth, because we preserve these rarities. We are a kind of old clothes men, who derive our glory from the cast-off garbs in our warehouses."

Amazan was willing to see the prince's palace, and he was accordingly conducted thither. He saw men dressed in violet coloured robes, who were reckoning the money of the revenues of the domains of lands, some situated upon the Danube, some upon the Loire, others upon the Guadalquivir, or the Vistula.

"Oh! Oh!" said Amazan, having consulted his geographical map, "your master, then, possesses all Europe, like those ancient heroes of the Seven Mountains?"

"He should possess the whole universe by divine right," replied a violet-livery man; "and there was even a time when his predecessors nearly compassed universal monarchy, but their successors are so good as to content themselves at present with some monies which the kings, their subjects, pay to them in the form of a tribute."

"Your master is then, in fact, the king of kings. Is that his title?" said Amazan.

"Your excellency, his title is *the servant of servants*! He was originally a fisherman and porter, wherefore the emblems of his dignity consist of keys and nets; but he at present issues orders to every king in Christendom. It is not a long while since he sent one hundred and one mandates to a king of the Celts, and the king obeyed."

"Your fisherman must then have sent five or six hundred thousand men to put these orders in execution?"

"Not at all, your excellency. Our holy master is not rich enough to keep ten thousand soldiers on foot: but he has five or six hundred thousand divine prophets dispersed in other countries. These prophets of various colours are, as they ought to be, supported at the expense of the people where they reside. They proclaim, from heaven, that my master may, with his keys, open and shut all locks, and particularly those of strong boxes. A Norman priest, who held the post of confident of this king's thoughts, convinced him he ought to obey, without questioning, the one hundred and one thoughts of my master; for you must know that one of the prerogatives of the Old Man of the Seven Mountains is never to err, whether he deigns to speak or deigns to write."

"In faith," said Amazan, "this is a very singular man; I should be pleased to dine with him."

"Were your excellency even a king, you could not eat at his table. All that he could do for you, would be to allow you to have one served by the side of his, but smaller and lower. But if you are inclined to have the honour of speaking to him, I will ask an audience for you on condition of the *buona mancia*, which you will be kind enough to give me." "Very readily," said the Gangarid. The violet-livery man bowed: "I will introduce you to-morrow," said he. "You must make three very low bows, and you must kiss the feet of the Old Man of the Seven Mountains." At this information Amazan burst into so violent a fit of laughing that he was almost choked; which, however, he surmounted, holding his sides, whilst the violent emotions of the risible muscles forced the tears down his cheeks, till he reached the inn, where the fit still continued upon him.

At dinner, twenty beardless men and twenty violins produced a concert. He received the compliments of the greatest lords of the city during the remainder of the day; but from their extravagant actions, he was strongly tempted to throw two or three of these violet-coloured gentry out of the window. He left with the greatest precipitation this city of the masters of the world, where young men were treated so whimsically, and where he found himself necessitated to kiss an old man's toe, as if his cheek were at the end of his foot.

Chapter 10: An Unfortunate Adventure in Gaul

IN ALL THE PROVINCES through which Amazan passed, he remained ever faithful to the princess of Babylon, though incessantly enraged at the king of Egypt. This model of constancy at length arrived at the new capital of the Gauls. This city, like many others, had alternately submitted to barbarity, ignorance, folly, and misery. The first name it bore was Dirt and Mire; it then took that of Isis, from the worship of Isis, which had reached even here. Its first senate consisted of a company of watermen. It had long been in bondage, and submitted to the ravages of the heroes of the Seven Mountains; and some ages after, some other heroic thieves who came from the farther banks of the Rhine, had seized upon its little lands.

Time, which changes all things, had formed it into a city, half of which was very noble and very agreeable, the other half somewhat barbarous and ridiculous. This was the emblem of its inhabitants. There were within its walls at least a hundred thousand people, who had no other employment than play and diversion. These idlers were the judges of those arts which the others cultivated. They were ignorant of all that passed at court; though they were only four short miles distant from it: but it seemed to them at least six hundred thousand miles off. Agreeableness in company, gaiety and frivolty, formed the important and sole considerations of their lives. They were governed like children, who are extravagantly supplied with gewgaws, to prevent their crying. If the horrors were discussed, which two centuries before had laid waste their country, or if those dreadful periods were recalled, when one half of the nation massacred the other for sophisms, they, indeed, said, "this was not well done;" then, presently, they fell to laughing again, or singing of catches.

In proportion as the idlers were polished, agreeable, and amiable, it was observed that there was a greater and more shocking contrast between them and those who were engaged in business.

Among the latter, or such as pretended so to be, there was a gang of melancholy fanatics, whose absurdity and knavery divided their character, – whose appearance alone diffused misery, – and who would have overturned the world, had they been able to gain a little credit. But the nation of idlers, by dancing and singing, forced them into obscurity in their caverns, as the warbling birds drive the croaking bats back to their holes and ruins.

A smaller number of those who were occupied, were the preservers of ancient barbarous customs, against which nature, terrified, loudly exclaimed. They consulted nothing but their worm-eaten registers. If they there discovered a foolish or horrid custom, they considered it as a sacred law. It was from this vile practice of not daring to think for themselves, but extracting their ideas from the ruins of those times when no one thought at all, that in the metropolis of pleasure there still remained some shocking manners. Hence it was that there was no proportion between crimes and punishments. A thousand deaths were sometimes inflicted upon an innocent victim, to make him acknowledge a crime he had not committed.

The extravagancies of youth were punished with the same severity as murder or parricide. The idlers screamed loudly at these exhibitions, and the next day thought no more about them, but were buried in the contemplation of some new fashion.

This people saw a whole age elapse, in which the fine arts attained a degree of perfection that far surpassed the most sanguine hopes. Foreigners then repaired thither, as they did to Babylon, to admire the great monuments of architecture, the wonders of gardening, the sublime efforts of sculpture and painting. They were charmed with a species of music that reached the heart without astonishing the ears.

True poetry, that is to say, such as is natural and harmonious, that which addresses the heart as well as the mind, was unknown to this nation before this happy period. New kinds of eloquence displayed sublime beauties. The theatres in particular reëchoed with masterpieces that no other nation ever approached. In a word, good taste prevailed in every profession to that degree, that there were even good writers among the Druids.

So many laurels that had branched even to the skies, soon withered in an exhausted soil. There remained but a very small number, whose leaves were of a pale dying verdure. This decay was occasioned by the facility of producing; laziness preventing good productions, and by a satiety of the brilliant, and a taste for the whimsical. Vanity protected arts that brought back times of barbarity; and this same vanity, in persecuting persons of real merit, forced them to quit their country. The hornets banished the bees.

There were scarce any real arts, scarce any real genius, talent now consisted in reasoning right or wrong upon the merit of the last age. The dauber of a sign-post criticised with an air of sagacity the works of the greatest painters; and the blotters of paper disfigured the works of the greatest writers. Ignorance and bad taste had other daubers in their pay. The same things were repeated in a hundred volumes under different titles. Every work was either a dictionary or a pamphlet. A Druid gazetteer wrote twice a week the obscure annals of an unknown people possessed with the devil, and of celestial prodigies operated in garrets by little beggars of both sexes. Other Ex-Druids, dressed in black, ready to die with rage and hunger, set forth their complaints in a hundred different writings, that they were no longer allowed to cheat mankind – this privilege being conferred on some goats clad in grey; and some Arch-Druids were employed in printing defamatory libels.

Amazan was quite ignorant of all this, and even if he had been acquainted with it, he would have given himself very little concern about it, having his head filled with nothing but the princess of Babylon, the king of Egypt, and the inviolable vow he had made to despise all female coquetry in whatever country his despair should drive him.

The gaping ignorant mob, whose curiosity exceeds all the bounds of nature and reason, for a long time thronged about his unicorns. The more sensible women forced open the doors of his *hotel* to contemplate his person.

He at first testified some desire of visiting the court; but some of the idlers, who constituted good company and casually went thither, informed him that it was quite out of fashion, that times were greatly changed, and that all amusements were confined to the city. He was invited that very night to sup with a lady whose sense and talents had reached foreign climes, and who had traveled in some countries through which Amazan had passed. This lady gave him great pleasure, as well as the society he met at her house. Here reigned a decent liberty, gaiety without tumult, silence without pedantry, and wit without asperity. He found that *good company* was not quite ideal, though the title was frequently usurped by pretenders. The next day he dined in a society far less amiable, but much more voluptuous. The more he was satisfied with the guests, the more they were pleased with him. He found his soul soften and dissolve, like the aromatics of his country, which gradually melt in a moderate heat, and exhale in delicious perfumes.

After dinner he was conducted to a place of public entertainment which was enchanting; but condemned, however, by the Druids, because it deprived them of their auditors, which, therefore, excited their jealousy. The representation here consisted of agreeable verses, delightful songs, dances which expressed the movements of the soul, and perspectives that charmed the eye in deceiving it. This kind of pastime, which included so many kinds, was known only under a foreign name. It was called an *Opera*, which formerly signified, in the language of the Seven Mountains, work, care, occupation, industry, enterprise, business. This exhibition enchanted him. A female singer, in particular, charmed him by her melodious voice, and the graces that accompanied her. This child of genius, after the performance, was introduced to him by his new friends. He presented her with a handful of diamonds; for which she was so grateful, that she could not leave him all the rest of the day. He supped with her and her companions, and during the delightful repast he forgot his sobriety, and became heated and oblivious with wine. What an instance of human frailty!

The beautiful princess of Babylon arrived at this juncture, with her phoenix, her chambermaid Irla, and her two hundred Gangaridian cavaliers mounted on their unicorns. It was a long while before the gates were opened. She immediately asked, if the handsomest, the most courageous, the most sensible, and the most faithful of men was still in that city? The magistrates readily concluded that she meant Amazan. She was conducted to his *hotel*. How great was the palpitation of her heart! – the powerful operation of the tender passion. Her whole soul was penetrated with inexpressible joy, to see once more in her lover the model of constancy. Nothing could prevent her entering his chamber; the curtains were open; and she saw the beautiful Amazan asleep and stupefied with drink.

Formosanta expressed her grief with such screams as made the house echo. She swooned into the arms of Irla. As soon as she had recovered her senses, she retired from this fatal chamber with grief blended with rage.

"Oh! just heaven; oh, powerful Oromasdes!" cried the beautiful princess of Babylon, bathed in tears. "By whom, and for whom am I thus betrayed? He that could reject for my sake so many princesses, to abandon me for the company of a strolling Gaul! No! I can never survive this affront."

"This is the disposition of all young people," said Irla to her, "from one end of the world to the other. Were they enamoured with a beauty descended from heaven, they would at certain moments forget her entirely."

"It is done," said the princess, "I will never see him again whilst I live. Let us depart this instant, and let the unicorns be harnessed."

The phoenix conjured her to stay at least till Amazan awoke, that he might speak with him.

"He does not deserve it," said the princess. "You would cruelly offend me. He would think that I had desired you to reproach him, and that I am willing to be reconciled to him. If you love me, do not add this injury to the insult he has offered me."

The phoenix, who after all owed his life to the daughter of the king of Babylon, could not disobey her. She set out with all her attendants.

"Where are you going?" said Irla to her.

"I do not know," replied the princess; "we will take the first road we find. Provided I fly from Amazan for ever, I am satisfied."

The phoenix, who was wiser than Formosanta, because he was divested of passion, consoled her upon the road. He gently insinuated to her that it was shocking to punish one's self for the faults of another; that Amazan had given her proofs sufficiently striking and numerous of his fidelity, so that she should forgive him for having forgotten himself for one moment in social company; that this was the only time in which he had been wanting of the grace of Oromasdes; that it would render him only the more constant in love and virtue for the future; that the desire of expiating his fault would raise him beyond himself; that it would be the means of increasing her happiness; that many great princesses before her had forgiven such slips, and had had no reason to be sorry afterward; and he was so thoroughly possessed of the art of persuasion, that Formosanta's mind grew more calm and peaceable. She was now sorry she had set out so soon. She thought her unicorns went too fast, but she did not dare return. Great was the conflict between her desire of forgiving and that of showing her rage – between her love and vanity. However, her unicorns pursued their pace; and she traversed the world, according to the prediction of her father's oracle.

When Amazan awoke, he was informed of the arrival and departure of Formosanta and the phoenix. He was also told of the rage and distraction of the princess, and that she had sworn never to forgive him.

"Then," said he, "there is nothing left for me to do, but follow her, and kill myself at her feet."

The report of this adventure drew together his festive companions, who all remonstrated with him. They said that he had much better stay with them; that nothing could equal the pleasant life they led in the centre of arts and refined delicate pleasures; that many strangers, and even kings, preferred such an agreeable enchanting repose to their country and their thrones. Moreover, his vehicle was broken, and another was being made for him according to the newest fashion; that the best tailor of the whole city had already cut out for him a dozen suits in the latest style; that the most vivacious, amiable, and fashionable ladies, at whose houses dramatic performances were represented, had each appointed a day to give him a regale. The girl from the opera was in the meanwhile drinking her chocolate, laughing, singing, and ogling the beautiful Amazan – who by this time clearly perceived she had no more sense than a goose.

A sincerity, cordiality, and frankness, as well as magnanimity and courage, constituted the character of this great prince, he related his travels and misfortunes to his friends. They knew that he was cousin-german to the princess. They were informed of the fatal kiss she had given the king of Egypt. "Such little tricks," said they, "are often forgiven between relatives, otherwise one's whole life would pass in perpetual uneasiness."

Nothing could shake his design of pursuing Formosanta; but his carriage not being ready, he was compelled to remain three days longer among the idlers, who were still feasting and merry-making. He at length took his leave of them, by embracing them and making them accept some of his diamonds that were the best mounted, and recommending to them a constant pursuit of frivolity and pleasure, since they were thereby made more agreeable and happy.

"The Germans," said he, "are the greyheads of Europe; the people of Albion are men formed; the inhabitants of Gaul are the children, – and I love to play with children."

Chapter 11: Amazan and Formosanta Become Reconciled

THE GUIDES HAD NO DIFFICULTY in following the route the princess had taken. There was nothing else talked of but her and her large bird. All the inhabitants were still in a state of fascination. The banks of the Loire, of the Dordogue – the Garonne, and the Gironde, still echoed with acclamation.

When Amazan reached the foot of the Pyrenees, the magistrates and Druids of the country made him dance, whether he would or not, a *Tambourin*; but as soon as he cleared the Pyrenees, nothing presented itself that was either gay or joyous. If he here and there heard a peasant sing, it was a doleful ditty. The inhabitants stalked with much gravity, having a few strung beads and a girted poniard. The nation dressed in black, and appeared to be in mourning.

If Amazan's servants asked passengers any questions, they were answered by signs; if they went into an inn, the host acquainted his guests in three words, that there was nothing in the house, but that the things they so pressingly wanted might be found a few miles off.

When these votaries to taciturnity were asked if they had seen the beautiful princess of Babylon pass, they answered with less brevity than usual: "We have seen her – she is not so handsome – there are no beauties that are not tawny

– she displays a bosom of alabaster, which is the most disgusting thing in the world, and which is scarce known in our climate."

Amazan advanced toward the province watered by the Betis. The Tyrians discovered this country about twelve thousand years ago, about the time they discovered the great Atlantic Isle, inundated so many centuries after. The Tyrians cultivated Betica, which the natives of the country had never done, being of opinion that it was not their place to meddle with anything, and that their neighbours, the Gauls, should come and reap their harvests. The Tyrians had brought with them some Palestines, or Jews, who, from that time, have wandered through every clime where money was to be gained. The Palestines, by extraordinary usury, at fifty per cent., had possessed themselves of almost all the riches of the country. This made the people of Betica imagine the Palestines were sorcerers; and all those who were accused of witchcraft were burnt, without mercy, by a company of Druids, who were called the Inquisitors, or the *Anthropokaies*. These priests immediately put their victims in a masquerade habit, seized upon their effects, and devoutly repeated the Palestines' own prayers, whilst burning them by a slow fire, *por l'amor de Dios.*

The princess of Babylon alighted in that city which has since been called Sevilla. Her design was to embark upon the Betis to return by Tyre to Babylon, and see again king Belus, her father; and forget, if possible, her perdious lover – or, at least, to ask him in marriage. She sent for two Palestines, who transacted all the business of the court. They were to furnish her with three ships. The phoenix made all the necessary contracts with them, and settled the price after some little dispute.

The hostess was a great devotee, and her husband, who was no less religious, was a Familiar: that is to say, a spy of the Druid Inquisitors or *Anthropokaies.*

He failed not to inform them, that in his house was a sorceress and two Palestines, who were entering into a compact with the devil, disguised like a large gilt bird.

The Inquisitors having learned that the lady possessed a large quantity of diamonds, swore point blank that she was a sorceress. They waited till night to imprison the two hundred cavaliers and the unicorns, (which slept in very extensive stables), for the Inquisitors are cowards.

Having strongly barricaded the gates, they seized the princess and Irla; but they could not catch the phoenix, who flew away with great swiftness. He did not doubt of meeting with Amazan upon the road from Gaul to Sevilla.

He met him upon the frontiers of Betica, and acquainted him with the disaster that had befallen the princess.

Amazan was struck speechless with rage. He armed himself with a steel cuirass damasquined with gold, a lance twelve feet long, two javelins, and an edged sword called the Thunderer, which at one single stroke would rend trees, rocks, and Druids. He covered his beautiful head with a golden casque, shaded with heron and ostrich feathers. This was the ancient armor of Magog, which his sister Aldea gave him when upon his journey in Scythia. The few attendants he had with him all mounted their unicorns.

Amazan, in embracing his dear phoenix, uttered only these melancholy expressions: "I am guilty! Had I not dined with the child of genius from the opera, in the city of the idlers, the princess of Babylon would not have been in this alarming situation. Let us fly to the *Anthropokaies.*" He presently entered Sevilla. Fifteen hundred Alguazils guarded the gates of the inclosure in which the two hundred Gangarids and their unicorns were shut up, without being allowed anything to eat. Preparations were already made for sacrificing the princess of Babylon, her chambermaid Irla, and the two rich Palestines.

The high *Anthropokaie,* surrounded by his subaltern *Anthropokaies,* was already seated upon his sacred tribunal. A crowd of Sevillians, wearing strung beads at their girdles, joined their two hands, without uttering a syllable, when the beautiful Princess, the maid Irla, and the two Palestines were brought forth, with their hands tied behind their backs and dressed in masquerade habits.

The phoenix entered the prison by a dormer window, whilst the Gangarids began to break open the doors. The invincible Amazan shattered them without. They all sallied forth armed, upon their unicorns, and Amazan put himself at their head. He had no difficulty in overthrowing the Alguazils, the Familiars, or the priests called *Anthropokaies.* Each unicorn pierced dozens at a time. The thundering Amazan cut to pieces all he met. The people in black cloaks and dirty frize ran away, always keeping fast hold of their blest beads, *por l'amor de Dios.*

Amazan collared the high Inquisitor upon his tribunal, and threw him upon the pile, which was prepared about forty paces distant; and he also cast upon it the other Inquisitors, one after the other. He then prostrated himself at Formosanta's feet. "Ah! how amiable you are," said she; "and how I should adore you, if you had not forsaken me for the company of an opera singer."

Whilst Amazan was making his peace with the princess, whilst his Gangarids cast upon the pile the bodies of all the *Anthropokaies*, and the flames ascended to the clouds, Amazan saw an army that approached him at a distance. An aged monarch, with a crown upon his head, advanced upon a car drawn by eight mules harnessed with ropes. An hundred other cars followed. They were accompanied by grave looking men in black cloaks or frize, mounted upon very fine horses. A multitude of people, with greasy hair, followed silently on foot.

Amazan immediately drew up his Gangarids about him, and advanced with his lance couched. As soon as the king perceived him, he took off his crown, alighted from his car, and embraced Amazan's stirrup, saying to him: "Man sent by the gods, you are the avenger of human kind, the deliverer of my country. These sacred monsters, of which you have purged the earth, were my masters, in the name of the Old Man of the Seven Mountains. I was forced to submit to their criminal power. My people would have deserted me, if I had only been inclined to moderate their abominable crimes. From this moment I breathe, I reign, and am indebted to you for it."

He afterward respectfully kissed Formosanta's hand, and entreated her to get into his coach (drawn by eight mules) with Amazan, Irla, and the phoenix.

The two Palestine bankers, who still remained prostrate on the ground through fear and terror, now raised their heads. The troop of unicorns followed the king of Betica into his palace.

As the dignity of a king who reigned over a people of characteristic brevity, required that his mules should go at a very slow pace, Amazan and Formosanta had time to relate to him their adventures. He also conversed with the phoenix, admiring and frequently embracing him. He easily comprehended how brutal and barbarous the people of the west should be considered, who ate animals, and did not understand their language; that the Gangarids alone had preserved the nature and dignity of primitive man; but he particularly agreed, that the most barbarous of mortals were the *Anthropokaies*, of whom Amazan had just purged the earth. He incessantly blessed and thanked him. The beautiful Formosanta had already forgotten the affair in Gaul, and had her soul filled with nothing but the valor of the hero who had preserved her life. Amazan being made acquainted with the innocence of the embrace she had given to the king of Egypt, and being told of the resurrection of the phoenix, tasted the purest joy, and was intoxicated with the most violent love.

They dined at the palace, but had a very indifferent repast. The cooks of Betica were the worst in Europe. Amazan advised the king to send for some from Gaul. The king's musicians performed, during the repast, that celebrated air which has since been called *the Follies of Spain*. After dinner, matters of business came upon the carpet.

The king enquired of the handsome Amazan, the beautiful Formosanta, and the charming phoenix, what they proposed doing. "For my part," said Amazan, "my intention is to return to Babylon, of which I am the presumptive heir, and to ask of my uncle Belus the hand of my cousin-german, the incomparable Formosanta."

"My design certainly is," said the princess, "never to separate from my cousin-germain. But I imagine he will agree with me, that I should return first to my father, because he only gave me leave to go upon a pilgrimage to Bassora, and I have wandered all over the world."

"For my part," said the phoenix, "I will follow every where these two tender, generous lovers."

"You are in the right," said the king of Betica; "but your return to Babylon is not so easy as you imagine. I receive daily intelligence from that country by Tyrian ships, and my Palestine bankers, who correspond with all the nations of the earth. The people are all in arms toward the Euphrates and the Nile. The king of Scythia claims the inheritance of his wife, at the head of three hundred thousand warriors on horseback. The kings of Egypt and India are also laying waste the banks of the Tygris and the Euphrates, each at the head of three hundred thousand men, to revenge themselves for being laughed at. The king of Ethiopia is ravaging Egypt with three hundred thousand men, whilst the king of Egypt is absent from his country. And the king of Babylon has as yet only six hundred thousand men to defend himself.

"I acknowledge to you," continued the king, "when I hear of those prodigious armies which are disembogued from the east, and their astonishing magnificence – when I compare them to my trifling bodies of twenty or thirty thousand soldiers, which it is so difficult to clothe and feed; I am inclined to think the eastern subsisted long before the western hemisphere. It seems as if we sprung only yesterday from chaos and barbarity."

"Sire," said Amazan, "the last comers frequently outstrip those who first began the career. It is thought in my country that man was first created in India; but this I am not certain of."

"And," said the king of Betica to the phoenix, "what do you think?"

"Sire," replied the phoenix, "I am as yet too young to have any knowledge concerning antiquity. I have lived only about twenty-seven thousand years; but my father, who had lived five times that age, told me he had learned from his father, that the eastern country had always been more populous and rich than the others. It had been transmitted to him from his ancestors, that the generation of all animals had begun upon the banks of the Ganges. For my part, said he, I have not the vanity to be of this opinion. I cannot believe that the foxes of Albion, the marmots of the Alps, and the wolves of Gaul, are descended from my country. In the like manner, I do not believe that the firs and oaks of your country descended from the palm and cocoa trees of India."

"But from whence are we descended, then?" said the king.

"I do not know," said the phoenix; "all I want to know is, to where the beautiful princess of Babylon and my dear Amazan may repair."

"I very much question," said the king, "whether with his two hundred unicorns he will be able to destroy so many armies of three hundred thousand men each."

"Why not?" said Amazan. The king of Betica felt the force of this sublime question, "Why not?" but he imagined sublimity alone was not sufficient against innumerable armies.

"I advise you," said he, "to seek the king of Ethiopia. I am related to that black prince through my Palestines. I will give you recommendatory letters to him. As he is at enmity with the king of Egypt, he will be but too happy to be strengthened by your alliance. I can assist you with two thousand sober, brave men; and it will depend upon yourself to engage as many more of the people who reside, or rather skip, about the foot of the Pyrenees, and who are called Vasques or Vascons. Send one of your warriors upon an unicorn, with a few diamonds. There is not a Vascon that will not quit the castle, that is, the thatched cottage of his father, to serve you. They are indefatigable, courageous, and agreeable; and whilst you wait their arrival, we will give you festivals, and prepare your ships. I cannot too much acknowledge the service you have done me."

Amazan realized the happiness of having recovered Formosanta, and enjoyed in tranquillity her conversation, and all the charms of reconciled love, – which are almost equal to a growing passion.

A troop of proud, joyous Vascons soon arrived, dancing a *tambourin*. The haughty and grave Betican troops were now ready. The old sun-burnt king tenderly embraced the two lovers. He sent great quantities of arms, beds, chests, boards, black clothes, onions, sheep, fowls, flour, and particularly garlic, on board the ships, and wished them a happy voyage, invariable love, and many victories.

Proud Carthage was not then a sea-port. There were at that time only a few Numidians there, who dried fish in the sun. They coasted along Bizacenes, the Syrthes, the fertile banks where since arose Cyrene and the great Chersonese.

They at length arrived toward the first mouth of the sacred Nile. It was at the extremity of this fertile land that the ships of all commercial nations were already received in the port of Canope, without knowing whether the god Canope had founded this port, or whether the inhabitants had manufactured the god – whether the star Canope had given its name to the city, or whether the city had bestowed it upon the star. All that was known of this matter was, that the city and the star were both very ancient; and this is all that can be known of the origin of things, of what nature soever they may be.

It was here that the king of Ethiopia, having ravaged all Egypt, saw the invincible Amazan and the adorable Formosanta come on shore. He took one for the god of war, and the other for the goddess of beauty. Amazan presented to him the letter of recommendation from the king of Spain. The king of Ethiopia immediately entertained them with some admirable festivals, according to the indispensable custom of heroic times. They then conferred about their expedition to exterminate the three hundred thousand men of the king of Egypt, the three hundred thousand of the emperor of the Indies, and the three hundred thousand of the great Khan of the Scythians, who laid siege to the immense, proud, voluptuous city of Babylon.

The two hundred Spaniards, whom Amazan had brought with him, said that they had nothing to do with the king of Ethiopia's succoring Babylon; that it was sufficient their king had ordered them to go and deliver it; and that they were formidable enough for this expedition.

The Vascons said they had performed many other exploits; that they would alone defeat the Egyptians, the Indians, and the Scythians; and that they would not march unless the Spaniards were placed in the rear-guard.

The two hundred Gangarids could not refrain from laughing at the pretensions of their allies, and they maintained that with only one hundred unicorns, they could put to flight all the kings of the earth. The beautiful Formosanta appeased them by her prudence, and by her enchanting discourse. Amazan introduced to the black monarch his Gangarids, his unicorns, his Spaniards, his Vascons, and his beautiful bird.

Everything was soon ready to march by Memphis, Heliopolis, Arsinoe, Petra, Artemitis, Sora, and Apamens, to attack the three kings, and to prosecute this memorable war, before which all the wars ever waged by man sink into insignificance.

Fame with her hundred tongues has proclaimed the victories Amazan gained over the three kings, with his Spaniards, his Vascons, and his unicorns. He restored the beautiful Formosanta to her father. He set at liberty all his mistress's train, whom the king of Egypt had reduced to slavery. The great Khan of the Scythians declared himself his vassal; and his marriage was confirmed with princess Aldea. The invincible and generous Amazan, was acknowledged the heir to the kingdom of Babylon, and entered the city in triumph with the phoenix, in the presence of a hundred tributary kings. The festival of his marriage far surpassed that which king Belus had given. The bull Apis was served up roasted at table. The kings of Egypt and India were cup-bearers to the married pair; and these nuptials were celebrated by five hundred illustrious poets of Babylon.

Oh, Muses! daughters of heaven, who are constantly invoked at the beginning of a work, I only implore you at the end. It is needless to reproach me with saying grace, without having said *benedicite*. But, Muses! you will not be less my patronesses. Inspire, I pray you, the *Ecclesiastical Gazetteer*, the illustrious orator of the *Convulsionnaires*, to say everything possible against *The Princess of Babylon*, in order that the work may be condemned by the Sorbonne, and, therefore, be universally read. And prevent, I beseech you, O chaste and noble Muses, any supplemental scribblers spoiling, by their fables, the truths I have taught mortals in this faithful narrative.